★★★★★

'Move over, Morse . . . police fiction gets no better than this'
Amanda, Netgalley

★★★★★

'Cara Hunter has become one of my favourite writers this year'
Helen, Netgalley

★★★★★

'I was hooked from the word go'
Ruchita, Netgalley

★★★★★

'I just couldn't put this one down'
Margaret, Netgalley

★★★★★

'I would give this more than a five-star rating if I could . . . it's a
wow wow wow book'
Marjorie, Netgalley

★★★★★

'Cara Hunter's books are made to be devoured'
Fiona, Netgalley

★★★★★

'For fans of Cara Hunter, you're in for a treat, and for those
who haven't read her yet . . . DO IT NOW'
Jacqueline, Netgalley

'Th...
Tony, Netgalley

ABOUT THE AUTHOR

Cara Hunter is the author of the *Sunday Times* bestselling crime novels *Close to Home* and *In the Dark*, featuring DI Adam Fawley and his Oxford-based police team. *Close to Home* was a Richard and Judy Book Club pick, and Cara's novels have sold more than half a million copies worldwide. She lives in Oxford, on a street not unlike those featured in her books.

No Way Out

CARA HUNTER

PENGUIN BOOKS

PENGUIN BOOKS

UK | USA | Canada | Ireland | Australia
India | New Zealand | South Africa

Penguin Books is part of the Penguin Random House group of companies
whose addresses can be found at global.penguinrandomhouse.com.

First published 2019
001

Set in 12.5/14.75 pt Garamond MT Std
Typeset by Jouve (UK), Milton Keynes
Printed and bound in Great Britain by Clays Ltd, Elcograf S.p.A.

A CIP catalogue record for this book is available from the British Library

ISBN: 978-0-241-28349-3

www.greenpenguin.co.uk

Penguin Random House is committed to a
sustainable future for our business, our readers
and our planet. This book is made from Forest
Stewardship Council® certified paper.

For Sarah
Because everyone needs a wonderwall

04/01/2018 00.55 a.m.

**Helmet camera footage, Firefighter Fletcher,
Oxfordshire Fire and Rescue Service**

*Incident at Felix House, 23 Southey Road, Oxford
Footage starts as two fire engines pull up in
suburban street. The houses are large. It's dark.
Sirens, flashing lights.*

DISPATCH FIRE CONTROL TO APPLIANCES:
This incident is persons reported. 999 call said
four people potentially in the dwelling. Two
adults, two children.

INCIDENT COMMANDER:
All received. Now in attendance. Ground floor well
alight.

*Camera swings right towards a house with black
smoke billowing out of right-hand upper windows and
fire visible on floors below. Half a dozen passers-by
and neighbours in the street. Sound of shouting
voices, more sirens. Police car draws up.
Firefighters are pulling down ladders, pulling off
the hose reel, strapping on breathing apparatus.*

INCIDENT COMMANDER TO CREWS:
None of the neighbours have seen the family so I
need two BA to go up and search the first floor.

BREATHING APPARATUS ENTRY CONTROL OFFICER:
All received. Alpha Team 1 are just getting ready
to enter.

*Flames now clearly visible through glass-panelled
front door. Breathing Apparatus Alpha Team 1 led by
Firefighter Fletcher proceed up the drive to the
house. A ladder goes up on left-hand side. Fletcher
ascends with a hose reel. Sounds of muffled voices
and radio interference. Heavy breathing in the BA
mask. Camera tracks over the windowsill into the
room. Thick smoke. Helmet torch beam swinging
left to right, picking out shelving, a chest of
drawers, a chair. No visible flames but carpet is
smouldering. Camera swings back round towards
window, shot of Firefighter Evans ascending ladder.*

BA ENTRY CONTROL OFFICER:
Alpha Team 1, any sign of casualties?

FLETCHER [*breathing heavily*]:
Negative.

*Fletcher moves towards door and exits on to
landing. Camera jerks from side to side, light beam
picks up three further doors and stairs leading to
an upper storey. Lower stairwell shows flickering
light from flames on the ground floor, sparks in the
air, smoke funnelling up the stairs and along the
ceiling. More crackling on the comms system, sound
of water from hoses as firefighters outside attempt*

to extinguish the fire. Fletcher moves to adjacent door, partially open. Football posters and single bed just visible through the smoke. Covers thrown back but no occupant. He searches the room and checks under the bed.

BA ENTRY CONTROL OFFICER:

Alpha Team 1, for information, neighbours say there's a boy, ten or eleven, and a toddler.

Fletcher moves back out to landing and along to next door. It's open. Smoke is much thicker here. Fire is well established – rug, curtains and cot bedding all alight. Fletcher rushes to the bed. There's a child, not moving. He returns quickly to first room and hands over child to Firefighter Evans on ladder at window. Gust of air into the room. Areas of carpet catch light.

FLETCHER:

Alpha Team 1 to BAECO. One casualty found and being brought out via ladder. Child. Unresponsive.

INCIDENT COMMANDER:

All received, Alpha 1. Paramedics on scene.

Fletcher returns to landing followed by Firefighter Waites. Moves to top of staircase. Firefighters Evans and Jones have also entered the building to search for casualties, and approach from other side.

FLETCHER:

You found anyone?

Evans gestures negative. Jones has hand-held Thermal Imaging Camera. Tracks around and starts gesturing urgently down the stairs.

JONES:

There's someone down there – near the bottom.

FLETCHER:

Alpha 1 to BAECO. Casualty identified at base of stairs. Could be the other kid. Going down.

Alpha Team 1 descend. Hall flooring is on fire and blaze is far advanced in all directions. They lift the casualty and retrace their steps up to the first floor where they pass him to Alpha Team 2, who carry him to the ladder. Sudden sounds of explosion and structural collapse as fire breaks through to upper storey. Shouts and alarm on radio. Flames now visible at bedroom door.

WAITES:

Shit – backdraught – backdraught!

INCIDENT COMMANDER:

Evacuate, repeat, evacuate.

FLETCHER [*gasping*]:

There must be other people in here – I'm going back in.

x

<u>INCIDENT COMMANDER:</u>

Negative, I repeat, negative. Severe risk to life. Get the hell out of there. I repeat: Get the hell out of there. Team Alpha 1 acknowledge –

Sounds of further explosion. Radio goes dead.

I bloody hate Christmas. I suppose I must have liked it once, when I was a kid, but I don't remember. As soon as I was old enough I'd walk – anything to get out of the house. I never had anywhere to go, but even walking the streets in circles was better than sitting around the living room staring at each other, or the exquisite torture of yet another *Only Fools and Horses* Christmas Special. And the older I've got the more I loathe this time of year. Cheery festive tat from the end of October to long after New Year. *You'll change your mind*, people said, *when you have kids; you'll see – Christmas with a child of your own is a magical time.* And it was. When we had Jake, it was. I remember him making the most amazing paper decorations, all on his own – reindeer and snowmen and polar bears in cut-outs and careful, intricate silhouettes. And we had holly, and oranges in the toes of knitted stockings, and little white lights strung across the garden. I remember it actually snowed one year, and he sat there, at his bedroom window, completely entranced as huge flakes swirled softly down, barely heavy enough to fall. So yes, it was magical. But what happens when you've lost the child who made it so – what then? People never talk to you about that. They don't tell you how to cope with the Christmas that comes After. Or the next, or the one after that.

There's work, of course. At least, there is for me.

Though Christmas is a crap time to be a police officer. Just about every crime you can think of goes up. Theft, domestic violence, public disorder. Mostly low-level stuff, but the amount of bloody admin it creates is still the same. People have too much to drink, too much time on their hands, and so much twenty-four-hour proximity to people they're supposed to love they find out that, actually, they don't. And what with that and everyone wanting to take leave, we're always short-staffed. Which is a very long way of explaining why I'm standing in a freezing cold kitchen at 5.35 a.m. in the dead zone at the fag-end of the holidays, staring out at the dark, listening to the Radio 4 news while I wait for the kettle to boil. There are dirty plates in the sink because I can't be bothered to empty the dishwasher, the bins are overflowing because I missed the change to the collection day and the food caddy has been upended all over the side path, possibly by next-door's cat, but more likely by the fox I've spotted in the garden once or twice lately, in the early hours. And if you're wondering what I've been doing up at such a godforsaken time, well, you won't have to wonder very long.

The radio switches to *Prayer for the Day* and I switch it off. I don't do God. And definitely not at this time in the morning. I pick up my mobile, hesitate a moment then make the call. And yes, I know it's stupid o'clock, but I don't think I'll wake her. She turns her phone off at night. Like a normal human being.

I hear the predictable four rings, the click, and the not-quite-human female voice telling me the person I am calling is not available. Then the tone.

'Alex – it's me. Nothing heavy. Just wanted to check

you're OK. That it's helping. I mean, having time to think. Like you said.'

What is it about talking to machines that makes supposedly intelligent people blither like morons? There's a sticky brown stain on the work surface I can't remember being there yesterday. I start scraping at it with my thumbnail.

'Tell your sister I said hello.' Then a pause. 'That's it, really. Look, just call me, OK?' I listen to the silence. I know it's impossible but half of me is hoping she's listening too. That she'll pick up. 'I miss you.'

I love you.

Which I should have said, but didn't. I'm trying not to remember exactly how long it is since she actually spoke to me. A week? More. I think it was the day after Boxing Day. I kept hoping New Year would make a difference. That we could put the whole thing behind us then, as if a completely arbitrary change in the numbering of the days could make the slightest difference to how she feels. How *I* feel.

The kettle boils and I poke about in the cupboard for coffee. All that's left is the jar of cheap instant Alex keeps for plumbers and decorators. Those poncey pod things ran out days ago. It was Alex who really wanted that machine. The cheap instant has some balls, though, and I've just poured a second when the phone rings.

'*Alex?*'

'No, boss. It's me. Gislingham.'

I can feel my cheeks redden. Did I sound as desperate to him as I did to me? 'What is it, Gis?'

'Sorry to call so early, boss. I'm at Southey Road.

There's been a fire overnight. They're still struggling to get it under control.'

'Casualties?'

But I know the answer before I ask. Gis wouldn't be calling me at 5.45 otherwise.

I hear him draw breath. 'Only one so far, boss. A little kiddie. There's an older boy too, but they managed to get to him in time. He's alive – just. They've taken him to the John Rad.'

'No sign of the parents?'

'Not yet.'

'Shit.'

'I know. We're trying to keep that from the press but it's only a matter of time. Sorry to drag you out of bed and all that, but I think you should be here –'

'I was already awake. And I'm on my way.'

* * *

At Southey Road, Gislingham puts his phone back in his pocket. He'd been in two minds whether to call at all. Though he'd never say so out loud and feels guilty even thinking it, Fawley has definitely been off his game recently. Not just short-tempered, though he's been that too. Distracted. Preoccupied. He didn't go to the station Christmas party, but since he always says how much he hates Christmas that doesn't necessarily mean anything. On the other hand, there's a rumour doing the rounds his wife has left him, and judging by the state of his ironing that's a distinct possibility. Gislingham's own shirt doesn't look much cop either, but they never do given he

4

does them himself. He still hasn't worked out how to do collars.

He turns and walks back down the drive towards the house. The flames have died back but firefighters in breathing apparatus are still sending jets of water arcing into the windows, pushing huge gusts of dense smoke into the dark sky. The air is thick with soot and the smell of burning plastic.

The Incident Commander comes towards him, his boots crunching on the gravel. 'Off the record, almost certainly arson, but it'll be a while before the investigation team can go in. Looks like it must have started in the sitting room, but the roof above has completely caved in so don't quote me on that.'

'So we might be looking at more bodies?'

'Could be. But there's three floors of rubble come down on that side. God knows how long it'll take to sift through it all.' He takes his helmet off and wipes his forehead on the back of his hand. 'Have you heard anything about the boy?'

'Not yet. One of my colleagues went in the ambulance. I'll let you know if I hear.'

The firefighter makes a face. He knows the odds; he's been doing this a long time. He takes a swig of water. 'Where's Quinn – on holiday?'

Gislingham shakes his head. 'This one's mine. I'm acting DS.'

The officer raises an eyebrow. 'I heard Quinn had got himself in the shit. Though I didn't know it was that bad.'

Gislingham shrugs. 'Not for me to say.'

The firefighter eyes him for a moment in the throbbing

blue glare. 'Takes some getting used to, doesn't it?' he says eventually. 'Being in charge.' Then he chucks the water bottle away and starts up towards the fire engine, tapping Gislingham's arm as he passes. 'You go for it, mate. Gotta take your chances in this life. No other bugger's gonna do it for you.'

Which is broadly what Gislingham's wife said when he told her. That and the fact that Quinn got himself in this mess, and they could do with the extra money now Billy's getting older, and what did he owe Quinn anyway? A question he'd (wisely) decided to assume was merely rhetorical.

He looks around for a moment, then heads towards the uniform standing behind the police tape. There are onlookers in the road, but given the time and the cold, it's only a straggle. Though Gislingham recognizes a journalist from the *Oxford Mail* who's been trying – and failing – to get his attention for the last ten minutes.

He turns to the constable. 'Have they started the house-to-house yet?'

'Just underway now, Sarge. We managed to rustle up three people. It's not much, but –'

'Yeah, I know. Everyone's on holiday.'

A car pulls up on the street and someone gets out. Briskly, officially, flashing a warrant card. And that's not the only thing that's flash. Gislingham takes a deep breath. It's Quinn's car.

* * *

6

Oxford Mail online

Thursday 4 January 2018 Last updated at 08:18

Fatality in Oxford house fire

A boy of three has died after a fire ripped through a seven-bedroom Edwardian home in Southey Road in the early hours of this morning. The cause of the fire is as yet unknown, but Oxfordshire Fire and Rescue Service are working closely with a police forensics team to determine exactly how it began. A second victim, identified by neighbours as the toddler's older brother, was taken by ambulance to the John Radcliffe hospital, believed to be suffering from smoke inhalation.

The emergency services were called to the house shortly after 12.40 a.m., when a neighbour saw flames issuing from a ground-floor window. Patrick Moreton, station manager at the Rewley Road fire station, said that the fire was far advanced by the time his crew arrived at the scene, and it took over four hours for the flames to be brought under control. He said it was far too early to tell whether combustible Christmas decorations could have contributed to the blaze, but added, 'This is a timely reminder of the importance of taking proper safety precautions when using decorations like

15-year-old boy arrested following stabbing in Blackbird Leys
A teenager is being questioned by police after the fatal stabbing of 16-year-old Damien Parry on New Year's Eve . . . /more

Transport disruption expected as more snow is forecast next week
The Met Office has issued a yellow weather warning as icy blasts are set to sweep in from Siberia next week . . . /more

Council announces new measures to reduce air pollution in Oxford
Oxford City Council is set to introduce a pioneering new scheme to cut diesel emissions in residential areas . . . /more

Oxford United beat MK Dons 3–1
Thomas, van Kessel and Obika all score in a lively home tie . . . /more

candles and flammable materials such as tinsel, and testing your smoke alarms at least once a week.'

Thames Valley Police have declined to comment on whether the two children were in the house alone.

* * *

It's only when I'm signalling left on the Banbury Road that I remember exactly where Southey Road is. Three turnings north of Frampton Road. Frampton Road as in William Harper and what we found locked in his cellar. The papers called him the 'Oxford Fritzl'. At least, at the beginning. It was eight months ago now, but I was still in court in December, and the file is still sitting on my desk, waiting to get shunted to archives. None of us are going to forget that one in a hurry. Least of all Quinn. Detective Sergeant Quinn as was, Detective Constable Quinn as now. Speaking of whom, his new black Audi is the first thing I see as I draw up in the street and turn off the engine. But then he's always been a bit of a swanky git when it comes to wheels. I couldn't tell you what Gislingham drives and I must have seen that damn car a thousand times. As for the scene, the fire may be under control but the place is a circus all the same. Two fire engines and three police cars. Nosy parkers. People taking pictures on their phones. Thank Christ they parked the undertaker's van out of sight.

Quinn and Gislingham are up by the house and they turn to face me as I walk towards them. Quinn is stamping his feet in the cold, but aside from that the body language is awkward, to say the least. He took to DS like a dog to water – zero hesitation, maximum splash – but he's having a lot more trouble going back down to DC. Well, you know what they say, trading up is easy, trading down is a different matter altogether. He's trying to balls it out, needless to say, but it's that part of his anatomy that got him into this mess in the first place. I can see he's itching to get stuck in, but Gislingham deserves a chance to prove he's up to this. I turn to him, perhaps a little too pointedly.

'Anything new, Sergeant?'

Gislingham stiffens a little and whips out his notebook, though I can't believe he actually needs it. His hands are trembling, ever so slightly. I suspect Quinn has spotted that as well.

'The house belongs to a family called Esmond, sir.

Michael Esmond, forty, is an academic. The wife is Samantha, thirty-three, and there are the two kids, Matty, ten, and Zachary, three.'

'How is he – the older boy?'

'Touch and go. He's pretty poorly.'

'And still no sign of the parents?'

Gislingham makes a face. 'Master bedroom's over there,' he says, pointing to the left-hand side of the house. 'It's still pretty much intact, but there's no sign of anyone. Fire boys say the bed wasn't even slept in. So I googled the family and this came up.'

He hands me his phone. It's a page from the King's College London website, advertising a conference on social anthropology taking place right now in London. One of the speakers is Michael Esmond: *'Death by Fire and Water: Sacrificial Ritual Practices in Latin American Vodou'*. Someone said, didn't they, that coincidence is God's way of remaining anonymous. Well, if that's the case, all I can say is he has pretty poor taste sometimes.

I give Gis his phone back. 'Call them and confirm he definitely showed. At the very least that means we have one less body to look for.'

'Hold the barbecue sauce, eh?' says Quinn.

I shoot him a look that wipes the smirk off his face, and turn again to Gislingham.

'What's the plan?'

He blinks a couple of times. 'Locate Michael and Samantha Esmond and establish their whereabouts at the time of the incident. Carry out an initial house-to-house in case one of the neighbours saw something. Talk to Boddie about the PM. Identify and inform other next of kin. Liaise with the fire forensic boys.' He points across the drive. 'And track down the car, of course.'

Quinn turns to look at him. 'What car?'

Gislingham raises his eyebrows. 'There are wheel marks on the gravel. Plain as day. The Esmonds definitely have a car. So where is it? No one in their right mind would drive into London from here so I reckon if we find that car we'll also find the wife.'

No prizes for guessing whose stock just went up a notch.

I nod. 'Good work, Sergeant. Keep me in the loop.'

I turn back to Quinn. Who's moved a yard or so closer to the house, presumably on the grounds that if you can't beat 'em, walk away. The house isn't really my taste, but if you like that sort of thing, I guess it's a desirable property. Or was. Right now, filthy water is streaming down the facade and all the ground-floor windows have gone. It's detached and double-fronted but the right-hand side is little more than a shell. The gable is still standing but only barely, and there's nothing behind it but blackened walls and a heap of bricks and roof timbers and shattered glass. What's left of the rest is pebble-dashed and overlaid with Tudorish wooden bits which must have been white before but are charred and soot-stained now. You can just about make out '1909' above one of the windows. As well as an Arsenal sticker still clinging to the broken pane.

'What are you thinking?' I ask Quinn.

He starts slightly. 'Oh, just the obvious, boss. How an academic gets to afford something that big round here. How much d'you think – five mill?'

More, if you ask me. Round here, houses are divided

into large, small, large-small and small-large. Safe to say this is large. *Large*-large.

'Could be family money,' I say. 'Worth checking, though.'

'Why don't you do that, Quinn,' says Gislingham.

Quinn shrugs. 'OK.'

And as I walk away I hear Gislingham say, under his breath, 'OK, *Sarge.*'

* * *

At 7.05, DC Erica Somer is standing looking at her wardrobe, trying to work out what to wear. She's only been in CID three months and Choosing the Right Clothes is a question that's getting more vexed by the day. She never liked her uniform, but it had its advantages. Uniformity being, of course, one of the most obvious. But now she's in 'plain clothes' and the best way to achieve that is anything but plain. How, she wonders for the umpteenth time, staring at the rack of hangers, do you manage to look serious but not frumpy? Professional but still approachable? It's a nightmare. She sighs. In this as in so much else, the blokes have it easy. An M&S suit and three ties will pretty much do you – Baxter being the living proof. Verity Everett's found her own way forward with a white-shirt-dark-skirt look that scarcely varies. Navy one day, black the next, grey the third and back to navy again. Flat shoes, and a cardi in winter. But on that basis you might as well go back to uniform and have done with it. And what about hair – is a ponytail too frivolous? A bun too school-ma'am?

She's just pulled out the black trouser suit (third time in five days – that'll be a uniform too if she's not careful) when the mobile rings. It's Gislingham. She likes Gislingham. Not brash (like Quinn) or gifted (like Fawley) but effective all the same. Methodical. Hard-working. And decent. Above all, decent. She really hopes he makes a fist of the sergeantship; he deserves it.

'What can I do for you, Sarge?'

'I'm at Southey Road.' The wind must have got up; his voice is catching in the gusts. 'There's been a fire. One fatality and a lad in Intensive Care in the John Rad.'

She sits down on the bed. 'Arson?'

'We don't know yet. But looks likely.'

'How can I help?'

'What with Christmas, we're really thin on the ground – Baxter's running the house-to-house but we've only got three uniforms.'

Somer knows what that's like and it's a shit of a job. Especially in this weather. She hopes to God he isn't about to ask her to pitch in. And he must have sensed something because he adds, quickly, 'But that's not what I was calling about. I'm stuck on-site right now, and Everett doesn't get back till this afternoon, so can you handle the PM?'

Why isn't Quinn doing that? she wonders. But she doesn't say so. She has her own history with Quinn – an ill-advised but mercifully brief relationship which she fears rather too many people know about. Notably Fawley.

'Sure. No problem.'

'Have you done a burns case before?'

She hesitates. 'No, actually I haven't.' She's only been to

one post-mortem, in fact, and that was a stabbing. Gruelling enough but insipid by comparison.

'First time for everything,' says Gislingham. 'You'll be fine.' He hesitates, then, 'Take some mints.'

∗   ∗   ∗

Interview with Beverley Draper, conducted at
21 Southey Road, Oxford
4 January 2018, 8.45 a.m.
In attendance, DC A. Baxter

AB: I believe you made the initial 999 call, Mrs Draper?

BD: Yes, that was me. My son woke me up – he was having a nightmare. His bedroom faces that way. I heard a noise – it sounded like a window breaking. I thought it might be a burglar so I pulled the curtain aside. That's when I saw the flames. I remember thinking it must have been on fire for quite a while to have got so bad, but there are so many trees you can't really see the house from the road. I suppose no one realized.

AB: And you called the emergency services at 12.47?

BD: That's right.

AB: You didn't see anyone near the house – or running away?

BD: No. Like I said, I'd been asleep until Dylan woke me. Do you know how they are – the family?

AB: We're not in a position to release any
    information at the moment.

BD: I saw them take Matty off in the ambulance,
    but they're talking on the internet about
    Michael and Samantha being missing. That can't
    be right, can it? I mean -

AB: As I said, we'll be making an official
    statement in due course. Can you tell me what
    you know about the family? They were here,
    were they, over Christmas and New Year? Not
    away visiting relatives? On a skiing break?

BD: I don't think they ski. And yes, they were
    here. The school did a carol singing thing the
    day before Christmas Eve and they were all
    there.

AB: Did they have visitors at all? Do you know of
    anyone else who might have been in the house
    last night?

BD: Well, I'm not sure -

AB: We just need to be clear who else might have
    been present. Family members? Friends? Take
    your time.

BD: [*pause*]
    To be honest, they don't do that much
    entertaining as far as I can tell. When we
    moved in we invited them round, like you do,
    and Samantha said she'd come back to me with
    some dates, but somehow it never happened. We
    had a party in the garden last summer and
    they came, but I think they were only going
    through the motions. They didn't stay long.

AB: What about family?

BD: Michael's father is dead, that I do know, and
    I think his mother's in a home. Somewhere out
    near Wantage I think. I've never heard
    Samantha mention her family.

AB: We also believe the family have a car, but it
    wasn't at the house.

BD: Oh yes, they definitely have a car. A Volvo
    estate. Quite old. White. But I don't know
    why it's not in the drive. That's where it
    usually is.

AB: You don't know anywhere Samantha might go?

BD: So she really *is* missing -

AB: Like I said, we aren't able to comment -

BD: Don't worry. I get it. But no. I'm afraid I
    have no idea.

AB: And there's no one else you can think of that
    we could contact?

BD: I'm sorry. We just weren't those kind of
    neighbours.

* * *

The air in the mortuary is even colder than it is outside.
Somer has two jumpers on under her scrubs; it was Everett who'd advised the extra layer ('Once your teeth start chattering, that'll be it – you won't be able to stop'). The body is on a metal bed. The toddler. Zachary. Though she realizes at once that giving him a name is only going to make it a whole lot worse. Shreds of blue blanket are still clinging to his skin, but underneath he's horribly

damaged. His body is lurid with mottled yellow and blistered red, scorched with patches of lumpy, sooty charring. His head is turned away, the soft baby curls burned off, the lips shrunken and waxy. She takes a deep breath and it comes out as something too close to a sob. One of the assistants glances across.

'I know. It's always doubly crappy when it's a kid.'

Somer nods, not trusting herself to speak. Right now, all she can think about is the smell. She's seen all those uber-realistic mock-ups on TV post-mortems but the one thing she hadn't been prepared for was the stink. Even behind her mask, the body smells like a hog roast. She sends up a silent thank you to Gislingham for the mints, and swallows, trying to keep control.

'Our first priority,' says Boddie, 'will be to confirm whether or not the victim was alive before the fire began. There being no obvious external injuries, I will therefore be examining the trachea and internal airways for evidence of smoke inhalation.'

He picks up a scalpel and looks across at her. 'So, shall we begin?'

* * *

Gislingham is still at Southey Road. The low winter sun is casting a deep rose glow over the wreckage of the house. There's frost in the air, but despite the cold the crowd in the road is larger. Perhaps twenty people, in scarves and gloves and big coats, their breath coming in chilly gusts. But they probably won't stay long – there's a lot less to see now. One of the fire engines has gone, and the firefighters who remain are damping down last areas of fire and loading kit back on to the truck. Inside, though, it's a different matter. As well as three members of Alan Challow's forensics team, there are two fire investigation officers, one of them with a video camera. The other is in the burnt-out breakfast room, with Gislingham and Challow. The heavy wooden table and chairs are still smouldering and there are flares of soot going up to the ceiling. Water is dropping through, and they can see through the joists to the room above. Winnie the Pooh wallpaper. The bare skeleton of a baby mobile. Gislingham is trying not to look at it.

'We'll need to do more analysis to be sure,' the fire officer is saying, 'but like I said, my money's on it starting in the sitting room. That would also account for the delay in the 999 call – there's no one overlooking the house at the back and, as far as we can tell, the neighbours that side are away.'

'And you think it was definitely arson?'

The officer nods. 'Based on the speed and spread, some sort of accelerant had to be involved, ably supported, no doubt, by the bloody Christmas tree. That would have gone up like the fourth of July. Must have been dry as a bone by now – might just as well have piled up a stack of kindling and have done with it. After that it was only a matter of time until *boom*: the whole place went up.'

'How long could that have taken?' asks Gislingham, making furious notes.

The fire officer straightens up. 'To reach flashover point? Three minutes? Possibly even less.' He gestures towards the stairs. 'Judging by the charring, I'm guessing they had some sort of garland draped down the banisters too. Holly or something. Which would also have been tinder dry by now, needless to say, making it about as good a trailing fuse as you're ever likely to get. Talk about bad timing. I mean, they'd have been taking it all down tomorrow, wouldn't they?'

Gislingham looks blank, then, 'Oh, of course, Twelfth Night. Bugger – I'd forgotten about that.'

His own house is festooned like a department store – Janet wanted it to be special for Billy's first Christmas at home. Gislingham's going to be up all night.

* * *

Verity Everett puts the phone down and sits back in her chair. She was half expecting to come back to a nearly empty office and the sad remains of the Christmas chocolates. But only half: this job has a way of catching you unawares. And to be honest, after several days of Uninterrupted Dad she's rather relieved to be back. Her flat really isn't big enough for the both of them. Especially not when he treats the place like a hotel, leaving his empty mugs wherever he's sitting and never making the bed (*her* bed, incidentally; she's had to make do with the futon, which is having the predictable effect on both her backache and her disgruntled cat). But tomorrow her father's going home, and today she's back where she belongs. Working. She scans the room, looking for Gislingham, but he obviously isn't back from Southey Road yet. And much as she hates going over his head, this can't wait.

A few moments later she's tapping on Fawley's door.

He's on the phone, but motions her forward. She stands there a moment, making a great show of not listening to what he's saying, but thankfully it doesn't sound personal. Not his wife, anyway. Fawley's started shutting the door when he's talking to her. She sneaks a sidelong look at him. He looks OK from a distance, but if you know him well enough you can spot the signs. And she does. Know him.

He puts the phone down and she turns towards him.

'You've got something, Ev?'

'Yes, sir. I spoke to the conference organizers at King's. Michael Esmond registered with them on Tuesday afternoon and attended the dinner that evening. And he was on some panel or other yesterday morning.'

'And after that?'

'The organizer said she saw him in the pub late last night. Around ten thirty.'

'So he's definitely in London.'

'Yes, sir. But he arranged his own accommodation so they don't know where he's staying.'

'Mobile phone?'

She holds out a sheet of paper. 'They gave me the number but it's just going straight to voicemail. I've left a message for him to call us.'

'When's his speech scheduled for?'

She has to hand it to him: he always gets to the key fact. 'Tomorrow afternoon, sir. Four o'clock.'

Fawley nods slowly. 'OK, keep me posted. And if Esmond phones in I want to be the first to know.'

* * *

It takes five hours to complete the post-mortem, and at the end of it Boddie decides he has more than earned a late lunch.

'Would you like to join us?' he asks Somer as they remove their scrubs. 'We'll be in Frankie's, just across the road.'

After he's gone, one of the assistants turns to her and smiles awkwardly. 'You may want to take a rain check on that invite. Boddie has this tradition. If it's a burns case, he buys us all barbecue ribs.'

'You cannot be serious – even when it's a *child*?'

'I know. Sounds callous, doesn't it. But it's just his way of keeping the horror at bay.'

* * *

We have our first team meeting at three. Somer has only just got back from the mortuary. She still looks a bit pale, and I see Everett asking a silent question and Somer replying with a grimace. Quinn is in the front row with his tablet in his hand and his pen behind his ear (yes, I know, it doesn't make sense, but that's what he does). Baxter is pinning pictures up on the whiteboard. Felix House, before and after the fire, the former clearly from Google Earth. Various shots of the fire damage inside: the dining room, the stairs, some of the bedrooms, what remains of the furniture – most of it hefty and old-fashioned. A floorplan for all three storeys, with cross marks where Matty and Zachary were. Photos of Michael and Samantha Esmond. From DVLA, I'm guessing. Esmond is upright, attentive, his hair dark, his skin pale. His wife's contrasts are softer: beige-brown hair, pinkish cheeks, light-coloured eyes, probably hazel. Then there are the pictures of the children, salvaged from the house, by the state of them. Matty in an Arsenal strip, holding a ball under one arm, his big glasses slightly awry. The toddler on his mother's lap, a mischievous smile and a mop of unruly bronze curls she probably couldn't bring herself to cut. And alongside the living child, the dead one. I think, not for the first time, what a cruel mutilator of human flesh fire can be. Believe me, you never get used to that, even when you've seen it as many times as I have. And the minute you do, it's time to quit.

Gislingham comes over. 'Do you want to do this, sir?' he asks under his breath.

I've noticed, by the way, that it's not 'boss' any more, or at least not in public. Always 'sir'. A small Rubicon, as Rubicons go, but a significant one all the same.

I sling my jacket over the back of a chair and sit down. 'No, you go ahead. I'll only chip in if I need to.'

Another Rubicon. And rather a bigger one, because the team will register it straight away. Gislingham nods, 'Right, sir.'

He goes to the front of the room and turns to face them. 'OK, everyone, let's get started.'

Every single person in this room knows this is the first big case Gis has done since he was made Acting DS. A couple of years ago, when Quinn was in exactly the same position, they were mildly sardonic; not hostile, exactly, but not about to bust a gut to help him, either. And more than happy to take the piss whenever the opportunity arose (which with Quinn is pretty much all the time). But this time round it's different. They like Gislingham, and they want him to make a fist of this. They're not going to let him mess it up – not if they can help it.

Gislingham clears his throat. 'OK. I'm going to do a quick summary of where we are on the Southey Road fire, and then I'll hand over to Paul Rigby, who's a watch manager from Rewley Road fire station and the designated fire investigation officer for this one.'

He nods to a man standing to one side by the door. Tall, balding, clean-shaven. I've definitely seen him before.

'Right,' says Gislingham, turning to the board, 'this is the house, 23 Southey Road. Home to the Esmond family – Michael, his wife, Samantha, and their children, three-year-old Zachary and Matty, who will be eleven in four days' time.' He stops, takes a deep breath, carries on. 'And for anyone who's not up to speed, Matty is still in paediatric Intensive Care. The John Rad have warned us the prognosis isn't that good, but they'll contact us straight away if there's any change.'

He turns back to the board and taps the pictures of the two parents. 'Still no sign of either Michael or Samantha. Michael is currently assumed to be in London at a conference –'

'Can't believe he hasn't seen the news by now,' says one of the DCs. 'It's all over the bloody place.'

'I can't either,' agrees Gis. 'But until we find him, we're just guessing. Same goes for Samantha.'

But the DC isn't finished. 'You really think they'd have left kids that young all by themselves?'

Gislingham shrugs. 'Well, *I* wouldn't, that's for sure. But right now we have no idea what might have gone on in that house last night. Something could have happened to that family we don't know anything about. Which is one reason why we need to track down their next of kin. Any progress on that, Baxter?' He flushes slightly at this first, very public, assumption of authority, but Baxter takes it in his stride. As he does with most things.

'Not yet, Sarge,' he says. 'Samantha was an only child so no brothers or sisters. The parents live in Cumbria but we haven't been able to speak to them yet. Michael's mother is in a home in Wantage. Alzheimer's, according to the manager. So, yes, we should deffo go and see her but I doubt we'll get very much.'

'Right,' says Gislingham, turning to Somer. 'And the PM on the little boy – Zachary?'

Somer looks up. 'Only one thing stood out. Boddie was surprised how little soot he found in his lungs. But apparently a child that young could have suffocated much more quickly than an adult. Especially if he had asthma or even something as minor as a cold. Boddie's running blood tests to be sure.'

There's a silence. Half of us are hanging on to the fact that it must have been over very fast; the other half know pain like that can't be calibrated in seconds. And cruel though it sounds, I do want them thinking about that – because I want them committed, angry, relentless. I want all their energy focused on getting to the truth. On finding out how something this appalling could possibly have happened.

'OK,' says Gislingham, looking around the room, 'I'm going to hand over to Paul now, and then we'll divvy up the jobs for the next couple of days.'

He steps to one side and Paul Rigby stands up and moves briskly to the whiteboard. He's a practised presenter, no question of that. He moves swiftly and succinctly through what they know, what they assume and what they can deduce.

'In conclusion,' he says, 'and as I said to the sergeant earlier, we're working on the basis that the fire was started deliberately.'

I see Quinn's head twitch at 'sergeant', which he covers by quickly turning it into a cough. But Gislingham saw it too.

'There's no chance it was just an accident?' says Everett, though less in hope than in despair. 'A dropped cigarette, a Christmas candle – something like that?'

Rigby nods. 'Freak accidents do happen, and I've seen some weird ones in my time, I can tell you. There was a case a couple of years back only a mile or two from this one – young boy took an unignited Molotov cocktail into the house. Apparently he said he "liked fireworks". It was in all the papers – you might even remember it.'

Of course we remember it. It was Leo Mason, Daisy Mason's brother.

'It was our case,' I say, quietly.

'Right,' says Rigby. 'Well, you'll know what I mean then. But this is different. This isn't just an accident. Or bad luck. The amount of damage, the speed of spread – I'd stake my mortgage we'll find some sort of accelerant under all that debris. And *significant quantities* of accelerant at that.'

I get up and walk to the front, then turn to face them.

'I probably don't need to say this, but I'm going to

anyway. What we have here is two crimes, not one. One we know for a fact, and one we're going to have to assume, unless and until we can eliminate it. The first is arson: we have to find out who set fire to that house, and why. The second is murder. Did the arsonist *know* there were people in that house, and if he did – or *she* did – what the hell could have driven them to burn down a building with two kids asleep inside?'

I turn to the whiteboard and pick up the pen.

ARSON
MURDER

And under those two words, I write one more.

WHY?

'One thing I still don't understand,' says Everett after a pause, 'is where you found him. The older boy, I mean.'

'That's a good point,' replies Rigby.

The DC sitting next to Everett nudges her, 'You're on fire today, Ev,' at which she blushes and swipes him one, and then suddenly he looks sheepish because he's realized quite how insensitive that comment must have sounded.

'I was coming to that,' continues Rigby, stony-faced. He must have heard every bad-taste fire pun a hundred times over. 'As far as we can ascertain, the fire must have started sometime soon after midnight – the 999 call was logged at 12.47. At that time of the night you'd expect the children to be in bed, but the older boy was found near the bottom of the stairs.'

'So what do we think?' says Somer. 'He woke up and wanted a drink of water or something?'

'Er, *hello*,' says Quinn, getting up and tapping at the photo of the boy's room. And irritated though I am with the performance, I have to acknowledge he's right: the room is snowed with soot and flakes of ash but you can still see the jug of water and beaker on the bedside table. Quinn rolls his eyes in Somer's direction and one of the DCs titters.

Somer's now gone red in the face and she's not looking at Quinn. She doesn't tend to, when she can avoid it. They're both keeping up the illusion that nothing ever happened between them, but the whole station knows it did.

'All I know,' she says, quietly but firmly, 'is there had to be a reason.'

'So given he's in a coma, how do you suggest we find out? Find a bloody psychic?' There's no mistaking Quinn's tone now. I see people shifting slightly.

'He could have heard something,' says Rigby evenly, apparently unaware of the undercurrent. 'Or perhaps –'

'Where are the phones?' says Everett suddenly.

Rigby turns to the floorplan. 'We found one mobile on charge here, in the kitchen, but it was completely burnt-out –'

'We're trying to find out whose that is,' says Gislingham quickly.

'– and according to BT, there was only one landline point.' Rigby indicates. 'In the sitting room. Here.'

'Oh my God,' whispers Everett. '*That's* what the boy was doing on the stairs. He must have woken up and realized what was happening and tried to call for help. But it was too late. He couldn't get out.'

Poor little sod didn't stand a chance. I can't be the only one thinking that.

I turn to the photos again. In the nursery there's still one patch of wallpaper that's almost untouched. Just a few scorch marks here and there among the Tiggers and the Eeyores and the Piglets. The burns look oddly like hand-prints. I can hear the room going silent behind me. I look across at Rigby.

'How long before you can officially confirm it's arson?'

He shrugs. 'A few days. Perhaps a week. There's half a house to work through. It's going to take time.'

'So what's the priority, sir?' It's Gislingham.

I turn and face him. 'Finding the parents. I want as many people as possible on that, including uniforms if we can get them. I want that car found, for a start. Where are we on the ANPR? And have we spoken to the Met about Esmond?'

Gislingham nods. 'They checked arrests and hospital admissions but came up empty. Other than that, there's not much they can do without any sort of address.'

'OK. But if we haven't tracked him down by tomorrow morning I want someone waiting for him at that confer-ence when he turns up.'

Gis glances across the room. 'DC Asante is going to pick up on that, sir.'

Someone in the back row looks up and our eyes meet. I remember now who Tony Asante is. Not long out of graduate fast-track entry, and newly hired from the Met himself. The Super says he's good, which is code for 'we didn't hire him just to up the BME numbers'.

Asante holds my gaze with a degree of confidence I hadn't expected. I'm the one, in the end, who looks away.

'And remember, it's not just about where these people are, it's *who* they are. I want everything we can dig up about this family. Social media, emails, phone records, the lot. Have we found anything useful at the house? Computers? Tablets?'

Gislingham shakes his head. 'Not yet. Esmond must have had an office or study or something but the fire boys haven't found it yet. If you ask me, it's under half a ton of rubble. But they'll let us know if they find anything.'

I look around the room. 'So in the meantime, let's talk to anyone who knew the family, lived near them or worked with them. How did they spend their time? And their money? Where did they come from and is there anything *at all* in their lives that could have provoked this?'

People are making notes, conferring quietly.

'Right. Everyone know what they're doing? Good. And DC Quinn? A word, please. In my office.'

*　*　*

'It's got to stop, Quinn. And don't pretend you don't know what I'm talking about.'

He glances at me, and then down.

'DC Somer is a good officer, doing a good job. In fact, the only mistake I'm aware she's made is having a relationship with you, however brief. But she seems to have moved on from that – what I don't understand is why you can't.'

He rakes a hand through his hair. He looks awful. I'm sure that's yesterday's shirt. It's certainly yesterday's tie. But who am I to talk. It takes one to know one.

'Sit down. Let's talk about this.'

He seems in two minds, but then pulls out a chair.

'I know being demoted must have been complete crap, but you really only have yourself to blame. That whole episode – sleeping with a suspect –'

'I *never slept with her* – how many more times!'

But he knows that's going too far. Shouting at me isn't going to help. And in any case, that was a classic Bill Clinton. And we both know it.

'Sorry, sir,' he says.

'You were offered the transfer and you decided not to take it.'

But I did sympathize with him on that one. Starting over somewhere else isn't that easy. He has a flat, a mortgage, a life. But if you stay, you have to suck it up, however sour.

'Look, Quinn, the only thing you can do now is deal with it. Focus on the bloody job. And don't take it out on Somer. It was nothing to do with her. You'd be really pissed off if the boot was on the other foot. She's being a model of restraint by comparison.'

He makes a face. 'I know. It's just that this time last year I was a DS and she was still in uniform. And now –'

Now they're both on the same level. And her trajectory is definitely up. As for his, well, I'm not putting any money on it.

'And the whole bloody station is *still* talking about it,'

he finishes, biting his lip. I think he may actually be close to tears.

I lean forward. 'I'm going to sound like your dad now, but the only reason everyone's still talking about it is because *you* keep reminding them. You took your punishment – you don't have to keep on taking it. So drop it – move on. And start by leaving Somer alone. OK?'

He's not looking at me. I drop my head, forcing his gaze. 'OK, Quinn?'

He breathes in, holds his breath a minute, then looks up. 'Yes, boss.'

He smiles. It's not much of a smile, but it's a start.

* * *

Andrew Baxter goes back to his desk and logs on to his PC. He checks his watch – he can get at least a couple of hours in before the end of the day. Right then, he thinks, let's start with the obvious. He logs on to Facebook and searches for Michael Esmond, grateful that – for once – he's looking for a relatively unusual name. The last search like this was for someone called David Williams; there were bloody hundreds of them. Esmond, on the other hand, throws up only a handful, and in less than five minutes he has his man. Not that it tells him very much. It's more like LinkedIn than Facebook – a self-congratulatory CV, a couple of stiff photos, some dull predictable Likes. There's also a Philip Esmond listed as a friend, though – as the name suggests – he turns out to be a brother rather than a mate. A year or so older and, judging by his Facebook presence, about as chalk to his brother's cheese as it's possible to imagine. He has the same colouring but there's an energy, a twinkle, that's entirely missing from his brother's face. He also has five times the friends and, on the face of it, at least three times the fun. Including sailing his boat single-handed to Croatia. It's a Jeanneau Sun Odyssey 45 called *Freedom 2*. There are shots of it just before departure, with people on the quayside waving Philip off (though, as Baxter notes, his brother isn't one of them), then some selfies taken on board and some shots of Atlantic winter sunsets that suggest he's no mean hand with a camera either. The last was posted a few days before, saying he might be out of reach of mobile phone comms but to leave a message if it's urgent. Safe to say the current situation probably meets the test.

Baxter writes down the details of Michael Esmond's dozen or so other FB friends, noting as he does so all he's posted in the last six months are a couple of updates on the book he was writing and four or five on the conference at King's. He obviously thought that was a pretty big deal. Samantha Esmond's page is much more animated, at least at first sight. A big photo album of pictures: in the garden, on the beach, feeding ducks on what looks like the Oxford canal, standing with another woman in a shop Baxter's pretty sure is in Summertown; then a whole series of school sports days and fetes, including a picture of a slightly lopsided cake tagged 'My effort' with a rueful emoji face. But looking more closely, most of the pictures were loaded more than four years ago. After that there are a few selfies of her heavily pregnant, her face blurred or half in shadow, and one of a newborn in a hospital crib, tagged 'At last'. No name, no weight, no sex. And after that, hardly anything. One or two brief updates talking about the baby, but hardly any photos after his first birthday, and in the last three months, nothing at all. Which, judging by Baxter's (admittedly limited) experience of the social media habits of proud new parents, strikes him as decidedly odd. Janet Gislingham's timeline bristles with Billy – no change is too minute to go unchronicled, no development too trivial to show the world. Quinn once observed sardonically that she might as well post his puke and have done with it, but he didn't get the laugh he was expecting. Too many people remembered how close Janet came to not having a son to photograph at all.

Baxter sits back and exhales a long slow breath. Then he sits forward and goes back through the photo album a second time. It starts when Matty was about three, and Baxter scrolls through watching him grow from a chubby contented toddler to a skinny kid with glasses too big for him. The little Matty beams up at the camera, holding out shells, pebbles, an ice cream, a snail; his older self seems to do his best to evade it, caught off-centre or looking away. In one he's hiding behind his father's legs, or at least you have to assume it's his father, since the man is cut off at the chest. Baxter frowns, and scrolls through again, registering for the first time how few shots Michael Esmond is actually in. A couple of the holiday snaps early on – playing cricket on the sand, on a fairground ride with Matty on his lap – but not much else. In one of the more recent ones Matty's in the garden with a dark-haired man in the background who's presumably Esmond, but he's mowing the lawn with his back to the camera and he's a long way away. Baxter scrolls back to the school

33

shots – dads don't get to duck that sort of thing these days – but he can't see Michael. It's only now he realizes that the school in question is Bishop Christopher's, and as he looks more closely he sees faces he recognizes from the Daisy Mason case. The head, one or two of the teachers, some of the children they interviewed, and finally, with a jolt, Daisy herself, coming second in the egg-and-spoon, her small face a model of furious determination. It's 2016 – the last summer term before she disappeared – and from what Baxter can see here, Matty Esmond was in the same class. It can't be connected – it can't even be relevant – but it brings something to the forefront of his mind which is always in the background for any police officer: after the case is solved, and the culprits apprehended, and the world goes back to 'normal', what then? Can anything really be 'normal' after a case like that? A child disappears and never comes back, and when her classmates start the new school year she isn't there. Everyone always says how resilient kids are, but is that just another lie adults keep repeating to make themselves feel better? This lad, Matty Esmond – he doesn't look 'resilient'. He looks fragile, vulnerable. How did he feel after Daisy went missing? How did he react when he heard what had really happened to her? However much parents might try to shield their kids, that sort of thing, it always gets out.

Baxter sighs, thinking – not for the first time – that he's glad he doesn't have children, then makes a few notes to add to the case file. Then he opens up his email and sends a message to Fawley, listing the information they're going to need which he'll have to OK. Financials, for starters. Phone and email records, medical files, internet histories. He's just closing down the machine when Everett arrives in a gust of cold air. She's been out to Wantage to see Michael Esmond's mother.

'How was it?' he says, glancing up. But one look at her face says it all.

'Doesn't matter how often I go to them or how good the staff are, those places always give me the willies.' She sits down heavily and starts to unwind her scarf. 'I mean, the manager couldn't have been nicer, and they obviously really care about the residents, but all those chairs pushed back against the wall, and the smell of piss, and the telly on sixteen hours a day. It's my idea of the second circle of hell.'

Though spending the last two weekends before Christmas trailing round every care home in a ten-mile radius probably didn't help. She'd been trying to find somewhere suitable for Dad – not that he knows that yet. Though it's been coming for a while. The forgetfulness, the sudden petulance, the defensiveness. And the loss of any sense of time. As soon as it gets light he's awake, and that means he has the TV on. He's been doing it the whole time he's been staying with her. Shuffling into the sitting room apparently unaware that she's still trying to sleep. Though she, at least, can keep hold of the volume control; his neighbours at home aren't so lucky. Two or three times a week they go round to complain, and with a four-month-old baby, Everett can't exactly blame them; they must be half hallucinating for lack of REM sleep. But her father refuses to answer the door when they ring, which means a thirty-mile round trip for Everett to sort it out. Something has to give. She's been telling herself for weeks that she'd have it out with him over Christmas, when they'd be alone and she'd have more time, but he's about to go home and she still hasn't done it. Like any good copper she can spot a coward when she sees one, and this time she doesn't need to look any further than her own mirror.

She looks up to see Baxter giving her a quizzical look. As well he might; she hasn't told anyone at work about all this. Though she'll probably need to say something soon. To Fawley, at least, if no one else.

'I did get to see Mrs Esmond,' she says, 'and I told her about the fire, as tactfully as I could, but I don't think she really took any of it in. Just smiled at me and said, "How nice, dear".'

'So she's not likely to be much help tracking Esmond down then.'

Ev shakes her head. 'I did tell her he was missing but she didn't seem very concerned. Just waved her hand about and said he'd "have gone off to that hut again".'

Baxter frowns. 'Scout hut? Nissen hut?'

Ev sighs. 'Could be bloody Pizza Hut for all I know. The staff were none the wiser. But they did warn me she probably wouldn't be much help.'

'Pity.'

Something about his tone makes her do a double-take. 'What – did you find something?'

Baxter makes a face. 'To be honest, it's more what I didn't find.'

* * *

Telephone interview with Philip Esmond,
4 January 2018, 5.46 p.m.
On the call, DC E. Somer

ES: DC Somer speaking.

PE: Hello – can you hear me? I think there's a
    delay on the line.

ES: I can hear you – is that Mr Esmond?

PE: Philip Esmond, yes. I got a message from the
    coastguard that someone at Thames Valley
    wanted to speak to me. It was something about
    Mike? Sorry about the line – I'm calling from
    a satellite phone in the middle of the Bay of
    Biscay.

ES: I'm really sorry to have to tell you like
    this, but there's been a fire at your brother's
    house.

PE: A fire? What do you mean, a fire?

ES: It broke out in the small hours of this
    morning.

PE: Jesus – not the kids –

ES: I'm so very sorry. Zachary, I'm afraid he
    didn't make it.

PE: And Matty?

ES: He's in intensive care. They're doing
    everything they possibly can –

PE: Fucking hell. I'll need to get back –
    [*pause*]
    Hang on a minute, why didn't Mike call? He's
    not dead too, is he? Jesus –

ES: No, sir. At least, not as far as we know.

PE: 'As far as you know'? What the hell does that
    mean?

ES: [*pause*]
    I'm afraid both your brother and sister-in-law
    are missing.

PE: What do you mean – *missing*?

ES: Your brother is supposed to be at a conference
    in London but we haven't been able to track
    him down and he's not answering his phone. We
    were hoping he'd been in contact with you.

PE: Last time I spoke to him was Christmas Day.

ES: How did he seem to you then?

PE: Fine. A bit hassled, but that's nothing new. I
    think he just had a lot on his plate.

ES: When did you last see him?

PE: Last summer. I stayed a few days. Mike had
    started smoking again and he was drinking a
    bit more than usual, but nothing, you know,
    heavy. And the kids were –
    [*pause*]
    He didn't, you know, suffer, did he? Zachary?

ES: We hope not. That's all I can really say.

PE: [*pause*]
    Shit.

ES: [*muffled noises at the police end*]
    Actually, Mr Esmond, there was one other thing
    we wanted to ask you. When we spoke to your
    mother she mentioned something about a hut. It
    was when we said Michael was missing. She said
    she thought he would have 'gone there again'.
    Does that mean anything to you?

PE: No. Sorry.

ES: She couldn't have been referring to your house, by any chance? We couldn't find a current address for you.

PE: I've been house-sitting for a mate the last six months. I move around a lot.

ES: Could Mr or Mrs Esmond be there?

PE: I don't see how – they don't have keys or anything. Like I said, it's not mine.

ES: They don't have a second home, do they? Country cottage, something like that?

PE: [*laughs drily*]

No, Constable, they don't. That house in Southey Road was more than enough, believe me.

* * *

Everett knows something is wrong the minute she opens the flat door. Something about that dry fizzing smell. She drops everything and races through to the kitchen. The gas is on full and the saucepan is empty. She snatches a tea towel and clatters the pan into the sink.

'Dad!' she calls, running cold water as the pan hisses in an angry spurt of steam. '*Dad!*'

There's no answer, and for a moment anger gives way to anxiety – she can't hear the TV – has he gone off wandering? Even though she told him to stay indoors? But then there's the sound of the toilet flushing and he comes bustling into the kitchen, still adjusting his trousers. There's a small wet stain near his fly that she wills herself not to notice.

'Dad, what the hell were you doing? You can't leave an empty pan on the gas –'

He frowns at her tetchily. 'It's not *empty*, Verity –'

'Oh yes, it is – I only just got to it in time –'

'I can assure you it wasn't. I was just going to boil myself an egg. Given there's absolutely no sign of any other kind of sustenance round here.'

'I had to work late. I *told you* –'

'That bloody cat gets fed better than I do.'

She feels her jaw tighten. 'You know that's not true. And if the pan really was full how come it had boiled completely dry? That didn't happen in five minutes. Where on earth were you?'

He looks away and starts hurrumphing about being cooped up all day and everyone being entitled to a little fresh air.

She takes a step towards him. 'This is *serious*, Dad. You could have burned the whole place down.'

He snaps a look at her at that. 'All this silly hoo-ha over a boiled egg. Your mother's right, Verity – you really do have a deplorable tendency to over-dramatize things; always have had, ever since you were a child. She was saying so only the other day.'

Ev turns away. There are tears in her eyes now. Not just at the unfairness of it but because her mother's been dead for more than two years. There's a voice in her head saying *You can't ignore this any more. Speak to him. Sit him down and speak to him. Right now.* She takes a deep breath and turns to face him.

'What would you like for tea, Dad?'

* * *

At 9.15 the following morning Gislingham and Quinn pull up on to the drive in front of the Institute of Social and Cultural Anthropology on the Banbury Road. A converted Victorian townhouse – as so many smaller Oxford departments are – rising four storeys above a lower ground. Dirty 'Oxford yellow' brick with ornamental woodwork in dark red paint. A bike rack, gravel greened with weeds, two industrial-sized recycling bins and a sign saying NO PARKING.

'Bloody hell,' says Quinn, pushing the car door shut and looking up. 'You wouldn't catch me working in there. It's like something out of *Hammer House of Horror*.'

Gislingham shoots him a look; it's on the tip of his tongue to observe that Quinn's just a tad underqualified for a university teaching post, but that's the sort of banter they'd have had in the old days. As Janet reminds him every morning, he has to act like Quinn's boss now.

They go up the steps to the door and ring the bell, hearing it echo somewhere inside. But that's all they can hear. They ring again, and wait again, then Quinn goes back down a step and squints into the venetian blinds on the upper ground floor.

'Can't see anything,' he says, finally. 'And there aren't any bikes out here either. Do you reckon anyone bothers to come in during the holidays?'

The answer, apparently, is yes, because suddenly the door opens and a woman appears. She has wispy grey hair in a French pleat, a tartan skirt and a coarse woollen jumper.

'I don't know who you are, but you can't park there.'

Quinn opens his mouth to speak but Gislingham gets

there first. 'We're the police, madam,' he says, flashing his warrant card. 'I'm Detective Sergeant Chris Gislingham and this is Detective Constable Quinn. May we come in?'

The woman takes the card and stares at it, then looks at Quinn. 'I suppose so,' she says eventually.

And as they follow her into the hallway Quinn mutters, in a voice calculated to be just about audible, *'Acting Detective Sergeant.'*

There's a room at the back overlooking the garden which clearly combines the woman's office, a reception area and a place for the coffee machine. She gestures towards two plastic chairs and asks them to wait while she finds Professor Jordan. 'I have seen her today but she was on the phone to China. We have a collaboration with a university in Hangzhou.'

'No worries, we can wait, Miss —'

'*Mrs* Beeton,' she says, tartly. 'And spare me the cookery jokes because I've heard them all before.'

She turns on her heel and marches back down the hall-way to the stairs, with Quinn grinning after her.

'She's a game old buzzard,' he says. 'Reminds me of my nan. She didn't take no shit from no one, even in her nineties.'

Must be where you get it from, thinks Gislingham. He has too much nervous energy to sit down, so he wanders over to the rack of magazines and journals. *American Ethnologist, Visual Anthropology Review, Comparative Studies in Society and History, Anthropological Journal of European Cultures.* He picks one up and scans down the list of articles. Even the titles are completely impenetrable: what the hell is 'performativity' anyway?

Quinn, meanwhile, is looking at the board on the wall with the names and pictures of the departmental staff. A good number of them are from overseas, if the names are anything to go by. There are one or two arty black-and-white photos, but most are standard colleague-with-a-digital-camera shots. Apart from Esmond's, which is definitely staged, and definitely professional.

'What do you think?' asks Quinn, staring at the picture. 'Bit up himself? Baxter seemed to think so, judging from his Facebook page.'

Gislingham considers. 'Strikes me as a bit insecure, to be honest. Over-compensating.'

Quinn makes a face. 'Not sure how much "compensating" you need to do when you've got a house like that. Must be rolling in it.'

'Speaking of which, did you check about the house?' *Like I asked you to*, hangs in the air.

'I did, actually,' says Quinn, with just the tiniest edge of sarcasm. 'Still waiting to hear. But my money's still on family dough. No way he could afford that place on what he earns. And where else would cash like that come from? Embezzlement's a no-no for starters.' He gestures round at the slightly shabby room, the ancient radiator, the MDF shelves. 'I mean, look at this place.'

'You're right, officer. Academic misdemeanours are rarely, if ever, pecuniary in nature.'

The voice is coming from the door. A tall thin woman with strong features and an arrangement of long dark clothes in layers. Wide trousers, tunic, overshirt. She has a chunky pewter necklace of geometrical shapes hanging low against her waist.

'I'm Annabel Jordan. Would you like to come up? Mary will bring us coffee. I, for one, could do with it.'

Her office is on the floor above, overlooking the street. What must once have been a family drawing room, complete with cornicing and a fireplace with a cast-iron surround. The walls are lined with untidy bookshelves, and she has two battered leather armchairs facing her desk. And on the wall a framed poster for an exhibition of Palaeolithic art at the Ashmolean museum – a carving of a woman, the hips and breasts bulbous, the head disproportionately small and without features.

'Do please sit down. I'm guessing you've come to talk to me about Michael. What a truly terrible thing to happen.'

'You heard about it?' asks Gislingham with a frown. They haven't released the family's name to the press.

She takes her own seat. 'I saw the news, Sergeant. I recognized the house. Michael had a drinks party soon after he moved in – the department, the post-grads – there must have been a hundred people there. It made my semi in Summertown look positively disadvantaged.'

Gislingham nods; no doubt that was part of the point.

'And your colleague is right,' she says with a gesture to Quinn. 'It was – is – family money.' She turns again to Gislingham, her face concerned. 'Is there any news on Matty?'

Gislingham shakes his head. 'Not that I've heard.'

'And that other poor child. Zachary. What a waste. What an awful, pointless, deplorable waste.'

'We believe Mr Esmond is currently attending a conference in London?'

She sits back, folds her hands. 'Yes, that's right.'

'You don't know where he might be staying in London? A friend's? A hotel he usually used?'

She shakes her head. 'No, I'm afraid I couldn't tell you. In fact, I haven't seen him for some time.'

She makes to get up but Gislingham hasn't finished. 'So what *can* you tell us about him, Professor Jordan?'

She sits back again, the ghost of a frown crossing her face. 'Diligent. Hard-working.' There's a pause. 'Perhaps a bit humourless. I don't think he makes friends easily.'

'He doesn't have any on the staff here?'

She starts playing with the necklace absent-mindedly, 'Not "friends" as such, no. I don't think so. There were some people he worked with more closely than others, but I suspect "colleagues" is the better word.'

'And what exactly does he work on?'

She hesitates. 'I'm not sure how much you know about anthropology, officer –'

Quinn smiles. 'Treat us like novices.'

She raises an eyebrow. 'That's rather more relevant than you realize. Michael specializes in the sacrificial and initiation practices of primitive and indigenous societies. Puberty rites, shamanic ordeals and so on. The various social, cultural, ritualistic and magico-religious factors that come into play –'

Quinn's eyes are already glazing over.

'– he wrote a very impressive doctoral thesis and got a post at Liverpool almost immediately afterwards. For a while his career looked unstoppable.'

'But?' says Gislingham.

Her eyes flicker. 'I'm sorry?'

'I've been doing this a lot of years,' he says drily.

She smiles, a trifle uneasily. 'Let's just say that he hasn't progressed quite as far – or as fast – as one might have expected. His research has stalled rather, and I happen to know he's applied for several other jobs in the last few months, both here and at other universities, but hasn't been shortlisted. That's confidential, of course,' she adds quickly. 'I was his referee, so I would have known.'

'And how did he feel about that?'

'I'm sure he was frustrated. Who wouldn't be?'

Something else Gislingham knows when he hears it is a professional evasion. He changes tack.

'How has he been lately?'

'I'm not sure what you mean.'

And there's another one. OK, he thinks, if that's how you want to play it.

'What's his mood been like? Any recent change in his habits or behaviour?'

She glances at him, then away. 'Michael is always very careful – very considered.'

'But?'

'But lately he's become, well, I suppose the only word is "loud". Outspoken, voicing quite controversial opinions. That sort of thing.'

'How long has this been going on?'

'I don't know, three or four months, perhaps?'

'Is there anyone in particular he's pissed off?'

'No. Not that I'm aware of. Nothing significant, anyway.'

The door opens and Mrs Beeton comes in with three mugs, a cafetière and a carton of semi-skimmed milk. She edges the tray on to the desk and leaves, though not without a meaningful look in Jordan's direction. Gislingham suspects she's been listening outside for a while. No kettle takes that long to boil.

'So what about the rest?'

'I'm sorry?'

Gislingham holds her gaze. 'You said "nothing significant". There's something else, isn't there? Something you'd rather not tell us. But believe me, Professor, it's all going to come out in the end. Far better you tell us now than we have to find out for ourselves.'

It's a line he'd heard Fawley say once, and filed away for future use.

They stare at each other for a moment, and then she says, 'I need to consult the university's legal team before I say anything more. It's a sensitive matter, and given what's now happened –'

She looks from one to the other and back again. She can see they're not buying it.

She sighs. 'Very well. In the very strictest confidence, we had a complaint from a student.'

'About Michael Esmond?'

She nods.

Jesus, thinks Gislingham, this is like drawing teeth.

'Getting a bit on the side, is he?' asks Quinn, who seems to have decided that there are advantages to his demotion, not the least of which is the freedom to be a bit of a tosser with complete impunity.

Jordan glares at him. 'I have no evidence for that whatsoever. Nor does the young woman in question allege anything of the kind.'

'So what was it?' says Gislingham. 'Sexting? Dodgy emails?'

Jordan hesitates. 'There seems to have been an unfortunate incident at the departmental Christmas party.'

'Just how "unfortunate" are we talking?'

She flushes. 'Some inappropriate comments and apparently some physical contact. All of which Michael vehemently denies. Unfortunately there were no witnesses.'

'So *he said, she said*, eh?' says Quinn.

'Quite. It was clear we were going to have to involve the legal department.'

'Were?'

'Sorry?'

'You said "*were* going to involve". Past tense.'

Another flush. 'Yes, well, the latest turn of events has put a rather different complexion on the matter.'

Right, thinks Gislingham. He suddenly has the absolute conviction that the call Jordan made earlier wasn't to China at all.

'You didn't see fit to inform the police?' he says.

'As I said, we haven't yet decided on the best course of action.'

Gislingham flips open his notebook again and writes a few words.

'When did you have this conversation with him – the one when he denied all knowledge?'

'I told him about the allegations at the end of last term and we met again on Tuesday.'

Gislingham can't disguise his reaction. 'Tuesday as in January 2nd? Tuesday as in less than *three days* ago? You just said you'd had no contact with him –' he flips back a couple of pages – '"for some time". I wouldn't call three days *some time*.'

She looks embarrassed now – embarrassed and outmanoeuvred. 'When I saw him before Christmas he was clearly rather overwrought, so I suggested he think it all over during the vac and we'd talk again in early January. He came here first thing on Tuesday on his way to London. I was hoping we'd be able to bring matters to a satisfactory conclusion.'

Gislingham starts to nod. 'I get it – you were hoping he'd resign, right? Give him the pearl-handled revolver and hope he'd do the decent thing?'

She bridles. 'Not at all. You're quite wrong about that, officer. Quite wrong.'

But the look on her face is saying something very different.

'So how did it go?'

She hesitates. 'Let's just leave it that we had a frank exchange of views.'

More like a slanging match, he thinks, to judge from her face. And that old bag Beeton must have heard every word.

'How were things left?'

'I said that, in the circumstances, I would now be consulting the University authorities and it would be up to them to determine the best course of action.'

'But he could lose his job, couldn't he.' It's Quinn. And it's a statement, not a question. 'I mean, sexual harassment of a student, in the current climate? "Me too" and all that. They'd hang him out by the balls.'

Jordan gives him a look of undisguised loathing. 'In

49

theory, it could lead to dismissal, yes. But we're a long way from that. At least at this stage.'

But that's not how Michael Esmond might have seen it. Quinn and Gislingham exchange a glance.

'Can we talk to the girl?' asks Gislingham.

Jordan frowns. 'She has not made a police complaint.'

'I'm aware of that, Professor. But you can appreciate why we'd like to talk to her.'

'Yes, I'm sure you would. But there are procedures – consents I have to obtain. I will speak to the lawyers, and then to the young woman, and I will come back to you as soon as I reasonably can.'

*　　*　　*

In Summertown, meanwhile, Everett has only just got back from dropping her father off at his house just outside Bicester. Anything involving him always takes five times longer than she allows for, and this morning was no different. And she hasn't spoken to him about the care home yet either. But she's looked up the number for his local Social Services and she's going to force herself to call them by the end of the day. Though right now she has a job to do. She pops back up to the flat to check on the cat (who's clearly as relieved as she is that normal service has been resumed) and then returns to the pavement, where she takes out the picture Baxter found on Samantha Esmond's Facebook page. He was pretty sure it was taken in one of the shops on the Summertown parade, and she'd agreed with him. She hasn't lived here for two years for nothing.

Five minutes later, she's pushing through the door. Candles, china, bathrobes, towels. If it's not white, it's glass. And it's all so delicate and refined and sweet-smelling she feels twice her normal size just standing there. Thankfully she doesn't have to do it for long; the girl behind the counter looks up with a smile. 'Is there anything in particular you were looking for? We have some of our discontinued items in the sale.'

Everett edges nervously round a display of ornate champagne glasses and pulls her warrant card from her jacket. 'DC Everett, Thames Valley. Could I speak to the manager?'

The girl looks alarmed. 'Is there something wrong?'

Everett's turn to smile. 'No, not at all. I just need to speak to the lady in this photo.'

The girl takes the picture and nods. 'Oh yes, that's Mel. She's on her break. I'll just get her.'

She disappears out the back, leaving Ev standing there staring at the champagne flutes. The ones she has at home were a gift from her mum when she first left home. They look like something out of a Babycham ad.

'Hello? I'm sorry, Jenna couldn't remember your name.'

She turns. It's definitely the woman in the photo. Mid height, strong, handsome features and well-cut dark auburn hair. Under the unforgiving lights the red is purplish.

'DC Everett,' she says, holding out her hand. 'Verity.'

'Mel Kennedy. What's this about?'

'The woman in this picture with you –'

'Sam? This is about Sam?'

Everett takes a deep breath. 'Did you see the news – the fire?'

The woman goes pale. 'Oh no – not those children – please don't say –'

'I'm very sorry.' She watches as Kennedy reaches half blindly for a chair and sits down heavily. She has her hand to her mouth. Her shock seems completely genuine.

'Take your time. Would you like a glass of water?'

Kennedy shakes her head. 'I just can't believe it.'

'When did you last see Mrs Esmond?'

Kennedy looks at her for a moment. 'You know, I can't honestly remember. Perhaps last summer?'

'This picture is a couple of years old, I think?'

Kennedy glances at it. 'At least three. She only worked here a short time. But we got on, you know? We really got on.'

Everett moves a little closer. 'We still haven't been able to track Mrs Esmond down. Do you have any idea where she might be?'

Kennedy shakes her head again. 'She's a very private person. She never talked much about her personal life.'

'No particular friends? No one she might be visiting?'

She shrugs, helpless.

Everett takes a deep breath; there's no easy way to broach this. 'Knowing Mrs Esmond – Sam – do you think she'd be likely to leave her children alone in the house?'

But Kennedy is already interrupting her. 'Sam would *never* have done that,' she says fiercely. 'Never.'

'Why did she stop working here?'

Kennedy gets out a tissue and blows her nose. 'It was when she got pregnant with Zachary. Her husband thought it would all be too much for her. What with Matty as well. But between you and me, I don't think he wanted her working here in the first place. Used to make snarky comments – "What the hell is shabby chic anyway?" That sort of thing. He's a bit snooty, I reckon. A bit of a snob.'

'You saw a lot of him?'

She shakes her head. 'No. He didn't come in much. Like I said, I don't think he approved of a wife of his doing shop work.'

'But they're happy, as far as you know? No problems at home?'

'Oh no. Nothing like that. He doted on her. She was always saying so.'

* * *

21 February 2017, 7.45 a.m.
317 days before the fire
23 Southey Road, Oxford

It's the clatter of crockery that wakes her. She'd slept unusually deeply, and surfaces from half-remembered menace like someone pulled from drowning. The other side of the bed is cold; Michael isn't there. That's unusual too – he never normally gets up first. And then she remembers. It's her birthday. That's what the noise downstairs is about. The boys are preparing her breakfast in bed. It's the same surprise every year, but she always manages to pretend she wasn't expecting it. She hauls herself to sitting position, and reaches to plump the pillows behind her. The air in the room is icy, despite the central heating. She sighs: the only way to insulate these houses properly is to take the plaster off the walls and start again. That's what the people in the house opposite did before they moved in. But they were renting somewhere at the time: they didn't have to live there while the builders were doing it. She got an estimate from the firm but when she broached it with Michael all he kept going on about was the mess.

There's the sound of their footsteps on the stairs now, and she can hear Zachary shouting and Matty saying 'Ssh, ssh!' A few moments later the door pushes open and Zachary rushes in yelling 'HAPPY BIRTHDAY!' at the top of his voice. He clambers on the bed, hurling himself at her, and his father says, 'Easy, Tigger.' Like he always does.

Michael perches on the edge of the bed and hands her the tray. Tea in one of the Wedgwood cups they were given by his mother, a boiled egg (Matty's contribution), three slices of toast laden with strawberry jam (Zachary's) and a rose in a little vase. Michael turns to his eldest son, who's hanging back, his face a little closed. 'Come on, Matty, stop skulking about over there.'

Matty pushes his glasses up his nose – Samantha knew they were too big for him, but the optician insisted. Her son sidles forward. He's holding two parcels.

'You wrapped yours yourself, didn't you, Matty?' says Michael, encouraging him closer.

'Come and sit with me, sweetheart,' she says quickly.

Matty puts the parcels on the bed and then climbs carefully across to his mother. She reaches out and pulls him to her, kissing him on the side of the head. Zachary starts to fidget, sending the tea slopping into the saucer.

'Mummy eat toast!'

'I will, sweet pea,' she says, catching the flicker of a frown on her husband's face. 'Let me just have this tea before it goes everywhere.'

The egg is almost hard-boiled and the toast is cold, but she eats it all, then breathes a silent sigh of relief as she hands the tray to Michael.

'Right,' he says, smiling. 'Presents!'

The boys have given her the same perfume they give her every year, and she kisses them both, then carefully folds the paper and detaches the gift tag Matty has written and puts it in her bedside drawer, making sure he sees. Things like that matter to him.

Michael's gift is in a small box. Silver earrings in the shape of tassels. She'd seen an actress wearing some like it a few weeks before and said how much she liked them. And he'd remembered. Remembered and spent God knows how long looking for them. She looks up and sees him smiling at her. There's hardly a strand of grey in his dark hair, and he's as slim as he was when they first met. That party in Hackney. She can't even remember now whose house it was. She was only a couple of months past graduation and he was already halfway through his PhD. There are times, even now, when she can't believe he really did choose her.

'They're beautiful,' she says softly.

He reaches forward and takes her hand. 'Just like you. I thought you could wear them tonight at Gee's. With that blue dress I got you.'

'Yes,' she says, smiling. 'Of course.'

'OK, boys,' he says, turning to his sons. 'Let's leave Mummy alone for a while now, shall we? She needs to rest.'

*　*　*

At 12.30, Professor Jordan goes up the steps to the University Offices. A building which, in a city of architectural wonders, promises much, but is actually a 1970s concrete slab that could just as easily be an inner-city comprehensive, a council office or the Ministry of Defence. Up on the second floor, there are three people in the meeting room already. The head of Esmond's college, and Nicholas Grant from the Proctors' Office. The third is introduced to Jordan as Emily McPherson, the director of the press relations department, a smartly dressed young woman in a black suit and a heavy set of pearls. Annabel has never had occasion to meet her before; it's not a good omen.

'Ah, Annabel,' says Grant. 'Thank you for coming in at such short notice, but in the circumstances, we do need to make sure we're all singing from the same hymn sheet.'

Jordan ticks off her mental bullshit bingo card. First sentence, and he's already got one in – that's good going, even for Grant. It'll be low-hanging fruit next.

Jordan swings her hessian bag down heavily on to the table and takes her seat opposite Grant.

'So,' he says, 'for Emily's benefit, perhaps you could summarize what we discussed on the phone?'

'Of course, Nicholas.' She turns to McPherson. 'At the end of last term, Ned Tate from Magdalen came to me to report an incident of alleged sexual harassment involving Michael Esmond and Lauren Kaminsky, one of our postgrads. Lauren is his girlfriend. It supposedly took place at the departmental Christmas party. Lauren and Michael both happened to be taking a cigarette break at the same time. He started flirting with her and it quickly escalated into something more serious. At least, that's her side of the story. She said Michael was very drunk at the time.'

'And has that been corroborated?' asks McPherson. 'The intoxication?'

Jordan sighs. 'I'm afraid so. I saw him that night myself.'

'But there were no witnesses to the alleged incident?'

'No. Lauren claims he started to touch her breasts and she pushed him away.'

'That's as far as it went?' says Grant.

'That's more than far enough, wouldn't you say?' she replies tersely.

'What did he say when you spoke to him?' asks McPherson. She has a soft Scottish accent. A very listenable voice.

'He denied it all. Vehemently. He swore a lot. Said she'd been drinking too, which is also true, incidentally. He was clearly in a highly emotional state – not just angry but paranoid. Rather alarmingly so. So I suggested he take some time to think about it all and we'd meet again after the vac.'

'It would have been better all round if he'd just bloody well resigned and had done with it,' says Grant.

Jordan flashes him a look. 'Better for you, maybe. But academic jobs don't grow on trees, you know. The man has a young family. And he may be telling the truth. It's not impossible.'

'What did the legal department say?' asks McPherson.

'I haven't talked to them about it yet. I was on the point of doing so when we heard the news about the fire.'

'It's still worth doing,' says McPherson with a sympathetic smile. 'If the press gets hold of this we'll need to know where we stand.'

'Is the girl likely to say anything?' asks Grant.

Jordan restrains herself from pointing out the many

and various crimes against political correctness 'girl' represents. 'Not at present. I will need to speak to her when she gets back from the US.'

'And I believe the police have been to see you?' asks the head of Esmond's college.

'Yes, two CID officers. I told them about the allegations, and if you are in agreement I will give them Lauren's name. In the circumstances, we can hardly refuse.'

He nods.

'So what's the game plan?' asks Grant. Jordan crosses off another weary bingo box.

'I don't think we can decide on an appropriate course of action,' says McPherson, 'until a) we know what's happened to Dr Esmond, and b) we know whether it was definitely arson. If it is indeed determined that the fire was started deliberately –'

'Which brings us,' replies Grant, 'to why we're here. I assume,' he says, turning to Jordan, 'that this other matter is *not* something you elected to share with the police?'

'Of course not,' she snaps. 'What do you take me for?'

'And have you spoken to him?'

'He called me in a panic as soon as he saw the news. I advised him that it would be preferable to pre-empt the inevitable enquiry by making a voluntary statement.'

'And is he going to take that advice?' asks McPherson.

'He says he will. And hopefully that will be the end of it.'

'You're sure?' says Grant. 'What about – the rest?'

'He swears he's removed all trace.'

Grant looks her straight in the eye. 'Well, I just hope you're right,' he says meaningfully.

Just after three, DC Asante emerges from Embankment tube station into sullen skies and a bitter wind off the water. Even the trees look huddled against the cold. He pulls on his gloves and heads north towards King's College. It's the first time he's been back to London since he joined Thames Valley three months before, and all the way in on the train he's been wondering how it would feel to be back. Not that this was ever his patch. Brixton police station may only be a couple of miles as the crow flies but it's a lot further by every other form of human measurement. And as for where he was brought up – that's another five miles west but it might as well be in a parallel universe. Not that his new colleagues in St Aldate's know about that. They just heard 'Brixton' and let assumptions do the rest. But he's not about to let a bit of casual racism like that bother him. Because, yes, his last station was indeed in South London but his school was Harrow, and his Ghanaian father is a former diplomat and his English mother the CEO of a pharmaceutical company, with a stucco-fronted town house in a Holland Park square. And they call him Anthony. With an 'h'. They're still rather bemused at his choice of career, but Anthony only ever saw the uniform phase as a means to an end. Everything's going to be different now – now he's in Oxford. He's clever and he's ambitious, and those are qualities he reckons that town will appreciate. Along with agility, both intellectual and social. But he's bright enough to know what to keep quiet, and how fast to push. For the time being, it's about watch and learn. And in his book, DI Adam Fawley is exactly the man to help him do it.

* * *

I'm checking my phone for what must be the hundredth time today when Gis knocks on the door.

'That mobile in the house,' he begins. 'The one that was charging in the kitchen.'

I'm still looking at my phone. Nothing from Alex. Again.

'Turns out it's hers,' he says, slightly louder. 'The wife's.'

He has my attention now. All of it. 'So it's possible –'

He nods. 'I reckon she could still be in there.'

I toss my own phone on to the desk. 'Jesus.'

He takes a step forward and puts a printout down in front of me. 'And we've been going through Esmond's mobile records. He's made no calls since 1.15 Tuesday lunchtime when he called his bank. He was already in London by that point. The phone is then off, until it goes back on again at 10.35 p.m. on Wednesday.'

'Wednesday? The night of the fire?'

'You got it. He was somewhere in the Tottenham Court Road area.'

He doesn't need to draw me a diagram: Esmond was fifty miles away when his home and family were wiped out. And whoever did it could well have known that.

'The phone was only on for about an hour though,' Gis says. 'He turned it off again at 11.45. And he didn't make or receive any calls in the meantime either.'

'And that's it?'

He nods. 'It's been off ever since.'

'Anything odd in the last few months?'

'Baxter's been through the call log and there are no obvious patterns.' He's flicking through a sheaf of print-outs. 'He used to phone home a lot during the day, but that's hardly unusual. Otherwise it was mostly mundane stuff like British Gas and his mother's care home.'

'Mostly?'

'Ah, that's the only vaguely interesting bit. He's been calling a pay-as-you-go mobile a fair amount lately, but we may struggle to find out who it belongs to.'

'When did the calls start?'

Gis leafs back. 'June last year. There's one or two that month, and then they become more frequent. At least two or three a week. The last one was on the morning of the 27th December.'

'Nothing the day of the fire?'

He shakes his head. 'Nope.' He shifts to another print-out. 'Though there've been a few calls to that number from the Esmonds' landline as well. The last of those was before Christmas. None from the wife's mobile, though. For the record.'

'I assume you've tried calling it – this mystery number?'

'Afraid it just rings out.'

'Do we know where that mobile was when Esmond was calling it?'

'It was in London on one occasion, but the rest of the time always in Oxford. Mostly in and around the Botley Road area. But without a name it'll be like looking for a black cat in the dark.'

Always assuming, of course, the damn cat is there in the first place.

I must have sighed because Gis hurries on. 'I've got the Tech unit monitoring Esmond's mobile in case he switches it back on again. But right now, wherever he is, he's not talking.'

I glance at him and then at my watch. In precisely twenty-five minutes Michael Esmond should be talking all right: he should be getting to his feet in front of a hall full of people.

'I know,' says Gis, reading my mind. 'Asante rang half an hour ago but there's been no sign of Esmond yet. But that doesn't mean he's not coming. He may just be one of those blokes who does everything at the last minute.'

But I can see from his face that he doesn't really believe that. And, frankly, nor do I.

* * *

At Southey Road, it's got so dark the fire investigators have had to turn on the arc-lights. It started to snow about an hour ago and, despite the makeshift tarpaulin, huge white flakes are drifting in, catching golden in the lamp beams and dropping softly on to the heaps of blackened debris.

Paul Rigby is outside on the phone when he hears the shout behind him. He turns to see one of the investigators beckoning urgently.

'Have you found something?'

The man nods and Rigby starts towards him, clambering up the rubble, roof tiles and shards of glass slipping and breaking under his boots. Three of the team are staring down at something at their feet. Rigby's seen that look too many times before to mistake it. Under the twisted window frame and the metal pipes and the sheet of scorched plasterboard, there's something else.

A human hand.

*   *   *

This time when Gis comes to my door, I only need to take one look at him to know there's something.

'What is it – did Esmond turn up?'

He makes a face. 'Nope. He was a no-show. Asante spoke to the organizers and they haven't heard a thing from him. No phone message, no email, nothing.'

I sigh heavily. And then realize that my overwhelming feeling right now is that I'm not surprised. At some level I must have been expecting this. Does that mean I suspect him? I didn't think I did – not consciously, anyway. But my gut instinct is clearly telling me otherwise.

Gis takes a step into the room. 'Though even if we haven't found him, we may have found *her*. That's what I came to tell you. Rigby called. There's another body at the site. Just like we thought.'

'Female?'

He nods.

'And they're sure it's her?'

'As sure as they can be. She was wearing some sort of nightdress. Looks like she must have been in one of the other bedrooms on the top floor. I hope for her sake she just went to sleep and didn't know anything about it.'

Unlike her son, who woke in terror and found himself alone.

I glance up at Gislingham and I can see he's thinking the same. 'No more news on Matty yet, boss,' he says. 'But we can always hope, eh?'

* * *

9 April 2017, 2.13 p.m.
270 days before the fire
23 Southey Road, Oxford

'Oh bloody hell!'

Michael Esmond drops the spade and it hits the grass with a metallic clang. The shrub he's trying to shift has wrenched the handle clean off. He stands there, staring down at the unyielding stump, breathing heavily. He really does have better things to do than this.

'Everything OK?' It's Sam, joining him. She hands him a mug of tea. It has 'Happy Birthday Daddy' on the side.

'Fine,' says Michael, a little tetchily: it was his wife's idea to replant this bloody border. 'Broken the sodding spade, but otherwise absolutely hunky-dory.'

Samantha looks down the garden to where her sons are playing. Matty is trying to interest Zachary in a game of football but the toddler is just running about after the ball, screaming with delight.

'You're supposed to be the goalie,' Matty is saying wearily. '*I'm* the striker.'

'Perhaps we should get someone in,' she ventures, 'for the garden.'

He turns to her. 'Gardeners round here cost a bloody fortune, you know that.'

'Not one of the firms,' she says quickly. 'Perhaps ask around at the faculty? There must be students who'd like to earn a bit of extra beer money.'

He's still staring at the wrecked shovel. 'It's all Dad's fault,' he says eventually. 'Why did he have to plant stuff like this?'

'I think he wanted to keep the weeds down,' she says, willing herself not to look across at the other borders, already spiked with the first signs of nettles. She doesn't want her husband to think he's being criticized, but a garden this size needs someone on it at least twice a week.

Michael drains his mug and turns to his wife, looking at her properly for the first time. 'How are you feeling?'

'OK,' she says at once.

'You do look a bit brighter. Better than yesterday, anyway.'

'I'm sorry, I was just so exhausted – I didn't mean to dump all that on you –'

'It's fine,' he says. 'That's what I'm here for. To look after you. You and the boys.'

She hesitates. 'You don't think I could –'

'No,' he says firmly. 'That's not a good idea. We can't go through all that again. You can't – *I* can't.'

'But I hate the way I feel – it's like living in fog – please, Michael –'

But whatever her husband was going to reply is drowned out by their youngest son, who suddenly careers into his father, waving the handle of the spade, shouting, 'Daddy, Daddy, you broke the spade! You broke it, Daddy!'

* * *

'Ah, Fawley, there you are. Take a seat.'

I was at the coffee machine when Superintendent Harrison's PA tracked me down and suggested I 'pop along' and give the superintendent an update. And like my inspector told me when I was just a DC, 'it's only a suggestion but let's not forget who's making it'.

'I thought we ought to give this Esmond case the once-over before the weekend,' he says. He must have something planned he doesn't want disturbing. 'And I've had a few calls – you know what I mean.'

Calls from the University is what he means. Probably not Annabel Jordan if I had to guess. More like one of the suits at Wellington Square, worried about their 'public image'.

'So, where are we, Adam?'

It doesn't take long. How could it – we have precisely sod all.

Harrison considers. He's thinking about the suits again. 'Anything on the car?'

'Nothing on traffic cams. Or ANPR.'

'Credit cards?'

'Still waiting on the bank. They're short-staffed because of the holidays.'

Just like we are.

He sits back in his chair and puts his fingertips together. 'So what now?'

But I'm prepared for this. 'There is one thing we could do, sir.'

* * *

66

Oxford Mail online

Friday 5 January 2018 Last updated at 18:11

BREAKING: Second fatality possible in Oxford fire; Police appeal for father to come forward

Residents of Southey Road earlier reported seeing an undertaker's van at the site of yesterday's fatal fire, in the wake of unconfirmed reports that the body of Mrs Samantha Esmond has been found at the house. Mrs Esmond, 33, has not been seen since before the fire broke out in the early hours of Thursday morning. Zachary Esmond, 3, died in the blaze, and his older brother, Matty, 10, remains in a critical condition in the John Radcliffe hospital. Both Mrs Esmond and her husband, Michael, 40, were initially thought to be missing, but it appears the police have called off their search for Mrs Esmond, adding weight to suspicions that the body is indeed hers.

Speaking to us this afternoon, Detective Inspector Adam Fawley made an appeal to Michael Esmond to come forward. 'We do not know where Dr Esmond is, and we are increasingly concerned about him and urge him to contact us as soon as possible. If a member of the public remembers seeing Dr Esmond at any time since 2 January,

Rail chaos after engineering work overruns between Oxford and Didcot
Commuters faced long waits for replacement buses after Christmas engineering work was not completed on time . . . /more

Plans announced to commemorate the centenary of the Armistice
Oxford City Council are to set out plans for events to mark 100 years since the end of the First World War . . . /more

Drivers warned to be more vigilant after car is stolen from the owner's drive
An Oxford man had his car stolen yesterday, after he left the engine running to defrost the vehicle . . . /more

Football: Oxford Mail Youth League, full reports and scores . . . /more

'Miracle baby' leaves John Radcliffe hospital
A baby girl born two months prematurely with a rare heart condition, will be leaving hospital with her parents today . . . /more

when he registered at a conference in central London, we would very much like to hear from them.' DI Fawley declined to comment on whether Dr Esmond is considered a suspect in the arson, or to speculate on the identity of the second victim. 'We will make a statement at the appropriate time,' he said.

Esmond, 40, is a member of the University's Anthropology department. The University offices in Wellington Square have issued a statement offering condolences to the Esmonds' family and friends.

213 comments

Tenant ofWildfell77
Where's the bloody father, that's what I want to know. He hasn't phoned – hasn't seen the TV – in all that time? Sorry, I'm not buying that.

nick_trelawney_40
Even if the mother was there after all it still looks off to me. Houses like that don't burn to the ground in five minutes

EchinasterGal556
My heart goes out to that poor kid. How's he going to feel when he wakes up and finds his Mum and his little brother are both dead?

VivendiVerve
Friends of ours house burned down because their down-lighters hadn't been fitted properly. People don't realise that they can overheat and set the whole place on fire. We checked ours afterwards and found ours were about to burn through too. It was a miracle we got to them in time. Get them checked – that's my advice!

* * *

Sent: Fri 05/01/2018, 19.35   **Importance: High**
From: Colin.Boddie@ouh.nhs.uk
To: DIAdamFawley@ThamesValley.police.uk,
CID@ThamesValley.police.uk, AlanChallowCSI@
ThamesValley.police.uk

Subject: Case no 556432/12 Felix House, 23 Southey Road

I have just completed the post-mortem of the female found
at the house. Provisional cause of death is asphyxiation as a
result of smoke inhalation, but I will need to run bloodwork
and toxicology before I can formally confirm this. Only
issue to note at this stage is a minor but recent bruise on
the right side of her neck. I would estimate it as having
occurred sometime in the preceding 48 hours.

If I clean her up a bit it should be possible to obtain
a formal identification from the next of kin.

*   *   *

At 8.30 on Saturday morning, Gislingham is sitting on the
floor in his front room. It looks like an asteroid hit on a
car boot sale. Cartons of decorations trailing tinsel, cards
heaped for recycling, fairy lights in tangled handfuls. And
in among it all, Billy. Hiding under the cardboard, picking
ornaments off the half-empty tree, pushing himself along
on his prized new plastic car. It doesn't matter how carefully Gislingham packs the boxes, as soon as he turns his
back Billy starts emptying them again. He clearly thinks
it's all the most amazing game, organized solely for his
benefit. In fact, it's the best fun he's had since he made

almost the same amount of mess opening the tsunami of presents with his name on.

Janet Gislingham comes into the room, wiping her hands on a tea towel. 'Make sure he doesn't hurt himself, Chris.'

Billy looks up from where he's sitting on the floor. He's wearing a miniature Chelsea football shirt with 'Champs 2017' on the back. Gislingham glances over. 'He's having a great time. Aren't you, Billy?'

Janet looks a bit closer. 'Is that chocolate he's got on his face?'

'I found a couple of uneaten Santas on the back of the tree.'

Billy grins and starts banging his hands on his car. Janet smiles. 'OK, I give in. I'll leave the boys to their toys. It would be good to get the decorations down at some stage, though. Perhaps in time for *next* Christmas? And *no more chocolate.*'

She gives Gislingham a meaningful look, then turns and goes back to the kitchen. Gislingham winks at his son, digs into his pocket and holds out another Santa wrapped in red and gold foil. 'Just don't tell your mum,' he says in a theatrical whisper, as Billy yelps with delight.

'*I heard that*,' calls his wife.

She can't ever remember being so happy.

* * *

Oxford Mail online

Saturday 6 January 2018 Last updated at 10.23 a.m.

Oxford house fire: No progress on identifying cause

Fire scene investigators have yet to confirm the cause of the house fire in Southey Road that has now killed two people. Three-year-old Zachary Esmond died in the fire, and his mother, Samantha, is believed to be the other victim found on the premises. Her older son, Matty, remains in intensive care at the John Radcliffe hospital.

Detective Inspector Adam Fawley has confirmed that fire officers are still at the scene but declined to speculate on the possibility of arson. He was, however, able to confirm that there was no cladding present on the building, and this was not, therefore, a factor in the speed of spread of the fire, which some commentators have raised as a concern.

The *Oxford Mail* understands that Michael Esmond, 40, has still not been located.

87 comments

nick_trelawney_40
'Still not been located'???? I told you – there's a lot more to this than meets the eye

MedoraMelborne
I thought they could get forensic results on this sort of thing
within hours these days.

Strictervictor_8_9
You've been watching too much crime TV. It can take weeks
to deal with a fire scene that size.

7788PlatinumPat
I met Samantha Esmond – Matty is at Bishop Christopher's
same as my two. She seemed such a nice woman.

* * *

When Gis rings I've just got back from Tesco. More
frozen pizza and meals for one. It's the third time I've
been in the last week. I keep telling myself Alex will be
back in a few days, that I don't want to end up with a freezer
full of this crap that will never get eaten. And yes, this is
probably about the time some joker chips in that 'denial'
is not a river in Egypt . . .

'I finally heard back from Professor Jordan,' says Gis.
'The woman Esmond was supposedly harassing is called
Lauren Kaminsky. She's a graduate student at Wolfson
College.'

'That's only just round the corner from Southey Road.'

'I gave them a call and she's been away for Christmas.
Went home to New York. But apparently she should be
back this weekend. They'll call me as soon as she's back
and we'll go up there. Better to do that sort of thing face
to face.'

'What about the appeal?'

I hear him sigh. 'I think we're up to thirty-five calls
already. Everywhere from Southampton to South Shields

and I doubt a single one of 'em is reliable. But the minute you ask the great British public – Well, you know how it is.'

I do. Indeed I do.

'And I'm afraid that's not the only thing, boss.' I can hear the diffidence in his voice now. Bad news, clearly. 'I was trying not to drag you in at the weekend but it's the parents – Samantha's parents.'

'We tracked them down?'

'Not exactly. They're here. Now. In the building. They got our message but they'd already seen the news on their holiday. They came straight from the airport.'

I dump the carrier bags, stand up, reset my brain. A shit job just got ten times shittier. 'OK, see them into whichever interview room looks marginally less crap than the others and organize some coffee, would you? I'll be there in twenty minutes.'

* * *

Interview with Gregory and Laura Gifford,
conducted at St Aldate's police station, Oxford
6 January 2018, 11.05 a.m.
In attendance, DI A. Fawley, DC V. Everett

AF: Can I start by saying how very sorry we are,
    Mr and Mrs Gifford. You may already be aware,
    but the fire investigators have found another
    body. I'm afraid we think it's your daughter.
GG: [reaching for his wife's hand. Mrs Gifford
    begins to weep]
    We feared as much. Whatever they said on the

73

TV, we knew Samantha would never have left the children alone. It was only a matter of time. We knew they'd find her in that house.

AF: I also want to apologize that we weren't able to inform you about the fire before you saw it on the news.

GG: Well, we were on holiday, weren't we. And that's how it is, these days. Wall-to-wall bloody news.

AF: All the same, I am sorry. I also need to tell you that these rooms are fitted with recording devices. With your permission, we'd like to keep a record of everything you say. I can't overstate how important this could be to our enquiries. And the last thing we want to do is have to drag you in here again later to answer more questions.

LG: [*still weeping*]
But I don't understand what we can possibly tell you. It was just an accident, wasn't it?

VE: We can't be 100 per cent sure of that yet, Mrs Gifford. The Fire Service are still at the house, carrying out their investigations.

LG: Are you saying that someone set the fire deliberately? With Samantha and those darling little children asleep inside? Who would want to do such a terrible thing?

GG: [*comforting his wife*]
Is that really what you're saying, Inspector?

AF: I know how frustrating this must be but at the moment it's impossible to be sure either way.

That's why we wanted to talk to you. You must
know far more about the family than anyone else.

GG: [*exchanging a glance with his wife*]
Well, I'm not sure what we can tell you. We
haven't seen Samantha that much recently.

VE: Was that normal?

LG: No, not really. We used to see them quite a
lot - we live in the Lakes so they'd come up
for holidays. Matty used to go out with Greg
in the rowing boat -
[*she breaks down again, crying into her
handkerchief, her voice muffled*]
He's such a sweet, sweet boy.

AF: When did you last see your daughter, Mr Gifford?

GG: It must have been late June. My wife's
birthday. They stayed overnight.

AF: That's quite a long time ago.

GG: It's a long way, Cumbria. At least, that's what
Michael's always saying.

AF: So you obviously didn't see them at Christmas?

GG: We did that Skype thing - so we could see
Matty and Zachary open our presents.

AF: And how did the rest of the family seem?

GG: Michael wasn't on the screen very much. He was
just in and out in the background.

LG: They were in the nursery. Samantha had it
decorated so beautifully. She had such a good
eye for things like that.

AF: And how were they when you saw them in June?

GG: OK, I suppose. Samantha was a bit quiet, but
she said Zachary had been keeping her awake

with a tummy upset, so she hadn't been getting
much sleep.

AF: And Michael?

GG: Much like normal.

AF: [*pause*]
Do you get on with your son-in-law, Mr Gifford?

GG: I've always found him a bit of a pompous shit,
if you really want to know –

LG: Greg – the man is missing –

GG: I *know that*, Laura. And our grandson is dead,
and if he had anything to do with it –
anything at all –

AF: What makes you say that, Mr Gifford?

GG: Oh, I don't know – he could have annoyed someone –

LG: Greg – please –

AF: Did you have someone particular in mind?

GG: [*pause*]
No.

AF: So he has no enemies, that you were aware of?

GG: That's not the sort of thing I'd know about.
All I can say is that I can see him getting up
someone's nose.

AF: Do you know if the family keeps any money or
valuables in the house?

LG: You think it was a burglary?

GG: Surely there'd be some evidence if someone had
broken in? Damage to the door or something?

AF: The degree of fire damage in this case means
it's going to be some time before we get any
definitive answers on that. So in the meantime,
as I said –

GG: You don't know either way. Right.

AF: There's no mortgage on the house, I believe. Is it a family property?

GG: They had a jewellery business – or did have. Sold it about twenty years ago, and made a packet. At least, that's what Michael said.

AF: So there might have been some expensive jewellery in the house?

LG: Michael has a gold pocket watch that must have been worth quite a bit. It was his great-grandfather's, I think. Had something on it in Polish. 'Blood is thicker than water' – something like that. Family was a really big thing with them.

AF: I'll check whether we've found a pocket watch at the scene. Was there anything else?

GG: I never saw anything. He never gave anything like that to Samantha, that I do know. They got her engagement ring at H. Samuel.

LG: They were just students, Greg –

GG: Don't you think I know that? They should never have got married so quickly. Samantha was far too young. And as for having a baby –

VE: I'm not sure what you mean? Did she have problems with the pregnancy?

LG: It wasn't so much that. It was a lot to adjust to, that's all. Most new mums take a while to get used to it. She doted on Matty.
[*starts to sob again*]

AF: I think we'll leave it there for now. DC Everett will arrange for an officer to take you

*　*　*

Out in the corridor I wait for Everett to shepherd them
along to reception.

'I said I'd go with them to the John Rad,' she says when
she comes back. 'Probably best if it's me – those units can
be pretty intimidating if you're not used to them.'

I remember, as I always do in these circumstances, that
Ev was training to be a nurse before she switched to the
police.

'If they're up to it, I'll take them to ID Samantha
afterwards.'

'So, what do you think?' I ask. She's good at picking up
undercurrents, Ev. It's one reason I wanted her there.

She takes a deep breath. 'No love lost with the father-
in-law, eh?'

I nod. 'The more I find out about Michael Esmond the
less I think I'd like him.'

'Me too, boss. But even if he did have a talent for hacking people off, it's a long way from that to someone setting
fire to his bloody house.'

In fact, you'd have to be some sort of sociopath. And
there's no one even remotely like that in the frame. Or at
least as far as we know.

*　*　*

THAMES VALLEY POLICE
Phone log
6 January 2018

Case no 556432/12 Felix House, 23 Southey Road (Michael Esmond)

Contact name:	Imogen Humphreys
Date and time of sighting:	4 January 2018, 11.30 pm (approx.)
Call summary:	Caller reports sighting of man answering to the description of Michael Esmond in the Covent Garden area of London. Said he appeared to be disorientated and possibly drunk, with a bleeding nose.
Follow-up required?	Sgt Woods to liaise with Met re. hospital admissions/homeless shelters

Contact name:	Tom Wesley
Date and time of sighting:	4 January 2018, 8.45 am
Call summary:	Possible sighting near Hythe. Caller saw man on beach when walking his dog. Looked as if he had been sleeping rough.
Follow-up required?	PC Linbury to check with Hants Police

Contact name:	Alan Wilcox
Date and time of sighting:	5 January 2018, 3.25 pm
Call summary:	Possible sighting of Michael Esmond in Grantham, Lincs. Shopping in Asda. Caller very definite that it was him.
Follow-up required?	Sgt Woods to speak to Lincs Police

Contact name:	Harriet Morgan
Date and time of sighting:	4 January 2018, 4 pm
Call summary:	Sighting of Michael Esmond in Northampton, waiting to use public phone box.
Follow-up required?	PC Linbury to check call records from phone box in question for any links to Esmond

79

Contact name:	Nick Brice
Date and time of sighting:	5 January 2018, 4.30 pm
Call summary:	Esmond sighted at King's Cross station, near Starbucks coffee shop.
Follow-up required?	PC Linbury to access CCTV from Network Rail
Contact name:	Sara Ellison
Date and time of sighting:	5 January 2018, 2 pm (approx.)
Call summary:	Possible sighting of Esmond in Hyde Park, accompanied by dog. Caller was some distance away.
Follow-up required?	No
Contact name:	Rhian Collins
Date and time of sighting:	6 January 2018, 9.20 am
Call summary:	Possible sighting near Beachy Head.
Follow-up required?	Sgt Woods to liaise with Sussex Police

* * *

At the John Rad, sharp winter sun is streaming through the windows of the Paediatric Intensive Care Unit. As they reach the door, the Giffords pause, daunted by the sheer weight of technology around each bed. The brightly coloured bedspreads and animal murals only seem to make it worse. The nurses move briskly but quietly between the patients, checking monitors, administering medication, conferring together in low voices. Laura Gifford puts her handkerchief to her mouth and Ev touches her kindly on the arm. 'I know it's a lot to take in but it's usually nothing like as bad as it looks,' she says quietly. 'The team here really are fantastic. Matty couldn't be in better hands.'

One of the nurses notices them and comes over.

'Mr and Mrs Gifford? We were told you were coming. Please come with me.'

Matty is in a bed by the window. His eyes are shut and he isn't moving. He has an oxygen tube taped to his face, and a clutch of wires attached to his chest. His whole body is swaddled in padding and bandages. They can see marks around his eyes where his glasses burned into his flesh.

'How is he?' whispers Laura Gifford.

The nurse looks up. 'He's sedated right now. We've done a bronchoscopy and X-rays and we've made him as comfortable as we can. But I'm afraid he is very poorly. The next twenty-four to forty-eight hours will be critical.'

Mrs Gifford starts to weep silently, and her husband puts an arm round her. 'They know what they're doing, love. This is one of the best hospitals in the country.'

'He looks so little, lying there.'

'It's these beds,' says the nurse kindly. 'They're so big, the poor children look lost and found.'

'Can we sit with him for a while?' asks Laura Gifford.

The nurse smiles. 'Of course. I'll arrange for a couple of chairs.'

As she disappears down towards the corridor Gifford puts a hand on his wife's shoulder. 'You stay here with the nurse, and me and the constable will go and find us all a cup of tea.'

Everett's about to offer to do the job herself, but one look at Gifford's face and she knows he just wants to get her alone.

As soon as they're out of earshot, he turns to her. His face is grey.

'You'll be needing an identification, won't you. For Samantha, I mean.'

Everett nods. 'I'm afraid so.'

'Is she here?' he says, his voice catching. 'In this hospital? Because I don't want Laura seeing that. It's bad enough as it is. I don't want her remembering her daughter that way.'

'I think you're very wise, sir.'

'So can we do it now – while she's with Matty? Can you get that sorted?'

Everett gets out her phone. 'I'll go down and see the pathologist now.'

*   *   *

Back at his desk, Gislingham is in a quandary. In theory he could go home – it is the weekend after all – but the rest of the team are in, and he's the DS. He doesn't want it to look like he's slacking. So when he opens up Google and types 'Michael Esmond' for a second time it's more to have something to do than because he actually thinks he's going to find anything.

Which appears to be borne out by the fact that ten minutes later, all he's found is what Baxter already got from Facebook. Routine references to Esmond's qualifications, links to conference speeches and publications. At the bottom of the sixth page Google tells him *'we have omitted some entries very similar to the 72 already displayed'*. Anyone else would give up – Quinn certainly would – but stubborn is Gislingham's middle name, so he scrolls back up and clicks on a few of the less-promising links. And that's when he finds it.

*   *   *

'You mean I don't have to actually go in there?'

Gregory Gifford is sitting in a small waiting room adjacent to the mortuary. There are no windows and thin institutional grey carpet on the floor. In front of him there is a table with a computer. The hospital's logo pings back and forth lazily across the screen. At least it's better than digitized fish.

Everett smiles at Gifford kindly. 'It's not like you see on the telly, thankfully. Much less dramatic. When you're ready, the attendant will bring up a photo on the screen here, and they'll ask you if it's your daughter. That's it – there's no need to do anything else.'

He swallows. 'OK. I see.' He drums his fingers on the table for a few moments. 'Right. Better get on with it. Laura will be wondering where we are.'

Everett nods to the attendant, who taps a couple of computer keys. An image appears on the screen. It's taken from above. The woman's face is visible, but the sheet is pulled up over her body. Not like it was when Everett first came down here. She's said it before and she'll say it again: whatever sort of death they died, there's always one thing about the dead that lodges in your mind and won't budge; some trivial little thing that captures an echo of who they once were. With Samantha Esmond it's the nail polish. Despite the damage and the dirt, Everett can see how much care this woman took of her hands. Clear varnish, neat cuticles. She's prepared to bet she kept a pot of hand cream by the side of her bed.

She hears Gifford draw breath beside her and turns to him. 'Is that your daughter, sir?'

He swallows again. 'Yes. That's Samantha.'

'Thank you. I know that can't have been easy.'

The image disappears. Gifford swivels round in his chair to face Everett.

'What about Zachary? Doesn't someone have to identify him too?'

Everett and the attendant exchange a glance.

'There are other methods that can be used which we think are more appropriate in his case,' says the attendant.

But Gifford's no fool. 'You don't want me to see him, do you? Because he's in such a terrible state, is that it?'

Everett starts to shake her head but she knows she's being disingenuous. She's seen the photos.

'There's no need to upset yourself,' she says. 'Really.'

Gifford sits back in his chair, and for one awful moment she thinks he's about to insist, but then his shoulders sag a little. 'OK,' he says. 'You know best.'

She makes a rueful face. 'I think I do. Sadly.'

* * *

'DI Fawley? There's someone down here to see you, sir.'

It's Anderson, the duty officer, sounding more than usually suspicious of the occupational hazard which is the General Public. Just came into reception. German bloke. Hasn't got an appointment. I can tell him you're not here – I mean, it is the weekend – you're probably wanting to get off back home –'

'No, it's OK, send him up.' Because let's face it, I don't have anywhere else I need to be.

Five minutes later the sergeant ushers the man into my room. He's tall – very tall, actually, probably six four – and that's the first clue. And when he introduces himself the accent clinches it. He's not German at all. He's Dutch. The last time I saw my brother he had a Dutch girlfriend. Her accent was exactly the same. And she was six foot two. Julian joked that he'd taken up mountaineering. Though obviously not in front of her.

'How can I help you?'

He sits down. Neatly, for someone of his height. 'It concerns the fire. The most unfortunate fire in Southey Road. If I am not mistaken, this is the house of my colleague, Michael Esmond.'

I'm intrigued. Not least by his evident anxiety.

He pushes his wire-framed glasses back up his nose. 'I believe you are what is called the Senior Investigating Officer?'

'I am, yes,' I say. He must have looked that up.

'As soon as I saw the news on TV, I knew at once that you would wish to speak to me. So I have pre-empted this request and come in myself.'

'Intrigued' bumps up a notch. What the hell is this all about?

* * *

Gislingham sits back. If what he's found is true, they're going to have to reassess the whole bloody case. Go through everything again. And not least the fact that Annabel Jordan lied to them. This isn't just pissing someone off; this is holing their career below the waterline. Gislingham leans forward, pulls up Google and keys in 'Jurjen Kuiper' again. Age, place of birth, qualifications and current position. A Facebook page, which mostly looks pretty anodyne (though a lot of it's in Dutch, and the automated translation may well be missing the nuance). There's also a Twitter feed, but that's all suitably academic too. No sign, in fact, that there is anything in the slightest amiss. Gislingham makes a face. Does that ring true? Is it really believable that a professional disaster of these proportions would leave no external trace at all? He sits thinking a moment. Then he shifts forward quickly and starts typing.

* * *

Ox-eGen

Your online source for University news, views, gossip and chit-chat

Posted by Tittle-Tattler 21 November 2017 11.56

Tribal warfare?

Latest rumblings on the departmental jungle drums suggest it's harpoons at dawn at a certain faculty building on the Banbury Road, after one of its inmates was stabbed in the front by a frankly blistering *TLS* review of his magnum opus. The culprit? None other than a member of his own tribe. Rather too close to home? One might well think so. After all, constructive criticism is one thing, live human sacrifice is quite another. Our sources tell us the atmosphere in the department is positively glacial, which doesn't, for once, reflect the primitive condition of the central heating system. Interested observers are now agog to see whether a rumoured TV contract will be the next casualty. Suffice to say that should such a catastrophe transpire, our amiable Dutchman's career will be less 'flying' than crashing and burning. One might well forgive him for fantasizing about the latter by way of revenge . . .

* * *

'So you understand, Inspector, why I had to come.'

I nod slowly. 'You're worried that we might think you had something to do with the fire.'

'Yes, yes,' he says, his cheeks slightly flushed. 'Even though that is ridiculous – unthinkable. Even if I had borne such a resentment of Dr Esmond –'

'It strikes me, Dr Kuiper, that you had a very good reason to feel aggrieved.'

He blinks. 'Yes, of course. Naturally. He had cast a slur upon my research. My professional integrity. I am sure you yourself would have felt no small annoyance should such a thing have happened to you.'

It has, by the way, and it went way beyond 'no small annoyance'. I was absolutely bloody incandescent. Which is, of course, a very unfortunate metaphor. In the circumstances.

* * *

Half an hour later, Gislingham is feeling decidedly smug. He's never been that good at lateral thinking but, this time, he really has surpassed himself. Though he did have to drag Baxter back in to help him with the techy stuff. Which turned out to be a good call, given what they've unearthed now. It's a Twitter feed with the ID @Ogou_badagri. That particular choice of identity may not mean much to them but the owner's name certainly does. 'Jurjen Kuiper' in Dutch is George Cooper in English, and it's a George Cooper who set up this account. And unlike Kuiper's official one, this Twitter feed is anything but academic.

* * *

'I do sympathize with you, Dr Kuiper.'

He inclines his head. 'Thank you. It is greatly distressing to have one's work impugned in such a way.'

'Impugned'. How many Brits would say that. Or even know what it means. But Kuiper does.

'All the same,' I continue evenly, 'we will, of course, have to eliminate you from our enquiries.'

A pale doubt flickers across his face.

'I'm sure it will be just a formality, in your case. But there are procedures we have to adhere to. I'm sure you appreciate that.' I pull my notebook towards me. 'If you could start by telling me where you were around midnight on Wednesday?'

He pushes his glasses up his nose again. 'I was hoping –'
He stops. Flushes.

'Yes?'

'It's a little delicate.'

I sit back. We're a long way past 'intrigued' now. This man has something to hide.

*　*　*

'Kuiper isn't just pissed off, sir – it's a lot more than that.'

It's Gislingham. Baxter's got the Twitter feed up on a projector in the incident room and Gis is scrolling down. Quinn has joined us too; he always thinks of himself as a bit of an expert when it comes to social media ('He bloody well should be,' as Ev said, 'the amount of time he spends on Tinder') but he's clearly worried Gis has got one over on him on this occasion.

'I googled that name as well,' says Gis, handing out printouts. 'Ogou Badagri is a Haitian voodoo spirit.'

I glance at the sheet and then back at Gis.

'Not only that,' he continues, 'but he just so happens to be the god of *fire*.' He gives me a meaningful look. '*And* apparently you can also ask him to help you out if you need to take revenge on someone who's pissed you off.'

Quinn starts laughing. 'Oh, come off it – no one seriously believes in that crap, do they? In this day and age?'

'That's not the point,' I say quietly. 'It's not about believing in it. It's about *using* it. Using it to send a message. Michael Esmond is an expert in Latin American voodoo, he'd have known exactly what this meant. And who was behind it.'

Gis nods. 'Looks like Kuiper was trolling Esmond for a while,' he says. 'As you can see, it's pretty full-on stuff too. He's also written some fairly savage blog posts, using yet another false name.' He picks up another printout. 'In one of them he says Esmond's research is "shallow, derivative, poorly footnoted and insufficiently recognisant of its indebtedness to antecedent sources".'

No one else could have written that: the vocabulary alone gives him away. But even if he chose a voodoo fire demon for a Twitter account, it doesn't mean he actually burned Esmond's house down. It was just a way to fantasize about doing it. In public. Without any apparent consequences. And that's the whole point, of course. Social media is a forcing ground for our darker selves. I sometimes think we're turning into that race on *The Forbidden Planet* – a supposedly advanced civilization who've created a machine to turn our thoughts into reality, only to find we've released the demon in our own minds. I don't have a Twitter account. As if you had to ask.

'So Kuiper wasn't above doing some heavy-duty impugning of his own,' I say, half to myself. Then I catch Gislingham giving me a quizzical look.

'Private joke. Sorry.' I turn to Baxter. 'And when did you say he deleted all this material?'

'Thursday morning, boss. Right around the time the news broke about the fire.' He shrugs. 'In theory, a deleted Twitter account is gone for good, but if you know what you're doing, you can usually dig them back up again.' And he does. Know what he's doing.

'Did Kuiper say anything about all this when he saw you, boss?' asks Ev.

I shake my head. 'He talked about the review but that's as far as it went. He was trying very hard to convince me he just wanted to be helpful. Though I suspected what he really wanted to do was stop a bunch of clod-hopping coppers turning up at his college and embarrassing him. Or, at least, that's what I assumed at the outset.'

'And later?'

'It was when we got to the alibi that he really got rattled. He said he was at home in bed but he didn't want us calling his wife to confirm it because she's pregnant. When I told him there was no way round that, he changed his story. Now he says he went for a drive. His wife woke him up tossing and turning and he couldn't get back to sleep so he went out.'

I pause and look at them, gauging how that went down.

'What, in that weather?' says Quinn, openly sceptical. 'It was cold enough to freeze your balls off Wednesday night. Even the joyriders on Blackbird Leys were tucked up with Horlicks.'

'His wife *is* pregnant though,' says Gislingham. 'I saw a pic of her on Facebook. And she's pretty big too. I buy that bit about her waking him up.' Quinn smirks at him and he blushes a little. 'Just saying. I know what it's like, that's all.'

'OK,' I say. 'Let's start by checking Kuiper's alibi, just like we would if this was any other case. With a particular focus on the speed cameras and ANPR within a mile or so of Southey Road. We need to establish if we can place Kuiper anywhere near the house that night – either in the car or on foot. And get him back in here to give us his fingerprints. That should show him we mean business.'

Gislingham nods to Quinn, but I'd put money on Quinn handing that one off to Baxter. Baxter always gets lumbered with the hard yards.

I pull my jacket off the back of the chair. 'I'm going home,' I say. 'But before I do that I'm going to make a house call on Annabel Jordan.'

* * *

The house is one of the Edwardian semis off the Banbury Road, just north of Summertown. It's not unlike Southey Road, albeit on a much smaller scale. The same bow windows, the same gabled roof, the same white woodwork over pebbledash. Quite a lot of academics live up here – those who were lucky enough to buy these houses when they could still afford them. These days it's Kidlington and beyond, and the huge Victorian piles originally built for academics are reserved for investment bankers. Or the Chinese.

When she opens the door, she clearly has no idea who I am. 'Yes? Can I help you?'

I flip open my warrant card. 'Detective Inspector Adam Fawley, Professor Jordan. May I come in?'

A frown creases briefly across her brows. She hesitates, and glances back down the passage. There's the sound of voices, children squealing, crockery. Lunch. That thing I forgot to do. Again.

'We have guests,' she says. 'My wife's family –'

'It won't take long.'

She hesitates. Then, 'Very well.'

The party is clearly in the back kitchen, and she shows me quickly into the front room. Artistic academic chaos. Over-stacked bookshelves, mismatched furniture, a scattering of colour supplements. A large chocolate Labrador looks up momentarily from his basket by the fire, then settles down again.

She closes the door behind her.

'How can I help you, Inspector? If this is about Michael Esmond, I've already spoken to your subordinates.'

'That's the point, Professor. You have already spoken to them and yet you completely failed to mention Jurjen Kuiper.'

Her gaze lights on me for a moment and then slides away. She walks over to the sofa and sits down.

'My officers specifically asked you if Michael Esmond was having problems with any of his colleagues, and you replied, "Not that I'm aware of". Are you really telling me you didn't know about this review Esmond wrote? Because if you are, I have to tell you, I find that very hard to believe.'

She sighs. 'Of course I knew. The entire thing was a complete nightmare.' She looks up at me. 'I blamed myself, if you must know. When the *TLS* asked me if I could recommend someone to review Jurjen's monograph I suggested Michael. I had no idea he'd do such a – such a –'

'Hatchet job?'

Her face is grim. 'I see you've had occasion to read it.' She folds her hands on her lap. 'In that case you will already know that Michael accused Jurjen of manipulating data to support his conclusions. In this admittedly rather small and self-obsessed discipline that counts as a high crime rather than a minor misdemeanour.'

'And did he? Falsify the facts?'

'The jury is still out. It would surprise me, knowing what I do of Jurjen. But on the other hand, the Michael I thought I knew would never dream of making such an accusation unless he had solid evidence.'

'And the TV series?'

She raises an eyebrow. 'You *are* well-informed. Yes, Jurjen had been approached to present a series for National Geographic. Not quite on the scale of *Blue Planet*, but prestigious, nonetheless, and a good deal better paid than academic publishing. Only it all fell through after that review appeared. They must have decided it wasn't worth the risk. But if you're suggesting for one moment that Jurjen could have had anything at all to do with that terrible fire –'

'I'm not "suggesting" anything. Merely attempting to establish the facts. I need hardly tell someone as intelligent as you that "facts" are even more important in my profession than they are in yours. And we've had to speak to you twice to get them.'

She flushes, flustered now. 'It's no secret that academic life can be very competitive, especially these days, but this isn't an episode of *Inspector Morse*, you know. People in this university don't go around *killing* each other for the sake of one bad review or a lost TV series, however lucrative. And as for torching a house full of people, including two innocent children – well, Jurjen simply isn't capable of that.'

I let the pause lengthen. 'What is he capable of?'

She looks up at me. 'What do you mean?'

'Would he be capable, for example, of making threats?' I'm watching her face carefully. 'Or orchestrating a concerted campaign of online trolling?'

Now she won't meet my gaze. 'I have no idea what you're talking about.'

But she does. I can see, now, that she knows full well. I extract the printouts from my jacket pocket and hand them to her. She glances at them and sets them to one side. Her mouth is set in a hard, irritated little line: she thought the material had been deleted. And she didn't think we'd be smart enough to find it. And that really pisses me off.

'Well?'

She takes a deep breath. 'He was merely letting off steam. Venting his frustration. In a controlled environment – relatively speaking. If you talk to him again, I'm sure he'll tell you that he realizes now how stupid that was, but that's *all* it was.'

I file away that 'again'. She knows Kuiper's been to see us. She may even have been the one who told him to do it.

'Unfortunately for you, Professor Jordan, Dr Kuiper is unable to prove that's "all it was". He began by telling us he was at home with his wife at the time of the fire, but when I told him she would have to corroborate that he rapidly changed his tune. He now says he was out for a drive. In the middle of the night. In the middle of winter.'

Doubt slips across her face and I know that this – for the first time in our conversation – is news to her.

'But presumably you can check – CCTV and so on?'

I nod. 'That is exactly what we are attempting to do. But it may not be possible to prove he is telling the truth. Indeed, we may well find that this, too, is not a "fact" but a lie. And if so –'

'If so?'

'You might want to dig out that crisis management manual your press office probably has gathering dust somewhere. I'm afraid real life is a great deal messier than *Inspector Morse*.'

* * *

'A terrible tragedy': Boy, 10, dies from injuries sustained in Oxford house fire

A spokeswoman from the John Radcliffe hospital has confirmed that Matty Esmond died in its paediatric Intensive Care Unit earlier this morning. Matty's mother, Samantha, and his younger brother, Zachary, 3, were also the victims of the fatal fire at the family's house last Thursday. The spokeswoman described the death as 'a terrible tragedy', and said that staff were providing support to members of the boy's family, who were with him when he died.

Neither Thames Valley Police nor Oxfordshire Fire and Rescue have yet issued a statement about the cause of the fire. Matty's father, Michael Esmond, 40, has still not been located despite a public appeal and what Thames Valley Police describe as 'concerted efforts' to find him.

More news on this as we get it.

* * *

The atmosphere in the incident room is grim. It doesn't get any shittier than the death of a child. Everett tells us the Giffords are distraught.

'I was there with them when he suddenly took a turn for the worse. You know what that's like – alarms going off, nurses all over the place, crash trolleys. It was bloody awful.'

I glance across at Gislingham – Billy had to be resuscitated twice when he was in the premature baby unit. They nearly lost him. His face is grey with the memory.

'They had to take the bandages off to give him CPR,' says Everett, 'so those poor bloody people saw the state he was in underneath. And now they won't be able to get that out of their minds.' She shakes her head. This job can be a bastard sometimes.

Gislingham forces himself back to the task in hand. 'OK,' he says, 'this is where we are. We still need to cover off the CCTV in the area round Southey Road to see if we can ID Kuiper in the area. And we need to speak to Lauren Kaminsky, who has – as of 10.30 last night – returned to Oxford. And just to get everyone up to speed, she's definitely *not* a suspect in any potential arson, as we've confirmed she was indeed on a flight to JFK on December 21st. Right,' he says, looking around the room. 'I'm about to go to see Kaminsky with DC Somer, and Quinn's on the CCTV.'

A couple of half-hearted sarcastic whoops at that. Quinn mouths *Yeah, yeah* and gives the other DCs the finger when he thinks I'm not looking.

'Have we managed to track down any of Esmond's friends yet?' I ask.

'We've left messages with a few,' begins Gislingham.

'There's the neighbours next door,' interjects Everett.

'They weren't at home last time I tried but I can have another go if you like.'

'Yes, do that. They may have seen something. OK, that's it for now. Everyone else gets the weekend to themselves. What's left of it.'

Gislingham goes back to collect his coat, and when he looks up he sees Somer has stopped to talk to Fawley. They're standing close together. She's saying something in a low voice and he's smiling. Gislingham realizes with a start that he can't remember the last time he saw the boss smile.

* * *

Interview with Ronald and Marion Young, conducted at 25 Southey Road, Oxford
7 January 2018, 1.16 p.m.
In attendance, DC V. Everett

VE: Thank you for making time to see me, Mr Young.

RY: I was going to call you first thing tomorrow anyway. We saw the card you put through the door as soon as we got back. I had no idea there'd been a fire. We're bloody lucky it didn't spread this far.

VE: You were away for Christmas?

RY: With our daughter, yes. In Barcelona. We left on the 22nd.

VE: Did you see the Esmonds before you left?

MY: I did. I popped over, just to say we'd be away and would they keep an eye on the house.

VE: Did you see both Mr and Mrs Esmond, Mrs Young?

MY: Just Samantha.

VE: How did she seem?

MY: A bit distracted. The little boy was crying, I remember that. She looked tired. But so do most new mums.

VE: Zachary was three, wasn't he? She was hardly a new mum.

MY: Well, it doesn't get any easier. Not when they're that age. Our Rachel –

RY: The constable doesn't want to know about all that, Marion.

VE: Were you aware if the Esmonds had anyone staying with them over the holidays? Any friends? Relatives?

MY: I wasn't aware of anyone. I'm here most of the time so I'd probably have noticed if someone had arrived before we left.

VE: No one unusual hanging around in the last few weeks?

RY: What do you mean 'unusual'?

VE: Someone you didn't recognize.

MY: No, no one I can think of.

VE: Did you get on with the Esmonds – as neighbours?

RY: She was all right. Bit anaemic. But he's a nasty piece of work.

VE: Really? What makes you say that?

MY: He was always very pleasant to me –

RY: [*to his wife*] *Pleasant?* He killed our bloody dog!

MY: You don't *know* that. Not for certain.

RY: [*to Everett*] Back in September we agreed to
    let them look after the dog while we were
    away. It was just for one night. The lad –
    Matty – he was always wanting to come round
    and play with her – take her for walks –

MY: Mollie was a lovely dog.

RY: We usually put her in kennels, but we thought,
    it was just the one night, what can possibly
    happen? And then when we got back the poor
    bloody dog was dead.

MY: She was fourteen, Ron.

RY: But she wasn't ill, was she? Hadn't been to
    the vet in years. Then all of a sudden she
    dies on the one night the Esmonds are looking
    after her? I'm sorry – I don't believe in
    coincidences.

VE: Neither does my DI.

RY: There you are, Marion, the constable agrees
    with me.

VE: I didn't mean by that –

MY: We couldn't prove anything, Ron. You know we
    couldn't.

VE: What did Mr Esmond say had happened?

RY: He didn't.

MY: Ron –

RY: Not really. He said the dog must have had a
    heart attack or something. He said he'd gone
    down to feed her in the morning and she was
    just lying there, dead. Load of bloody
    rubbish.

VE: You didn't have a post-mortem done?

RY: Do you know how much that would've cost?

MY: I thought it was best to assume it was an accident. Having poor Mollie cut up wasn't going to bring her back, and I didn't want to make things difficult with the Esmonds. They're our neighbours, after all. We still had to live next door to them.

VE: I completely understand that, Mrs Young.

MY: And Michael did give us some money. He said he was very sorry and gave us £100.

RY: [*contemptuous*] A hundred measly quid.

MY: The saddest thing about it is that we hardly ever saw Matty after that. He was distraught about Mollie. Poor little boy, I can't get it out of my mind, him dying in such a horrible way. I remember the day they moved in like it was yesterday – he was so excited about the garden. I don't think they'd ever had one before.

VE: Have you lived here long, Mrs Young?

RY: Ten years now. No, twelve.

VE: So you knew Mr Esmond's parents?

RY: I never got on with Richard but Alice Esmond was a very nice woman.

MY: She was completely under his thumb, Ron, and you know it. What do they call it these days? Controlling – that's it. He was very controlling.

VE: So he could have been like that as a father too? When the boys were growing up?

MY: It wouldn't surprise me. Michael was very quiet, certainly. But from what I've seen of

him, Philip is quite the opposite. Very
lively. Outgoing. I remember seeing him in the
garden with Matty last summer. They had the
paddling pool out and Philip was trying to
teach him to body surf or whatever it's
called. There was water everywhere. Even
Samantha was laughing. That's how I want to
remember them. Laughing in the sunshine. Just
a normal happy family.

* * *

It was supposed to be Quinn looking for Kuiper on the
CCTV, but it's no surprise to find it's Baxter doing the
heavy lifting. There are several cameras on the Banbury
Road and outside some of the shops on the Summertown
parade, but nothing on the side streets, and if Kuiper had
any sense he'd have gone that way. Their only chance is
the route he must have taken to get there from where he
lives in Littlemore. Whether he went round the ring road
or through the centre of town, they should still be able to
pick him up. Always assuming, of course, that he used his
own car.

Baxter loads up the first set of footage and glances
across at Quinn, who's fiddling about with his mobile.

'Can you do me a favour and check the taxi firms? Kuiper might have got a minicab.'

Quinn makes a face. 'Really? So he gets in the back seat
saying *"Don't mind the petrol can, mate, I'll pay extra if I soil the
seats"*?'

Baxter's turn to make a face. 'OK, OK, but you know

what I mean.' He turns back to his screen. 'And it'll give you something useful to do,' he mutters.

* * *

Lauren Kaminsky has a room in one of Wolfson's modern blocks overlooking the Cherwell and the Rainbow Bridge. That's modern as in 1970s; in this town a college founded in 1379 is still called 'New'. There's frost clinging to the trees and two swans are gliding silently with the current. A whirl of seagulls circle above the water, screeching like witches. The room itself is small but comfortable. No clutter, very little sign of personal preferences. A kitchenette, a tiny bathroom glimpsed through a half-open door. As for Lauren, she's as self-contained as her surroundings. Petite, with short brown hair in a pixie cut. She catches Somer glancing around and smiles, a little wearily.

'I'm not here much. My boyfriend is a don at Magdalen. I spend most of my time there. I mean, this place is fine and all that, but it's hardly "Oxford", is it?'

She gestures them to take a seat. The sofa is only just big enough for two and Somer is uncomfortably aware that she is thigh to thigh with Gislingham.

'I'm guessing you want to talk to me about Michael Esmond? It's truly terrible, what happened.'

Everyone has said that. Sometimes in exactly the same words.

'It was your boyfriend who reported the sexual harassment, I believe?' says Gislingham.

She nods. 'I wasn't going to make a big thing of it, but

Ned was furious. He wanted me to go to the police, file an official complaint – the whole nine yards.'

'I gather Dr Esmond denies anything happened.'

She takes a seat, but sits on the edge, as if poised for escape. 'Well, he would, wouldn't he?'

'You haven't spoken to him about it yourself?' asks Somer.

She shakes her head. 'No, not since that night. It was way too embarrassing. I decided it was better to let the department handle it. That's what they're paid for.'

'And how had he been with you before that?' asks Gislingham. 'Did he ever –'

She smiles at his discomfiture. 'Come on to me? No. He was always really – what is it you Brits say? – *stand-offish*. Buttoned-up. Until that night. I think it must have been the drink talking.'

'That's no excuse,' says Somer, frowning.

'No, of course not. He behaved like a sexist shit. But, hey, I liked the guy. The whole thing was totally out of character. Like I said, I'd have left it at that but Ned wasn't having any of it.'

'So there was absolutely no flirtation before that – nothing to suggest he was interested in you in that way?'

'Uh-uh,' she says, stifling a yawn. 'Sorry, jet lag kicking in.'

'Is there anything else?' asks Somer. 'Anything that struck you about Dr Esmond in the last few months? Other people seem to think he was under a lot of strain. Did he appear that way to you?'

She considers. 'I didn't see him a whole lot. But I guess

he did seem a bit off. That whole Kuiper review thing can't have helped, but you can't say he didn't bring that on himself. You do know about that, right?'

Somer nods. 'Is there anything you can tell us about it? Something we might not already know?'

Kaminsky yawns again. 'I doubt it. Look, can we take a rain check? I'm totally wiped out. If I think of anything I'll give you a call.'

Somer glances at Gislingham: they're not going to get much more here. They get up to go.

'Thank you, Miss Kaminsky,' Gislingham says at the door. 'And do phone us, won't you? Even if it's something that doesn't seem significant.'

They go down the stairs and out into the cold air. Somer pulls on a beanie and Gislingham smiles at her. 'You look just like my kid sister.'

She glances across. 'I didn't know you had one.'

'Yeah, she's seven years younger than me, so she was always the baby of the family. You?'

'Older sister.' But something about the look on her face means he doesn't ask any more.

'So, what do you think?' asks Somer, as they reach the porter's lodge and Gislingham pulls open the heavy glass door.

'I can't see why Kaminsky would lie. And we know she wasn't in the country when the fire started.'

'And only fifteen per cent of arsons are committed by women,' says Somer thoughtfully.

'Right, so this is just ticking a box, isn't it? Or am I missing something?'

Somer is silent for a moment. 'What about the boy-friend?'

'The bloke at Magdalen? Ned whatsit? What about him?'

'He was obviously seriously pissed off at Esmond. Wouldn't you be – if it was Janet?'

'Yeah, course I would. But I wouldn't set his bloody house on fire. Trust me. This is a dead end.'

Up at her window, Lauren Kaminsky watches the police officers down the path and out of sight. Then she picks up her mobile.

'Ned – call me back, will you? The police have been here.'

She ends the call but remains standing at the window. Her face is troubled.

* * *

Back at St Aldate's, Everett has taken one for the team and volunteered to go through the calls they've been tak-ing on the tip line, which has to be in the dictionary under 'thankless task'. After an hour of it she realizes her foot has gone numb and stands up to get herself a coffee, limp-ing down the corridor to the machine as the pins and needles kick in.

'You all right?' asks Quinn, who's contemplating the selection. He has his pen behind his ear. Like he does.

'Fine,' she says. 'Trying to stop the rest of me falling asleep as well as my foot.'

'That good, eh?'

'What about you?'

He kicks the machine. 'Nada. No sign of Kuiper anywhere that night. Doesn't look like he took a cab either, though we haven't covered all of them yet. How many bloody taxi firms are there in this city?'

'There's never one at the station when it's raining, though,' says Everett with a sigh.

Back in the office she sits down next to Somer. 'Anything useful?' she says, looking across at what's on the desk in front of her.

'Just seeing if I can find out anything about Lauren Kaminsky's boyfriend.'

Everett raises her eyebrows. 'You think he could be a suspect?'

Somer gives a wry smile. 'No, not really. But I'd just like to put a big fat tick in the box marked "Cast-Iron Alibi".'

'Somer?' calls Baxter from the other side of the room. 'Call for you, line three.'

* * *

Telephone interview with Philip Esmond, 7 January 2018, 4.55 p.m.
On the call, DC E. Somer

PE: DC Somer? It's Philip Esmond again. I saw the news. About Matty.

ES: I'm so sorry.

PE: I just wish I could have got back in time.

ES: His grandparents were with him. If that helps.

PE: That's something, I suppose. They must be
     devastated. First Zachary, then Sam, and now
     this.
     [*sighs*]
     Well, at least all those shits online will
     stop abusing her for being a bad mother now.

ES: I know it's hard but you just have to ignore
     all that stuff. They don't know you. They're
     just venting in a vacuum.

PE: Yeah, I know. Easier said than done, though,
     if it's happening to you. Look, the main
     reason I phoned was because I remembered
     something. Last time you mentioned a hut?
     Something Mum said?

ES: That's right. She seemed to think your brother
     might be there.

PE: Well, if you ask me, *that* is highly unlikely,
     but I think I know what she might have meant.
     When we were kids we went to the south coast
     on holiday once. Dad hired us a beach hut on
     Calshot Spit.

ES: A beach hut?

PE: Right. But what with the Alzheimer's, she does
     get pretty confused. She's probably forgotten
     Michael is forty, not fourteen. I know he did
     love that place. But it probably fell to bits
     years ago. If you ask me, there's sod-all
     chance he's there, but I thought you ought to
     know.

ES: Can you text me exactly where it is – the hut?

PE: Sure.

ES: And obviously if you hear from your brother –
PE: Of course. And as soon as I dock at Poole I'll
    come straight to Oxford. Should be no more
    than a couple of days, with a fair wind.

* * *

The house is dark when I get back. It's what I expected, but my heart is still heavy as I turn the engine off and walk up the drive. I can barely get the door open for the junk mail. Estate agents' flyers, something from the Liberal Democrats which is going straight to recycling, offers of gardening services, pizza takeaway menus. Though I can't really complain about the latter; I've been living on the bloody things. I turn the lights on, stick a frozen meal in the oven and switch on the laptop on the kitchen island. I make a cursory effort to clear away last night's debris, but the dishwasher is already full so there's nowhere for it to go. I open a bottle of wine. I thought there was one in the fridge but I must have finished it last night. That seems to be happening a lot these days.

The doorbell rings. I decide not to answer it. Alex has a key, and I'm not in the mood for Jehovah's Witnesses. Or ex-cons selling from suitcases – the one thing I don't need right now is more dishcloths. The bell rings again. And then again.

I throw the door open, but it's not a Nottingham Knocker. It's Somer.

'I'm sorry to bother you at home, sir. I tried your mobile but it's just ringing out.'

Bugger. I must have forgotten to charge it.

109

'I just wanted to run something past you,' she says, tentative.

'Oh yes?'

'It's something Philip Esmond said. He called this afternoon.'

It occurs to me I'm still holding my glass of wine. And that sharing the bottle with someone else is probably the only way I'm going to avoid finishing the whole lot on my own.

I stand back. 'Do you want to come in?'

She hesitates and glances down the passage behind me. 'What about your wife, sir –'

'She's visiting her sister.'

She smiles. 'Well, if you're sure. Why not.'

I follow her down to the kitchen, watching as she takes in the decor, the furnishings, the ornaments. She's making judgements – of course she is. That's what we're trained to do. Pick up nuances, intercept signals, interpret appearances. But you don't need police training to draw some pretty obvious conclusions from the state of this place. The mess, the empties lined up by the back door, the fact that I haven't bothered to shower since I got home. I should care that she's seeing all this, but somehow I don't.

'Glass of wine?' I say, gesturing to a stool.

'Just a half,' she says. 'I'm driving.'

I reach for the bottle and a clean glass. 'So what's this about Philip Esmond?'

'When DC Everett told Esmond's mother he was missing, she said something about a hut. Turns out it's a beach hut on Southampton Water.'

'So?'

'I know it sounds far-fetched, but don't you think we should check it out? Just to be sure?'

'Why on earth would he go there, of all places?'

'I know, it makes absolutely no sense. But I just keep remembering that one of those sightings on the tip line was at Hythe. That's not far from Southampton.'

And on that, she has a point.

'OK,' I say. 'I'll get on to Hants Police first thing – won't do any harm to rule it out.'

Upstairs, the landline starts ringing.

'Excuse me a minute.'

I want it to be Alex. I'm telling myself it's Alex – that she's ringing the landline because she wants to make sure I'm at home, on my own, so we can talk –

But when I lift the receiver I hear the irritatingly cheery tones of the bank's automated credit card security system. I have a moment's ironic amusement that their algorithm has already detected an unprecedented preponderance of fast-food outlets in my recent spending habits, but reconfirming my last four transactions takes longer than I want it to, and by the time I get back downstairs, Somer is stacking the dishwasher. The clean stuff sits in neat piles on the counter.

She blushes. 'I didn't want to start opening your cupboards. I hate it when people do that.' She sees my face and bites her lip. 'Sorry – I didn't mean to intrude. Just trying to make myself useful ...' Her voice trails off. 'Sorry,' she says again, her cheeks bright red now.

I make a face. 'I hate that too, actually. But thank God you tackled that bloody dishwasher; I've been putting it off for the best part of a week.'

She smiles, clearly relieved. 'I'll trade you clearing the stuff in the sitting room for another glass of wine.'

'I thought you were driving?'

'I can get a cab. Pick the car up on my way in tomorrow.'

My turn to smile. 'Well, if you put it like that.'

* * *

2 May 2017, 12.27 p.m.
247 days before the fire
23 Southey Road, Oxford

Sam is sitting on the bed in the top-floor spare room, staring out of the window. She's taken to coming up here on the bad days. As if she can box them up and keep them closed in this echoey half-empty room no one's used for years. As if by doing that she can stop them leaking into the rest of the house – the rest of her life. Though the room is chilly, outside the sun is shining and there are flowers in the garden despite the weeds. A flurry of tulips all down one border. Blowsy scarlet petals with black spikes in their hearts. But inside, in this room, there is a weight of grey cloud somewhere just above her peripheral vision. A telltale tenderness at the base of her skull. But Michael said he might pop back to check on her at lunchtime. She doesn't want him to find her up here. He would only worry, and he has enough to deal with already.

She hauls herself to her feet, reaching for her cardigan. That's when she hears it. Downstairs. The soft thud that could be a door swinging to or something falling or a step on an old board, muffled by carpet. Not the children because they're not here. Not a draught. She stands there, listening fiercely. It's happened before but never indoors, never *inside* the house. Once, it was on the side path. The last time, outside the kitchen. A flicker just beyond her eye. A movement that wasn't the wind or a bird or a squirrel running along the fence. She tastes metal in her mouth and realizes she's bitten her lip so hard it's bleeding. But she is not going mad – she is *not* going mad –

She forces herself to move quickly, reaching the door and throwing it open. She goes down the stairs, clinging to the banister like an old woman, then works her way through every room on the floor beneath, throwing open every cupboard and wardrobe until she is breathless with the effort.

Then she hears the front door bang and her husband calling for her.

'Sam? You upstairs?'

'I'll be down in a minute,' she replies, her voice half strangled. 'I'm just sorting the washing.'

When he looks up a few moments later she is coming down the stairs smiling at him with the laundry basket under one arm.

'Hello, darling, how was your morning?'

* * *

On Monday morning I spend half an hour on the phone tracking down the right person at Hampshire Constabulary, and explaining what we need to do. I can hear the man's irritation levels rising. 'We're not complete turnip tops down here, Inspector.' Well, he didn't actually say that, but he might as well have done.

As I put the phone down there's a flurry of wind against the window. Outside, the sky is yellowish; we may even get snow. But probably only enough to cause havoc, not enough to justify it. There's no town in England that looks more beautiful under really heavy snow: Christ Church Meadow, the Magdalen deer park, Radcliffe Square. But in this job, all you tend to think about is the body count going up. Rough sleepers die in snow, and they do it here just as much as anywhere else.

* * *

Telephone conversation with DI Giles Saumarez,
Hampshire Police, 8 January 2018, 11.26 a.m.
On the call, DI A. Fawley

GS: DI Fawley? We've checked out that beach hut for you and there's definitely someone there. Male, apparently arrived a few days ago, but we don't know exactly when. Couple of locals noticed a bonfire on the beach and called it in. We showed them your man's picture and they're sure it's the same guy.

AF: Your officers haven't attempted to speak to him?

GS: Nope. There haven't been any signs of life this morning but we'll just babysit him till your guys get here. Makes the paperwork a hell of a sight easier for a start.

AF: OK - we'll get there as fast as we can. And thank you.

GS: No worries. We've got two officers parked up on the road in case he makes a run for it. Though

```
it's not as if he can get out any other way.
        Not without a boat, anyway. I'll send a link
        to the dashboard cam so you can see for
        yourself.
AF:     What's the area like?
GS:     Calshot? It's a bit of a nothing place to be
        honest. The Spit is busy in the summer, but
        this time of year, it's as dead as a dodo.
        Four times last week I had the next beach
        down completely to myself.
AF:     Walking?
GS:     Swimming.
AF:     Christ, in this weather?
GS:     [laughs]
        No better way to clear your head. I go most
        mornings - it's only about five miles away from
        where I live. Ironic, really.
AF:     Ironic?
GS:     Where I live - it's called Fawley.
```

* * *

I go back to the incident room to tell them it looks like
we've finally found Esmond and there's a moment of
silence followed by a surge of questions.

'Calshot? What the hell is he doing there?'

'So the bastard killed his entire bloody family and ran
away to the sodding seaside?'

'He must have known we'd track him down eventually –'

'Trust me – the man's lost it – it'll be a white-coats job,
just you wait –'

But under the anger there's also a palpable ripple of relief. And I don't blame them. We were beginning to wonder if we were chasing a ghost. A couple of the DCs pat Somer on the back and she flushes and tries to play it down. Which she shouldn't, of course, but getting the right balance between being a pushover and a push-aside is fiendishly difficult in this job. Especially for women. Needless to say, I tell her she should be the one to go to Calshot with Gislingham, and after they've gone I go back to my office and sit for a moment staring at the dashboard cam link Saumarez sent over.

A flat expanse of scrubby bushes and wind-flattened grass on one side, and on the other, a line of huts in bright primary colours. A litter bin. A carrier bag caught in a tree. Other than that, no movement, no cars, no people, nothing. It's only the swooping seagulls and the billowing plastic that prove it really is a live feed.

* * *

At 2.30, Gislingham pulls up on the main road leading towards Calshot Spit. Fast grey clouds, salt in the air and a slicing wind coming off the water. There's an unmarked police car parked a few yards away and a rather beaten-up black Land Rover just behind it. The driver's door swings open. The man who gets out is in plain clothes. Probably mid-forties but he looks a lot younger. Slim, athletic-looking, and with the year-round tan of someone who lives by the sea. Gislingham catches the look on Somer's face, and when he gets out of his own car he's uncomfortably aware that he's holding his stomach in.

'DI Saumarez,' the man says, coming up and shaking their hands. 'I spoke to Adam Fawley earlier.'

'DS Gislingham, DC Somer. Any news on Esmond?'

'Haven't seen any movement since I got here. Though the lads tell me they could hear someone inside earlier so presumably he's still in there.'

Saumarez turns and points. 'It's that red one halfway down. There are no windows this side so I doubt he knows we're here.'

Gislingham starts towards the hut then realizes Saumarez isn't moving.

'You not coming?'

The DI shrugs. 'Your collar, as the Americans say.'

Gislingham eyes him narrowly; he's starting to wonder if he's taking the piss. That physique of his certainly is. Gislingham squares his shoulders and moves slowly down the side to the front of the hut. The door is shut, but it's definitely been broken into. The wood is badly splintered and the handle is hanging off.

Gislingham knocks, then stands there, his head against the door, straining to hear above the wind. He knocks again. And now there's definitely movement inside. The sound of scraping, and then the door opens a couple of inches.

'Who is it?'

'Mr Esmond?'

'No, I'm afraid you've come to the wrong address. I am a different person entirely.'

The man laughs – it's a slightly manic laugh, and he's slurring. Gislingham can smell the alcohol.

He takes out his warrant card and pushes it against the

gap in the door. 'Detective Sergeant Chris Gislingham, Thames Valley Police. Can we come in?'

'Fuck off – I told you – I'm not whatever his bloody name is –'

The door starts to close and Gislingham wedges his foot against it. 'We know it's you, Mr Esmond – people have identified you.'

Somer glances round; despite what he said, Saumarez has followed them. And behind him there's a uniformed officer. With a battering ram in one hand.

Gislingham can feel the strain against the door. 'Mr Esmond, I really don't want to have to force this open.' He knocks again. Silence now. He turns and gestures to Somer – why doesn't she have a go. She steps up to the door, absurdly self-conscious that Saumarez is watching all this.

'Mr Esmond, my name is DC Erica Somer. Can you open the door for a moment? I'm sure we can sort all this out.'

There's a moment when everyone seems to be holding their breath. And then the door suddenly swings wide open.

A table and two ancient folding chairs; the man is slumped in one of them. He's wearing a cord jacket and chinos but they're creased and dirty. There's a candle wedged in a Coke bottle, a scatter of crisp packets and sandwich wrappers, and an empty bottle of whisky upended on the floor. The tiny room reeks of sweat and piss and drink.

The man is eyeing them, struggling to keep his gaze steady.

'I told you, fuck off.'

Somer takes a step forward. Now her eyes have adjusted to the gloom she can see him properly. He's the right age, the right height, the right colouring. But he's not Michael Esmond. They've come all this way for nothing, and it's all down to her. She bites her lip, trying to come up with the least-worst way to say that to Gislingham, when the man lurches suddenly forward, his body doubled up.

'Oh fucking hell,' says Somer, as he vomits all down her.

* * *

12 May 2017, 11.49 a.m.
237 days before the fire
23 Southey Road, Oxford

Michael Esmond kicks the front door open and dumps two carrier bags in the hall, then goes back to the car, lets Matty out of the back, and goes round to the other side to unstrap Zachary from the car seat. The little boy has been crying all the way back from the supermarket.

'Matty – can you come back and carry one of these bags?' Michael calls, lifting his youngest son out of the car. His skin feels hot to the touch.

Matty comes back out of the house, dragging his feet.

'Is your mum up?' asks Michael.

Matty shakes his head.

'OK, just take one of these bags, will you – the green one isn't very heavy.'

Five minutes later he has the shopping stacked on the kitchen floor and Zachary balanced on one arm while he sticks macaroni cheese in the oven for lunch.

Matty comes in from the hall. He's still wearing his outdoor clothes.

'Can I take Mollie for a walk, Dad?'

'You know you can't take her on your own, Matty. She's too big. She might pull you into the road.'

'You come with me then.'

'I can't,' says Michael, exasperated. 'I've got to unpack this lot, then sort the lunch out, and this afternoon I absolutely *have* to do some work.'

'Ple-ee-ease, Dad!'

'I said NO, Matty,' Michael snaps. He's just realized one of the yogurt pots has broken in the carrier bag. There's white goo seeping on to the floor. He stifles an expletive; he never swears. And certainly not in front of the kids.

'You're *always* saying that,' wails Matty. 'I never get to do *anything.'*

'You know that's not true –'

'Yes it is. You said we were going to the zoo and then we didn't because Zachary was sick and then you said you'd play football with me and you didn't. It's not *fair*, you only care about Zachary. *No one* cares about me.'

Michael flushes. 'Look,' he says, gentler now. 'We talked about this, didn't we? I told you that Mummy hasn't been very well and you and me need to do our bit to look after her and keep things going until she gets better. That means being a Big Boy and helping me with things like tidying your room and not making too much noise when she's trying to sleep.'

Zachary is crying now in a dull weary drone as if he hasn't the energy to scream. Michael hitches him a little higher. 'Look, why don't you go and play on your Xbox for a bit while I get

Zachary settled? And if he's feeling better later perhaps we can take the dog out. The two of us.'

'Promise?' says Matty, sceptical.

'Promise.'

Michael carries Zachary up the stairs to the nursery, where he pulls off his clothes and tries to find his Winnie the Pooh pyjamas. There's a rash across the little boy's stomach that he doesn't like the look of. Zachary curls up under the duvet and Michael sits a moment, stroking his hair, before getting up and going along the landing to look in on his wife. She's in her dressing gown, lying on top of the covers, her eyes closed. Her hair looks lank and he wonders if she's even bothered to shower today. He's turning to go when she stops him.

'Are the boys OK?' Her voice is heavy, as if she's half asleep.

'They're fine. Do you want some lunch?'

She turns over slowly, her back to him. 'Not hungry,' she murmurs.

Michael pulls the door to, and is about to go back down the stairs when he hears something that stops him. It's coming from the nursery. Michael frowns, then starts back along the landing. He can hear exactly what it is now. Matty, talking to his brother, his tone irritated and impatient over the little boy's cries.

'You've *got* to have some because if you don't I can't take Mollie for a walk.'

Michael rounds the corner into the room. Matty is sitting on the bed. He has one arm round his brother, and with the other hand, he's pushing a spoon at his mouth. Something pink and sticky. There are huge gouts of it smeared all over Zachary's face, and he's squealing and twisting away, his body rigid.

'Jesus Christ!' yells Michael. 'What the fuck are you doing?'

He yanks Matty aside and grabs Zachary.

'How much did you give him?'

Matty shrinks back against the wall. 'Not much.'

Michael looks at him; his heart is pounding with ambulances, 999 calls, stomach pumps – 'How much is "not much"?'

Matty shrugs.

Michael lurches forward and grabs Matty by both shoulders. '*How much?* This is *important* – can't you understand that?'

Matty is squirming. 'You're hurting me.'

'I'll hurt you even more if you don't tell me the truth,' shouts Michael, shaking his son. '*How much did you give him?*'

'Just one spoon,' mutters Matty, sullen now.

'You're *absolutely sure*?'

The boy nods. He's not looking at his father.

Michael slowly releases his hold. He hadn't realized his grip was so tight.

He goes back to Zachary and takes him on his lap. The little boy is grizzling and grinding his eyes with his fists. There's a smell of pee.

'What's all the noise?'

Michael swings round. Sam is standing in the doorway, steadying herself against the door frame.

'Nothing,' Michael says quickly. 'I just spilled some Calpol, that's all.'

She looks at Matty, then at her husband, and frowns a little. 'You sure?'

'Absolutely,' says Michael, smiling reassuringly. 'There's nothing to worry about. We're all fine, aren't we, Matty?'

Matty is clearly very far from fine, but his mother doesn't seem to have the strength to argue.

'OK,' she says, and trails off back to her room.

Michael puts Zachary back into bed and turns to his oldest son.

'I didn't mean to shout at you, but you have to understand, Calpol is not like juice – it's *medicine*. You can't give it to him – not *ever*. Only Mummy and I can do that. Is that clear?'

Matty flickers a glance at his father, then nods briefly. His face is tight and closed.

It's only much later, when he finally gets to his desk and manages to start on the draft that he should have submitted to his publisher three months ago, that Michael realizes. In all the chaos and the panic, Matty never apologized. Not once.

He never said sorry for what he had done.

* * *

There's a small crowd gathered by the beach now. The police cars have their lights flashing. Two officers are trying to load the man from the hut into the back of one of the cars, and Somer is leaning against the litter bin doing her best to get the sick off her clothes. Though that, as Gislingham puts it, with his characteristic eloquence, is a bit like pissing on a blast furnace.

Saumarez comes across the road from the police car.

'I'm not sure how much good that tissue is doing,' he says, eyeing her.

She makes a face. 'Yeah, well, that'll teach me.'

Gislingham finishes talking to one of the officers and comes back towards them. 'Looks like our man is a well-known local rough sleeper. Goes by the name of Tristram, apparently.'

Saumarez smiles. 'Yeah, well, we have a better class of tramp round here.'

Gislingham ignores him. 'You coming?' he asks Somer, perhaps a little pointedly.

'Tell you what,' says Saumarez, turning to Somer, 'why don't you come with me and we can stop off at my house — you'll go past the door anyway so it's not out of your way. It'd mean you could clean up a bit.'

Somer glances at Gislingham. 'Is that OK with you, Sarge? To be honest, I doubt you want to sit in a car with me all the way back to Oxford smelling like this.'

'OK,' says Gislingham reluctantly, though even he can't argue with that. He's nearly gagging three feet away. 'I'll follow you. Just as long as it doesn't take too long. We've wasted enough bloody time today already.'

Unlike the outside, the inside of Saumarez's Land Rover is impeccably clean. Which, in Somer's experience, has to be a first. Not just for male police officers but men in general. Even Fawley has crap in his car. Ten minutes after leaving the beach they're slowing down and turning on to what looks like nothing more than a farm track. Low trees, a ploughed field, wire fencing. There's no sign of habitation at all.

'This is why I have this car,' says Saumarez, as they jolt into a rut. 'You need a four-by-four to get up and down here in winter.'

It's a steep unmade drive for the first hundred yards and suddenly the trees open out and Somer can see an area of gravel and a line of white single-storey houses. A wooded slope down to the water on one side; on the other, and far closer, the power station: vast unforgiving blocks of concrete and a chimney towering above. And beyond all that, in the distance, the oil refinery, as large as a small town. Metal chimneys bristling with lights and gantries. Low white gas canisters dotted like a gigantic draughts board. Plumes of smoke against the indigo sky.

Saumarez gets out and comes to join her. 'What do you think?'

'I can't decide if it's beautiful or obscene.'

He laughs. 'Me neither. It's one reason why I live here. Stops me getting complacent. And, of course, it's cheap. Most people don't consider that to be much of a view.'

When he opens the front door, ducking to get inside, she realizes that what had looked like three or four cottages is actually one. Someone – Saumarez? – has knocked them all together into one huge open-plan space. Stone fireplaces, piled logs, stripped floors, tongue-and-groove walls. White and shades of grey. Pale stripes. Mirrors with driftwood frames.

'I like it,' she says, suddenly aware how filthy she is.

Saumarez is busy turning on the lights. 'The bathroom's through at the back,' he says, gesturing. 'If you want a shower there are towels, and I can find you something to wear.'

It's all a bit clichéd – how many romcoms has she seen with a scene just like this? – but ten minutes later she opens the bathroom door gingerly to find a T-shirt on the floor outside. Not one of his, that's for sure. She does what she can with her hair and ventures back out. Through one of the windows she can see Gislingham standing by his car, talking on the phone. Probably telling Fawley what a fuck-up she made sending them on a 200-mile round-trip for nothing.

'All done?' asks Saumarez, from the other side of the room.

'Thanks for the shirt.'

'Not mine, as you've probably guessed.'

'Thank your girlfriend then.'

He smiles. 'My daughter. My eldest daughter, to be precise. Olivia is only ten. But Claudia's nearly as tall as you. Or she was last time I saw her.'

'Pretty names.'

He gives a sardonic smile. 'My wife's choice. She said I'd have called them Girl A and Girl B given half a chance.'

'Do they live a long way away?' she asks, wondering about that 'last time'.

'Vancouver far enough for you?'

There's something in his face now and she bites her lip. 'Sorry – I didn't mean –'

'It's not a problem. Not for me anyway. I miss them, but it's a fabulous opportunity. I grew up on an island twelve miles long. I want wider horizons for my girls.'

He sees her eyes stray towards the window and laughs. 'Everyone does that – assumes I must mean the Isle of Wight – but it was actually Guernsey. A lot smaller and a lot further away.'

'How often do you get to see your daughters?'

He shrugs. 'We Skype every week and I get to be Hero Dad once a year when they come over. It works. OK, it's not quite what I had in mind when they were born, but it works.'

There's a knock on the door then and Saumarez opens

it to Gislingham, who makes a great show of looking at his watch.

'Can we go now?'

He's staring at her T-shirt. It says *Beyoncé* in pink and blue sequins. She blushes. 'The DI was kind enough to lend me this.'

'One of my daughter's,' says Saumarez genially. Which makes Gislingham suspicious, straight away. Because as he clocked over an hour ago, the DI's not wearing a ring.

There's a pause that threatens to become embarrassing, then Saumarez clears his throat. 'If there's anything else I can help with, you know where to find me.'

'Talk about up himself,' says Gislingham as they walk towards his car.

Somer flushes a little. 'Oh, I don't know. Seems OK to me.'

It's on the tip of Gislingham's tongue to ask what Fawley would think of her making nice with another DI but he stops himself just in time. After all, he doesn't actually *know* there's anything going on between her and the boss. And what she does in her private life is her business. *Obviously.* But all the same, there's no getting away from the fact that he's pissed off, and pissed off that he's pissed off, and doubly pissed off that she knows he's pissed off and she probably thinks it's all because she sent them on this bloody wild goose chase.

The journey back is all but silent.

* * *

Telephone interview with Stacey Gunn,
9 January 2018, 9.11 a.m.
On the call, DC E. Somer

SG: Hello? Who's that?

ES: My name is Detective Constable Erica Somer.
The switchboard put you through to me - I'm
part of the team investigating the fire in
Southey Road.

SG: Right. Good. I saw the appeal you put out. On
the local news. That's why I'm calling.

ES: Did you know the Esmonds, Ms Gunn?

SG: Just her. Samantha. We did Pilates together. I
never knew where she lived so I didn't realize
it was her house in that awful fire. But I saw
him once - her husband. He picked her up after
a session. That's why I recognized him on the
TV.

ES: When did you last see Mrs Esmond?

SG: She hasn't come much recently. To the class, I
mean. She stopped when she got pregnant and
she hasn't really been back since.

ES: So you haven't seen her for over three
years?

SG: Sorry, I'm not making myself very clear. I saw
her at the doctor's - the one off the
Woodstock Road. Must have been about two
months ago. She had both the kids with her.
But to be honest, I almost didn't recognize
her. She looked awful. Hair all rats' tails,
no make-up. She'd always been so beautifully

turned out before. Even for a Pilates class. I think her husband liked it that way.

ES: What makes you say that?

SG: That day he turned up – he helped her put on her coat, and then he stepped back and looked at her, and tucked a strand of hair behind her ear. It was a bit creepy, to be honest.

ES: Did she ever talk to you about her husband?

SG: Not really. Nothing more than general stuff. But looking back at it now it was as if she was being really careful what she said about him. Making sure she didn't say anything out of place.

ES: I see. You said you saw Mrs Esmond at the doctor's. Did she say what she was there for?

SG: Well, I know it wasn't for the kids. When she went in it was her name they called. But if you ask me, it was pretty obvious.

ES: Yes?

SG: Post-natal depression. A cousin of mine had it. She looked exactly the same. Like the light had gone out in her eyes.

* * *

Somer puts down the phone and sits there for a moment. Then she gets up quickly and leaves the room. Five minutes later Everett pushes open the door to the Ladies and finds her motionless, staring into the mirror.

'You OK?'

Somer sighs. 'Was it that obvious?'

Everett smiles drily. 'Probably not to most of the blokes. But if you're still worrying about the Calshot thing, then seriously, don't. It was a good call. Imagine what would have happened if he'd actually been there and we didn't bother checking it out –'

'It's not that,' says Somer quickly. 'I was just talking to one of Samantha Esmond's friends. Or what I suspect was the nearest thing she had to a "friend".'

Everett comes over to join her, leaning against the basin. 'You're right. I hadn't thought about it before, but no one else who knew her has come forward, have they?'

'I get the impression her husband doesn't "approve" of friends very much.'

'So what did this woman say?'

Somer turns to face her. 'She saw her at the doctor's. Samantha didn't say why she was there but her friend thinks it might have been post-natal depression. She recognized the signs – she knew someone who'd had it.'

The two women are silent for a moment. Somer has turned away again but Everett is still watching her. Suddenly, several stray observations she's made about Somer since they became friends fall into place.

'You do, too. Don't you. Know someone, I mean.'

Somer glances up. 'My sister. She's three years older than me.'

'What happened?' asks Everett softly.

Somer sighs. 'It was bloody awful. Kath was always one of those people you struggle to keep up with. Completely gorgeous to look at, for a start –'

Which might explain something about Somer, too, thinks Everett. For someone so attractive, Somer's never

130

seemed at all fixated by her looks. But if she has a stunner for a sister, perhaps that explains it.

'Kath was always top stream at school – she got a great degree, a job in a major law firm, married a guy who adored her. Then she hit thirty and decided that if she was going to have a baby she'd better get on with it. She had all these plans – she'd hire a live-in au pair, go back to work, have it all. And the baby was beautiful – the most gorgeous little girl you've ever seen. And Kath could hardly bear to look at her.'

Everett reaches out and touches Somer lightly on the shoulder. She knows how much she isn't saying; how hard this must have been. 'How old is the baby now?'

'Eighteen months. And it's taken Kath most of that time to crawl back to who she used to be. But she's still not back at work. They had to sign her off on long-term sick leave. Most people have no idea how long PND can last.'

Everett makes a face. 'It must have been really tough. Especially on her husband.'

'Stuart? He's a bloody hero. I dread to think how she'd have coped without a partner like him.'

They're both silent now, but they're both thinking the same thing: what kind of partner did Samantha Esmond have?

The door opens again and one of the uniform PCs comes in. She and Somer exchange a nod.

'OK,' says Everett more briskly as the cubicle door closes. 'What now?'

'First thing tomorrow I'm going to talk to her GP,' says Somer. 'See what they can tell us.'

'It's a bit odd, isn't it, that Samantha's parents never said anything?'

Somer shakes her head. 'It was months before Stu told my parents. Sometimes a problem shared just makes things twice as bad – especially if people live a long way away and can't do anything practical to help.'

There's a hinterland of pain here that Everett knows better than to trespass on.

At least not now.

* * *

I'm in the car when the phone rings. Queuing to get past the ring road. It doesn't matter which way you try to get into this city in the morning rush hour (and believe me, I've tried them all), you always end up waiting in line. I'm not in the best of moods, and in two minds whether to answer the damn phone. Until I see who it is.

'Alex? It's fantastic to hear from you. How are you? How's your sister?'

Too much, Fawley, too much.

There's a pause. This isn't good.

'Alex?'

'Who is she, Adam?'

I'm not sure what freezes my heart more: the question or the tone she asks it in.

'Who's who? Sorry, you've lost me.'

'Oh, don't give me that. You're an awful liar, you always have been.'

'Seriously, I haven't a clue what you're talking about.'

I hear her draw breath. Ragged, angry breath. 'I came by the house this morning to pick up my post –'

'You should have said – I'd have waited. Why didn't you say?'

'– and as I was leaving I saw Mrs Barrett.'

Who lives opposite us and is a right old busybody with far too much time on her hands. This isn't good either.

'She said she saw you – with *her*.'

'*Who?* Look, Alex, I'm not bullshitting you – I don't know what you're talking about. Seriously. And why you'd believe that Barrett woman rather than me –'

'Because *she* has no reason to lie!'

My turn to draw breath. We need to slow this down. Take some of the emotion out of it.

'Alex, I swear. *I. Do. Not. Know.* And as for seeing another woman – you think I even have *time*?'

But I know even before the words are out that was the wrong thing to say.

'Please – don't hang up. We haven't talked in weeks and now this? I swear to you I have *not* been seeing anyone else. I love *you*; I want you to come home. How many more ways can I say that? What can I do to make you believe me?'

Silence.

'Look, I know we have some problems. I know you want to adopt and I wish with *all my heart* that I felt the same way about it as you do, but I don't. And I can't let us build a family on a fault line like that. It's not fair to you, and it's not fair – above all – to any child we might take on.'

I don't need to say that. I've said it, and she's heard it, time out of mind. Back in November, she made me listen to a radio series about finding adoptive parents for a brother and sister of two and three. The foster carer, the diligent, careful social worker, the new parents who were at one and the same time overjoyed to give a home to these tiny children they'd never met and fearful they might not even like them, and the final episode, recorded months later, when the four of them had made themselves into a family, with all the same love and muddle and working-it-out-as-you-go-along every family has. I knew why Alex wanted me to hear it; of course I did. She wanted to prove to me that not everyone feels the same way as I do about being adopted. That it's possible to find love and belonging and acceptance. The proof was there, in that episode: all the people who wrote in because they were touched and moved, and those who'd felt vindicated in their own decision to adopt themselves, whatever the challenges. But then, at the end, there was a woman in her fifties who described adoption as a life sentence, who described the guilt at feeling always different 'like some ghastly kind of cuckoo', the sense of disconnection, and the pain which only gets worse, not easier, the older you become. Alex stood there, frozen to the spot. I couldn't bear to look at her so I walked to the window and stared down at the garden it was too dark to see. Three days later, she told me she was leaving.

And now there's silence at the end of the line.

'Alex –'

'It was Sunday.' Her voice is icy. 'Mrs Barrett was putting out the bins and she saw a woman leaving the house. She said you two seemed very "pally".' There's bitterness now. 'Blonde. Late twenties. *Very attractive*,' she adds. 'Apparently.'

And now I know. Both who that was and why it's causing Alex so much pain. She thinks I'm trying to replace her. With someone young enough to give me a child.

'That was Somer. Erica Somer. She's on the team. You know that.'

But Alex has never met her. She wasn't at my birthday drinks.

'Mrs Barrett didn't say anything about a uniform.'

'That's because Somer's CID now. I told you.'

'So what was she doing there? At *our house*? On a *Sunday*? At *ten o'clock at night*?' But there's a hesitancy now. She wants to believe me. Or at least I want to think so.

'She wanted to check something with me. And the place was a state, so she offered to help clear up a bit. That's all it was. Really.'

Silence again.

'It did look tidier than I expected,' she says eventually. 'This morning.'

'I can't take the credit for that. I was going to, of course, but you've rumbled me now. And like you say, I'm a terrible liar.'

I try to put a laugh into my voice. To draw her in.

In front of me, the traffic is suddenly moving and the car behind is sounding its horn.

'Look, why don't you come over later – I can get a takeaway. Bottle of wine. We can talk properly.'

She sighs. 'I don't know, Adam.'

'But you believe me – about Somer?'

Her voice is dull, unhappy. 'Yes. I believe you. But I'm not ready to come home. Not yet. I'm sorry.'

And the line goes dead.

* * *

The waiting room is packed. And hacking. Testy coughs, leaky sniffs. January germs. The surgery is a converted house off the Woodstock Road. One of those Victorian semis that look quite narrow from the street, but go back a long way. The waiting room is at the rear, looking over a garden that's probably quite nice in the summer, but is ankle deep in dead and rotting leaves. The large tree at the bottom is encircled two inches thick by dingy rust-coloured needles. What's the point in a conifer, thinks Somer, if you still have to sweep up all the crap?

Even though she arrives before surgery starts she still has to wait half an hour for Dr Miller to be free. The woman is clearly frazzled. She has slate grey hair in a severe bob and a pair of glasses perched on the top of her head. Somer is prepared to bet she forgets where she's put them at least twice a day.

'Sorry, officer,' she says, moving things about on the desk distractedly. 'The week after the holidays is always a bit like this. What can I do for you?'

'It's about Samantha Esmond.'

The fidgeting stops.

'Ah, yes. That was truly appalling.' The distress in her pale green eyes is genuine.

'We've now spoken to one of Samantha's friends, who

thinks she might have been suffering from post-natal depression. Is that true?'

The doctor starts to tap her biro on the desk. 'That is, of course, confidential medical information. I assume you have obtained the appropriate authorization?'

'I can assure you the paperwork is entirely in order. I have a copy, if you want to see it.'

She doesn't expect the doctor to take her up on it, but the woman holds out her hand. Somer reaches into her bag for the sheet. Miller pulls down her glasses, snagging her hair as she does so. She reads the page once, and then again, then puts it down on the desk and removes her glasses.

'Yes,' she says with a sigh. 'Samantha did have PND. And it wasn't the first time. She'd had the same problems after Matty was born, though from what I could tell from her notes, it was much worse with Zachary. And went on much longer.'

'How did it manifest itself?'

'The usual symptoms. Listlessness, feeling inadequate, crying for no reason, problems sleeping.'

'Was she on medication?'

'Yes. I recently started her on temazepam to help her sleep and she was also taking sertraline to help with the anxiety.'

'So you considered it severe enough to need anti-depressants?'

Dr Miller eyes her. 'Yes, I'm afraid it was. We tried various alternatives before deciding that was the most appropriate one for her.'

Somer hesitates, but it has to be asked. 'Did you ever think she might harm herself? Or the baby?'

Dr Miller sits back. 'To be completely honest, we *were* beginning to be concerned about Zachary, but not for that reason, I hasten to add. He was having rather too many stomach upsets. We were trying to get to the bottom of it.'

'I see –'

'But there was no suggestion he was being abused, if that's what you're thinking. As for Samantha, she was just – well, overwhelmed. She had Matty to deal with as well, remember. It was all too much for her.'

'She had her husband to help, didn't she?'

'Michael? He was exemplary. He couldn't do enough for her. Shopping, washing, cleaning, taking Matty to school. He did the lot. He was extraordinarily supportive.'

Or extraordinarily controlling, thinks Somer.

'I don't know how he managed to do it all and still hold down such a responsible job,' says the doctor, a little tersely. Perhaps she has sensed Somer's scepticism. 'It would have defeated most people. Me included.'

'Did he show signs of being under stress?'

Dr Miller's eyes narrow. 'Dr Esmond was not taking medication for stress, depression or any other similar condition. As for Matty, he was a rather nervous child, but clearly loved and well cared for. What more do you want me to say?'

This is new. 'You say Matty was nervous – how did that manifest itself?'

Miller starts tapping her biro again. 'He was a bit fretful. Took things a bit too much to heart. Impressionable and, I imagine, easily intimidated.'

'Intimidated? You mean, he was being bullied?'

She shakes her head. 'No. I'm fairly sure that wasn't the case. The school nurse did get in touch with me last year, and I'm sure she would have mentioned that if it had been any sort of issue.'

'So if it wasn't that, why did she want to talk to you?'

Miller sighs again. 'Matty was worried about his mother. He told his teacher she was seeing ghosts.'

* * *

Gislingham is on his way in to the station when his phone rings. One glance at the screen and he knows he has to take the call. He pulls over and picks up the handset.

'DS Gislingham.'

'Chris? It's Paul Rigby. I'm at Southey Road. Where are you?'

'In the car. But I can be there in twenty minutes.'

'Good. Because I think you'll want to see this as soon as possible.'

* * *

13 June 2017, 2.13 p.m.
205 days before the fire
23 Southey Road, Oxford

When Sam gets back from the park with the boys, Michael is in the garden. After a grey start the sun has come out, and it's now so hot that she's had to bring the children home early. She gives them a juice each in the kitchen and it's only when she goes to the sink to rinse the glasses that she realizes her husband is not alone. There's a young man with him she's never seen before. He's tall and good-looking, in cargo shorts and a pair of loafers. Even at this distance he looks at ease with himself. Intrigued, she encourages the boys outside, and follows them down the lawn.

'I'm Harry,' he says as she approaches, holding out his hand. She's seen that smile many times in this town. The sort of smile that springs from a lot of attitude – from deep-set assumptions about your own worth and your place in the world, and the reception you think you're going to get.

'Harry replied to the ad,' says her husband. 'The one I put up in the newsagent's about getting some help in the garden.'

'You never told me you actually did that,' says Sam, openly incredulous. Her husband has never put a card on a shop noticeboard in his life. He's always saying you never know what you might be letting yourself in for.

'Mr Esmond was hoping I could get the grass cut before you got home,' interjects Harry. 'As a surprise. But the mower ran out of petrol.'

'I told you we should keep a spare can,' says Sam, keeping her tone light. She doesn't want Michael to think she's nagging. Especially in front of someone else.

'So you're a student, are you, Harry?' she says, turning to him. He nods. 'Only an undergrad, hence needing the money,' he says with a rueful face.

Matty has by now sidled up to the adults. He has his ball under his arm and starts dragging at his father's sleeve. '*Da-ad.*'

Michael turns to him. 'I'm busy, Matty. We're talking.'

'You like football, Matt?' says Harry, and Sam sees her husband stifle a wince. No one calls their son Matt. They've worked really hard to make sure of that.

Harry reaches forward and takes the ball, walks away a few paces and starts doing tricks. Bouncing it on his knee, catching it on his shoulder blades. Matty is beside himself.

'Can you teach me to do that?' he says, almost gasping.

Harry gathers up the ball. 'Sure,' he said. 'How about now?'

Sam sees her husband open his mouth to say no but Matty is already jumping up and down, pawing at him, squealing, 'Can I, Dad? Can I?'

Zachary hurtles towards them and starts shouting, 'Me too! Me too!'

Sam turns to Harry. 'Are you sure you're up for this?'

That smile again. 'Sure. No problem. I didn't have anything else planned. And I always wanted a brother when I was growing up.'

An hour later the boys are exhausted and Michael's retreated to his study. In the kitchen, Sam pours Harry a beer.

'Nice place,' he says, wandering through to the sitting room and looking round at the furniture, the grandfather clock, the piano with its framed photographs.

'It's Michael's family's house,' she says, wondering why she feels the need to apologize. 'Nothing much has been changed in here since his grandmother died.'

Harry lifts the lid of the piano and plays a few notes, then makes a face. 'Needs tuning.'

She sighs. 'I know. We keep meaning to get it organized but you know how it is. Matty wants to learn, though.'

Harry looks up. 'Really? You should encourage him. It's a great age to start.'

He closes the lid and picks up a picture of her son playing in a sandpit with his uncle. Matty must have been about four, grinning from ear to ear. Sam realizes with a sudden lump in her throat that he hardly ever smiles like that any more. Until this afternoon, that is.

'So you'll definitely come back?' she says quickly. 'For the garden?'

* * *

Bishop Christopher's Church of England Primary still has a tired post-Christmas look to it. The bins bulging with recycled decorations aren't helping, and there are bits of tinsel still sellotaped to some of the windows. Somer and Everett get out of the car; Somer has never been here, but Everett has. It's why Somer asked her to come.

'Has it changed much?'

Everett shakes her head. 'No. I suppose some of the kids will be different by now, but the place is just the same.'

Just the same as when Daisy Mason went missing and Everett and Gislingham came here to question her teachers and classmates. And now the school has lost another child and the questioning will start all over again.

Everett leads the way inside: it's a warren of corridors but she knows exactly where she's going. And they are – clearly – expected. Alison Stevens is waiting restlessly in the reception area outside the head teacher's office.

'DC Everett,' she says, coming towards them with an outstretched hand. 'How nice to see you again, despite the tragic circumstances.'

'This is my colleague, DC Somer.'

Somer shakes the woman's hand, noting how cool her skin is and how anxious her smile.

'Do please come in. I've asked Matty's teacher to join us as well.'

Everett doesn't recognize the woman waiting inside. She has large round glasses, a splashy floral-print dress and heavy cardigan, with unflattering flat shoes, in sharp contrast to the elegant and understated Stevens.

'This is Emily West,' says Stevens. 'She joined us last year.'

So she never knew Daisy Mason. Stevens doesn't say it, but she doesn't have to. Then she turns to the desk and starts occupying her nervous energy by pouring tea. There's a picture of her daughter by the computer, her hair in elaborate crochet braids. She must be about the same age as Matty Esmond.

Everett and Somer take a seat. Emily West seems a good deal less anxious than the head.

'You wanted to know about Matty?' she asks.

'I saw his doctor this morning,' says Somer. 'She says you were concerned about him. Concerned enough for the school nurse to call her.'

Somer has deliberately left out the bit about the ghost. She's intrigued to see how – and if – they raise it.

West smiles. 'I know you're probably assuming it was something to do with bullying,' she begins and Everett sees anxiety flicker across Stevens's face, though she says nothing. 'But honestly, it was nothing like that. He was concerned about his mother. He said she wasn't very well. That it felt like someone had "put her under a spell". But what was really worrying him was that she'd told him she thought there was a ghost in the house.'

'Did he say why she thought that?'

West nods. 'Apparently she'd heard noises.'

'That was all?'

West shakes her head. 'No. She'd seen it too.'

Everett sits forward. 'Where, precisely?'

'Once in the garden, I think. And she thought she heard him indoors.'

Somer and Everett exchange a glance.

'So it was definitely a "he"?'

West shakes her head again. 'No, not necessarily. Apparently she didn't get a good look. I gathered it was more like catching a glimpse out of the corner of your eye.'

'Was she the only person who'd seen it?'

West pauses. 'That's a good question. It's possible Matty had – or thought he had. It's hard to remember the exact words he used, but I got the sense he thought he'd seen something.'

But then again, thinks Somer, this is a boy described as 'impressionable'. If his mother told him there was a ghost, it's quite possible his imagination did the rest.

'Did you speak to either of his parents about this?' asks Everett.

West nods. 'I spoke to Dr Esmond one morning.' She glances at Stevens. 'We wanted both Matty's parents to come in for a proper meeting but he said he was very busy and Samantha was unwell. He said she was on medication and sometimes it made her a bit spaced out, but it was all under control and there was nothing for us to worry about. But he did promise to talk to Matty. He was a bit short with me, to be honest, but he is a scientist after all. I suppose stories of ghosts and ghoulies are a bit beneath him.'

Not for an anthropologist, surely, thinks Somer. He would have understood what 'stories' like that can signify.

'He hadn't seen anything odd himself?'

West is quick to reply. 'No, absolutely not. The whole thing was clearly news to him. In fact, I think that was one reason he was annoyed – that we knew something about his family that he didn't.'

Everett takes out her notebook. 'And when was this, that you spoke to him?'

'Last summer term, I think it was. Yes, definitely around then.'

'And how was Matty when he returned to school in the autumn?'

'Actually,' interrupts the head, 'he seemed much happier. He'd struggled to make friends before but he seemed much more confident.'

'Was there any particular reason for that?' asks Somer, looking from one woman to the other.

'No,' says West. 'But it can happen that way. Especially with boys. They can grow up in fits and starts.'

'Or not at all, if some of our colleagues are anything to go by,' mutters Everett, which elicits a wry smile from Stevens.

Somer takes a deep breath; in for a penny and all that. 'And Matty got on OK with his father?' She keeps her voice light – she doesn't want to influence the answer.

West smiles. 'Dr Esmond was obviously quite strict,

but Matty clearly idolized him. He was *always* talking about him. How clever he was and what an important job he had. Last year he was the only child in the class with an academic for a father.'

'My dad's job's bigger than your dad's,' says Everett.

West grins. 'Something like that. You know how competitive kids can be.'

Something isn't adding up here, thinks Somer. But I'm damned if I know what it is.

'So you weren't aware of anything that was troubling him at the end of Christmas term?' she continues calmly. 'No problems at home?'

West looks blank. 'No, nothing. He was just excited about the holidays. Like all the kids were. I'm sorry. I don't know what else I can say.'

Everett and Somer get to their feet. No one has touched the tea.

* * *

Rigby is waiting at the end of the drive at Southey Road when Gislingham draws up. He's wearing a black jumpsuit and a hard hat, and has a face mask slung round his neck.

'We didn't find it until an hour ago,' he says as they walk up towards the house, past the team of three on their hands and knees picking over the slag heap of rubble. 'But to be honest, we had other priorities.'

They come to a halt in front of the garage. It's several yards from the house, so apart from the soot marks and the blistering to the paintwork it's almost untouched.

There's a padlock hanging off the door handle, but as Gis sees at once, it's not been closed properly.

'And before you ask,' says Rigby as he pushes open the door, 'it was already in that state when I got here. And I've been wearing gloves. If there are prints, they'll be intact.'

He reaches for the light switch inside and the neon strip stutters and plinks on. It may have been built as a garage but it's being used as a shed. Wheelie bins, a couple of ancient shovels, boxes of assorted household detritus, a wheelbarrow, bicycles, a garden table and chairs, and a parasol, furred with spiders' webs.

'Looks like it's true what they say,' says Gislingham, looking around, 'junk really does expand to fill the available space.'

But even as he says it he knows that's not why they're here: pushed against one corner is a lawnmower. A motor mower.

'Judging by the stains on the floor,' says Rigby quietly, 'I reckon there was a spare can of petrol for that mower in here. A spare can that definitely isn't here any more.'

Gislingham's face is grim. 'But I bet I know where we're going to find it.'

Rigby nods. 'And it's not just that. There's something else.' He starts to pick his way across the junk and gestures Gislingham to follow. There's a door in the back wall. A door that opens into a completely different kind of space. Pale walls studded with children's drawings, brightly coloured kelims on a tiled floor, and glass doors opening on to the garden.

'We didn't even realize it was here,' says Rigby. 'They have roller shutters on those doors so as far as we could

147

see it was just the back of the garage.' He looks round. 'Pretty nice man-cave, eh?'

Gislingham is staring. At the desk, the filing cabinets, the shelves of textbooks.

It's not a man-cave. It's Michael Esmond's study.

* * *

When Gis calls me from Southey Road I can tell from the echo that he's indoors.

'We've found his desktop PC and the charger for a laptop, though I assume he has the machine with him. And there's a stack of paperwork. And I do mean a *stack*.'

I take a deep breath. 'OK, bring the computer back here and we'll have a look at it. And I'm afraid we're going to have to go through all those bloody papers as well.'

'Right, boss. I'll get it organized.'

I wonder, in passing, who he'll dump with that one. If I were a betting man, my money'd be on Quinn.

'There was something else too, boss. We've finally picked up Jurjen Kuiper's car on the ANPR cameras that night. He was at the Littlemore exit of the ring road at 12.10 a.m. That must have been just after the fire started, so I really don't see how he could have done it. It'd take fifteen minutes from there to Southey Road, even at that time of night, and the car definitely wasn't speeding.'

I still find it hard to comprehend why Kuiper was out driving so late in such treacherous conditions, but that's looking like another story we'll never know the end of.

* * *

Everett and Somer are only just in time for the team meeting at 4.30. Somer leaves Everett to park the car and makes her way across to the police station. It's started to rain again and Everett struggles to find a space; when she turns the engine off and looks up she can see Somer talking to someone in the doorway. In the gloom and the downpour it's another few seconds before she realizes who it is.

Fawley.

Everett's not nosy by nature. She's not interested in tittle-tattle, and she tries to live and let live. But she can't stop herself watching. He and Somer are standing close together, but it's impossible to tell if that's just to keep out of the rain. The light above their heads casts deep sharp shadows and Fawley's bending his head now, talking to Somer in an urgent, intimate way she can't ever remember seeing before. He usually holds back – keeps his distance, in every sense. But not this time.

She opens the door and gets slowly out of the car. Then reaches into the back seat for her umbrella, which she opens as extravagantly as she can manage. She wants to give them as much chance as possible to see her coming. Which they evidently do, because by the time she reaches the door, Somer is alone.

'Who was that?' asks Everett casually, shaking out the brolly.

'Oh, just one of the uniforms. He wanted to know how the case was going.'

Everett's heart sinks. As any halfway decent police officer knows, people don't bother lying if they've nothing to hide.

* * *

149

Sent: Weds 10/01/2018, 15.45   **Importance: High**

From: Colin.Boddie@ouh.nhs.uk

To: DIAdamFawley@ThamesValley.police.uk,
CID@ThamesValley.police.uk, AlanChallowCSI@
ThamesValley.police.uk

Subject: Bloodwork and toxicology: Case no 556432/12 Felix House, 23 Southey Road

I have just had the toxicology results on the three victims. To summarize: there were no untoward findings in relation to Matthew Esmond. Zachary's bloods showed a relatively high level of acetaminophen (paracetamol) but one which would still be consistent with a therapeutic dose of a paediatric medicine such as Calpol.

Bloodwork from Samantha Esmond detected the presence of desmethylsertraline (i.e. the antidepressant sertraline) at a concentration consistent with ongoing therapeutic use. However, there were also very significant levels of both alcohol (a BAC of 0.10%) and benzodiazepine (i.e. temazepam). For the avoidance of doubt, the latter was not inconsistent with a therapeutic dose, but in combination with the alcohol would have quickly rendered a woman of her height and weight drowsy. There's one final test outstanding on Samantha, which I will forward to you as soon as I get it.

I've also had results from Zachary Esmond's bloods. The level of carbon monoxide detected is significantly lower than I would have expected. I cannot, therefore, rule out the possibility that Zachary was already dead before the fire took full hold. There being no other obvious signs of injury, the most likely cause of death in that case would have been suffocation.

* * *

It's fair to say I'm probably not on top form at the team meeting. Alex's call is still distracting me. I tried to phone her back three times today and got nothing but voicemail. And then I stopped because I knew it would just make me look desperate. Even though I am. Even though part of me wants her to know I am.

So if I lose the thread of the discussion a couple of times, that's why. It's not an excuse. But it is an explanation. And I only manage to wing it because there's so little *to* discuss. Despite the appeal, the tweets, the thankless door-knocking, despite the hundreds of calls that have come in and a running total of man hours I don't even want to think about, we still have no bloody idea where Esmond is. And I say as much. I notice Everett eyeing me once or twice. Especially when Somer is reporting back on the meetings with the school and the family doctor.

'So,' she says, summing up, 'we now know that Samantha Esmond was suffering from post-natal depression. But the doctor insists she wasn't a risk to herself or her children.'

She's not saying so explicitly, but we all know what she means: if anyone was thinking of putting Samantha forward as a possible suspect, as far as Somer is concerned you can forget it. It wasn't her who set that fire.

'Are you sure about that?' says Baxter, googling on his phone. 'It says here that severe cases can lead to paranoia and hallucinations, and if it goes untreated up to four per cent of mothers will commit infanticide.'

There's a flicker of unease round the room at that. They're remembering what Boddie said: Zachary could have been dead before the fire even started. And suffocation is one of the commonest ways women kill their children.

'You're talking about post-partum *psychosis*,' says Somer, slightly abruptly. '*Not* post-natal depression. Samantha was never diagnosed with PPP.'

'All the same –' begins Baxter, but she doesn't let him finish.

'Post-partum psychosis almost always starts within two weeks of having the baby. Zachary was *three*. The number of cases where PPP comes on without warning that long after birth is vanishingly small.'

Baxter looks from me to Somer. 'Could her post-natal depression have turned into this PPP? Is that possible?'

She shakes her head. 'No. They're entirely different. And the one doesn't lead to the other.'

'So if Samantha really was seeing things, it wasn't down to that?'

'Not that, no. I guess the medication she was on may have been a factor. But even if that were true, there's a huge leap from seeing ghosts to deliberately killing the entire family.'

There's something in her face – the way she says

it – that stifles further disagreement. I just wish I had her certainty.

* * *

25 June 2017, 4.30 p.m.
193 days before the fire
23 Southey Road, Oxford

Sam can tell at once something's up.

'I brought you a beer,' she says carefully, easing the bottle on to the edge of the desk. The study is a beautiful space at this time of year, the glass doors open to the garden and the light and the scent of cut grass. A red admiral butterfly has landed on the printer and is opening and closing its wings in the warmth. But her husband is frowning.

'What is it?'

He makes a face. 'Just Philip. He emailed to say he'll be here on the 13th July.'

'How long is he staying?'

'He says two days, but you know him. It could just as easily be two weeks.'

'Well, we can hardly say no – what with –'

'I know, I know,' Michael says tetchily.

Sam bites her lip. She knows better than to offer any defence for Philip. Last time she tried she found herself on the wrong end of a twenty-minute tirade about what a waster he is, bumming about the world from one tropical beach to the next and never being around to do any of the heavy lifting. Like Dad's funeral. Like getting Mum into a home. The first time Michael ever really opened up to her had been about Philip. They'd only been together about six weeks and up till then his whole persona had been so carefully crafted she was beginning to think he was too good to be true. *Always* courteous, *always* patient, *always* considerate. And then she got to his flat early one night to find him on the phone to his father. He'd rung home to tell him he was about to get his first article published in an academic journal, but by the time he finished the call he was almost in tears.

'What do I have to do?' he'd said. 'Philip's the one who flunked even getting *in* to Oxford. Philip's the one who's never bothered doing a proper day's work in his life because he's been living off money my grandfather left him. *Philip* should be the disappointment. And yet to listen to my father you'd think I was sleeping rough under Charing Cross station.'

She'd remonstrated, sitting close, her arm round him.

'He's so proud of you. You know he doesn't mean it.'

He'd looked up at her, angry through the tears. 'Oh yes he does. It's always *Philip* this and *Philip* that. All the time I was growing up Dad called him Pip. He'd tousle his hair and say he had "great expectations". It was years before I knew what he was getting at – and all that time I thought it meant that he had higher hopes of Philip than he did of me. I don't think he had the first bloody idea the impact something like that can have.'

Her heart had broken, then, for the sad little boy he had been and the furiously ambitious man he'd turned that into. And she'd felt, as she never had with Michael before, that she was the strong one – she was the one with something to give, the one to protect, not be protected. It was the first time she'd ever felt that. And it would be the last.

* * *

Somer stops by her desk to collect the bag of shopping she left there at lunchtime. Some of the fruit has rolled out under her chair, and she has to get down on her hands and knees to retrieve it. When she finally straightens up she's surprised to find Quinn standing there. She's flustered a moment, conscious that she's red in the face and her hair has come loose.

'Can I help you?'

He looks diffident. A word she's never associated with him before.

'I just wanted to check you were OK.'

She stares at him, not sure she heard him right. 'Why wouldn't I be?'

He shrugs. 'It was just, well, what you were saying back there. It sounded like it was coming from somewhere – you know – personal.'

She hesitates, not sure she wants to open up on this. At least to him. But there's something in his face.

'My sister had it – *has* it,' she says eventually. 'Post-natal depression, I mean. It's been tough. On all of us.'

He nods.

'And there's such a terrible stigma attached to it, even now. Far too many women don't come forward and get help because they're worried about what people will say. They're frightened they'll be labelled as bad mothers or "hysterical" or one of those other words men only use about women and never about other men.' She stops, aware she's even redder in the face now.

'I know,' he says quietly. 'About PND. My mother had it.'

Now that really does floor her. She opens her mouth, then closes it again.

'You never mentioned it. When we –'

He shrugs. 'Like you said. There's still a lot of prejudice. And ignorance.'

And it must have been even worse a generation ago.

'They ended up sectioning her,' he says, reading her thoughts. 'My dad had to cope for six months with a newborn baby and an eight-year-old. He didn't know what'd hit him.'

He looks up, meeting her eyes properly for the first time.

'You were only eight?'

He smiles weakly. 'Dad kept telling me I had to be a big boy. That he had enough to worry about without me acting up. No one in the family ever spoke about it. It was as if she'd done something shameful. Or criminal. It was years before I found out what had really happened.'

She nods, struggling to find the right thing to say. But it explains a lot about Quinn. His strident self-sufficiency, his intolerance of weakness, his inability to admit any vulnerability.

'Anyway,' he says, straightening his shoulders a little. 'I just wanted to check.'

He starts to go, but she calls him back. 'Quinn?'

He turns. 'Yeah?'

'Thank you. For telling me. That can't have been easy.'

He shrugs. 'No worries.'

And then he's gone.

* * *

11 July 2017, 10.23 a.m.
177 days before the fire
23 Southey Road, Oxford

'Hi,' says Philip, when she opens the door. 'I got back to Poole a bit earlier than I expected.'

She's only seen him once or twice since the wedding, where he'd been, rather to her surprise given Michael's loud and frequent reservations, an exemplary best man.

He's thinner than when she last saw him, but it suits him. Sun-bleached hair, a deep tan, shirt open just a bit too far. There's a heap of dusty rucksacks and duffel bags at his feet. A black cab is just turning out of the street on to the Banbury Road.

He sees her face and looks sheepish. 'Sorry. I know I'm a couple of days early. But if it's a problem I can leave all this crap here and lose myself for an hour or two.'

She smiles. 'No, it's fine. You just took me by surprise, that's all.'

'I did try Mike's mobile but he's not answering.'

She makes a face. 'He does that. Turns it off to save the battery and then forgets and wonders why no one's calling him.'

Philip grins. 'Always was a bit of a throwback. In a nice way, of course,' he adds quickly.

One of the neighbours has stopped on the other side of the street. She's pretending to fiddle with her shoe but Sam can see her clocking Philip and doing the mental maths that puts two and two together and makes extra-marital affair.

She stands back. 'Come in,' she says quickly. 'Do you need a hand with all that –?'

'Absolutely not,' he says firmly. 'Dad always used to say, only travel with the bags you're prepared to carry yourself.'

*

157

By the time Michael gets home they're sitting in the garden with the bottle of Chablis Philip brought with him. Zachary is sitting at their feet, playing with his toy fire engine. Harry must have been too, because the lawn has been mowed and the cuttings stacked in a bag by the wheelie bin. Michael frowns, then goes to the fridge for a beer before heading outside. Whether deliberately or not, Philip has positioned his chair so he can see the house. He gets to his feet at once.

'Mike! Sorry to turn up unannounced like this,' he says, reaching to give his brother a hug.

'No problem,' says Michael, a little stiff in the embrace.

Samantha looks up, alert to the acerbity. But there's a colour in her cheeks Michael hasn't seen for weeks.

'We brought you out a chair,' she says, gesturing. Smiling.

He puts his beer down on the table. 'Where's Matty?'

Philip makes a face. 'On his Xbox. I did try to tempt him out but he seemed completely engrossed.'

'Yeah, well,' says Michael. 'That won't be the first time.' He turns to his wife. 'What are we going to do about dinner?'

'All sorted,' says Philip quickly. 'Getting a Deliveroo from Brown's. Least I can do.'

Two hours later the sun is going down and the chairs have been shunted to one side so that Philip can play football with Matty.

Michael stands at the sink, rinsing the plates before they go into the dishwasher.

'They haven't had so much fun for ages,' says Sam, coming in with a tray of glasses and a sleepy Zachary wedged on one hip. 'Apparently Philip is Ronaldo and Matty is Messi.'

There's a shout from the garden; Philip has just scored a goal and is running round the lawn with his T-shirt over his face.

'Prat,' says Michael. But not out loud.

'He's going to take us punting tomorrow,' says Sam casually.

Michael glances at her. 'Really? Are you sure he knows how? Must be years since he did it last.'

She shrugs. 'He says he does.' Then, 'I thought you'd be pleased. It'll give you some peace and quiet to get some work done.'

And, of course, it will.

'Do you need me to do some shopping?' he says, making more of an effort. 'I can get some picnic stuff from M&S in the morning –'

'Don't worry, Phil said he'd do it. Just you focus on the book.'

She touches him lightly on the arm, then goes back outside. The sounds of laughter blossom in the air.

* * *

At Southey Road, Quinn pushes open the door to Esmond's office and stands there looking around. Judging from what's left of the rest of the house, he was expecting a pompous roll-top desk, an antique leather chair and one of those reading lamps with green shades. But he couldn't have been more wrong. Everything in here is light, modern and well designed, right down to the sleek Dyson heater, the Bose CD player and the gleaming Nespresso machine. Complete with supplies. He slings his jacket over the back of the chair and turns the heater on full. Maybe this won't be such a crap job after all.

* * *

Sent: Weds 10/01/2018, 18.45   **Importance: High**

From: Colin.Boddie@ouh.nhs.uk

To: DIAdamFawley@ThamesValley.police.uk,
CID@ThamesValley.police.uk, AlanChallowCSI@
ThamesValley.police.uk

**Subject: Bloodwork and toxicology: Case no 556432/12
Felix House, 23 Southey Road**

I've had that final test back on Samantha Esmond. Her
bloods showed slightly raised levels of human chorionic
gonadotropin (hCG). This can be produced by cancerous
tumours, but in the absence of any such abnormalities I see
no reason to deviate from the simplest clinical explanation:
Samantha Esmond was pregnant.

Given the level detected, and the fact that nothing was
discovered in the uterus, I would estimate a gestation of no
more than four weeks. At that stage the foetus would be
little more than a cluster of cells.

* * *

'So, do you think she knew? About the baby?'

It's Gislingham, in the incident room. And whether he
realizes it or not, he's looking at Ev and Somer.

Everett shrugs. 'I'm not the one to ask. I've never been
pregnant.'

Somer flushes slightly and I wonder suddenly if she
has, at some point in her past.

'Impossible to say, sir,' she says. 'Though I think the
doctor would have told me, if she'd done a proper test.'

But that doesn't mean anything. Alex only got to that stage once, in all the years we tried. All those days of hope, month after month. Days when she'd buy one of those kits and lock herself away. Days when I'd hear her sobbing. Days – the worst days – when she'd emerge, dry-faced and silent, her hands cold and her body rigid in my arms. And then there was the blue line that was Jake and a new more desperate hope and a ferocious caution and pacts with a God I don't believe in. I've often wondered, since, if that's where I went wrong. I only begged to have Jake; I never begged to keep him.

'Might give her a reason though,' says Baxter, breaking into my thoughts. He's looking at Somer. 'I mean, I know you said she couldn't have set that fire, but that was before we found out she was in the club again. If she'd had such a bad time with the previous two, she might not have been able to face having a third.'

Somer looks at him icily. 'That's not a reason to kill herself. And it's *definitely* not a reason to kill those children.'

Baxter puts up both hands. 'OK, OK, I was just saying.'

Somer opens her mouth to reply but Everett cuts in. Peacemaker mode. 'There's no point in us arguing about it. The simple fact is we have no way of knowing if she even knew about the pregnancy.'

'Can we do a DNA test?' asks Asante.

I shake my head. 'Good try, but no. Way too early.'

'So we don't know Esmond was definitely the father,' he continues. 'I mean – if it was someone else and her husband found out –'

'He was in London, though, wasn't he?' says Gis quietly.

'And we haven't come across any other men in her life,

either,' I say. 'And as far as I can see she was barely up to leaving the house, never mind carrying on a secret affair.'

Asante backs off. He clearly knows when to stop digging. But he's right about one thing. That pregnancy is a wild card we hadn't allowed for. And it's nagging at me like a stone in my shoe.

The door opens and the duty officer looks in, scanning the room.

'DC Somer? Someone in reception for you. A Mr Philip Esmond.'

* * *

12 July 2017, 4.43 p.m.
176 days before the fire
23 Southey Road, Oxford

Philip and Matty are on their third chorus of 'What shall we do with the drunken sailor?' when Michael finally gives up trying to work and goes back up to the house. In the kitchen, Philip has Zachary on his shoulders and Sam is at the sink scraping food into the caddy. The debris from the picnic is scattered all over the kitchen.

'*Way! Hey! and up she rises, Way! Hey! and up she rises, Way! Hey! and up she rises, Ear-ly in the morning,*' bellows Philip, before turning and seeing his brother at the door.

''Gain! 'Gain!' shouts Zachary, banging his hands on Philip's head. 'Want it 'gain!'

Philip swings him down on to the table and grins at Michael. 'Sorry – did we disturb you? Just got rather into the nautical spirit, if you see what I mean.'

Sam looks up from the sink and smiles. 'It was fabulous – I can't think why we don't do it more often. It's only ten minutes' walk.'

Michael eyes his brother. His T-shirt is dripping wet.

'Did you fall in?'

Philip makes a rueful face. 'Well, you know what they say – you're not doing punting right unless you get soaked.'

'Uncle Philip was *really* good,' says Matty. 'We went faster than anyone. And there was a big fat man who fell in and made the most huge splash, and someone else got his pole stuck in the water.'

Michael nods. 'Sounds like you all –'

But Matty hasn't finished. 'And then there was the *fox*. That was *awesome*.'

Michael frowns. 'There must be a better word than that, Matty.'

'Actually,' says Philip, 'it *was* pretty awesome. In the literal sense, I mean. We'd just turned round up past the Vicky Arms and were on the way back and suddenly there was this drowned fox in the water. It must have literally run into the river only a minute or two before.'

'It was *wicked*,' breathes Matty, his eyes wide and round. 'It was like a wizard had turned it into stone.'

Sam turns, wiping her hands on a tea towel. 'I've never seen anything like it. It was actually quite spooky, the way it was hanging there. Like the river had turned to ice.'

Michael frowns. 'As far as I was aware, foxes can swim.'

Philip shrugs, then swings the squealing Zachary back on to his shoulders. 'Well, all I know,' he says, 'is that this one defin-itely couldn't.'

In the weeks that follow, Michael thinks a lot about that fox. Did it really just plunge straight into the water? Was it running after something or away from something? He even dreams about it once.

He was in the punt with Philip; it was cold, the trees hanging close, and wisps of mist coming off the water. Everything wishy-washy in black and grey. Except the fox. That was burning with colour. And so close to the boat he could reach out and touch it. He could see the whiskers, the coarseness of the fur, the air bubbles caught about its mouth, and the eyes. Wide open and staring into death.

* * *

There are four people in the reception area and Somer doesn't need telling which one is Philip Esmond. An old man with a greyhound, a young black guy in a hoodie playing a game on his phone, his leg jiggling up and down, a female journalist she recognizes from the *Oxford Mail*, and a man in his forties, pacing. At a distance, the resemblance to Giles Saumarez is striking. The same stature, the same tan, the same physical confidence. But Philip Esmond's face is lined with anxiety. When he turns and sees her, he comes forward at once.

'DC Somer? I'm Philip Esmond. I came straight here.'

Somer glances around. 'Look, shall we go for a coffee or something? It might be easier.'

'What about Michael? Have you found him?'

She shakes her head. 'No. I'm afraid we haven't.' She can see the journalist eyeing them with interest, and she drops her voice. 'Seriously, I think it would be better to talk about this somewhere else.'

He stares at her a moment, nonplussed, then, 'Sure. OK. If you think that's best.'

The cafe is only a few yards away up towards Carfax and it's all but empty. They're on the point of closing. Somer buys the coffees, waving away Esmond's offer to pay, and they take a table in the window, looking up towards Christ Church cathedral, floodlit against the sallow grey sky. There's rain in the air.

'So,' says Esmond, sitting forward in his chair, his face anxious. 'What can you tell me?'

She sighs. 'Very little, I'm afraid. We've made every possible effort to find your brother but we're getting absolutely nowhere. Is there *anything* you can think of – anything that's occurred to you since we last spoke – anything at all that could help us?'

He shakes his head. 'I've been racking my brains, but really, there's nothing. We weren't exactly close – I mean, I loved him – he was my kid brother – but there's been a lot of water under the bridge one way or another.'

The cafe door opens and a mother struggles in with a baby in a pushchair and a little boy holding tight to her coat, one finger in his mouth. The children are younger than Michael Esmond's, but not by much. Philip shuts his eyes briefly then turns back to face Somer.

'What can I do? I must be able to do *something*.'

'Perhaps you could talk to your mother? We've tried but I'm sure it would be better coming from someone she knows.'

Philip nods. 'Yes. I'm sure you're right. First thing tomorrow, I'll go down there.' He picks up his spoon and starts fiddling with it. 'I need to go anyway. Not just to see her. I have to talk to her about the funerals. Though I doubt she'll be in any state to come.'

Somer nods. That's pretty much what Ev said.

'I suppose I'll have to see the Giffords as well.'

'You don't get on?'

He lets the spoon fall with a clatter. 'Oh, that's not really it. I hardly know them, to be honest. But Mike always found them a bit overbearing. Well, *him*, anyway. I think he got on OK with Laura.' He glances up and sees her face. 'Don't worry. I'm not about to make things any worse than they already are. For them or for me.'

* * *

When I get home, the house seems doubly empty. It shouldn't make a difference, but it does: knowing Alex has been here so recently, but isn't here now. I can even smell her perfume. Or perhaps that's just my mind playing tricks on me. Wishful thinking.

There's half a pizza in the freezer and half a bottle of red in the fridge, so that's my evening taken care of. I stick the pizza in the microwave and go round closing the curtains. I'm uncomfortably aware that I'm turning into my own father. He drove us mad in the winter – every morning, like clockwork, going from room to room with a cloth, wiping the windows for condensation. Though I tell myself I'm not quite that programmed. Not yet.

In the sitting room, I stop for a moment, aware that something's out of place. I haven't been in this room for a few days – not since Somer was here. And that must be what it is. When she was clearing up she must have moved things about. Not much, but enough for me to notice. And now it's obvious: the photographs on the mantelpiece are in a different order. I have a sudden mental image of her standing where I am now, looking at the pictures, seeing the private part of my life for the first time. Our wedding: Alex in a long tight-fitting ivory satin gown that literally took my breath away when I turned to see her at the end of the aisle. Our honeymoon in Sicily: tanned, happy, sharing a bottle of champagne against the sunset at Agrigento. And Jake. Of course, Jake. As a baby; on his first day at school; on the beach, with a sandcastle it took him all day to build. He'd be twelve now. At senior school. He wouldn't be building sandcastles any more. He'd be starting to fret about girls.

We have one of those software programs at CID – the ones they use to age photos of missing children. Alex asked me, once, to put a picture of Jake through it, but I said I couldn't – that they log each use and in any case it wouldn't be ethical. What I didn't tell her was that I'd already done it. One night, after everyone else had gone home. It was the picture I took two weeks before he died. So close up you can see the fine down on his upper lip. A moment before he'd been frowning and the camera has captured the ghost of it: the shadow of a furrow between his brows, his dark eyes still thoughtful. I've wondered, since, if he was already planning it – if he knew by then what he was going to do. The doctors told us it was unlikely – that children who take their own lives so young, rarely think about it so far in advance. Even so, the picture still gives me pain. Perhaps that's why I chose that one to put through the software. And it was eerie, sitting there, in the darkened empty room, watching that precious face lengthening, the soft contours hardening. I saw him at fifteen, twenty, thirty-five. I saw how he would have looked when he became a man, when he made me a grandfather. I saw him at the age I am now. The real boy may be frozen in time, but in my mind he and I are growing old together, hand in hand.

* * *

The following morning's meeting takes no more than ten minutes. The case is turning ground-hog now. Round and round and round we go. Dead ends, false starts, blind alleys. Paperwork, legwork, phonework. Though we do have one new angle: the Esmond financials have finally come through. And as Gislingham always says, if it's not love, it's money – though unfortunately for Baxter, money's a lot less interesting to investigate. When I look into the incident room later he has his chin resting on one hand, staring at his computer screen. And beside him there's a coffee and one of those chocolate bars his wife doesn't know he's still eating. But I won't tell if you don't.

* * *

At 9.45 a.m. Quinn kicks open the door to Esmond's study and dumps his bag on the floor. This time he's fully prepared. Not just more pods for the coffee machine, but an almond croissant from the French patisserie in Summertown and a sandwich in case he gets peckish. As he stands making the espresso, he can hear the clatter of rubble as the investigators tip debris into wheelbarrows and cart it away. The sky is bright and there's even some doomed blossom on the trees, but he's bloody glad he's in here in the warm and not outside freezing his balls off and up to his knees in crap. The only thing he's going to have to contend with is boredom: Esmond was obviously one of those people who file every bit of paper they're ever handed. There are till receipts and card statements in bulldog clips, organized by month, and utilities bills and council tax arranged by year. There's even a box file with family photo albums and some of Esmond's old essays and school reports from the Griffin. According to his fourth-form history teacher he was already 'driven and uncompromising' when he was fourteen, and by the time he was doing A levels the woman who taught him geography was referring to him as 'pushing himself, if anything, a little too hard'. Which chimes pretty well with the man Annabel Jordan described.

Quinn digs a little deeper into the box and finds a ring binder from what must have been Esmond's first year at the school. The first sheet is headed up 'My Family'. Intrigued, Quinn takes it out, leans back in his chair and starts to read.

*   *   *

My Family

I think family is very important. It's important to know where you come from. I am very proud of my family. It goes back to Victorian times. My great-grandfather came to England from Poland. His name was ZACHARJASZ ELSZTEJN. He came here because he wanted to be a success. He had a dream that he would have his own company and make a lot of money. He started a ~~jewetry~~ jewellery shop in the East End of London. It was called Zachary Esmond and Son. He had to change his name because no one in England knew how to spell the other one. He bought two more shops to start with and then he bought another one in ~~Nightsbridge~~ Knightsbridge. It was near Harrods. It was

169

very small but it was in a good place. After that he was very successful. My father has a gold watch that belonged to my great-grandfather. It is a big watch with a chain. You don't wear it on your wrist like now. It has a motto on it in Polish. It says 'Bliższa koszula ciału'. In English that is 'the body is closest to the shirt'. My Dad says it means that the things that are closest to us are the most important, and family is the most important of all.

My family have lived in Oxford since 1909. My great-grandfather came on a visit to the city and thought it was very beautiful. There were houses being built in Southey Road then and he bought one. He was the one who gave it its name. It is called Felix House which means 'lucky' in Latin. It's because he felt lucky to live here. We are the only family who have ever lived in it. I don't think there are any other houses like that round here. My grandfather also worked in the company and my father does now. I think my older brother Philip will do it too. When I grow up I would like to go to Oxford University. That is MY dream.

* * *

Before HM Coroner Oriana Pound
Oxford Coroner's Court
County Hall, New Road, Oxford.

Inquests conducted: Wednesday 10th January 2018
11 a.m. – Samantha Esmond, aged 33, and Zachary Esmond, aged 3, died 04/01/2018 in Oxford; and Matthew Esmond, aged 10, died 07/01/2018 in Oxford.

Following representations from the Crown Prosecution Service, the inquest was adjourned pending further enquiries by the police. Given the possibility of criminal charges, Mrs Pound ordered a second post-mortem on the three deceased, so that the bodies can be released to the family for burial.

* * *

Telephone interview with Jason Morrell, Walton Manor Motors, Knatchbull Road, Oxford
11 January 2018, 11.50 a.m.
On the call, DC A. Asante

AA: This is DC Asante. The switchboard said you have some information for us – something relating to the Southey Road fire?

JM: Yeah, it's about the car. If you're looking for it, it's here. At the garage. We did the MOT last week and it's been on the forecourt ever since. Had to change one of the tyres but otherwise it passed OK. It's parked out the front ready to go.

AA: I see. When did Mr Esmond bring the car in?

JM: Must have been Tuesday sometime. Mick booked it in – hold on –
[*muffled noises*]
Yep – definitely Tuesday 2nd. About 9.15 in the morning.

AA: Did any of you speak to him after that?

JM: I left a couple of messages about the tyre

back end of last week. Just to say it had to
be done to get the car through so to call me
if there was a problem, otherwise I'd just go
ahead. He didn't call back.

AA: Your colleague – Mick – does he remember
anything unusual about Mr Esmond that
morning? Anything that struck him?

JM: Blimey, now you're asking. Hold on.
[*more muffled noises*]
Just said he was in a hurry. A bit offhand.
But they're all like that round here, mate.
Par for the course.

* * *

15 July 2017, 3.12 p.m.
173 days before the fire
23 Southey Road, Oxford

Michael leans back in his deckchair and closes his eyes, the
sun warm on his skin. After the barbecue and that couple of
beers he doesn't feel much like working. He hadn't been relish-
ing the prospect of Philip's visit but it's actually been a good
few days. Sam was looking better than she has for weeks, and
Matty's spent more time outside and less time on that bloody
Xbox.

He can hear the summer hum of the lawnmower further down
the garden and, closer, the shrieks and splashes of excitement
from the paddling pool. Philip is teaching Matty to body surf.
With pretty limited success as far as Michael can see. He opens
his eyes briefly, sees Philip at the tap filling the pool again, then

leans back. He must have dozed off because when he comes to he can hear his wife and Philip talking a few yards away. They're speaking low, so they must think he's asleep. He was going to open his eyes but something makes him change his mind. At first the talk is just trivial stuff. Where Philip's planning to take the boat in the autumn. How Mum is doing. Then, suddenly, the mood changes.

'Look,' he says, tentative, 'you can tell me to sod off and mind my own business if you like, but is everything OK?' There's a creak in the deckchair; he must be leaning towards her.

'What makes you say that?' she says, wary.

'I don't know – I just get the impression you have something on your mind. You seem unhappy. To me, anyway.'

There's a silence. Sam must have gestured towards her husband because Philip says, 'Don't worry, he can't hear you. All that Stella – he's been out for the count for the last half hour.'

Michael's grip tightens on the side of his chair, but he doesn't move. All his other senses are sharpened. The bee veering close. The dog barking in the garden next door. The smell of cut grass.

'How long's that been going on, by the way?' continues Philip. 'The drinking, I mean.'

'It's not *drinking* as such –'

'It is, compared to what he used to do. He barely drank at all in the old days.'

'He has a lot on his plate – you know that –' She takes a deep breath. 'He told you, didn't he, about the problems I've had?'

'The depression?' he says, his voice softer. 'Yes, he told me. But I thought – well – after all this time –'

'That's why I never tell anyone,' she says sadly. 'They'd just assume I should have got over it by now. "Pulled myself together." That Zachary's over two and it must have gone away. But it hasn't.' There are tears in her voice now. 'I'm starting to wonder if it ever will.'

'What does the doc say?'

'She has me on medication, but I *hate* it, Philip – I hate it. It's like I'm living in fog – I can't think straight, can't *do* anything. And then Michael has to look after the kids as well as doing his job and his research, and it's not fair. It's too much – the cooking, the school run, the house –'

'Yeah, right,' says Philip heavily, 'the bloody house.'

'So I came off them –'

'You came off the meds – without telling your doctor?'

Michael stops breathing. This is the first he's heard about his wife not taking her medication.

'I was desperate – only not taking them was even worse.'

'I'm not surprised –'

'No,' she says miserably, 'you don't understand. That's when it started. The – other stuff.'

The chair creaks again. She's crying; he must have put an arm round her.

'You can tell me,' he whispers.

'I kept losing things. Putting them down and finding them later somewhere else where I'd looked already.'

'That could be anything – *I* do that –'

'It's not just that. I started hearing things too. In the house. Like there was someone there. And last week I suddenly smelt burning but nothing was on fire –'

'Someone's barby? It's that time of year.'

'No, like I said, it was *inside* the house.'

He starts saying something about the possible side effects of coming off the meds but she's crying hard now.

'Have you spoken to Mike about this?' he says gently. 'Or the doctor?'

'I'm too scared.'

'Scared? Scared of what?'

'I went on Google,' she says, her voice breaking, 'and there were all these websites saying that hallucinations can be a symptom of post-partum psychosis, and I was frightened they'd take Zachary away if they knew. That they'd think I might harm him and he wouldn't be safe with me, and you know that's not true, don't you, I would never harm my children –'

She breaks down now, and Michael can hear Philip soothing her, telling her it's OK.

And then the sound of the football bouncing on the dry earth. Close. Closer still.

'Why's Mummy crying?' says Matty.

'She's just a bit upset,' says Philip. 'Nothing to worry about, Matt.'

'Can we play Ronaldo and Messi again?'

'In a minute. I just need to talk to Mummy first. Why don't you go and get a juice from the fridge and bring one for Zachary too.'

Matty whines a bit at that, but Michael eventually hears his footsteps retreating towards the house.

'Sorry about that,' says Sam. 'It all just got on top of me.'

'No need to apologize to me. Seriously. But I think you really do need to go back on the meds.'

'I did. I went to the doctor. I didn't tell her – you know – what had happened. Just said the pills weren't agreeing with me. She put me on something different.'

'And are they better?'

A pause. She must have nodded.

'And there hasn't been anything since – none of that weird stuff?'

Another pause.

'Well, that has to be a good sign, doesn't it – if it only happened when you weren't on the medication?'

'I suppose so.'

'But I really do think you should talk to your doctor about it – all of it. Just to be on the safe side. You don't need to worry. Nothing bad's going to happen.'

'Do you promise?' she whispers.

Michael's heard enough; he shifts a little in his chair, feigning waking. And when he opens his eyes he sees his brother holding his wife's hand.

'I promise,' Philip says.

*   *   *

At the John Rad, Alan Challow's assistant, Nina Mukerjee, is pulling on a clean set of scrubs. Ray Goodwin, the appointed pathologist, has just arrived to conduct the second autopsies and she's been asked to sit in and observe, in case something new comes up. No one's expecting anything – it's just standard procedure in case there's a trial. But right now, any sort of trial seems a very long way off and Nina's steeling herself for a gruesome afternoon that gets them precisely nowhere.

The door swings open. 'Miss Mukerjee?'

He's younger than she expected – a lot younger. And definitely not the usual tweedy type. More rogue than brogues, by the look of him, with his hipster beard and earring. In fact, she's pretty sure she can see a tattoo.

'You ready?'

She nods.

'Then let's get this party started.'

*   *   *

By five, Baxter is rather pleased with himself. He's no accountant but he's done a few courses and he's got quite savvy with numbers, over the years. Enough to get by, anyway. If it's a really big one, like fraud or money laundering, then they call in the experts, but usually it's just about getting a clear picture of the cash. The haves, the have-nots, and the desperately wanna-haves. And with this bloke Esmond it only took him an afternoon to get a pretty good idea, even if 'pretty' is hardly the word, in the circumstances. He picks up the phone and calls Fawley, and a couple of minutes later the DI pushes open the door and comes towards him. He looks frazzled, which seems to be par for the course these days. Baxter's heard the same rumours the rest of the station has, and even if he tends to be sceptical about office gossip it's hard not to see Fawley's frayed nerves as evidence that something's gone badly wrong on the home front.

Gis stands up from his desk and comes over to join them.

'OK,' says Fawley, 'what have we got?'

Baxter gestures at his computer. 'The last time Esmond's credit card was used is late afternoon on the 31st December. The Tesco in Summertown. No unusual transactions recently as far as I can see, though he was close to his credit limit, and only paying off the minimum most months.' He changes the page. 'And this is Esmond's current account. As you can see, only a couple of hundred quid in it.' He scrolls down. 'Nothing untoward in terms of incomings or outgoings until about two months ago, when there's a transfer in from the savings account of £2,000, which goes straight back out again three days later. In *cash*.'

'Who needs that sort of cash these days?' wonders Gislingham.

'And this,' says Baxter, switching to another page, 'is the savings account. After that last withdrawal, all that's left in it is,' he leans forward to read, 'three hundred and seventy-six pounds fifty-four pence. Eighteen months ago there was over fifteen thousand in there, but by last October it was all but gone, apart from that final two grand.'

'So what was he spending it on?' asks Fawley.

'I've looked at the individual transactions and most of it has been going on care home fees. That place in Wantage where his mother is? That's one of the most expensive ones round here.' Which is probably, thinks Baxter, why Everett hasn't bothered checking that one out. She still hasn't said anything to him about her dad but he's seen the brochures in her desk drawer and he knows the old man's been struggling.

Fawley, meanwhile, has been studying the numbers. 'So if the cash ran out in October, how's he been paying the fees since?'

Fawley's sharp, no question. Even when he is distracted.

Baxter sits back and places his fingertips together. 'Short answer? He hasn't. I spoke to the home's account-ant and there's two months' bills outstanding. They asked Esmond to come in and see them in December and he said he was "making arrangements" but no actual dosh has yet been forthcoming.'

'I thought the family were supposed to be wealthy?' says Gislingham.

Baxter glances up at him. 'You and me both. So I did a bit more digging. I couldn't get full financials on the fam-ily business because it was a private sale but judging by how little Esmond's father sold it for it must have been in big trouble. And he lived on the proceeds for the rest of his life – by the time he died the cash must have pretty much dried out.' He makes a face. 'You know that saying – first generation makes it, second generation spends it and third generation blows it. Looks like Esmond's father blew it big time.'

'So why not sell the house?' says Gislingham. 'I mean, I know it's the family silver and all that, but if his mum needed care –'

'He can't.'

It's Quinn, at the door, still in his coat. He holds up a sheaf of papers.

'I found this at the house.'

He walks over and hands the papers to Fawley, who reads the top sheet slowly, then looks up at Quinn. 'Good work,' he says. 'Bloody good work.'

* * *

Last Will and Testament

This is the last will and testament of Horace Zachary Esmond, of Felix House, 23 Southey Road, Oxford.

1   I appoint as the Executors and Trustees of this my Will ('the Trustees') the partners in the firm of Rotherham Fleming & Co of 67 Cornwallis Mews, Oxford.

2   In this Will, where the context admits:
    i.   Beneficiaries' shall mean my son Richard Zachary Esmond, his children, and their subsequent issue;
    ii. 'Property Beneficiary' shall mean my son Richard, and upon his death, his oldest surviving son (or if none, daughter), and so on for each succeeding generation;
    iii. 'Property' shall mean Felix House, 23 Southey Road, Oxford;
    iv. 'Residual Property' shall mean all of my property and assets, personal and commercial, with the exception of the Property.

3   The Trustees must hold the Property on trust for the Property Beneficiary for the term of his life, and allow him to occupy the Property rent-free so long as he (i) pays all outgoings on the Property; (ii) keeps the Property in good repair; and (iii) keeps the Property insured in the Trustees' name and to their satisfaction.

4   Subject to clause 5 below, the Trustees must not sell the Property.

5   In circumstances where (i) the Property Beneficiary dies without any surviving issue, or (ii) the Property is required to be demolished (whether due to fire, flood, subsidence, act of God, or a compulsory purchase order of a Local Authority or other public body in accordance with statute or otherwise), the Trustees shall sell the Property and distribute the proceeds to each of the Beneficiaries in equal parts.

6   The Trustees shall, after paying all debts, funeral and testamentary expenses and Inheritance Tax on all property that vests in them, distribute the Residual Property to my son Richard Zachary Esmond.

Testimonium and Attestation

Dated this 14th day of April, 1965.

Signed by the above named Horace Zachary Esmond as and for his last Will in our presence and by us in his.

H Z Esmond

Peter Clarence
Peter Clarence
Partner, Rotherham Fleming & Co

N H Dennis
Norman Dennis
Partner, Rotherham Fleming & Co

First Codicil

I, Horace Zachary Esmond, of Felix House, 23 Southey Road, Oxford, DECLARE this to be a first Codicil to my last Will, dated the 14th day of April 1965 ('my Will').

> MY WILL shall be construed and take effect as if it contained the following clause: I give free of Inheritance tax to: Philip Zachary Esmond, my grandson, born 11th October 1975, the sum of One Hundred Thousand pounds (£100,000).

IN ALL other respects I confirm my Will dated 14th April 1965. IN WITNESS whereof I have hereunto set my hand on this 27th day of November 1975:

H Z Esmond

And for a first Codicil to his Will in our presence, and by us jointly attested and subscribed in his presence:

N H Dennis
Norman Dennis
Partner, Rotherham Fleming & Co

Benjamin Turner
Benjamin Turner
Partner, Rotherham Fleming & Co

* * *

Long after most of the team have gone home I'm still at my desk, looking at the will and wondering about the man who drafted it. What sort of mind must you have to draw up something like this – to go to such lengths to ensure generations you'll never even see will conform to your own conception of the family, to your idea of its legacy and its position. And yes, clearly there was plenty of money in the sixties – a hundred grand would have been a fortune back then – and Horace Esmond probably couldn't even imagine a time when his descendants might actually need to sell that house, but that's no excuse. I sit back in my chair, feeling, for the first time, genuinely sorry for Michael Esmond. Then I reach forward and pick up the phone. Because suddenly I have an excuse to call. A reason to speak to my wife that's not about her or me or some impossible possible child, but about what she *does*. Because at times like this, in cases like this, I always talk to my wife. Not only for her lawyer's training, but because she has one of the most acute minds I've ever known. A quite staggering ability to home in on the key facts – both those we have, and those we don't. And if I'm hesitating to call her now, it's because I'm not sure I can face listening to her applying that relentless intellect to argue herself out of what remains of our marriage.

'Alex, it's me. Can you give me a call back? It's not about – it's about a case. I just need someone to tell me that a document means what I think it means. And yes, I know I could ask the legal people here, but I'd rather ask you. I'd *always* rather ask you.'

* * *

At the John Rad, the second autopsies are over. Zachary's was especially grim, but it was always going to be. Yet in the face of such horror, Ray Goodwin had an unexpectedly calming way with him. And for once it wasn't down to CDs of string quartets or amplified whale song. Just a quiet, measured manner that managed to be both gentle and professional at the same time. Nina had to admit, she was impressed.

Afterwards, as they're stripping off their scrubs, he asks how long she's been a forensics officer, and it turns out they have acquaintances in common, and somehow or other they end up having a drink in town. Nina doesn't notice, but Gislingham and Everett are on the far side of the same bar. He with a lager and she a glass of Chardonnay. But the drinks have been sitting there for over an hour. And unlike Nina, their day has not gone unexpectedly well.

* * *

'So what do you think is up?' says Gislingham.

Ev glances at him. 'What do you mean "up"?'

'You know. With the boss. Don't tell me you haven't noticed.'

Everett sighs. 'Of course I have. It just seems a bit shitty talking about it behind his back.'

'People are just concerned, Ev.'

'I know. And so am I. But we're not going to solve it, are we? Whatever it is.'

Gislingham picks up his glass. 'Baxter thinks his wife has left him. Says he overheard Fawley leaving a message for her.'

'That doesn't necessarily mean anything. Whenever I've seen them together I've never thought they were having problems. Though, to be fair, I haven't seen her for a while.'

She thinks back. It must have been at Fawley's birthday drinks. Last October, a couple of dozen of them crammed under the low ceilings of the Turf Tavern, the air thick with the smoke from the braziers outside. Fawley's wife arrived half an hour before the end, saying she'd been held up at work. She'd looked amazing, as always. High heels, scarlet suit, long dark hair in one of those swept-up-and-falling-down things that Everett couldn't manage even if she had the hair for it. Or the time. Alex Fawley had drunk half a glass of warm Prosecco and teased Gislingham about his promotion and smiled at her husband when they did a toast and he'd looked at her in a way no one has ever looked at Everett, her whole life. And then they were gone. No one seeing the Fawleys together would have said there was anything wrong. But then again, anyone can keep up a facade if they only have to do it for half an hour.

'Look, it may still be nothing,' says Everett. But the look on her face says the opposite. The sound system is now playing 'Saving All My Love For You'. She's always hated that song, and right now, the lyrics have become horribly apposite.

Gislingham makes a face. 'Well, I never had Fawley pegged for a cheater. And after that car crash with Quinn, I'd have thought Somer would have had enough of shitting on her own doorstep.' He glances at Everett. 'You two are mates – has she said anything to you?'

Everett shakes her head. 'Not a squeak. But I wouldn't either, if I was shagging the boss.'

They're silent for a moment. Everett makes circles on the table with her glass.

'Look,' says Gislingham eventually, 'I'm going to have to go. I told Janet I wouldn't be late.' He gets up and drags his coat off the back of the chair. 'And, Ev? Not a word, right? There's enough bloody gossip at the station already.'

She gives him a 'what sort of a person do you think I am' look, and drains her glass.

'I'll come with you.'

* * *

Sent: Thurs 11/01/2018, 21.35   **Importance: High**
From: Alexandra.Fawley@HHHlaw.co.uk
To: DIAdamFawley@ThamesValley.police.uk

Subject: Your email

I've had a look at it. It's not the sort of arrangement we would ever recommend these days – it's far too restrictive. But basically your assumptions are right:

- A life interest in the house passes to the oldest son of each generation, and failing that, the oldest daughter.
- He (or she) is entitled to live in the house, but cannot sell it (it being the property of the Trust).
- However, according to clause 5, if the house has to be demolished due to circumstances beyond the Trustees' control (such as a catastrophic flood), the house and plot are to be sold and the proceeds distributed among all the direct heirs living at the time.

If this is the Southey Road house we're talking about, in my opinion the conditions of clause 5 have more than adequately been met.

Hope that helps,
A

Alexandra Fawley I Partner I Oxford office I Harlowe Hickman Howe LLP

Not even an 'x' at the bottom. Something she'd do without thinking even for friends, but must have stopped herself doing for me.

I don't think I've ever felt more wretched.

* * *

20 July 2017, 11.45 a.m.
168 days before the fire
23 Southey Road, Oxford

The man on the doorstep is in overalls, with a stepladder and a toolbox.

'Mrs Esmond?'

'Yes,' she says warily. There's a van parked by the kerb with 'D&S Security' painted on the side.

'Your husband booked us in,' he says, seeing the look on her face. He reaches into his pocket for a sheet of paper. 'Side gate, alarm system, new deadlocks to windows and exterior doors throughout.'

'He never said anything about it to me.'

At least, she can't remember him doing so.

He looks up and smiles. 'Feel free to check with him. You can't be too careful, that's what I always say.'

'If you don't mind, I will.'

She closes the door and goes into the sitting room. She can see the man through the front window. But, as usual, her husband's mobile is off.

'Michael – can you call me back? There's a man here to do something to the locks. You never mentioned he was coming.'

She puts the phone down and goes back to the door.

'All OK, then?' says the man, cheerily.

'I couldn't reach him. Do you mind – could I see that piece of paper?'

'Office said he came in earlier this week,' he says, handing it to her. 'Tuesday, I think it was.'

The day after Philip left. Two days after she'd confided in him that she thought there'd been someone in the house. Only Michael didn't know about that. Did he?

'See?' says the man. 'That's his signature right there.'

She stares at the paper. And he's right. It is Michael's signature.

'What did you say you were doing again?'

'New side gate, state-of-the-art alarm system and new door and window locks.' He glances to the side of the house. 'I mean, anyone can just walk right in as it stands, can't they? And this time of year, you could be upstairs, with your back door open, and any Tom, Dick or axe murderer could walk straight in. A house this big, you might not even realize. In fact, didn't your husband say you'd had a burglary?'

She flushes. 'Not a burglary, no – not as such –'

'All the same, like I said, Mrs Esmond, you can't be too careful. Not these days. Some of those weirdos aren't interested in nicking stuff. They just want the kick of knowing they're somewhere they're not supposed to be.'

* * *

187

'So why the fuck didn't he tell us?'

No prizes for guessing who that is: Quinn, at peak bolshie.

'Seriously,' he continues, looking round at the rest of the team, 'Philip Esmond has known all about this will right from the start and yet he hasn't even mentioned it. Not a bloody word.'

'But how is it relevant?' says Ev. 'Philip couldn't possibly have set fire to the house because he was in the middle of the sodding Atlantic.'

'Do we actually *know* that?' Quinn again.

Ev flushes. 'Well, no –'

'Well then,' he says.

I turn to Somer. 'What day did you first speak to Philip?'

'On the Thursday afternoon, sir. A few hours after the fire.'

'Right. Could you double-check the exact co-ordinates of that satellite phone call, please? Just to be sure.'

Meanwhile Ev's got a second wind. 'In any case, why would Philip want to trash the place? There's no suggestion he was in need of the money.'

'Even a hundred grand at compound interest will run out sometime,' says Asante. 'Especially at his rate of burn.'

He's not wrong – it's not just the shiny new boat, it's the go-as-you-please lifestyle, and all without any visible means of support.

'That's as may be,' says Baxter grimly, 'but it sure as hell gives *Michael* a motive, though, doesn't it?' And he's right too: setting fire to that house would have solved his financial problems for good and all. But would he really go so far as to burn it down? A building so intimately bound up with his sense of self and his place – quite literally – in the world? If you're asking me, that's one hell of a stretch. Even if his family hadn't been inside. Even if I didn't know he was fifty miles away at the time.

'Why don't I ask him about it,' says Somer eventually. 'Philip, I mean. I can give him a call.'

'No,' I say. 'Go and speak to him in person. I want to know how he reacts. And before you go, put in a call to Rotherham Fleming & Co. I want to know everything they're prepared to tell us about the Esmonds.'

She looks doubtful. 'They'll probably say it's confidential –'

'I know. But there's nothing to stop us asking.' I look around the room. 'Anyone else have anything new and/or useful?'

'Challow called,' says Gislingham. 'About the fingerprints they took off the garage door. Most were Michael's and match a lot in the study, but the rest were just partials. And for the record, none were remotely like Jurjen Kuiper's.'

'I've had a call from that Oxford friend of Michael's we were trying to talk to,' says Everett. 'He could have seen me later today, but luckily he's also around tomorrow morning.'

She doesn't bother saying why this afternoon is out because we all know. I'm going to have to dig around in my desk drawer and find my black tie.

* * *

'Can I help you – have you come to see a resident?'

The attendant at the care home reception smiles a

neat professional smile that doesn't quite reach the rest of her face.

Somer takes out her warrant card. 'DC Erica Somer, Thames Valley Police. I believe Mr Esmond is here at the moment, with his mother?'

The woman nods. 'They're in the side lounge.'

She heads down the corridor, her plastic shoes squeaking on the wooden floor. The whole place has the feel of a faintly rundown country hotel. The sweep of gravel drive, the slightly over-large wooden staircase, the brocade curtains with their tasselled tie-backs and the heavy furniture that wouldn't have been out of place in the Southey Road house. Somer wonders for a moment whether that was the point – whether Michael Esmond wanted his mother to spend her last days in a place as much like her old home as possible. The only difference is that all the chairs here have plastic seat protectors and the heavy scent of artificial air freshener is masking something worse.

The Esmonds are sitting in a bow window overlooking the garden. On the terrace outside, there are pots of crocuses placed close to the window so the residents can see them, and in front of them there's a pot of tea and two cups. With saucers. Somer can tell, even though he has his back to her, that Philip is already wearing his funeral suit.

He's clearly pleased to see her. Despite the circumstances. He gets to his feet. 'DC Somer – Erica – thank you for coming.'

She smiles. 'It's no problem. I know you have a lot to deal with at the moment.'

'This is my mother, Alice.'

Mrs Esmond looks up at her. She must be one of the youngest residents here. No more than seventy, perhaps as little as sixty-five. But her eyes are those of an old woman.

'Hello, Mrs Esmond,' says Somer, holding out her hand.

'Is this your girlfriend?' Mrs Esmond asks, ignoring the hand and turning stiffly to her son.

'Bit of a looker, isn't she?'

'No, Mum,' he replies quickly, flushing and shooting Somer a glance. 'This is a lady from the police.'

Mrs Esmond's mouth falls open and she appears about to say something but they're interrupted by the attendant, asking Somer if she'd like tea. 'There should still be some in the pot.'

'OK, thank you. Why not.'

The attendant goes in search of extra crockery and Philip turns to face her. 'What was it you wanted to talk to me about, DC Somer? Must have been something important.'

'We found a copy of your grandfather's will at the house.'

Philip's shoulders sag a little. 'Oh, that.'

'You didn't tell us about it.' She keeps her tone light and her smile in place. 'Was there any reason for that?'

He looks bewildered. 'It didn't have any relevance. How could it?'

'Just so I'm clear, the terms of the will stipulate that the house has to pass to the eldest son. That means you, doesn't it? But you weren't living there.'

Philip sighs. 'Well, like I said, I move around a lot. It would have been standing empty half the time. And

Michael had more need of that place than I did. He's the one with the kids.'

He seems to realize suddenly what he's just said. 'Jesus,' he says, dropping his head into his hands. 'What a fucking nightmare. Sorry. I don't normally swear that much. I'm just struggling to process all this.'

'Don't mind me. I've heard a lot worse. I used to teach in a secondary school.'

He glances up with a sad, rueful smile. She hadn't realized before how blue his eyes are.

'So you agreed that your brother and his family could live in the house?'

'It wasn't official or anything. But yes. It made sense all round, what with him working in Oxford as well.'

'And the clause about the house being demolished?'

'I know it looks a bit odd, but that will was done in the sixties. Right around the time the government were planning the ring road. One of the routes they were considering would have gone straight through Southey Road – the house would have been compulsorily purchased. The lawyers told my grandfather he ought to have a provision for an eventuality like that – something outside anyone's control. Look, is that it, Constable, only I have a funeral to go to –'

'Just one more question, sir. Presumably the fire means clause five does actually now apply. The house will have to be pulled down, won't it?'

'I suppose so. I really hadn't thought about it.'

But she's not letting up. 'So that means it'll be sold. The land, I mean. That'll be worth a huge amount of money, in that part of Oxford – a building plot of that size.'

Philip shrugs. 'Probably. But like I said, that's really not my top priority at the moment –'

'You haven't spoken to your insurance company? It's going to be a huge claim. Surely they'll want to send an adjuster –'

'Look, I just want to find my brother. Which, if you don't mind me saying, is what the police should be doing as well.'

'The police?' says Mrs Esmond suddenly. 'Are you from the police?'

'I told you, Mum,' he says patiently.

'Is it Michael?'

Somer and Philip exchange a glance. 'Yes, Mum,' he says quietly. 'It's about Michael.'

'I thought your father had sorted it all out,' she says, gripping her son's arm.

'Sorry,' says Philip in an undertone. 'This is what happens. She seems OK and then she starts getting the past confused with the present. Or she just starts getting confused, full stop.'

'He told me he'd spoken to the doctor,' Mrs Esmond continues, louder now. 'That Mr Taverner. And then *he* spoke to the police and it was all sorted out.'

'Here you are then,' says the attendant cheerily, bending over to make space on the tray. 'And I've brought some biscuits too. Only garibaldis but beggars can't be choosers, eh, Mrs E?'

'I told him, the doctor, Michael's never done anything like that before,' Mrs Esmond is saying. 'He's always been such an honest little boy. Always owns up when he's been naughty. The very idea that he could do something like that and then just run away –'

Somer frowns. This isn't confusion – this is something specific. She turns to Philip. 'Do you know what she's referring to?'

'Seriously – I've no idea.'

'It could be important.'

The attendant looks at Philip and then at Somer. 'Well, if it helps, I think I know what she means. Alice told me that story a while ago.' She straightens up. 'It was when your brother was still at school, wasn't it?'

There's an awkward silence. Philip Esmond looks away.

The attendant glances at him and then at Somer. 'Just shows you what going private can do,' she says heavily, before turning and moving briskly away.

Philip isn't meeting Somer's eye.

'Mr Esmond, are you still asking me to believe you don't know anything about this?'

He shakes his head, then takes a deep breath. 'No. But we can't talk about it here. Not where Mum can hear.'

* * *

With Fawley, Everett and Somer all due at the funeral, Baxter is having an unusually quiet afternoon. He has a cup of tea (proper tea, brought up from the canteen), and a half-eaten snack bar. It's one of those protein things, and in his book that counts as health food not chocolate, which means it doesn't have to be confessed to his wife and written down in that bloody Weight Watchers log she's running for him. He's been doing the diet for two months now, and he can tell his wife is disappointed the pounds aren't rolling off. She asks him, some days, if he's sure he's remembered everything he ate at the office, and he always looks her straight in the eye. All those years questioning professional liars have finally come in useful.

He finishes the tea, and turns again to trying to crack the password on the PC they found in Michael Esmond's office.

* * *

'OK, so talk to me.'

Outside in the garden it's bright but cold. Here and there, smudges of snow linger in shaded corners of the borders. There are snowdrops and the succulent first tips of hyacinths.

Philip shoves his hands in his pockets. It's too cold to sit so they keep walking. Somer can see his mother staring at them from inside. It occurs to her that she probably still thinks she's her son's girlfriend.

'When I said I didn't know anything about it, I wasn't exactly lying.'

'Not *exactly*? What does that mean?'

'It means I was in Australia at the time. Having a gap year. Only it turned out to be just a "year", since I never ended up going to uni at all.'

'So what happened?'

'Mum and Dad were always really cagey about the whole thing, but Mike told me about it in the end. Not all at once – it came out in dribs and drabs.' He takes a deep breath. 'Basically, my dad caught him with another boy.'

'Another *boy*?' Whatever she thought she was expecting, it wasn't this.

'They were in the summerhouse. The one at the bottom of the garden. I don't think it was actual – you know – *sex*. Look, he was seventeen, they were probably just experimenting. But Dad went off the deep end. Threw the other kid out, started shouting and bawling and telling Mike he didn't bring him up to be a pervert – that he was a disgrace to the family name – shit like that. I'm sure you can fill in the blanks.'

And she can. Just as she can imagine how close to home words like that would have gone.

'So what happened?'

'Mike ran back to the house, grabbed the car keys and left. Five minutes later he knocked a little girl off her bike on the Banbury Road.'

'Oh Lord.'

'I know. Poor bastard.'

'And was she all right? The little girl?'

'Yes, she was fine. Just a few bruises. But she was knocked unconscious for a few minutes. Mike thought he'd killed her. He completely panicked. Just got back in the car and drove away. They didn't find him for three days. And when they did, he couldn't remember a thing about it.'

And suddenly it all clicks. 'He was at Calshot Spit, right?'

Philip flushes, then nods.

'Why didn't you tell me all this when I asked you about the hut?'

He makes a rueful face. 'I'm sorry. I should have been more open with you about that, I realize that now. But it was over twenty years ago – I couldn't see how digging it all up again was going to help anyone. Least of all Michael. It just didn't seem in the slightest bit relevant.'

'That's for us to decide, Mr Esmond. Not you.'

He stops walking and turns to face her. 'I'm sorry. Really. I'm not a liar. That's not who I am. If you knew me better, you'd know that.'

She elects to ignore the covert message and moves on again. 'And that doctor your mother mentioned?'

'My parents were panicking about the whole thing trashing Mike's chances of getting into Oxford so they paid for him to see someone in Harley Street. That way it stayed out of his NHS records. He said Mike was in a state of extreme emotional disturbance at the time of the accident and then went into some sort of traumatic amnesia afterwards – "dissociative fugue", I think was the phrase. He wrote a letter to the police and they accepted it. And since the little girl was basically unharmed, my parents managed to make it all go away.'

He catches her eye. 'And yes, I suspect the latter did involve a fairly hefty cheque.'

'And afterwards?'

'Mike saw the shrink for the rest of that summer and sat his entrance exams that autumn. The rest, you know.'

'And the other boy –'

Philip gives an ironic laugh. 'Totally redacted. I don't even know the poor little sod's name. And the way Mike went on afterwards, well, let's just say it was about as un-gay as you can get. He'd only had one girlfriend up till then. Janey – Jenny – something like that. But suddenly he was seeing them left, right and centre. Well "seeing" is perhaps an exaggeration. It was just sex, as far as I could tell.' He grins sheepishly. 'I was pretty envious, if you must know.'

'So you were back from Australia by then.'

He nods.

'And how did your brother seem to you?'

'The same – and different. I'd never have guessed what had happened just from looking at him.'

'I don't follow.'

'Well, something like that – you'd expect it to knock you back, wouldn't you? But with Mike it was the opposite. It wasn't just the sleeping around. He was more confident, more assertive. You know, just *louder*.'

Just like the last six months, thinks Somer. Coincidence? Or has history been repeating itself?

* * *

However different our lives are, the way we leave them doesn't vary much. Not these days. Crematoria are like McDonald's. Identical in every town. Same layout, same chairs, same acrylic-looking curtains. And in most cases, the same embarrassing sense of one group of mourners being bundled out the back just as the next lot are coming in the front door. But not this time. The Esmonds' funeral is going to be all over the press this time tomorrow and the crematorium has clearly freed up the entire afternoon. I get there early, before Everett and Somer, but the vestibule is still packed, and I scan the crowd wondering who a lot of these people are. The smattering of smartly dressed women in their thirties is probably parents from Matty's school, but I reckon most of the rest are journos, sporting over-worn blacks and over-practised grief faces.

I'm doing my best to blend into the background, leaving Everett and Somer to manage the official presence. And they do it well, in their different ways. Somer is prompter to approach people, and I see her starting conversations, asking questions. I watch men underestimating her because she's attractive and in a uniform, and I watch her registering that fact and using it to her advantage. Everett, on the other hand, is more outwardly passive, as well as a good deal less comfortable in her uniform, which she keeps tugging at every few minutes. She does more listening than talking, making people feel they're the ones controlling the flow of information. But she's gathering it, all the same.

As the three hearses draw up outside, there's an unseemly jostling as the press photographers push forward to get the best angle. Samantha's coffin is covered in pink lilies and those tiny white flowers. Baby's breath. In the second car, Matty's is draped in an Arsenal flag, with a wreath of red roses I'm told was sent on behalf of the club. Apparently they're going to wear black armbands for the next game. That's social media for you. And finally Zachary's, the tiny coffin overwhelmed by his name picked out in cushions of daisies.

There's rain in the air, but the clouds part momentarily and a shaft of sunlight slants down across the grass and the shrivelled winter plants. There's a solitary blackbird at the edge of the gravel, darting at the municipal bark chips and digging out shreds of wood. I find myself staring at it as the bearers move forward, so I hear rather than see the swell of emotion as Gregory Gifford steps up to take his little grandson's coffin. It's Zachary who has the women in tears, but it's Matty I'm shrinking from. Any parent who's lost a child will tell you the same. Widows, orphans – there are names for people who've lost wives, lost husbands, lost parents. But there's no name for a parent who's lost a child. And so I avoid funerals when I can, and children's even more. It's bad enough at the time, when you're half dazed with the wreckage of your life, but reliving it in the rawness of someone else's grief is all but unbearable. I don't want to think about that day. I don't want to remember Alex's white tearless face, my parents clinging to each other, and the flowers, wreath upon wreath of them sent from all those people we'd asked not to come – people we'd asked not to send flowers. And yet they sent flowers all the same, because they had to do *something*. Because they felt as helpless as we did in the face of such unthinkable pain.

The procession forms now, the bearers adjust under the weight and the minister comes forward. I hang back, letting the last stragglers go before me, avoiding the eye of the one or two hacks I recognize. The music they're playing is classical. Bach, I'm guessing, but something richer, less austere than I usually find him. We had Handel for Jake. Handel and Oasis. The Handel was Alex's choice. 'Lascia ch'io pianga', 'Let me weep over my cruel fate'. I loved it once, but I can't listen to it any more. The Oasis was down to me. 'Wonderwall'. Jake listened to it all the time. I always thought he played it so much because he was hanging on to the idea that we would save him. But we couldn't. *I* couldn't. I wasn't any sort of wall for my son. In the end, when he needed me, I wasn't there.

I slip into a seat in the back row. A seat with a view over the entrance and the grounds. Because that's the main reason I'm here. Michael Esmond's entire family is being cremated today, and we've done whatever we can to ensure that wherever he is, he'll know that. His wife, his two sons – it takes a special kind of coldness to turn your back on that: even hardened killers I've known couldn't do it. So I position myself where I can scan the long drive and the bleak flat parkland that quarantines this place of death and parting from the ordinary, busy, self-absorbed life going on outside. The words of the funeral service push into my brain – *Devoted mother and wife . . . Popular with all his classmates . . . Taken so tragically soon* – but all I can see is the blackbird. With its intent beady eye and its brutal stabbing beak.

* * *

Oxford Mail online

Friday 12 January 2018 Last updated at 17:08

Funerals held in Oxford house fire

The funerals of Samantha Esmond and her two sons, Matty, 10, and Zachary, 3, were held at the Oxford crematorium this afternoon. Residents stood in silence in the streets as the cortège passed, and the large crowd of mourners included family, friends and colleagues, as well as representatives from Bishop Christopher's School, where

Fears for future of Covered Market
Traders in the historic market are concerned for its future after several high-profile closures . . . */more*

Football: Oxford Mail Youth League, full reports and scores . . . */more*

Man held after rape allegation
A 45-year-old teacher has been arrested after one of his pupils made an allegation of rape. The girl, who cannot be named for legal reasons . . . */more*

Matty was a pupil. There was also a significant, if discreet, police presence. However, if officers were hoping Michael Esmond might make an appearance, they were disappointed.

Despite police appeals for him to come forward, the Oxford University academic has not been seen since the evening of 3 January, at an academic conference in London. Earlier that week he is thought to have attended a meeting with his head of department. Sources close to the faculty have suggested that Dr Esmond had been accused of sexual harassment by a female student, and could have faced a serious reprimand, if not dismissal.

New community centre to open in Littlemore
Littlemore's new £3.4m community centre will be officially opened in April, offering local residents a range of facilities . . . /more

92 comments

CallydonianGal0099
It breaks your heart, it really does. Those poor children

MedoraMelborne
The father killed them. Killed them and then killed himself. Just you wait – I know I'm right

> **5656AcesHigh**
> I'm with you. I reckon the vicious SOB murdered the lot of them.

HillBilly_889
The more you hear about this the worse it gets. Now that bloke's a sex pest? You couldn't make it up.

* * *

I wait by the car, catching a smoke. Everett and Somer are seeing off the last of the mourners and the car park is nearly empty. The wind is getting up and I see Somer holding on to her cap as they round the side of the building and come towards me.

'Did you get anything, sir?' says Everett as they reach me. 'Because I don't think we did.' She pulls at her jacket again, shunting it back down.

I shake my head. 'Nothing concrete. And you, Somer?'

'Not really, sir.'

'Did you speak to the lawyers?'

She nods. 'Nothing doing, I'm afraid. They said they're unable to divulge anything about their clients' affairs. Even if they wanted to.'

I'm not surprised, though it was worth a try.

'But I did have a very interesting conversation with Philip Esmond. Not here,' she adds quickly. 'This morning, at the care home.'

Which may explain an idle observation I made more than once during the last hour and a half. The way Esmond was looking at her, and the way she wasn't looking at him.

It doesn't take long to give me the gist of it. The incident with the boy, the accident on the Banbury Road and the panic flight to Calshot, the one place where Michael Esmond felt safe. And by the end of it she's not the only one who's starting to see a pattern.

'I know he didn't actually go to Calshot this time,' she finishes, flushing slightly at the memory, 'but the rest of it – do you think he saw the news about the fire and went into another fugue state? It must be a possibility, surely. Though I suppose we'd have to talk to a psychiatrist to be sure –'

'I can call Bryan Gow. Remind me – when did Annabel Jordan say she noticed a change in Esmond?'

'Last summer, boss,' says Ev with a meaningful look. 'Which was exactly the same time the teachers at Bishop Christopher's noticed a change in Matty.'

Michael, Matty – there's something there, I'm sure of it – only just out of reach –

'OK, let's do a bit more digging. Something happened in that family last summer and I want to know what it was.'

* * *

Interview with James Beresford, conducted at
12 Feverel Close, Wolvercote, Oxford
13 January 2018, 11.16 a.m.
In attendance, DC V. Everett

VE: Thank you for making time to see me on a
    Saturday, Mr Beresford.
JB: No problem. Happy to help. Though I'm not sure
    what use I can be. I don't see Michael much. I
    mean, we were at school together, but that's a
    long time ago now. We were never exactly
    'friends'.
VE: When did you last see him?
JB: I've been thinking about that, ever since I
    saw the news. It was about three months ago.

He emailed me out of the blue. It must have been four or five years since I'd heard from him before that.

VE: So was there a particular reason why he got in contact this time?

JB: It didn't seem like that to start with. We met up in one of those bars on South Parade. We had to sit outside because he wanted to smoke. I thought he'd given up years ago, but anyway, we must have been there at least an hour talking about nothing, and then he finally comes out with it. Says he wants to pick my brains. Professionally, I mean.

VE: He wanted your advice?

JB: Yeah, well, he didn't put it like that, of course. Michael would never want you to think you knew better than he did.

VE: But he did want your help?

JB: I was gobsmacked, if you really want to know. He'd never made a secret of the fact that he thought what I do is a load of crap. Not a 'proper' academic discipline. Not like his.

VE: What is it you do?

JB: I'm a psychotherapist.

VE: I see. So he wanted – what? A recommendation of someone he could see?

JB: Basically, yes. Though he kept saying it was for someone in the family, not for him. But he would say that, wouldn't he?

VE: In fact, we have now ascertained that his wife was suffering from post-natal depression. Do

you think it might have been her he had in
mind?

JB: Right, I didn't know that. In that case, yes,
he could well have been thinking of her.

VE: Can you give me the name? The person you
recommended?

JB: I gave him a list actually – six or seven
people locally. I can get you that.

VE: Do you know if he ever contacted any of them?

JB: They wouldn't tell me, even if he had.
Confidentiality. And like I said, I haven't
heard from him since.

VE: And how did he seem, in general, that night on
South Parade?

JB: He looked bloody awful, actually. Hadn't
shaved, sweat under his armpits. That sort of
thing.

VE: And that was unlike him?

JB: [makes a face] I should say. It was always
all about appearances with Michael. He had
to be the one with the best exam results,
the best job, the most beautiful home,
the most beautiful wife. You get the picture.
Actually –

VE: Yes?

JB: The first thing I thought when I heard the
news was that he'd done it himself. You know,
taken the ultimate way out. To be honest, if I
didn't know he was in London at the time, I'd
still think that. He always did have the cork
in too tight.

28 July 2017, 10.45 a.m.
160 days before the fire
23 Southey Road, Oxford

Michael Esmond opens the study doors and stands for a moment, staring down the garden. It's one of the hottest days of the year but he had to have the doors closed while the grass was being cut because it was too noisy. But he can let some air into the room now that Harry is on his hands and knees doing the borders. And he's doing a good job, no question: the garden looks better than it has for years. It would almost be worth having another party for the department. Almost, but not quite. He knows from experience that events like that are always far more work than you've bargained for, and Sam probably still isn't up to it. Not to mention the cost. He turns and goes back to his desk, and for an hour all he can hear is the snip of the secateurs, the birdsong and an occasional bark from the dog next door. He's so engrossed he doesn't notice the sounds of gardening have stopped; he doesn't even look up until a shadow falls across the page in front of him. He glances up.

'Present from Sam.'

Harry is standing in front of him, holding out a can of lager. And a glass. He has a can of his own in his other hand.

'Thanks,' says Michael, sitting back. 'You're doing well – with the garden, I mean.'

Harry smiles. 'Most of the heavy lifting's done now, but you have to keep on top of it at this time of year.' He wipes the cold can across his forehead like he's a model in a soft drink ad. And modelling might well be a viable option if he put his mind to it. He has the looks, the height, the six-pack. The tan. There's a line of sweat along his upper lip and he wipes his hand across his mouth. Michael looks away quickly, realizing he was staring. He feels himself redden.

'I didn't realize you had tatts,' he says, desperate for something to fill the silence.

Harry looks down at where his shirt is open. There's a small tattoo just visible on his left pectoral. 'Just the one,' he says, touching it. 'It's for the woman in my life.' He winks.

Later, when his wife brings him out a sandwich, Michael asks her if Harry has a girlfriend.

'Not that I know of,' she says, looking down the garden to where he's bagging up the grass cuttings. He's taken his shirt off now. 'Why?'

'Oh, no reason. It was just something he said. About that tattoo of his. He said it was for the woman in his life.'

'Oh, *that*,' she says, smiling. 'He told me about that. It's for his mother. It's a reference to her name. She brought him up on her own so they're very close. A bit classier than "I love my Mum" in big letters, don't you think?'

Harry is coming up the garden now, the bag over his shoulder. The tattoo is clearly visible. A tiny sprig of berries on sharp dark shoots.

'Don't worry,' says Samantha, seeing her husband's face. 'I won't let Matty get one.'

'No,' he says, without turning to look at her. 'I should hope not.'

* * *

Telephone interview with Belinda Bolton,
14 January 2018, 2.55 p.m.
On the call, DC V. Everett

VE: Hello? DC Everett speaking.

BB: Oh, hello, it's Belinda Bolton. I spoke to you
at the funeral on Friday. You gave me your
card, do you remember? My son Jack is in
Matty's class.

VE: Oh yes, I remember. You said they were good
friends.

BB: Only in the last term, really, but yes, we did
see Matty quite a few times.

VE: So how can I help you?

BB: You said, at the funeral, that it was possible
Jack might remember something. That he might
have heard or seen something but not realize
how important it was.

VE: That often happens, with children. It can
sometimes be better not to push it - to
let them come out with it in their own good
time.

BB: Yes, well, that's just it. I just dropped him
off at one of his friend's, and just as he was
getting out of the car he said something
really odd. I was a bit distracted because I
was parked on a yellow line and I wanted him
to get a move on.

VE: What did he say?

BB: I think he'd been talking about one of

his video games. To be honest, I pretty much switch off when he starts on about that stuff, and then he was halfway out of the car –

VE: Mrs Bolton – what did he say?

BB: It sounds mad, saying it now, but I'm sure he said something about Matty wanting to kill Zachary.

* * *

'It was just a game. It's not *real*.'

The four of them are sitting on a bench in the Bishop Christopher's school playground. Everett, Somer, Alison Stevens and Jack Bolton, Matty Esmond's friend. They can hear voices from the classrooms and, somewhere, piano music and children singing. There was a hard frost overnight and the rather scrappy perimeter hedge has turned into a glittering fortification worthy of a fairy castle. A weak sun has just emerged from the clouds, but it's still cold. The boy is swaddled in a blue puffa jacket, scuffing his trainers against the tarmac.

'You like playing games online, don't you, Jack?' says Everett.

'Sometimes,' he says warily.

'Which do you like best?'

A little more energy now. '*Fortnite*. But *Minecraft* is cool too.'

Everett and Somer exchange a glance.

'That was Matty's favourite, wasn't it? His dad said something about that.'

Jack is still scuffing the tarmac. 'Matty was ace at it.'

'You said something to your mum yesterday – something about killing Zachary,' says Everett. She says it lightly, as if it's not that important.

Jack looks up briefly. '*Attack Zack*.'

'What's that then?'

'Matty made it for *Minecraft*. It was *awesome*.'

'You played it with him?'

Jack shrugs. 'A few times.'

'Did he tell you why he called it after his brother?' asks Everett.

Jack glances up; he's obviously perplexed by the question. 'It was just a name. It didn't *mean* anything.'

He's closing up now and the presence of the head teacher probably isn't helping. Everett elects to try a different tack. 'Mrs Stevens said you have a little brother, too, Jack. Is that right?' asks Everett.

He nods. He's avoiding her eye.

'I'm sure you love him, don't you?'

A pause. 'Babies are stupid. They're really *boring*.'

'But you still love him, don't you?'

A shrug. 'He just lies there. And he cries. All the time. It's really *boring*.'

Somer rubs her hands together against the cold. Her gloves don't seem to be helping much. One of her old boyfriends said she needed mittens. He was into adventure sports and said mittens are better because they allow your fingers to touch. Conserves your body heat, apparently. But how the hell does a grown woman get away with wearing mittens? Never mind a bloody police officer. She wonders in passing, surprised she's even having the thought, if Giles Saumarez has an opinion about mittens.

'Did Matty talk to you about his brother?' Everett asks.

Jack nods. 'Not much. Sometimes.'

'What did he say?'

Another shrug. 'He said his mum cared more about Zachary than she did about him.'

'But Zachary was very little,' says Somer. 'He needed someone to look after him. Just like Matty had, when he was little.'

No reply at all this time. Jack is still scuffing the ground. Alison Stevens is clearly itching to ask him to stop.

'I *told* you,' he says eventually. 'It isn't *real*. Nobody *dies*.'

Fifteen minutes later the three women are walking back towards the head's office. Everett stops a moment and looks back at where Jack is now playing football with four or five classmates. They look just like all the other kids who've kicked a ball about on this playground over the years. But are they really? Has there ever been a generation so inured to violence, so habituated to casual brutality? All those specialists she reads about in the Sunday papers, with their dire warnings about the impact of playing video games and the erosion of empathy – judging by what she's just seen, they don't know the half of it.

* * *

5 September 2017, 7.15 p.m.
121 days before the fire
23 Southey Road, Oxford

The kitchen is full of overenthusiastic dog. The elderly golden retriever is capering like a puppy as Matty throws treats into the air for her to catch. Zachary is laughing and squealing, and Samantha is at the sink, turning occasionally and smiling.

Michael puts his laptop case down on the table and joins his wife. 'I gather the Youngs said yes.'

'They said we can do it again if it works out OK this time.'

'Can we, Dad?' says Matty at once. 'Can we?'

'Let's see how it goes tonight first.'

Matty drops to his knees and wraps his arms round the dog's neck, resting his cheek against the gentle face.

'You remember the rules, don't you, Matty?' says Michael.

The boy nods.

'Tell me.'

'Mollie can't go on the furniture and I have to take responsibility for feeding her.'

'That's right. And she has to sleep down here, in the basket, not in your room.'

Matty seems about to say something to that, but clearly thinks better of it. 'OK, Dad.'

Two hours later, Michael goes upstairs to check on his son to find Mollie curled up on the end of the bed. She opens one eye, then settles down with a doggy sigh.

'Don't wake him,' whispers Sam, appearing at her husband's elbow. 'He looks so happy.'

'That duvet cover will be taking a beating.'

'It's fine,' she says softly. 'There are more important things in life than a bit of dog hair.'

* * *

'That lad wasn't just playing games online,' says Baxter. 'He was *seriously* into it.'

I'm standing behind him, looking down at his computer. Everett and Somer are on the other side.

'He used his own name for his profile, too,' continues Baxter, 'which is why he was so easy to find.'

I glance at him with a frown. 'But don't you need a credit card to play online? A subscription or something?'

'Not with *Minecraft*. Once you buy the game you can play online for free, no problem,' says Baxter, still staring at the screen. 'Most parents think it's pretty innocuous. And it is, at least compared to something like *Call of Duty* or *Mortal Kombat*. It can actually be quite educational – people have built 3D versions of places like the Louvre, specially for *Minecraft*. And there's a really cool Escher thing, too.'

He pulls up a screen and there it is: one of my favourite optical illusions recreated in tiny Lego-like bricks. Impossible staircases, irresolvable walls. I had no idea you could do something like that in a video game and I think sadly how much I'd have loved Jake to see it. I did try to get into it – the whole idea left me cold but Alex said that I had to make an effort, that it was something Jake and I could do together. But it never really worked. Alex says the problem is I can't suspend my disbelief. Perhaps that's one reason I'm a good copper: I refuse to lose touch with reality. I can't let it go, not completely. Even when I was a kid I couldn't unsee the strings on *Thunderbirds*. But looking at Baxter's screen now, at something I've always loved and didn't know existed, I wonder whether Jake and I could have shared this after all, just as Alex wanted. But then it occurs to me that perhaps Jake knew about it all along. He just didn't tell me. He didn't think I'd be interested.

'Impressive, eh?' Baxter is saying, typically oblivious. 'As is this. In rather a different way.'

He changes the screen. The avatar I'm now staring at looks exactly like Matty. It's still made of bricks, but it's clearly him. In fact I'm impressed how cleverly he's resolved his face into square blocks of colour. A rather endearing caricature. The glasses, the hair, the nose. The likeness is slightly unnerving.

'Is it easy to do something like that?' asks Everett.

'It's fiddly,' Baxter concedes. 'But he clearly had quite a talent. Though probably not one his father had much time for. Strikes me he was a three Rs kinda guy.'

'So what about this "Attack Zack" thing,' I ask. 'Where does that come in?'

He swivels his chair round to face me. 'How much do you know about the way *Minecraft* works?'

'I'm guessing it's a bit like *The Lord of the Rings* on acid?'

Somer suppresses a smile.

'Right,' says Baxter. 'Weird creatures all over the place. Some of them are dangerous, like spiders and zombies. And Creepers. They're the worst kind of Mob –'

'Mob?'

'Sorry – it's short for Mobile. Basically, anything that's supposed to be a living creature. Like farmyard animals, which you can kill and eat, or use to make weapons and stuff.'

My new-found enthusiasm for gaming is already diminishing. 'So?'

He turns back to the computer again, then sits back and points. 'Look.'

The creature on the screen is labelled 'baby pig'.

And it has Matty's brother's face.

* * *

6 September 2017, 8.11 a.m.
120 days before the fire
23 Southey Road, Oxford

He should have realized something was wrong from the silence. He checks his watch – gone eight. The kids are always awake by now, and what with having the dog in the house, he's surprised it isn't a riot downstairs by now. He sighs, rolls over and hauls himself out of bed. At his side Samantha stirs but doesn't wake, dulled to the world. It's starting to get cold in the mornings and he pulls on his dressing gown, tying it as he makes his way across the landing. There are sounds from the nursery. Zachary baby-talking to himself. He hesitates at the top of the stairs, wondering whether to make tea for Sam first, but something prompts him to change his mind and go along to the nursery door. His son is sitting on the floor surrounded by scraps of silver foil. His face is smeared with chocolate, and the dog is lying at his side. At first glance Michael assumes it's asleep, until he notices the dregs of vomit around its mouth and the congealing half-glazed eye.

'Wake her up, Daddy!' cries Zachary, raising his arms towards his father. 'Wake the doggy up!'

Michael is on his knees at once, feeling the dog's body for a pulse, but there's nothing. He turns to Zachary. 'Did you give the doggy some of your chocolate?'

Zachary nods, his eyes wide. 'She liked it. She had lots.'

'And when was that, do you remember?'

Zachary puts his finger in his mouth. His face starts to pucker.

'Don't worry,' says Michael quickly, getting to his feet, his heart pounding. There's only one thing that matters now and that's getting the bloody dog out of here. Before everyone else wakes up. Before Matty sees this and realizes what's happened.

He lifts Zachary back on to his bed, then bends to pick up the dog. Its body is already stiffening and starting to go cold. He staggers a little, under the weight, then turns towards the door.

It's Matty. In his Arsenal pyjamas. His face pale and closed, and his knuckles clenched so hard the skin is white. Michael has no idea how long he's been standing there.

* * *

I'm still looking at the screen. I'm not sure I want to know the answer to the next question, but I'm going to have to ask it.

'Baxter – these animals on *Minecraft* – you said people kill them? And that's part of the game – you're *supposed* to do that?'

'Yeah,' he says, looking slightly uncomfortable now. 'You get pork chops if you kill a pig.'

Pork chops. Just like in real life. Only this is much worse, somehow.

'So if I wanted to kill that baby pig – the one on that screen – how would I go about doing it?'

'Well, you could stab it or drown it or blow it up.' He takes a deep breath. 'And there's another way, too.'

It's as if I'm having to drag it out of him, word by word. 'Like *what*, Baxter?'

He looks embarrassed. 'You could set it on fire.'

'*Set it on fire?*'

He flushes. 'That way you get your pork chops ready cooked.' He glances back at me. 'You want me to show you "Attack Zack"?'

'No,' I say, swallowing. It feels like I have grit in my throat. 'Round up the rest of the team first. We all need to see this.'

* * *

Milo's Minecraft Mobs

Posted 11 Dec 17

fear the creeper . . .

So we all know that Creepers are just about the scariest Mob out there, right? But how much do you really know about this icon of Minecraft? Don't worry – right here is all you need to know . . .

Creepers may be mega-fear-provoking, but they actually came about by accident (cool, eh?). Apparently Notch, Minecraft's creator, was really trying to create a pig 🐷, only – holy crap – something went wrong and it came out tall and thin instead of long and fat. And GREEN! Just has to be the luckiest accident <u>ever</u>.

Creepers are worse than just about any other hostile Mob because unlike zombies and skeletons 💀 they can operate in daylight (they spawn at night, tho'). Even worse than that, they're pretty much silent too, so they can get real close before you even know they're there, and if they get close enough they BLOW UP! That's right – they don't attack you, they just 💥 **explode** 💥. The only warning you get is this creepy hissy noise, then they start to flash and swell up and BANG!

Amazingly enough, Creepers can actually climb ladders and stairs and get across lava pools, though they can't go through doors and they're scared of cats (Tip: Get yourself a cat 🐱).

The best way to kill a Creeper? Light a 🔥 fire 🔥 and lure it in . . .

Next post: Zapping Zombies

*   *   *

It takes Baxter ten minutes to connect his computer to the Incident Room projector. Ten minutes while I prowl up and down like one of those bloody Creeper things. First rule of technology: if it can blow up in your face, it will try its darnedest. And then finally Baxter's desktop appears on the screen and he starts to pull up the images. Matty's avatar, which has people glancing at each other and smiling sadly. And then the mutant piglet with Zachary's face, Zachary's mop of curly hair. And now there are no smiles at all.

'And he made that pig thing himself? On his own?' says Gislingham, who's struggling to get to grips with all this.

'Customization,' says Asante. 'All those games do it.'

'Bit more than that in this case,' says Baxter. 'It's relatively easy to change your own avatar, but to do that piglet he had to make his own Mod.'

Mobs? Mods? I'm losing the plot now. 'Mod? What the hell is that?'

'Stands for modification. Basically *Minecraft* stuff made by players themselves, which they allow other people to use.'

He navigates to an internet page and scrolls down a whole list of customized add-ons. Everything from deluxe battleaxes to new and especially nasty hybrid creatures. Right down the bottom of the page Baxter stops. It's the link 'Attack Zack'.

You could hear a pin drop in this room right now.

Baxter glances at me then clicks on the link and pulls up a video. It's a farmyard of some sort. Barns and outhouses and animal pens. In the foreground, the Zachary piglet is staring straight out of the screen, moving its head, flicking its little tail. And then the game begins. In the background, a nasty high-pitched voice is singing the nursery rhyme.

> *This little piggy went to market*
> *This little piggy stayed at home*
> *This little piggy had roast beef*
> *This little piggy had none*

We watch as the piglet is chased through the maze of farmyard buildings until it's cornered, unable to escape.

It's an animation, nothing more than bright pink pixel-ated bricks, but the screams, the panic, are horrifyingly realistic. And just as we're getting to the point when we can't watch it any more, the player throws something at the piglet and it's consumed in flames. Flames that even I believe in.

The tinny voice is cackling now.

This little piggy went BOOM!

'Jesus Christ,' says Gislingham, turning away. 'Christ knows how parents keep their kids safe, with all the shit there is out there.' He sighs. 'I suppose all you can do is love them. Love them and hope they'll talk to you. You know, before they do anything really stupid –'

He stops, frozen, realizing what he's said.

'Shit, I'm sorry, boss. I didn't mean –'

I swallow hard and wave it away. 'Don't worry, I know you didn't.'

No one ever does. But they do it all the same.

Everett is still staring at the screen. 'I know children can resent new babies, but this? This – this – it's horrific.'

'But it could make sense, couldn't it?' says Somer, glancing around. 'As a motive, I mean. Boddie said it was possible Zachary was suffocated before the fire even started, didn't he? What if that was *Matty*?'

Silence, then 'I buy it,' says Baxter sturdily. 'He's angry, he's resentful. Wouldn't take much to set him off. And when he realizes what he's done he panics and starts the fire to cover it up.'

'He wouldn't be the first person to do that,' continues Somer. 'And it wouldn't have been that difficult either.

He'd have known where the petrol was. And once the Christmas tree caught –'

'Would a kid like him really be capable of that?' asks Gislingham. He doesn't want to believe Matty did this, but he's a good copper. He'll go with the evidence, even if that takes us somewhere very dark indeed.

'And what about that therapist?' says Baxter. 'Esmond said it was for someone in the family and we all assumed it was the wife. But what if it was the *son*?'

'You mean he *knew*?' says Ev, her eyes widening. 'Esmond actually *knew* about all this Attack Zack stuff?'

'Hang on,' says Gislingham suddenly. 'Wasn't Matty on the wrong side of the flames? If it started in the sitting room like the fire boys said, what was he doing coming down the stairs? That doesn't make any sense –'

But Asante has an answer. 'Maybe he underestimated how quickly the fire would spread? Perhaps he thought he had time to go upstairs and wake his mother or get his Xbox or whatever. But all at once it's a conflagration.'

Baxter, meanwhile, has been flicking through videos on YouTube. He opens one into full screen: a *Minecraft* player moving around a huge virtual mansion shooting fire in all directions – floors, walls, ceilings – effortlessly moving upstairs, downstairs, inside, out. The blaze looks surprisingly realistic, but there's no heat, and no harm.

'Perhaps he thought escaping a real fire would be that easy too,' says Gislingham grimly.

'But it's still a *huge* leap,' says Everett. 'And if we're going to build this whole case on the theory that a *ten-year-old boy* set that fire we're going to need a hell of a lot more than wild assumptions backed up by no evidence whatsoever.'

I get up and start walking again. Behind me, the silence extends. I need to think. We all do. Because even if that child had nothing to do with the fire, something was very wrong in that house. Something was very wrong indeed.

'OK,' I say eventually. 'Get Challow to double-check the forensics. If Matty really did set that fire there should be some sort of evidence. A boy that age – he'll have got petrol all down himself.'

Like Jake used to do. Milkshake, juice, cola. You name it, he wore it.

There's the ping of a text on Gislingham's phone. He reads it then looks up to me, his face suddenly alert. 'It's the Tech unit, boss. Esmond's phone just went back on.'

* * *

25 September 2017, 5.49 p.m.
101 days before the fire
23 Southey Road, Oxford

When Michael gets home his wife is in the kitchen making a spaghetti bolognese.

'You're early,' she says. 'I wasn't expecting you for an hour at least.'

The nights are starting to draw in but it's still light enough for Matty to be in the garden. He's playing football with Harry. Michael watches them for a moment then turns to his wife. 'How much time is he spending here?'

She glances up, a little confused. 'Harry? He comes twice a week. Like we agreed.'

'No, I meant how much extra time is he spending here? I mean, he must have finished the garden hours ago.'

She flushes. 'Well, he's been doing some of those other jobs you've been struggling to get round to. The tap upstairs, the DIY –'

'I wasn't talking about the DIY.'

'And once or twice he's played football with Matty.'

There's a shout from the garden and the sound of Matty yelling, '*Goal! Goal!*'

Michael leans back against the kitchen counter and folds his arms. 'Sounds like it's been a lot more than "once or twice" to me.'

She frowns. 'I'm not with you.'

'When I dropped Matty off at school this morning his teacher came bowling up to me to say how pleased they are with him at the moment. How he's getting better marks and making new friends and getting invited to things after school.'

'That's good, isn't it?'

'Of course it is. It was just that she appeared to be putting this spectacular transformation down to all the activities I've been doing with him at home. The science experiments I've shown him and the magic tricks I've taught him and the educational games I've created for the two of us to play.'

Her flush has deepened. 'Oh. I see.'

'So it was Harry? All that stuff was Harry?'

She nods. 'He said he'd really like to do it and there didn't seem any harm in it – and of course Matty was over the moon.' She bites her lip. 'I'm sorry, I should have said.'

'So the marvellous scale model of the solar system with a bag of apples, a melon and a ball of string was Harry? The one they replicated in class because it was so "inventive and imaginative"?'

She nods.

'And the trick with the candle making water boil inside a balloon, that was Harry too?'

She says nothing.

Michael takes a deep breath. '*I'm* his father, not Harry.'

'I know, but you're so busy and you have so much on your plate and Harry genuinely seemed to enjoy doing it and like I said I couldn't see the harm.' It all comes out in a rush. And then she stops. 'And in any case, you and Harry are so close. I assumed he'd told you. I thought it might even have been your idea.'

'What do you mean, "we're so close"?'

She turns to the pan and adds salt to the sauce. 'Well, you are, aren't you? I've seen you.'

'Seen me what?'

She's still staring at the pan. 'You know, talking. Laughing.'

'Sam, you're not making any sense. He's the *gardener*, not my bloody BFF.'

She picks up a spoon. 'But that's exactly what I mean. You don't really have any friends, do you? Not really. So I thought, you and he – that it might be like –'

'Like what exactly?'

'That boy you knew. At school.'

His face has turned to stone. 'Who told you about that?'

'Philip. When he was here. He said it was a shame you'd never had any close mates and I asked if it had always been like that and he said yes, apart from the friend you had at school. Look, I didn't mean –'

'And what else did he say?' His voice is perilously low.

Her cheeks are burning now. 'Nothing. That was it. He didn't even remember the boy's name.' She turns away, pretending to do something to the pasta. 'And in any case,' she says, fake-casual, 'what difference does it make?'

Her husband is silent so long that by the time she turns to face him Matty has already come bounding through into the kitchen yelling, *'I won! I won!'*

'Is everything OK?' says Harry, in the doorway.

'Absolutely,' says Michael quietly, not looking at him. 'Everything is fine.'

* * *

Gislingham picks up his phone and looks at me. 'OK?'

'Just get on with it,' mutters Quinn.

We're all standing round Gislingham's desk; he's dialling Michael Esmond's mobile number.

'The Tech unit say it's still in London,' he says, covering the mouthpiece and glancing up at me. 'Somewhere near Regent Street.'

'Oh, hello,' he says suddenly. We start looking at each other – after all this time, Esmond actually *answered*?

'Is that Dr Esmond?' There's a pause then Gis frowns. 'This is DS Chris Gislingham of Thames Valley Police. We're trying to track down Dr Esmond. That's right, he's the owner of this phone.' A pause, then, 'Yes, it is the same man on the news.'

He picks up a pen and makes a few quick notes. 'Do you have his number? Great, thanks. I'll be in touch.'

He puts the phone down and looks around. 'You are *never* going to guess who that was.'

'Oh for fuck's sake,' begins Quinn, until he catches my eye and shuts up.

'His name is Andy Weltch,' says Gislingham. 'Or rather *PC* Andy Weltch. He works the desk. At West End Central police station.'

* * *

25 September 2017, 8.48 p.m.
101 days before the fire
23 Southey Road, Oxford

'No, you can't stay up to watch the end.'

'But, *Dad* –'

'Stop whining, Matty. We agreed you could see the first half, but now you have to go to bed. It's a school night. You know the rules.'

Michael Esmond is loading the dishwasher. His son is standing in the kitchen door. He's in his Arsenal pyjamas: the team are playing West Bromwich Albion tonight.

'But we're winning!'

Michael straightens up. 'That's not the point, Matty. We had an agreement and now you're trying to change it. Life isn't like that. You can't have everything your own way all the time.'

'But yesterday you told Zachary he couldn't play in the sand-pit and then you changed your mind.'

Michael takes a deep breath; kids always manage to check-mate you one way or another. 'That was different.'

'*How? How* was it different?'

'Because I originally said no because I thought it was going to rain and then it didn't. So the circumstances changed.' He flushes a little; the real reason was because Zachary was screaming the place down, but he's not about to admit that to

Matty. 'And in any case, Zachary is too little to understand. Not like you.'

'That's what you *always* say,' wails Matty, his face red. 'You always say that I have to be a big boy but he's too little and he gets away with *everything*. It's not fair, it's not *fair*!'

He stares at his father. Michael is waiting for him to mention the dog. He never has, not once, all these weeks. Not once since that horrible morning when he stood dry-eyed to listen to his father lie.

They stare at each other a long moment, then Matty turns and runs back down the hall without a word.

* * *

'Apparently a taxi driver handed the phone in a couple of hours ago,' says Gislingham. 'Weltch turned it on to see if anyone rang it – in case they could track down the owner that way.'

'Well, that worked a treat, didn't it,' says Quinn sardonically.

'How long had the cabbie had it?' I ask, ignoring Quinn.

'Ah,' says Gis, 'that's the point. He found it on the evening of *January 3rd*.' He watches us piece it together. January 3rd – the night of the fire. The night there was a signal from Esmond's phone in the vicinity of Tottenham Court Road and we assumed that's where he was.

'So it wasn't Esmond who turned the phone on that night – it was this cabbie?'

'In one, boss. He must have tried the same thing as Weltch, only he didn't have any luck either.'

'So – what – he just drives around with it for ten days?'

Gis shrugs. 'He's been away for a week in Las Vegas and he didn't manage to hand it in before he went. And to be fair, he had no idea it was important – he was already in the States by the time we made the appeal. Apparently the phone had slipped down the side of one of the back seats – he didn't have a clue how long it had been there.'

I nod. That's what bedevils most investigations. Not the out-and-out lies and the deliberate evasions, just the inadvertent sloppiness of the day-to-day.

'But I've got the taxi driver's mobile,' continues Gislingham. 'I'll give him a call and text him a picture of Esmond. If we're lucky, he'll remember the fare.'

It's something. Possibly more than something.

'And the Met are sending the phone up here overnight,' Gis adds, clearly trying to be as positive as possible. 'That might give us more to go on. Remember that pay-as-you-go number Esmond was calling? If he stored it with a name we may be able to track them down. Always assuming Baxter can get into the bloody thing, of course.'

Baxter makes a gesture of false modesty and there's a ripple of subdued laughter. But I'm not listening. I walk up to the whiteboard and look at our timeline, doubt clutching my gut for the first time. Is it possible we've got this all wrong? That we've had it back to front, right from the start?

I turn back to Ev. 'That witness who saw Esmond in the pub on the night of the fire – the organizer woman? It was you who spoke to her, wasn't it?'

Ev frowns. 'Yes, boss. What about her?'

'She was *absolutely sure* it was him?'

Ev has gone a little pale. 'She seemed to be. But I can speak to her again if you want.'

'Yes. I do want. And as soon as possible please.'

* * *

Telephone interview with Tony Farlow, 15 January 2018, 6.55 p.m.
On the call, Acting DS C. Gislingham

CG: Mr Farlow? I'm calling from Thames Valley Police. It's about the phone you handed in at the Savile Row police station.

TF: Thames Valley? Bit out of your range, isn't it?

CG: This is important. I'm going to send you a photo. This is the man who owns that phone. Can you look at the picture and tell me when you think you picked him up?

TF: Seems a lot of fuss over a poxy phone, but it's your funeral.
[pause - sound of text arriving]
Oh yeah, I remember this bloke. Picked him up on Great Queen Street. Figured he was staying at one of those hotels round there.

CG: When was this?

TF: Now you're asking. Definitely a couple of weeks now, what with the holiday and that.

CG: Tuesday 2nd? Wednesday 3rd?

TF: Must have been the Wednesday. I remember now. I had a doctor's appointment first thing so I

started later than usual. He was one of my
first fares.

CG: So you picked him up when?

TF: Lunchtime. Around 12.

CG: And do you remember where you dropped him?

TF: Victoria station. Rail, not bus.

CG: Did he say where he was heading?

TF: Nope. Didn't talk to me at all. He was looking
at something on the phone most of the time.
That must have been when he dropped it.

CG: Did he have luggage with him?

TF: Nah. Just one of those poncey laptop bags. I
reckoned that wherever he was going, he wasn't
planning to stay.

* * *

'Once we knew where to look, we found him almost
immediately.'

It's Baxter, in the morning meeting. He's projected an
image on to the screen: CCTV footage at Victoria station
on the afternoon of 3 January. It's the usual grainy quality
but there's no doubt: it's Esmond.

'That's him getting on to the 14.30 to Brighton.' He
flips up another image. 'And this is him at Brighton station at 15.24, after getting off that train. He stays two
hours, then he's back at the station at 17.40 for the London train at 17.46.'

'Brighton?' says Quinn. 'What the fuck was he doing in
Brighton?'

'Search me,' says Baxter. 'We haven't turned up any

sort of Brighton connection so far. Nothing on Facebook, that's for sure.'

'And we're sure he came back to London? He didn't get off somewhere on the way?'

'Like bloody Gatwick, for instance,' mutters Quinn. Who knows darn well we've checked all ports and airports and yet says it all the same.

'Well, we haven't spotted him at Victoria that night yet,' says Baxter. 'There was a derailment just outside Haywards Heath. They had to get lights and lifting gear and God knows what. Everything was at a standstill for two hours. The train didn't get back to London till gone nine and by then the whole place was chaos. We're still going through the footage.'

'OK,' I say, 'keep at it. We need to know *exactly* where Michael Esmond went that night. Even if it was only back to that pub.'

I turn to look at Ev, and she's gone slightly red about the cheeks.

'I just spoke to the organizer again, boss. I'm afraid she's gone flaky on us. She still *thinks* it was Esmond, but he had his back to her and she can't be absolutely certain. Apparently it was the jacket she recognized more than anything – she never actually saw his face.'

'Oh, for fuck's sake,' says Quinn. 'Who bothers looking at a sodding *jacket*?'

Somer shoots him a look that says *That's rich, coming from you*, but no one says anything.

'One thing we *do* know,' I continue, 'is that Michael Esmond made this mystery trip to Brighton only a few hours before his whole house went up in flames. I'm not

232

about to put that down to coincidence until we prove it really was one.'

A ripple of nods and wry exchanges of looks; they know how I feel about coincidences.

'We need to liaise with Sussex police on checking cabs and buses – see if we can establish where Esmond went after he left the station. Why don't you do that, Quinn – nothing like sea air to blow the crap away.' A couple of smirks at that, but he deserves it, he's been a pain in the arse all morning. 'Even better – you get to drive that flash new car of yours.'

* * *

Sent: Tues 16/01/2018, 10.54   **Importance: High**
From: TimothyBrownTechUnit@ThamesValley.police.uk
To: DCEricaSomer@ThamesValley.police.uk

Subject: Case no 556432/12 Felix House, 23 Southey Road – satellite phone tracking

Hi Erica,
We've managed to trace the call you were asking about. The phone in question was definitely offshore when the call took place. I won't bother you with the techy stuff, but *Freedom 2* was twenty miles off the Portuguese coast at the time.

Let me know if you need anything else – always happy to help.

Cheers,
Tim

* * *

Having heated seats in your car has its downsides. It makes for a more comfortable ride, but you sure as hell notice it when you get out. And with the temperature below freezing and the wind off the sea, Brighton is as chill as charity.

Quinn locks his car and walks up to the police station. Architecture-wise it could have been separated at birth from the Thames Valley HQ. Squat, square, functional. And it's much the same inside as well. Quinn signs in and kicks his heels for fifteen minutes; he's just about to go up to the desk again when a uniformed constable appears.

'DC Quinn? PC Alok Kumar. Your DS told us you were coming.'

It takes Quinn a moment to realize that he must mean Gislingham. Old assumptions die hard. As they walk through the office area, people glance up from their computers. Most do little more than register a stranger. A couple of the women gaze a little longer. One of them smiles. Quinn's day starts to look up a bit. Though he's still bloody freezing; the room is icy, everyone else is wearing jumpers.

'Sorry about the cold,' says Kumar genially, 'the heating's on the blink again.' He pulls up a spare chair for Quinn, then sits down at his computer and navigates to the video player. 'Here you are. The bus company sent over all the CCTV from their vehicles for that day.'

'Great, thanks.'

'And when you're ready we can go down to the station and talk to some of the cabbies.'

He smiles. He has amazingly good teeth.

'Coffee?'

Quinn looks up. 'That'd be great –'

'The machine's in the kitchen. Second door on the left.'

* * *

In Oxford, Gislingham's parked just off the far end of the Botley Road. He has coffee too – two coffees in fact: take-aways from a cafe in the shopping centre. He gets back to the car and hands Everett the cardboard tray. She seizes one of the cups and wraps her hands round it. Gislingham pulls the door shut and the car starts to steam up.

'Your nose has gone bright pink.'

She makes a face at him. '*Hey, Eddie,*' she says in a squeaky American accent. '*How come you're such a big hit with the girls?*'

'Showing your age, Ev,' he grins. 'That ad must be thirty years old.'

'More like forty,' she says, grimacing. 'Not that *I'm* that old, of course. And I'll forgive you your lack of gallantry, because of the coffee.' She takes a sip. 'So, where next?'

Gislingham turns to his notebook. Esmond's mobile phone arrived by special delivery from the Met that morning, and for once, they had a bit of luck: the password was almost the first combination Baxter tried. 1978, the year Michael Esmond was born. As Baxter observed grimly, 'Never underestimate the stupidity of supposedly intelligent people.'

The phone got them into Esmond's texts (nothing doing), his private email account (another password, not yet cracked), and last but not least, his contact list, which included the elusive pay-as-you-go mobile he'd been calling since the previous summer. It's logged in the phone as 'Harry', a name which left them all looking at each other blankly when Baxter read it out. There's been no Harry anywhere – not in his list of colleagues, his current students or his Facebook contacts. And when Somer called Philip Esmond to ask him, he was none the wiser. And that in itself has piqued their interest. Sometimes absence is as telling as discovery. And so, for the last two hours, they've been checking the locations where 'Harry' was when Michael Esmond called him, but so far they've come up completely empty: no one knows anything about a Harry. And now there's only one location left to check. Gis looks across at the houses opposite. 'I think it must be one of those.'

'OK, just let me finish this.'

They sit there a moment, watching as a bunch of teenagers wander past, laughing, seemingly oblivious to the cold.

'Must be nice, being a student,' says Gislingham.

Ev peers through the glass. 'They're not students. Well, not from here, anyway. They're from the youth hostel.' She nudges him and whispers, *'The backpacks rather gave it away.'*

Gislingham is all fake astonishment. 'Hey, have you ever thought of a career as a detective? Because, you know, I think you might have a talent for it.'

She digs him in the ribs and they fall silent again. A few drops of rain start to spatter the windscreen.

Everett finishes her coffee. 'OK – you set?'

By four o'clock Quinn has had enough. It's pissing down with rain and he's pretty sure he has a cold coming. He's spoken to seventeen taxi drivers and four station staff, and not one of them recognizes Michael Esmond or has the slightest idea where he went after the CCTV showed him leaving the station, hitching his bag over his shoulder and heading for the exit. By the time Quinn's walked back to police HQ for his car, his shoes are wet through and his mood has hit rock bottom. And the sight of a smiling (and very dry) PC Kumar coming towards him does nothing to improve it.

'DC Quinn – did you have any luck?'

Quinn glares at him. 'No, I sodding well didn't.'

Kumar's smile falters. 'Oh, sorry to hear that. You want to come in and dry off?'

'If it's all the same to you, I think I'll just get going.'

Kumar hesitates. 'I did have one idea . . .'

'Oh yeah, what was that then?'

'I looked at that footage again. There are two cameras at the station – one outside and one inside. At 3.26 the inside camera shows him walking across towards the exit and disappearing out of view.'

'Yeah, and?'

Quinn's tone was a bit shorter than he intended and Kumar looks a little dashed. 'It's just that he doesn't appear on the outside camera for another two minutes fifteen seconds. So I was trying to work out what he could have been doing during that time.'

'Went to the Gents?'

Kumar shakes his head. 'The station toilets are in the other direction.'

'OK, so what's the answer?'

'I think he was looking at the map of the local area. It's by the doors, just out of camera range. I reckon he didn't know exactly where he was going. It was somewhere he hadn't been before.'

Quinn opens his mouth and closes it again. He's underestimated this guy. 'OK, so let's say you're right. Where does it get us?'

Kumar brightens up. 'Well, I reckon it rules out visiting a friend. And given we can't find a bus or taxi who picked him up, I think we need to assume he was on foot.' He pulls a map out of his jacket. There's a circle marked on it with red pen, with the railway station dead centre. 'This is as far as he could have got at a reasonably fast pace in thirty minutes.'

Quinn takes the map. 'On the basis that he walked around half an hour, spent an hour wherever it was, then walked back?'

Kumar nods. 'Seems a fair enough place to start. And we can probably get CCTV for most of the obvious routes. At least for the first mile or so. Which is something.'

Quinn is still staring at the map. 'And of course we do have one other thing on our side.'

Kumar frowns. 'What do you mean?'

Quinn looks up and grins at him. 'Half this circle is in the bloody sea.'

* * *

Sent: Tues 16/01/2018, 19.35   **Importance: High**

From: AlanChallowCSI@ThamesValley.police.uk

To: DIAdamFawley@ThamesValley.police.uk,
CID@ThamesValley.police.uk

**Subject: Case no 556432/12 Felix House, 23 Southey
Road – additional tests**

I have carried out the additional tests you requested on
Matthew Esmond's clothing. There were no traces of any
kind of accelerant. Nor was anything discovered on his
hands during the PM. It is, of course, possible that he was
very careful and/or wore gloves, but with a boy that age, I
suspect that degree of planning/foresight is very unlikely.

*   *   *

'The last address was a non-starter,' says Everett. 'No one
had ever heard of a "Harry", never mind Michael
Esmond. Though it was obvious the bloke we spoke to
recognized the picture. But he said it must have been from
the news.'

8.15 a.m. Gis is perched on the radiator in my office,
trying to warm up. Outside, it's only just starting to get
light. The stone is orange in the street lights.

'Did you believe him – this bloke?'

Gis considers. 'Seemed straight up.'

'Anything else useful on Esmond's phone?'

He shakes his head. 'Baxter's been through it. Nothing
doing, I'm afraid. Last call was a voicemail from the wife
on the 3rd. All she says is she's sorry she didn't call the

night before, she was too tired, but she's at home and Zachary's been ill so could he call her. Which, of course, he never did.'

'Because he'd already lost the phone by then.'

'Right.'

'What about the Brighton angle?'

He gives me a heavy look. 'You'll have to ask DC Quinn that. When *and if* he deigns to grace us with his presence.'

* * *

At Southey Road, Paul Rigby is organizing the tasks for the day ahead. After nearly two weeks on-site, the investigation team is finally hitting pay dirt. Though that's an unfortunate idiom in the circumstances. The rubble from the top two floors has been painstakingly sifted, documented and carried away, and they're getting to the sitting room now: the sitting room where the blaze must have started. The combination of the heat of the fire and the sheer weight that came down has left most of it little more than black and broken shards. But they know what they're looking for, and they'll know how to read it when they find it.

'OK,' says Rigby, running down the list on his clipboard one last time, 'let's get this area sectioned off and get to work.'

* * *

Gareth Quinn is feeling a good deal better. Not just about his job, but life in general. Fawley was right – getting out of the office was a good idea. Gave him a fresh perspective. Not to mention the phone number of that female officer who was giving him the eye. And as for Alok Kumar, well, he's going to be very useful: more than happy to do the donkey-work and so far away he'll never know he isn't getting any credit for it. So there's a bit of the old swagger in Quinn's stride when he swings into the incident room at half past nine.

Gislingham glances up from his desk. He knows that look well.

'Nice of you to turn up,' he says.

Quinn tosses his car keys on to the table. 'Got stuck in traffic.'

'Well, now you *are* here, do you want to brief me on what you got in Brighton?'

Quinn smiles. 'Sure. Just let me get a coffee.'

Ten minutes later Quinn wanders into the meeting room, pulls out a chair and slides his tablet and his coffee on to the table. Then he opens a paper bag and starts eating a croissant. A chocolate croissant. Gislingham knows he's being wound up, but knowing it is one thing; rising above it is quite another.

'I thought you got stuck in traffic?' he says, eyeing the croissant. The smell is making his stomach rumble.

'Yeah, well,' says Quinn, his mouth full.

'So, go on then. What did you find?'

Quinn puts down the paper bag and fires up the tablet.

'No luck on cabbies or bus drivers,' he says, spraying crumbs, 'so the inference has to be that Esmond walked from the station. And given he was only there two hours, that gives us a maximum range of about three miles.' He twists the tablet towards Gislingham and takes another bite. Shreds of almond drop on to the table.

Gislingham forces himself to stare at the map on the tablet screen. 'What do the yellow marks mean?' he says after a moment.

'CCTV cameras,' replies Quinn, finishing the croissant and wiping his hands. 'Shops mostly. Sussex are collecting the footage for the relevant times, but it might take a few days to get it all.'

'How much do you have so far?'

Quinn considers. 'About half. Maybe a bit less. No sign of Esmond so far.'

Gislingham looks at the map again. Quinn's done a decent job of this, no doubt about that. It's good, solid police work.

'OK,' says Gislingham, getting to his feet and moving towards the door. 'Keep me posted.'

As soon as he's out of sight Quinn smiles to himself, screws the paper bag into a ball and lobs it at the waste-paper bin.

'Yesss!' he says as it drops dead centre. 'Still got it.'

*   *   *

I'm in the middle of a tedious update call with the Super when Baxter appears at my door, gesturing urgently.

I make my excuses to Harrison and get to my feet. 'What is it?'

'Sir,' he says, half out of breath. 'I think you should see this.'

I follow him to the incident room at the closest thing to a run I've ever seen Baxter manage. In fact, I've never seen him so animated. He beckons me to his screen and stands there, pointing. But it's just another still of a railway station. People in scarves and gloves, backpacks, duffel bags, suitcases. A scattering of cheap Christmas decorations –

'Hang on – this isn't Brighton.'

Baxter's nodding. 'No, boss, it's *Oxford*. On *the night of January 3rd*. And that man there,' he says, pointing, 'is *Michael Esmond*. He didn't stay in London that night like we thought. For some reason we don't yet know about, he *came home*. And I reckon, whatever he was up to in Brighton, it's to do with that. Has to be.'

I look at the time code on the bottom of the screen. 23.15.

Less than an hour later, his house was on fire.

*   *   *

Sent: Weds 17/01/2018, 14.35   **Importance: High**
From: PRigby@Oxford.fire.uk
To: DIAdamFawley@ThamesValley.police.uk,
     AlanChallowCSI@ThamesValley.police.uk,
     CID@ThamesValley.police.uk

**Subject: Case no 556432/12 Felix House,
23 Southey Road**

Just to say we have now located the main front door to the house. The four glass panels are broken, but there are no obvious signs of a break-in – none of the damage we would expect to the wood, and the door was fitted with high-quality deadlocks. The question, therefore, comes down to the glass panels and whether someone could have broken one of those and accessed the house that way. We'll do more tests, but the pattern of fragments suggests to me that the glass broke from the inside out (i.e., it blew as a result of the fire) rather than from the outside in. Add to that the security alarm and the height of the side gate, and I think it unlikely someone broke into the house. Whoever set that fire had their own means of getting inside.

*   *   *

Bryan Gow meets me at a coffee shop round the corner from the university psychology department. He tells me he's working on a seminar series on personality profiling and psychopathology, though I suspect the profile he's really interested in is actually his own. My private theory is that all the academic stuff he does is just a stepping stone. What he really yearns for is TV. A credit at the end of *Line of Duty*, one of those talking heads on *Britain's Darkest Taboos*. He's done a bit with novelists over the years, straightening out the misconceptions, toning down the implausibilities, but there's no real money in that. I remember him saying once how much it amused him that the bloodiest books were always written by the meekest authors. Mousey middle-aged women or well-heeled yummy mums up to their Boden-clad elbows in decomp fluid. I told him there was a seminar series in that too, but he just thought I was joking.

'I don't have long,' he says as we sit down. 'I got bogged down in family stuff over Christmas and didn't get as much done as I planned.' He pulls the sugar bowl over. 'How's Alex?'

He doesn't usually ask. In fact he's never even met her. He looks up, sensing the hesitation.

'Everything OK?'

'Yes, fine. I'm just a bit stressed out. This case, you know.'

'The fire? In Southey Road?'

In the street outside two students are walking up towards New College. Laughing, despite the cold, muffled up in coats and scarves and those bobble hats with ear flaps and pom-poms. They get to the street lamp and stop, as if by silent signal, and the boy bends his head and takes the girl's face in his hands, tilting her mouth up to meet his. The movement is as beautiful as ballet.

Gow follows my gaze and raises his eyebrows. 'Personally, I can't think of anything worse than being twenty-one again. Anyway, that fire – was that what you wanted to talk to me about?'

I nod. 'Something about it isn't adding up.' I fill him in on what we've found out so far – about Esmond, the family, the allegations, the money. Or lack of it.

'I thought he was sighted in London that night?'

'So did we. But when we spoke to the witness again she started to backtrack and now she can't be certain whether it was him after all.'

'I see. So all this time, you've been looking in entirely the wrong place.'

He says it neutrally enough but it still rubs me the

wrong way. Not least because the Super said almost exactly the same thing not half an hour ago.

Gow is still considering. 'It's definitely arson?'

'Still waiting for conclusive proof. But it's the working assumption.'

'And you're sure the family were all alive when the fire started?'

It might seem an odd question, but if I'm right, it's not the non sequitur it might appear.

'The mother and the older boy, definitely. The PM wasn't so conclusive on the younger child.'

Gow sits back in his chair. 'I'd need to know a hell of a lot more about this man Esmond before I could be sure –'

'But?'

'But the hypothesis I'd start with is Family Destroyer.'

Which is exactly what I was expecting him to say. It all adds up. It's been in my mind for days, but every time I ran up at it I couldn't get round the fact that Esmond was in London. The phone, the witness – the evidence seemed conclusive. Only now, we know better.

'He sounds – in theory – like a textbook candidate,' continues Gow. 'Almost too perfect, in fact. Highly educated, successful, massively invested in how the world perceives him, suddenly facing bankruptcy or prosecution or some other cataclysmic loss of social or professional standing. Even the fact that he had just turned forty. You'd be surprised what an impact that can have. Especially for men whose self-esteem is predicated on status and success. They start asking themselves – is this really all I've achieved? Is this really all there is?'

Been there, done that, got the disenchantment.

'The actual act of familicide,' Gow continues, 'is typically preceded by a noticeable change of behaviour in the preceding months: the man in question becomes impulsive, erratic, aggressive, sexually promiscuous, just like your man –'

'Even though Esmond actually denied that allegation.'

'Precisely. Even though he denied it. From what you say, his whole world was about to fall in.'

'*His* world. Not his family's. Even if he wanted to end his own life he didn't have to take them with him.'

Gow shrugs. 'Some of these men tell themselves that they're actually doing their family a favour – sparing them public shame or the loss of their comfortable lifestyle.'

'And the others?'

'There can be rather darker motives. Some appear to take the view that "if I can't have them, no one will". That's why so many set light to the family home – it's as much a symbolic act of destruction as an actual one. A way of regaining command of a situation that's got completely beyond their control.'

'But how do they rationalize doing something like that?'

'They don't – not in the way you mean, anyway. Once they've decided on suicide the normal rules simply cease to apply. Even when it's a deep-seated taboo like killing their own children.'

'But Esmond didn't commit suicide. Not as far as we know.'

Gow raises an eyebrow. 'Maybe you just haven't found the body yet.'

It's not impossible. There are woods round here where corpses can go unnoticed for months.

'But if he wanted to end it all,' I continue, 'why go to such elaborate lengths to kill his family, and not take the same way out himself?'

Gow picks up his cup. 'In fact, only about seventy per cent of Family Destroyers commit suicide themselves. Not a lot of people know that. Some try to, and either fail or lose their nerve at the last minute. Google Jean-Claude Romand – absolutely fascinating case – they're making it into a film –'

'But if they don't die, what do they do?'

He stops and looks at me over his glasses. 'They run away,' he says. 'Usually. And if they're caught they claim diminished responsibility – some sort of psychotic break or sudden overwhelming moment of insanity.'

I don't need reminding that Esmond has already had one dissociative episode as a teenager. Was Somer right when she asked me if it could have happened again? When I tell Gow the story he nods. 'I couldn't rule it out. Not without talking to him myself. Some sort of post-traumatic reaction might well have occurred. *After* the event, of course.'

'What about before – could he have had some sort of breakdown, a psychotic break like you just said?'

Gow makes a grim face. 'To quote Jack Levin, one of the experts in this particular field, "These killings are executions. They are *never* spontaneous."' He finishes his coffee. 'That's why I asked if the wife and children were definitely dead when the fire began. A Family Destroyer doesn't tend to take the risk of anyone surviving. Same applies to the fire. Some even barricade themselves in to make doubly sure there's no chance of firefighters getting to them in time. And there's usually huge quantities of accelerant. Classic overkill.'

And that rings true too: it's exactly what Paul Rigby is expecting to find.

Gow gets out his phone and scrolls through a few pages. 'I'll send you a link. You probably remember the case, but it might be useful background.' He puts the phone down on the table. 'Have you had the toxicology results?'

'The wife was on antidepressants and had been drinking. We have to hope she didn't know anything about it. She was also pregnant.'

Gow nods. 'Another straw on the dromedary's back. Assuming Esmond knew, of course. And that showdown with Jordan about the harassment would have been the final trigger. After that, things would have moved very quickly.'

We sit in silence for a moment. The couple opposite have moved on. Their breath follows them down the street in a soft white cloud.

'The other thing to remember,' says Gow, pushing away his empty cup, 'is that these killings are almost always meticulously planned, sometimes months in advance. Especially if the perpetrator is looking for a way out rather than a way to end it.' He starts to gather his things. 'If I were you, I'd have a very close look at his financials – see if he's been moving money around. That'd be a big red flag: if he was planning a nice shiny new life, he may well have tried to salt some cash away before everything went tits up.' He glances at me. 'That's a technical term, of course.'

'Baxter's been through them. Esmond took out two grand in cash a few weeks ago. But that wouldn't last long.'

Gow considers. 'Long enough to regroup, organize a new identity? Don't ask me, I'm just a psychologist. You're the detective.'

Touché.

'Is there anything else we should be looking for? Apart from him, of course?'

'There may have been a record of domestic abuse. Probably the sort you can't see, and his wife almost certainly never reported it. But she may have told someone she was close to. A friend, a sister?'

'Her parents haven't said anything. Her father clearly didn't have a lot of time for Esmond so I doubt he'd have held back if he suspected there'd been anything like that going on.'

'Ask the mother then. When the father isn't present.'

I should have thought of that myself. 'I'll call Everett. She's doing the family liaison. Though to be honest, the Giffords don't seem to want us around very much.'

Gow gets to his feet. 'I'll be on my mobile if you need me.'

When I get home I stick a frozen meal in the oven, switch on the laptop on the kitchen island and open up the link Gow gave me. It's an episode of *Crimes That Shook Britain.* I allow myself a smile: no surprises he's been boning up on shows like that. But he's right about the case: it's ten years ago but I do remember it. Christopher Foster, the millionaire who had a manor house in Shropshire, a garage full of fast cars, a suite of barns and stables, and a fine collection of shotguns. And that's what he used. First on his animals, then on his wife and daughter. There's chilling CCTV footage of him moving silently about his yard at three o'clock in the morning, killing the horses, carrying cans of petrol, starting up the horsebox so he can block the drive. A calm, determined figure, his face bleached white of all features by the poor quality of the film. A few minutes later the house and outbuildings are ablaze, and Foster is lying on his bed, still alive, waiting for the flames.

The oven alarm goes off and I go to get my anaemic-looking lasagne. Then I start the video again. It's the people who knew Foster I find most compelling. The personal assistant who calls him competitive and controlling, the brother who says he abused him as a child. And then there's a psychologist talking about whether it wasn't only the imminent financial ruin that pushed Foster to do it – whether there'd been another side to his personality that he'd never been able to reveal, and was suddenly threatened with public exposure –

Then the doorbell rings and when I open the door I'm momentarily thrown. Fluorescent yellow waterproof, black leggings, bumbag, cycling helmet. He looks like one of those Deliveroo guys.

'Sorry, you must have the wrong house. I didn't order anything.'

'DI Fawley?' he says. 'It's Paul Rigby. The Fire Investigation Officer?'

'Shit – sorry. I didn't recognize you.'

'I hope you don't mind me calling unannounced. I only live a mile or so from here so it was easier than phoning.'

'Of course,' I say, standing back to open the door. 'Come in.'

He steps over the threshold and starts wiping his feet on the mat.

'I can't stay long,' he says. 'My wife's out tonight so I need to be back for the kids. But we've had some results that I think you'll want to know.'

I gesture towards the kitchen and follow him down. He declines to join me in a glass of wine but accepts the solitary low-alcohol beer I find at the back of the fridge.

He glances at the laptop and the screen paused on an image of Foster's house after the fire; the roof collapsed, the whole building a smouldering shell, and a forensics tent over where the bodies were found.

'That's not Southey Road, is it.'

'It's the Christopher Foster house.'

Evidently I don't need to say any more. He nods. 'It seems my team aren't the only people who think it was an inside job. You've got there too, have you?'

I pass him the bottle opener. 'We've just found out Esmond came back to Oxford that night. In plenty of time to set the fire.'

'With his wife and kids inside.' But it's a statement, not a question. Rigby's been doing this job a long time.

I take a deep breath. 'So what did you want to talk to me about?'

He reaches back and pulls his phone out of his bumbag, and flicks through the photo app.

'We found this.'

It's a cigarette lighter. Blackened, like everything else in that house, but underneath metallic. Golden.

'Made in 1954, according to the hallmark,' says Rigby.

I look up with a question and he nods. 'Solid gold. Must be worth a bomb.'

'And you found this where?'

'In the sitting room. We haven't cleared the whole area yet, but I assumed you'd want to know about this straight away. We didn't realize what it was until we scraped the crap off it.'

'I assume it's too much to ask if there'll be any fingerprints?'

He shakes his head. 'Fire will have done for that. But there is something else.'

He finds another picture and hands me the phone. One side of the lighter is engraved.

To Michael, On your 18th birthday, Love Mum & Dad.

I look up at Rigby and he shrugs. 'There is, of course, no way of knowing where it was before the ceiling came down. It could have been in one of the upper rooms, on a coffee table, anywhere.'

'But he'd have carried it about with him, wouldn't he – as a smoker?'

'Don't you?'

Of course I do. It's one of the things I check automatically, without even thinking: keys, phone, lighter.

'But if he set the fire he wouldn't have left the lighter behind, surely? He must have known we'd find it eventually.'

Rigby shakes his head. 'I've seen this before. People completely underestimate how suddenly an accelerant can ignite. It's like recoil – the heat hits you so fast you'll more than likely drop anything you're holding. And if you do, there's no way you're going to get it back.' He makes a face. 'Even if it is a bloody heirloom.'

* * *

'So he just burned down his life,' says Baxter, 'and swanned off to start a new one somewhere else? Just like that?'

It's the morning meeting and I've just spent the last half an hour going through what Gow told me, and what Rigby found.

'Well, *I'm* not buying it,' says Quinn. 'If Esmond wanted to start all over again he'd need money. *Lots* of money. And OK, he did take out that two grand in cash, but that wouldn't be anywhere near enough. *No way.* And why do it on a day when his car's in the garage?'

Everett shakes her head. 'He wouldn't have used his own car anyway. Far too easy to trace.'

In the silence that follows Gislingham picks up the marker pen and goes over to the whiteboard to mark up the new evidence. The new hypothesis, the new questions we need to answer. As he writes the word 'Escape' and adds a question mark, Somer speaks into the silence.

'He didn't need to murder his family, if all he wanted was to start again.'

I glance across at her. 'No, he didn't. But the picture everyone is painting is of a man under acute strain. Remember, he's run away before.'

'That time it didn't involve burning his own kids to death,' mutters Everett, in an icy undertone.

254

'A lot of men who walk out on their lives are really walking out on their *wives*,' begins Somer.

'True,' says Gislingham. 'Most blokes don't want to live on their own – they're crap at it.'

'Worked out how to use the washing machine yet, Sarge?' someone calls out at the back to general laughter.

Gislingham grins – a flash of the old Gis. 'Hey, I even know what the "Delicates" setting is for. So there.'

I wait for the noise to subside. 'We've found no suggestion Esmond had a girlfriend.'

'What about this "Harry"?' says Ev, giving me a meaningful look. 'We've been assuming he must be the plumber or something –'

'Unlikely,' says Baxter stolidly. 'Esmond was calling him far too often for that.'

'– but what if he's the lover? What if Esmond is gay?'

Quinn folds his arms, clearly sceptical. 'All the while playing the happily married man in public?'

Ev shrugs. 'Well, it's not absolutely impossible, is it?'

'There was that incident when he was still at school,' says Somer quietly. 'His brother thought it was just teenage experimenting, but what if he's wrong? What if Esmond has had those feelings all his life? Only now, finally, he can't hide them any more.'

'Right,' says Ev. 'And if he did have a gay lover he strikes me as the sort who wouldn't have wanted people to know.'

'Have we found any other communications between him and Harry?' I ask, looking around. 'Social media? Emails?'

'I'm still waiting for access to his university account,' says Baxter. 'But there isn't likely to be, is there. Not if what Ev says is true.'

'What about the private one?'

Baxter flushes a little. 'Still haven't worked out the password for that, boss. Sorry – it didn't seem a priority –'

'Well, it is now.'

He nods. 'On it, sir.'

I turn to the rest of the room. 'If Michael Esmond is still in Oxford – with or without this "Harry" character – then where is he? And if he *isn't* here, how did he travel? He hasn't used his credit cards so he must be paying his way in cash.'

'That two grand could be coming in useful after all,' says Ev, nodding heavily at Quinn.

'We'll start checking trains and buses,' says Gislingham. 'Or rather, DC Quinn will.'

Quinn rolls his eyes, which I pretend not to notice.

'And Ev, talk to Mrs Gifford again, will you? See if Gow was on to anything when he said there might have been domestic abuse. If she confided in anyone, it could well have been her mother.'

I look around the room. 'OK, that's it. But for the time being we keep the news about Esmond within these four walls, all right? I don't want it getting out until we're ready to announce it.' I look across at Everett. 'And that includes the Giffords. At least for now.'

She nods. 'OK, boss.'

The phone rings and Asante picks it up, then looks across at me. 'Message for you, sir. You're wanted, you and the DS. At Southey Road.'

* * *

Telephone interview with Laura Gifford,
18 January 2018, 11.15 a.m.
On the call, DC V. Everett

VE: I'm very sorry to bother you again, Mrs Gifford.
Things must be awful for you right now.

LG: I don't know what I'd do without Greg. I can't
get my head around it all. You never think you'll
have to do it, do you? Sort out the death of
your own child. Never mind your grandchildren.
Was it Greg you wanted to talk to?

VE: Actually, I was hoping to catch you on your own.
I know these things can be difficult to talk
about, but most girls confide in their mums.

LG: I'm sorry, I don't know what you mean.

VE: It was a happy marriage, was it? Some of the
things you both said, I got the impression
there may have been some difficulties.

LG: No more than anyone else. Michael was a very
loving husband, and a *very* good father. I know
Greg was a bit harsh when we spoke before but
you know what fathers can be like, especially
about their little girls.

VE: Samantha never said anything to you that
might suggest Michael had been — I'm sorry
there's no easy way to ask this —

LG: Abusing her? Hitting her? Is that what you mean?
Absolutely not — whatever gave you that idea?

VE: I didn't mean to upset you, Mrs Gifford,
truly. But violence isn't the only way problems
in a relationship can show themselves. Would

you say Michael was controlling? Did Samantha
ever say he was trying to dictate how she
behaved?

LG: *Of course she didn't.* You people are all the
same - going round poking your noses in
looking for problems when there aren't any.

VE: Mr Esmond is still missing, Mrs Gifford. We're
just trying to eliminate him from our
enquiries - I'm sure you can understand -

LG: No, I *don't* understand. Why aren't you
concentrating on finding out who did this?
That's what I want to know. My daughter is
dead - my *grandsons* are dead - and you people
haven't the first clue who's responsible -

VE: Mrs Gifford -

[*the line goes dead*]

* * *

When Gis parks up in Southey Road there's hardly anyone around, just an elderly man shuffling along in a heavy
tweed overcoat and a woman pushing a buggy with a little
blond boy inside. He's wearing a baseball cap with 'anti-
hero' printed on the front. He must be about the same age
as Zachary Esmond. It's drizzling now, and I turn up my
collar as I trudge up the gravel after Gislingham. The
house looks even worse than it did last time I was here,
the windows running dark stains like weeping clown
eyes. You can feel the wet soot in your throat.

Rigby comes towards us through the rubble, his boots
crunching at each step.

'Sorry to drag you out here, but I think you'll be glad I did.'

He hands us both hard hats. 'No one allowed on-site without one of these.' He waits until we fit them, then turns. 'This way.'

The only access is through the back, and we pick our way across to the sitting room over a floor still strewn with ash and debris and broken plaster, with here and there a tarpaulin rigged up over the last few sections they haven't yet cleared. Rigby stops and crouches down, pointing at what's left of the blackened boards. 'See that? It's spill pattern. Once you know what you're looking for you can see it all over in here. The place was *doused* in the stuff.'

'Petrol?' asks Gislingham, making notes.

Rigby nods. 'Almost certainly. We've sent samples to the lab to see if we can match it to the lawnmower. We also found the can. I doubt there'll be prints, given the state it's in, but it's worth trying.' He straightens up again. 'What the spill pattern tells us is that the arsonist stood in the middle of the room and started to back towards that door over there, throwing petrol to left and right.' He starts mimicking it, flinging his arms from side to side as he retreats. 'But this,' he says, coming to a halt, 'is where he stopped.'

Gis frowns. 'How do you know?'

Rigby gestures at the tarpaulin at his feet, then bends to lift it. Underneath there's a heavy wooden beam, and what's left of an ornate Victorian mirror, the gilding still glinting through the soot. My reflection stares up at me brokenly from the splintered glass.

And it's not the only face I can see.

*   *   *

Oxford Mail online

Thursday 18 January 2018 Last updated at 13:11

BREAKING Oxford fire: Investigators discover a fourth victim

In a shocking turn of events, the fire investigation team at Southey Road are believed to have discovered a fourth victim in the burnt-out remains of the Edwardian house. Neighbours report seeing an undertaker's van, and a body bag being removed on a stretcher. The fire team have been on-site since the fire broke out in the early hours of the morning on 4 January, and have been painstakingly sifting through the collapsed ruins of one side of the house, looking for clues as to the fire's possible cause. Mrs Samantha Esmond, 33, and her younger son, Zachary, 3, perished in the blaze, and her older son, Matty, 10, later died of his injuries in the John Radcliffe hospital.

Speculation is mounting that the fourth victim is Michael Esmond, 40, an academic in the University's anthropology department, who has not been seen since before the fire, despite a nationwide police appeal asking for him to come forward. Those with knowledge of fire investigation procedures have suggested that the newly discovered body must have been in

Millions to be invested in Oxfordshire's roads
The government will be making significant investments in the country's roads over the next five years as part of . . . /more

Headington resident celebrates 100th birthday
Friends and neighbours have gathered to celebrate the centenary of Hester Ainsworth, of Carberry Close, Headington . . . /more

Local schools to raise money for Sport Relief
A number of local schools and colleges are planning special events to raise money for Sport Relief this spring . . . /more

the sitting room on the ground floor, given the length of time it has taken to locate the remains. The fire is also thought to have started in that part of the house.

Thames Valley Police have so far declined to make a statement, nor was anyone at the University offices in Wellington Square available for comment.

670 comments

WittenhamWendy66
Am I missing something completely obvious here or are they actually suggesting the father did it – set light to the house with his little children asleep upstairs? That's beyond belief – what sort of monster does something like that to his own kids?

> **Turner_Rolland**
> They're called 'Family Annihilators'. If you watched as much trashy American crime TV as my wife you'd know all about them.

> **Metaxa88**
> There's a good article about it – based on some research done by a team at Birmingham uni. Apparently there are four types – 'self-righteous' ones who are usually going through a divorce and blame the mother for breaking up the family and usually call her to taunt her with what they're about to do (nice), 'disappointed' ones who think everyone has betrayed them, 'paranoid' ones who think they're under some sort of threat, and 'anomic' ones (no, I didn't know what it meant either) who see the family as a symbol of their own success, but then find themselves going bankrupt or something and everything crashing down around their ears. Here's the link http://www.wired.co.uk/article/family-killers

> **AndEveSpan1985**
> And they're all men. Now there's a surprise.

* * *

'I'd have sold tickets,' says Boddie, glancing up at the viewing gallery and then back down at me, 'if I'd known you were bringing a posse.'

I would say something darkly ironic by way of retort, only right now I'm focusing on not gagging in front of my entire team. I should have copped out and stayed upstairs with the rest of them, but sometimes leadership really is thrust upon you.

The body on the table in front of me is charred blue-black, but here and there the skin has split open in long slicing gashes like ruptured fruit. You can see the pale grey bone of the skull, the yellowish coils of the intestine.

'As we can see,' says Boddie, his voice muffled by his mask, 'the cadaver exhibits the classic pugilistic attitude typically observed in severe burns victims. Supine position, clenched fists, raised knees and so on.' He glances up and raises his voice. 'And for the benefit of the in-génues among you, he wasn't going one last round with the Grim Reaper. The extreme heat causes the proteins in the muscles to coagulate and contract, resulting in this rather quaintly combative appearance.'

He moves round towards the head of the table. 'I can confirm that the body is male, but I will not be able to give an accurate estimate of weight or height, given the shrinkage consequent on the fire damage. Likewise, with this degree of charring, I doubt I will find any exterior distinguishing marks worthy the name. Apart, perhaps, from this.' He indicates one of the clawed hands. 'As the more observant among you will already have spotted, there is a ring on the fifth finger of the left hand.' He looks up at the gallery. 'What I imagine Detective Sergeant Gislingham would call his "pinky".'

I can't hear the laughter but I can see it. Ev is nudging Gislingham, who's managing to grin.

'We must hope Alan Challow will uncover some useful identifying mark on it by way of inscription,' continues Boddie, leaning over the skull, 'because our friend appears to have lost most of his jaw.'

'One of the joists came down on top of him,' I say, through gritted teeth.

'So I see,' says Boddie drily. 'How very unfortunate. I'm afraid there's far too much damage here to attempt a reliable identification through dental records. I will, of course, conduct routine X-rays to see if there are any bones with healed breaks that might assist with identification, but our best bet is probably DNA. There's a brother living, I believe?'

I nod.

He bends again, inspecting the skull from different angles. 'Interesting. I suspect we may have a significant fracture in the right temporal area.' He raises his voice again. 'For those up in the cheap seats, bones often crack in intense heat, which can make it difficult to determine whether the injury to a burns victim was pre- or post-mortem. Many an otherwise competent officer has come a cropper on that one.'

'You're saying someone could have hit him?'

'I'm saying it's *possible*. Just as it's *possible* he hit his head when he was overcome by the fumes.' He picks up his scalpel. 'So shall we take a look?'

As the blade pierces the blackened flesh I glance up to see that most of them have turned away or found a sudden urgent need to check their phones. With one exception. DC Asante. He's taking notes.

FIRE SCENE EXAMINATION – EXCAVATION

RESTRICTED WHEN COMPLETED

Draft extracts from full report

FRS Incident No.	87/1434	**Date of Incident:**	4 / 1 /2018	**Time of Call for incident:**	00 : 47 **HRS**
Address:	23 Southey Road, Oxford OX2				
Use of Premises	Domestic / residential				
Name of Occupier:	Michael Esmond				

Fire Investigation Officer

Name:	Watch Manager Paul Rigby	**Service No:**	667	**FRS:**	Oxfordshire

INCIDENT AND INVESTIGATION SUMMARY SHEET / OVERVIEW

Date / Time FIO Mobilised	00 : 52 **Hours** 4 / 1 /2018		**Date / Time of Arrival of FIO**	01 : 15 **Hours** 4 / 1 /2018	
Cordon Established	Y	Yes	**Cordon Established by**	✓	**FRS**
		No			**Police**
Scene Secured	Y	FRS	**Police Incident Log started at:**		
	Y	Police			
FRS Incident Commander	Station Manager G Lowe				
Police Incident Commander	DS C Gislingham	**Reason for Investigation**	Fatality/possible arson		
Police Investigation Officer Name	A Challow	**Workplace**	St Aldate's		
Appliances attending	Oxford fire appliances Slade fire appliances	**Call signs and time in attendance**	21P1 at 00:55 21P2 at 01:01 30P1 at 01:15 30P2 at 01:30		

Primary Witness – Before Arrival of Fire and Rescue Service			
Name of person discovering the fire	Mrs Beverley Draper	**Contact address**	21 Southey Road, Oxford OX2
Contact phone No.	01865 003425	**How was the fire discovered?**	Visible from window
Was an alarm sounding?	No	**Time discovered**	00.45
Who called the FRS?	Mrs Draper	**Were any actions taken before the arrival of the FRS?**	No

Incident Description

The 999 call from the adjacent house indicated that there could be four persons present in the property, including two children. The first appliance booked in attendance at 00:55, with a first impression message of smoke issuing from the right-hand first and second storey of the property, with flames visible at the lower level. SM Lowe instructed his crew to lay out a hose reel and Firefighters 354 Fletcher, 143 Evans, 176 Jones and 233 Waites to get ready in breathing apparatus sets. These firefighters immediately ascended to the first floor by ladder, making entry through a window. Zachary Esmond was located by 354 Fletcher in a room identifiable as a nursery and immediately removed and handed to the care of paramedics. Shortly afterwards, Matthew Esmond was discovered at ground level, on the staircase. Zachary Esmond was pronounced dead at the scene. Ambulance staff administered first aid to Matthew Esmond before transfer to John Radcliffe A&E. During this time, additional firefighters wearing breathing apparatus were committed into the property to fight the fire at ground floor level. Access was only possible from the rear left-hand side (kitchen), due to severe fire in the hall and front entrance.

At 01.15 WM Rigby was appointed Fire Investigation Officer. At 02.45 SM Lowe reported back to Control as follows: "Severe fire in right-hand rear ground floor, leading to significant structural collapse above. Fire and smoke damage to rest of property. One child fatality, and one casualty. One firefighter suffering slight smoke inhalation treated at scene. Eight breathing apparatus wearers, four hose-reels, one strike jet and PPV fan in use. Incident remains Offensive and to be left open – cause currently unknown – awaiting SOCO."

Casualty / Fatality Information		
Name	Age	Type of Injury / Treatment at Scene / Receiving Hospital Treatment or Check-up
Zachary Esmond	3	Fatality
Matthew Esmond	10	Casualty. Hospitalised at JR. Subsequently deceased

CONSTRUCTION AND OCCUPANCY DETAILS				
Type of Premises	Single-occupancy house		Use of Premises	Family home
Construction – External walls	Brick		Construction – Roof	Pitched tiled
Internal walls	Brick			
No. of Floors	3		Age of Construction	1909
Occupied at time of fire	✓	Yes	By whom and by how many? Two children discovered during course of fire, one deceased. Remains of two adults discovered during excavation	

Lifestyle of occupier	Evidence of:		Details:	
	✓	Smoking	Time of Last Cigarette: Not known	
		Non-Smoking		
	✓	Alcohol Consumption		
		Drug use		
Address / Occupant(s) known to Police			No	

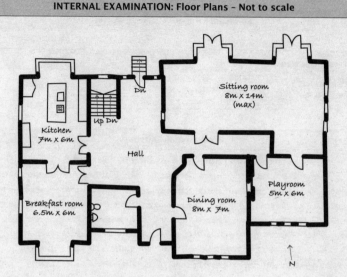

GROUND FLOOR

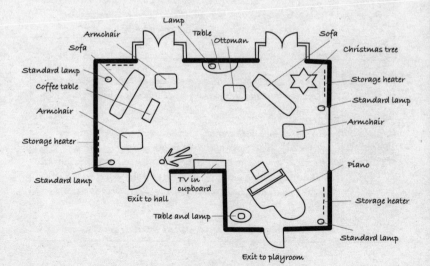

SITTING ROOM (not to scale)

FIRE SCENE EXAMINATION – EXCAVATION

Date and time started		Date and time Complete	
In attendance (add names)	▪ FIO Paul Rigby	▪ CSI/SOCO M Paice, D Thatcher (FRS), C Conway (TVP)	

Excavation description

The excavation process began approx 32 hours after the site was pronounced safe. Two floors had collapsed on the right-hand side of the building, which required the careful removal of debris and construction materials, in order to preserve forensic evidence. The remains of Mrs Samantha Esmond were discovered at approx 16:30 on 5/1/2018. The position of the body suggested she had been asleep in one of the smaller bedrooms on the top (2nd) floor, immediately above the seat of the fire. On the morning of 18/1/2018, the remains of an adult male were discovered in the sitting room (see floor plan). The body was badly charred and visual identification at the scene was not possible. Further excavation and investigation in this room revealed evidence of accelerant and the presence of a cigarette lighter belonging to Mr Michael Esmond. The burn patterns detected on the flooring and what remained of the furniture in the room indicated that the accelerant had been deployed by a single individual, moving across the room towards the door to the hallway. It was not possible to determine why the individual found in this room had not been able to exit safely. When the main front door was located there were no signs of forced entry (as was also the case in the rest of the house).

How the fire spread	<u>Ignition</u> The fire was started by the deliberate ignition of petrol accelerant on the floor, rug and adjacent furniture in the ground-floor sitting room. <u>Development</u> Due to the combustible rug materials on the floor and the dry and highly combustible Christmas decorations in the room, the fire development would have been swift and significant. The fire quickly spread through the ground floor and up the stairs, gaining in energy from the Christmas garlands used to decorate the wooden stair banisters. No smoke detectors were fitted anywhere within the house.

Signed: Paul J Rigby   **Date:** 18/1/2018

Copies to: D Supt J Harrison (Thames Valley)
DI A Fawley

Baxter is the only one who wasn't at the post-mortem, but he did have a good excuse.

'Cracked that password, boss,' he says as soon as I get to the incident room. 'The one for the email account. *And* the one for the home PC.'

A cheer goes up behind me and Baxter blushes, but he's chuffed all the same. 'I leant on the Anthropology department IT guys and they eventually gave me the password he was using for his university emails. That turned out to be Xfile9781. The one for the private account is a variation of exactly the same letters and numbers.'

'So, what – he was some sort of sci-fi fan?' asks one of the DCs.

'More likely a Gillian Anderson fan,' says another with a nudge. 'I mean, aren't we all.'

'Good try, lads,' smiles Baxter. 'But it's actually an anagram. Xfile is an anagram of Felix. The name of the house.'

'And the number?' I ask.

'I'm guessing it refers to 1978,' says Baxter. 'The year he was born. Just like with his phone.'

The house and him, locked together. Passwords can be so revealing.

'But the bad news,' continues Baxter, 'is that there was sod all on the personal emails either. No evidence of a dodgy relationship, female *or* male.'

'No messages to Harry? None at all?'

He shakes his head. 'Nowt. Esmond seemed to use it mainly for ordering stuff from Amazon and doing his Tesco order.'

God, this man is dull. Nothing about his life was as interesting as his leaving of it.

But Baxter's not done yet. 'I went back and looked at his old passwords and turns out it's always the same – a different combination of Felix and 1978. Though he only put a password on the home PC for the first time in November. The last time he updated that was 2 January. Judging by the time, it must have been just before he left the house that morning.'

On his way to the meeting with Jordan, and the conference in London, and – as we know now – someone or some*thing* in Brighton. The timing can't be insignificant.

'So what's the password now?'

'Xlife9718. As in "ex-life". As in dead.'

It could just be a coincidence. But as I'm sure you know by now, I don't believe in coincidences.

* * *

29 October 2017, 2.48 p.m.
67 days before the fire
23 Southey Road, Oxford

'Everything OK?'

It's Sam, standing in the door of the study. Behind her, the wind is whipping through the bare branches. One is creaking against the roof above like a rusty violin.

Michael looks up and frowns. 'It's the bill from the care home.'

Sam comes further in and goes to stand at his shoulder, staring at the screen.

'It's the extras that are doing it,' he says. 'Hairdressing, chiropodists, eye tests. Where does it end?'

'Perhaps we should think about somewhere cheaper?' she says, tentatively. 'Philip said –'

'Philip said what?'

She flushes. 'Only that she'd probably be happy anywhere where they were kind and she was warm and well fed. It's not as if she really knows where she is.'

She expects him to blow up at that, but he just sits there, staring at the screen.

'I know she's settled there, but if it's becoming a problem –'

Her husband sits back in his chair. There are dark circles under his eyes. She wonders, suddenly, how much sleep he's been getting.

'There's enough in the savings account for this month, but after that –'

He looks up; she's biting her lip.

'I was going to tell you,' she says.

'You were going to tell me what?'

'I've taken some money out of the savings account. Sorry. I should have said.'

He's frowning again. 'How much, exactly?'

She's gone very red. '£2,000.'

He stares at her. 'But what could you possibly need that sort of money for?'

'It wasn't for me. It was just a loan. I'll be getting it back.'

'A loan? Who the hell for? Surely your parents –'

'Not my parents. Harry. I lent the money to Harry.'

'*Harry?*'

'His mother's been ill and he's been sending her money.'

'Did you have to give him quite that much?'

'I'm so sorry, Michael – I didn't realize it was going to be a problem – I mean, you never said – I never see the statements –'

'That's because I don't want you worrying.'

Her heart turns over. He's under so much pressure. Not just his mother but his job and the book she knows must be at least six months behind schedule.

She folds her arms about him, feeling the tension in his shoulders, the pulse in his neck. 'Please don't worry. He said he'd definitely pay it back by the end of the month. We'll have it in time for Christmas. He promised.'

* * *

'Boss? There's something you should see.'

It's Baxter. I didn't even realize he was still here. I was about to leave myself but he clearly has something. Though it's giving him no pleasure to tell me so.

'What is it?'

'It's Esmond's PC.'

The incident room is deserted, and I avoid making any reference to the bag of crisps and Mars bar on Baxter's desk.

He sits down in front of the machine. It's not very new and has seen a good deal of use, if the scratches on the screen are anything to go by. There's a faded blue sticker saying 'The Best Dad in the World', and another with the name of a PC-servicing company: 'Honest practical help for all your IT problems'.

Baxter opens a YouTube page.

'It was buried in his browsing history,' he says quietly. 'Press Play.'

The soundtrack is a heavy disco beat and the film isn't much more than a home video with primitive Comic Sans captions and jerky transitions from one frame to the next. But it gets its message over all the same.

5 Truly Awesome Tricks 2 Start A Fire!

Fire-starters made of matchbooks, time-delay devices using firework fuses, balloons filled with petrol strung up over candles. A pair of close-up hands like some sort of perverse *Blue Peter* show while a chirpy American voiceover proffers handy tips (*'Careful, guys – too much fuel in the balloon and you can actually put the candle out!'*) then three smiley emoticons go up in flames and we're on to the next Truly Awesome Trick.

It's only then I realize that the pounding music is 'Burn Baby Burn'.

'Jesus Christ.'

Baxter makes a face. 'I know.'

'And Esmond definitely looked at this?'

Baxter nods. 'Back in November. The 4th, to be precise.'

I push the keyboard away. The sticker is still there.

'The Best Dad in the World.'

* * *

'Took a while to clean it up, but it's not in bad nick, all things considered.'

Alan Challow hands me the plastic evidence bag and a magnifying glass. 'Take a look.'

273

The ring is silver, or perhaps white gold, with a smooth dark-blue centre. It's dented and scratched, but the inscription on the enamel is clear: two initials, ornately engraved and overlaid on top of one another. An M and an E.

'I think that's pretty conclusive, don't you?'

I look up at him. 'I'll show it to the brother. If this is Esmond's he must have seen it before.'

Challow nods. 'Good idea. In fact, you can do that right now. He's outside, waiting to have a swab taken.'

* * *

After the best part of three days, Quinn is on the point of giving up on the whole Brighton angle. PC Kumar's been struggling to find the time to review the CCTV footage and Quinn's not about to volunteer. But when he gets back from lunch there's a Post-it stuck on his computer screen. Kumar's called: there's an email in his inbox. Quinn sits down and opens up his screen. The CCTV clip is only thirty-five seconds long and it's not exactly definitive. The quality is pretty poor and the man's face is partly concealed by an umbrella, but the laptop bag looks like the one Esmond was carrying when he left Brighton station. Quinn picks up the phone.

'Kumar? It's Quinn. You think that's our guy?'

'The timing is right. He'd have got about that far if he'd been walking at normal pace.'

'So where was he – where was he going – any ideas?'

He can hear Kumar exhale. 'That's a bit trickier. This camera is on a corner shop in a residential neighbourhood north-west of town. As to where he was going, it could have been anywhere, to be honest. I've checked and there are no more cameras on that stretch of road for another couple of miles, and there's nothing on any of those.'

Quinn sighs. Loudly.

'Look, I'll do a bit of digging,' says Kumar. 'But I think my luck may have run out.'

Not just yours, thinks Quinn.

* * *

'Where did you find that?'

Philip Esmond is looking at the signet ring lying in my palm. He's gone very pale.

'It was on that body, wasn't it? The one they were talking about on the news.'

'I'm afraid so.'

He swallows. 'So he's dead then. My brother is dead.'

'Do you want a glass of water? This must be quite a shock.'

He shakes his head; there are tears in his eyes. 'I mean, I was expecting it – especially after the news, but –' His voice breaks and he looks away.

And I know what he means. Suspecting is one thing, knowing is another. You cling on to the faintest, most fragile hope, because hope is all you have.

'So he killed them. He really did kill them. And then he killed himself.'

I feel my own heart clutch at his pain. 'I'm so very sorry. But yes, it's looking very much like that's what happened.'

And as the PM results have just confirmed, he was still alive when the fire started. But I'm not about to tell his brother that. He's got it tough enough.

'I'm sorry to bring this up now but we do still need you to give us a DNA sample. Just to be sure. Are you OK to do that now? It's only a mouth swab.'

He blinks the tears away. 'Sure. No problem.'

He gets up from the chair. 'I suppose I can at least give him a decent funeral now.'

'I'm sure the coroner will do everything she can to speed up the inquest. Though –' I stop, not quite sure how to broach it. 'You might want to think about where – for the funeral, I mean. I'm not sure how the Giffords would feel if –'

'– if I put Mike right next to the daughter and grandsons he killed? Don't worry, I'm not about to make things ten times worse.'

He reaches out a hand, half awkwardly. 'Thank you. For everything you've done.'

'It's my job. And we'll make sure the ring is returned to you as soon as possible.'

He smiles wanly. 'Thanks. I'd appreciate that.'

Ten minutes later I stand and watch him as he walks across the car park. He stops at the car and fumbles in his pocket for the keys. It's a rental, I'm guessing, because it takes him too long to find the one he needs and get the door open. Then he stands there, one hand leaning on the roof, his shoulders sunk. I just hope he has the sense to opt for a private funeral a long way away. Social media is tearing his brother apart.

* * *

4 November 2017, 7.14 p.m.
61 days before the fire
23 Southey Road, Oxford

Michael Esmond is late getting back, so he's not surprised to find the house in darkness: Sam said she was going to take the boys to see the new Lego movie. He stands in the hall a moment, dumping his keys. He can still smell the faint chemical odour of the new floor varnish. Varnish, and now, something else.

Burning.

From upstairs.

He's up the stairs without even thinking – running solely on reflex. It's coming from Matty's room. Jesus, he thinks – what the hell is he doing – we've told him a hundred times about playing with flames. And when he rounds the corner into the room, his son is sitting there, cross-legged on the floor.

His hands are on fire.

'What the fuck –' he yells. Though he never swears. Not in front of the kids. Not ever.

And then he realizes Harry is in the room too. Harry, who is staring at him, calm as you like.

'Hi, Mike,' he says, smiling.

Matty starts dropping the pale blue flame from one palm to the other and Michael realizes the fire is coming from something the size of a ping-pong ball. And that his skin is completely unmarked.

'Isn't it ace?' breathes Matty. 'It's like the fire chargers in *Minecraft*.'

'Cool, eh?' says Harry. 'Something for the kids for Bonfire

Night. We found it on the web, didn't we, Matt? If you soak a fabric ball in lighter fuel you can actually hold a fire in your hands.'

'I can smell the burning all the way up the stairs.'

'Yeah, sorry about that. We had a couple of false starts.'

'You could have burned the bloody house down.'

Harry smiles again, a little more coolly now. 'The house is perfectly safe. I know what I'm doing.'

'You just said you found it on the sodding internet –'

Harry reaches out and takes the fireball from Matty, then closes up his fist like a magician and the fire goes out.

'Go downstairs, Matty,' says Michael, not looking at him.

'But, Dad –' he begins.

'Do as I say. And close the door. I want to speak to Harry.'

Matty gets up slowly and drags his feet towards the door. Harry glances across. 'It's OK, Matt. I'll be down in a minute.'

The door closes behind him and they hear the boy moving slowly down the stairs.

'Don't you ever put my son in danger like that again.'

'Really?' says Harry, raising one eyebrow. 'Sounded like it was just the house you were worried about.'

'You know precisely what I mean. What you were doing is reckless and completely irresponsible. What if he tries it on his own – what then?'

Harry uncrosses his legs and gets up. 'He won't,' he says. 'He's not stupid.'

'I know that. But he's still a kid. A *ten-year-old kid*.'

'I told him not to do it on his own. That he could only do it if I was with him so I could make sure we were doing it safely. With the right stuff.'

'Oh, well, that's all right then.'

'You worry too much,' Harry says, putting his hands in his pockets. 'Just chill. It's all under control.'

'And what did you mean by "we"?'

'Sorry – not with you.'

'You said "*we* found it on the internet".'

Harry is unfazed. 'Oh, right. Yeah, it was me and Matt. We did it together.'

'On your phone?'

He frowns. 'No, on the computer.'

'*My* computer. In *my* office.' Michael is visibly struggling to keep his temper.

'What's the big deal? Matt said you wouldn't mind.'

'That's not for Matty to say.'

Harry shrugs. 'If it bothers you so much you should use a bloody password. Though it's not as if you have anything interesting on it as far as I could see.'

Michael takes a step closer to him. 'You were looking through my files – my *documents* –'

'Not looking through. I just happened to notice. Look, Mike –'

They're inches apart now. Eye to eye. 'I told you before. Don't call me Mike.'

'Fine by me,' says Harry evenly. 'Do you have something else in mind?'

* * *

Quinn is in the coffee shop on St Aldate's, staring at his tablet. But it's not his Facebook page (even though he's started up rather a promising connection with one of the female DCs in Brighton). He's on something else. Maybe even *on to* something else.

He stares at the image, clicks the zoom to the maximum it will go, and stares again.

* * *

'I just need a bit more time, Adam. It's complicated – there's something – I need to be sure –'

Of all the days she chooses to call, it's a crap day like today. And even though I know I'm doing it, I'm starting to lose my temper. 'Sure about what, Alex? About me? About us? How the hell can you be sure about anything when you won't even talk to me?'

'Please,' her voice is pleading now. 'I'm not doing this to hurt you –'

'Really? You should try being on the receiving end for a change.'

And then I do something I never do. Not to anyone. And certainly not to Alex.

I cut the line.

Because suddenly I've had enough. Of this case, this place, this absurd situation with Alex. I get up and move towards the door, almost colliding with Quinn, who clearly wants to speak to me.

'Boss?'

'Not now. I'm going out.'

He stares at me. At the jacket I'm not wearing. 'It's bloody freezing out there – just saying –'

'I don't care.'

*

I stride out on to the pavement and stop, still breathing heavily, and uncomfortably aware quite what a stupid idea this is. Everyone else is in hats and scarves and gloves. Including the man standing on the other side of the road, staring at the building. He's young – probably not much more than twenty. A crew cut, thin hips, and his scarf is in one of those hip knots they apparently call 'the Parisian' (I have Quinn to thank for that information, as if you couldn't guess). He looks at his phone and then at the police station again. I cross the road quickly, narrowly missing a bike, and make my way towards him. At least I don't have a uniform to scare him off. Though I wouldn't blame him if he thought I was some sort of nutter, outside in shirtsleeves in weather like this. Close up, he looks nervous. He's biting his lip as he looks at his phone. He's wearing black nail varnish.

'Can I help you?'

He looks up; his eyes widen.

'I work in there. The police station. Is there something you want to talk to us about?'

He flushes. 'I don't want to waste your time. It may be nothing.'

'You're worried enough to stand out here freezing your balls off wondering what to do. That doesn't sound like nothing to me.'

He opens his mouth then closes it again.

'Come on. At least it's warm in there. And if it's nothing, well, it's nothing.' I try a smile. It seems to work.

'OK,' he says.

*　*　*

12 December 2017, 3.54 p.m.
23 days before the fire
23 Southey Road, Oxford

'Hey, careful, don't want you falling off!'

Sam is standing on the stepladder, with Harry holding it steady beneath her. She's decorating the Christmas tree. When she answered the front door an hour ago Harry was standing there, with one of the biggest trees she'd ever seen. It must be eight foot tall.

'Well,' he'd said, after they'd dragged it inside. 'All these high ceilings – might as well make the most of them.'

'It's wonderful, Harry. I can't thank you enough.'

'I'll take Matt out later to look for holly. We can make something for the hall. You think he'd like that?'

'He'd love it – of course he would.'

She'd stood and watched him then as he'd hauled the tree upright in the sitting room, biting her lip and remembering the Christmas before when she'd barely got out of bed for three days and Michael had had to roast a chicken from the freezer. But this year, she told herself, it would all be different. She'd get a turkey and mince pies and a cake. And a Yule log. Michael always said he preferred Yule log to Christmas cake, but if they got a cake as well she could ice it with the boys like her mother used to. She could buy some cake ornaments – let the boys decorate it like she did when she was little.

And now she's on the stepladder, surrounded by the decorations Harry brought down from the attic. She's never liked the way this house is furnished – she'd wanted to do a complete refurb when they moved in but Michael wouldn't hear of it. But, for once, his mania about keeping everything the way his grandparents had it has paid dividends. The decorations are exquisite. No tacky tinsel or shiny plastic but beautiful hand-painted china figurines of snowmen and Father Christmases, folded paper angels and snow-flakes, tiny shoes embellished with lace and fake pearls, gold bells that ring. Some of them are so delicate she's afraid to touch them.

'They'll be fine,' Harry said. 'Just put them higher up. Out of Zachary's reach.'

She hangs a little yellow feathered bird now, and leans back to see the effect. 'These things are so beautiful, aren't they? We just had plastic tinsel tat when I was a child. That and a bag of Brazil nuts my dad always insisted on buying and no one ever ate.'

'At least you *had* a dad,' says Harry, passing up another feath-ered bird.

She flushes. 'I'm sorry – I didn't mean –'

He waves a hand, dismissive. 'What you've never had, you don't miss. And my mum did her best to make up for it. Always did a ton of baking – traditional recipes and stuff she'd got from her grandmother. I was always the most popular kid in class.'

'Sounds lovely. I always feel inadequate, not making the boys' cakes myself. It just seems such hard work.'

He laughs. 'Get them to help – they'd love it. I remember making these cute little doughnut things that we'd deep fry and dip in sugar. There was flour everywhere, but Mum never seemed to mind.'

It still sounds too much like hard work to Sam, but she doesn't want to say that.

'Thank you, by the way,' she says, trying to change the sub-ject. 'That pirate show you saw online? I gave them a call and they have tickets after Christmas. I'm going to make it a surprise for Matty's birthday. We can stay over – go to that Spaceport place he keeps on about. It'll be nice to go back to Liverpool – I haven't been back at all since we left.'

'Oh,' she says suddenly. 'Michael – you're early! Isn't this fabulous?'

Her husband is standing in the doorway. She has no idea how long he has been there. Or why he has such a strange expression on his face.

* * *

I could leave the young man to the duty officer but something keeps me there, listening.

'So it's your boyfriend that's gone missing, is it?' says Woods, heavily.

The young man frowns. 'Not my *boyfriend*. I told you, we'd only met three or four times. I just wanted to check if he's been reported missing. He doesn't have any family here so I thought –'

'When did you last see him?'

'New Year's. He came over to my place. We arranged to meet the following weekend, but he never showed.'

'So that would have been the 6th?'

The young man nods. His name is Davy. Davy Jones. I asked him if his mum liked The Monkees and he looked at me as if I was deranged. I feel about 104.

'And he's not answering his phone?' continues Woods. 'No. Not for days.'

'You sure he doesn't just want to,' Woods looks flustered, 'you know, break up with you?'

Davy flushes. 'There wasn't anything *to* break up. I *told* you. It was just a hook-up.'

'Do you have a picture?' I say.

He turns to me in obvious relief and pulls one up on

his phone. The young man on the screen is extraordinarily good-looking. Dark hair, light blue-violet eyes, a wide, confident smile.

I nod to Woods. 'Have you got the MissPers list for the last couple of weeks?'

THAMES VALLEY POLICE
Missing Person Report

Date: 2 January 2018

Name: Robert 'Bobby' Bell
(Rough sleeper)

D.O.B. 1956?

Address: NFA

Description: Approx 5' 5", thin, several teeth
missing, scar under left eye

Last seen wearing: Rough trousers and jacket,
trainers, woollen hat

Last seen by: Adrian Close, manager, Oxford
Night Shelter

Last seen date/location: 23/12/17, Oxford Night Shelter,
approx. 3 pm

Mr Bell is a well-known rough sleeper, with both drink and
drug issues. Mr Close is concerned because Mr Bell did not
turn up as expected for the Night Shelter Christmas lunch.
He has not been seen in any of the locations where he
usually sleeps, and has not been in good health.

Logged by: PC Sandy Wilson

THAMES VALLEY POLICE
Missing Person Report

Date: 3 January 2018

Name: Jonathan Eldridge

D.O.B.   18/04/1976

Address: 88 Moffat Way, Kidlington

Description: Medium height and build, dark
                          hair (balding), brown eyes

Last seen wearing: Tracksuit, running shoes, bumbag

Last seen by: Jenny Eldridge (wife)

Last seen date/location: 3/1/18, Moffat Way, Kidlington,
                          10.30 am

Mr Eldridge is a husband and father with a steady job, and
no pressing financial difficulties. His health is good. He
is a keen runner and was last seen leaving his home on the
morning of 3 January. After he did not return by noon, his
wife became concerned. He had only a phone and house keys
on him. His wallet, car keys and passport remain at the
house. Local hospitals have been checked.

Logged by: PC Anne Shields

THAMES VALLEY POLICE
Missing Person Report

Date: 5 January 2018

Name: Ben Perrie

D.O.B. 02/10/1998

Address: St Peter's College

Description: 6' 2", athletic build, blond
hair, blue/green eyes

Last seen wearing: Dark denim jeans, light-coloured
jacket, red scarf

Last seen by: Maurice Jennings (porter,
St Peter's)

Last seen date/location: 2/1/18, St Peter's lodge, approx. 1 pm

Mr Perrie is a first-year student. He returned to college
immediately after Christmas to study for upcoming
exams. He had not been having any problems academically
and his tutor says he showed no sign of anxiety. He had,
however, recently broken up with his girlfriend. His
parents have been informed, as have the police in Hartle-
pool (his home address).

Logged by: PC Sandy Wilson

I skim-read the three sheets, then read them again just
to be sure, but it's pretty obvious Davy's absent friend is
not a MissPers. Not officially anyway. The student's the
wrong colouring, and I don't give the homeless guy very
good odds in this weather. It was minus five last night.

The happily married man is more of an enigma. Looks like he just did a runner. Literally. But we'll probably never know. This job is like that. Like I said before, don't become a copper if you want to know What Happened In The End.

'So he's not there?' says Davy, reading my face.

'No. But a lot of people are still away. It could be a while yet before it becomes clear someone's not where they're supposed to be.'

And yes, I'm acutely aware that I've just described my own wife.

I hand the sheets back to Woods. 'I think we should log this one, Sergeant. Can you take the full details from Mr Jones?'

Woods sighs. 'If you say so, sir.'

The door swings open behind me and reception is suddenly thronged with people – half a busload of American tourists clamouring for directions. But I should thank them, because the extra time it takes me to get through the crowd means I'm still in earshot when Woods asks his next question.

'So what's this friend of yours called, Mr Jones?'

*   *   *

23 December 2017, 3.12 p.m.
12 days before the fire
23 Southey Road, Oxford

Downstairs, Sam can hear the sound of voices. Her sons, and Harry, who's having the usual skirmish getting them into coats

288

and hats and mittens. They're going to the Christingle service at St Margaret's. She'd asked Michael if he wanted to come too but he said it would be hypocritical. He doesn't believe in God. 'Not a God that behaves like this one, anyway.' He had an odd look in his eyes as he said it and she hadn't pushed him, though she has no idea what he meant. He's been like this for days. Not just pre-occupied but watchful. Watching. But now, at least, he can't. She's alone. She needs to be. For this. She doesn't want him getting even the slightest hint of it.

She locks the bathroom door and gets the packet out from where she hid it under the clean towels. Her cycle has been off the last few months and she doesn't really think there's any chance – after all, she and Michael have hardly even –

She puts the plastic stick on the shelf and turns away, willing herself not to fixate on it. She washes her hands and applies hand cream, then checks her make-up in the mirror.

There's the sound of feet on the landing outside, and Zachary starts banging on the door. *'Mummy! Mummy!* Where are you?'

She reaches for the stick. 'I'll be out in a second, sweet pea.'

When she comes down the stairs ten minutes later her face is so white Harry asks if she's seen a ghost. She gives a bitter little laugh. 'The ghost of Christmas future, you mean?'

'You sure you're OK?' he says then, unsettled by her tone. 'I can take them on my own if you don't feel up to it.'

She shakes her head. 'No, I'm fine. Just something I need to sort out.'

* * *

Twenty minutes later I'm back upstairs in the incident room.

'So this bloke that Davy whatsisname was seeing is the same one Michael Esmond was calling at the back end of last year?' It's Gislingham, still processing what I've just told them.

'The one Esmond logged in his phone as "Harry". That's right. His full name is Harry Brown.'

'And they're definitely one and the same person?'

'No question. It's the identical mobile number.'

'Actually, I wanted to talk to you about the phone, boss,' says Quinn quickly. 'I've been looking at that footage again – the CCTV from Brighton station. I didn't notice it before but when Esmond comes back for the train just before six he's got something with him he didn't have when he arrived.'

'Which was?'

'A carrier bag. From Carphone Warehouse.'

He stops, waiting for the reaction he knows he's going to get.

'What,' says Baxter, 'Esmond bought himself another phone? *That afternoon?*'

Quinn nods. 'So then I had another look at Harry's phone records. He got a call the night of the fire from another pay-as-you-go mobile. It was just after nine o'clock. And while *he* was in Oxford, the *caller* was somewhere near Haywards Heath.'

He doesn't need to spell it out. It was Esmond, stuck on a train behind the derailment. Desperate, for reasons we still don't understand, to speak to Harry. So desperate, in fact, that he bought another phone rather than waiting to see if his was handed in. And whatever those reasons were, they're connected with that visit to Brighton. Because he could have bought another phone in London, when he realized he'd lost his, but he didn't. It was only after those two hours he spent in Brighton that the need to make that call became so urgent.

'Has Esmond used that phone since?'

Quinn shakes his head. 'Nothing since that call.'

'This Davy character, boss – does he know where Harry was living?' asks Gislingham.

I shake my head. 'They never went to his place. Davy says he got the impression there was someone else in his life, and that was probably the reason. A live-in lover, maybe even a husband.'

'Or someone else's,' says Ev darkly. 'Samantha Esmond's, for instance.'

'There's something else too,' I continue. 'Davy says he met Harry at the bar where he was working in Summertown. But later he told him he was also doing a bit of gardening on the side for extra cash.'

Realization dawns. Somer first, then the others.

'So *that's* the link,' says Ev. 'Harry was doing the Esmonds' garden. The neighbours said there was someone. We just didn't make the connection.'

I nod. 'Right. But we can easily confirm it one way or the other.' I go over to the board and pin up a picture of Harry Brown, then turn to Gis. 'Speak to the Youngs again. Ask them if they recognize this man. Ev, can you pick up on the bar in Summertown – it's the Volterra on South Parade. See what the staff can tell us about him. And Quinn?'

'Boss?'

'That was excellent, lateral-thinking detective work. Keep it up.'

2 January 2018, 8.30 a.m.
Two days before the fire
23 Southey Road, Oxford

'You're going to miss that train at this rate,' calls Michael, checking his watch. He's standing at the bottom of the stairs, surrounded by holdalls and carrier bags. Matty has been waiting for at least ten minutes. They can hear Zachary whining upstairs.

'Mum said I shouldn't wear my Arsenal scarf,' he says sullenly.

'Well, it might not be a great idea, not in Liverpool. They're pretty proud of their own team up there.'

'Here we are,' says Sam, coming down the stairs with Zachary on her hip, still grizzling.

'Is everything OK? You were ages up there.'

He scans her face, wondering when she's going to tell him. *If* she's going to tell him. She'd wrapped the pregnancy test in a wodge of toilet paper and stuffed it in the bottom of the bin but he found it all the same. Because he can read her like a book and he knew there was something. Something she was keeping from him.

'There's enough stuff here for half a dozen kids,' he says, eyeing the baggage. 'Just as well you only have two.' He keeps his voice light but she doesn't meet his gaze, doesn't take the bait.

'You know what it's like,' she says distractedly. 'You always need three times more than you think. Right,' she says, turning to Matty, 'are we all set for our pirate adventure?'

Michael loads the luggage into the car as she straps Zachary into the child seat.

'Remember, you'll have to get a cab on the way home. I doubt I'll be back before you, and in any case, the car will still be in the garage.'

'It's fine,' she says, closing the door and getting into the front. 'We like black cabs, don't we, Matty?'

'They make a funny noise,' he replies. 'Like a Dalek.'

Michael gets in and puts the key in the ignition.

'Have you got everything for your presentation?' she says brightly, eyeing her husband.

'Yes, it's all sorted.'

'And that meeting with Professor Jordan, when was that again?'

'Ten fifteen. But it's nothing. Just routine admin stuff.'

She turns to pull on her seat belt.

'I'm sure your talk will be brilliant. They always are. Give me a call to let me know how it goes.'

'Oh, I meant to mention – on that score, don't worry if you can't get me on the mobile. I'll probably be in the library quite a lot of the time.'

She frowns. 'I thought you said the talk was all sorted?'

'It is,' he says, starting the engine. 'This is something else. Something I need to check.'

* * *

All in all, Quinn tells himself as he walks down the corridor, that went as well as it was probably ever going to. And at least he's shown some initiative. Some smarts. Which is more than he can say of the rest of them, right now. Who knows, perhaps he might make it back to DS after all.

When his mobile rings ten minutes later he's in two minds whether to answer it at all. He stares at it for four rings, then heaves a heavy sigh and sits back in his chair.

'Quinn here.'

'DC Quinn? It's PC Kumar.'

'Yeah. I know that,' says Quinn, making a face at the phone.

'I had half an hour spare so I took another look at that area where we last spotted your suspect.'

Quinn starts doodling on his pad. 'Thought you said it was just residential?'

'Ah, but that's just the point.'

'Sorry – not with you.'

'One of the buildings further along that street is a residential care home. Fair Lawns, it's called.'

'So you think –'

Kumar's excitement is obvious now. 'I don't think. I *know*.'

* * *

Sent: Fri 19/01/2018, 13.28   **Importance: High**
From: AlanChallowCSI@ThamesValley.police.uk
To: DIAdamFawley@ThamesValley.police.uk,
          CID@ThamesValley.police.uk

Subject: DNA results: Case no 556432/12 Felix House, 23 Southey Road

Those DNA results you wanted a rush on: we've compared the sample from Philip Esmond to the DNA extracted from the male corpse at Southey Road. As you know, familial identification isn't as clear-cut as a simple yes or no, but in this case the results are entirely consistent with the two men being brothers.

* * *

Quinn's carefully crafted persona is way too suave to do urgent, so when he comes hurtling into my office without even knocking I know something's really up.

'I know where Esmond went,' he says, slightly out of breath. 'In Brighton. It was an old people's home. Fair Lawns. His name isn't on the visitor log for that day, but when we emailed over a picture of him the staff recognized him at once. He was visiting an old lady by the name of Muriel Fraser. Claimed he was her nephew or something but we know for a fact he isn't.'

'So if she's not his aunt, what the hell was he doing there?'

'I haven't turned up any connection yet. But the staff at the home say she definitely knew him.'

I'm on my feet already. 'Get Asante to phone through. Tell them we're on our way.'

* * *

2 January 2018, 10.45 a.m.
Two days before the fire
CrossCountry train service, just outside Birmingham

'Is there anything I can do to help?'

The woman in the tartan coat means well but, right now, the last thing Samantha wants is more attention. Zachary has been screaming at the top of his voice for twenty minutes and the carriage is crowded. The surreptitious looks have become openly hostile. Several people have taken to earphones. She can hear their voices in her head. *Can't she control that brat? You shouldn't bring kids on trains unless they know how to behave.*

'I'm sorry,' she says to the woman in tartan, raising her voice loud enough for the rest of them to hear. 'He has a tummy ache and I can't remember which bag I put the Calpol in.' There's one holdall open at her feet and another squashed beside her, but just her luck, it's in neither. 'It must be in the one on the rack.'

Matty is hunched in the window seat, staring out at the dull landscape. He looks wretchedly embarrassed, as only ten-year-olds can.

'Do you want some juice, Zachary?' says Sam. He's twisting and writhing, his face red and blotchy. He shakes his head vehemently, squeezing his eyes shut.

'I'm getting off at Birmingham,' says the woman, 'but do you want me to take him for a minute while you get his medicine?'

'Oh, would you?' says Sam in a gush of relief. 'I'll be really quick.'

She lifts the screeching Zachary and manages to get him on to the woman's lap, though she gets a kick in the neck in the process.

'Oh dear,' says the woman, struggling to keep hold of the little boy. 'Are you all right?'

'It's nothing,' Sam says quickly. 'Happens all the time.'

She reaches up to the bag and pulls it down on to the seat, then starts to dig about in it. The train lurches and judders as it starts to slow down, and suddenly the woman opposite lets out a strangled cry.

Zachary has been sick all over her.

* * *

Judging by what Somer told me, Fair Lawns is a world away from the home where Michael Esmond put his mother. You could get them under trade descriptions for the 'lawns' for a start: there's asphalt on every flat surface. Tired 1970s architecture, and that nasty textured glass in the front door. It reminds me horribly of where my grandmother ended up. I used to dread being dragged there once a month as a child, sitting for the required hour and a half while my father said the same things he said the previous time, in a terrifying bright and happy voice. Even now, I can't bear the smell of disinfectant.

Quinn locks the car door and heads off to reception. He seems intent on proving to me just how efficient he can be and, hey, I'm not complaining.

The young woman on the desk has a heavy East European accent. Romanian, if I had to guess. She also has perfect skin and small, exquisite features that must have the old ladies yearning for their past youth, but Quinn seems determined to be Mr Professional. He doesn't even smile when he introduces himself.

'DC Quinn, DI Fawley, Thames Valley Police. To see Muriel Fraser?'

'Ah yes,' she says. 'We spoke to your office. Please come this way.'

Mrs Fraser is having one of her good days, she tells us, as we follow her down the corridor, but all the same we shouldn't expect too much. 'She is ninety-seven, after all.'

She leaves us with the care assistant in the 'lounge', who's serving tea from the sort of trolley I haven't seen since I was

297

a constable. She's much older than the receptionist – one of those competent motherly types we must all be thankful are prepared to work for minimum wage in places like this. *Jeremy Kyle* is on full volume in the corner and the newspapers are untouched on the coffee table. One old chap has a chessboard on a table in front of him and a book about the Spassky/Fischer world championship open in one hand. I don't want to think about the state of his inner life.

'Mrs Fraser's long-term memory is still pretty good,' says the assistant. 'Though she struggles with more day-to-day things. But she really is a sweet lady.' She smiles. 'One of the easy ones. Never complains.'

Muriel is in a chair by the window, hunched up against a cushion, her thin arms shrunk into a baggy sugar-pink cardigan.

'You made that cardi yourself, didn't you, Muriel?' says the assistant kindly, seeing me looking at it. 'Though her knitting days are long gone now, I'm afraid.'

She reaches down to pat Muriel's clawed-up brown hands and the old lady smiles up at her.

'You have some visitors, Muriel. Two nice gentlemen from the police.'

The old lady's eyes widen and she stares first at Quinn and then at me.

'Nothing to worry about, lovey. They just want to check a few things with you.' Then she pats Muriel's hand again. 'I'll see about getting you all some tea.'

We pull up the hard plastic visitor chairs and sit down.

'I think you had someone else come to see you recently, didn't you, Mrs Fraser?' asks Quinn.

She smiles at him. I think there's even the ghost of a wink. 'I'm not completely gaga, you know. It was that Esmond boy.'

In the background, Jeremy Kyle is losing his patience. *'It's a simple enough question. Did you sleep with her or didn't you?'*

Quinn sits forward, clearly startled to have got so far so fast.

'That's right,' he says. 'How do you know him?'

'He's Jenny's boyfriend.' She folds her hands then, disapproving. 'Or *was*.'

Quinn and I exchange a glance. Jenny. The girlfriend Philip mentioned. The one Michael Esmond dumped when he went on his shag spree.

'And remind me, who is Jenny?' I ask, keeping my voice light.

'My granddaughter, of course. Ella's girl. Though why she took it into her head to marry that horrible man I'll never know.'

'Jenny?'

'No,' she says, clearly impatient with my stupidity. *'Ella.'*

'Jenny went to school in Oxford, didn't she?'

Her chin lifts. 'That's right. She goes to the Griffin. It's supposed to be a very good school. Very expensive, that I do know.'

I've seen this before. With my grandmother, with other old people as frail as this. The past is blurring with the present: Jenny can't have been at that school for more than twenty years.

'They say it's a punishment,' she says suddenly. Loudly. The assistant looks up from the other side of the room. 'They keep telling her that she *deserves* it. Even brought in a damn *priest* to tell her so.'

Quinn glances across at me, but I shrug; I've no more idea than he does.

'What did she do, Mrs Fraser? Why does she need to be punished?'

Muriel makes no attempt to conceal her disdain. '*She* didn't do anything. It isn't *her* fault, whatever they say.'

Quinn waves a finger at his ear and mouths, '*Gaga.*' Muriel doesn't see him do it, but the assistant does. He gathers his papers and makes to get up, but I catch his eye and stop him. There's something here, I'm sure of it.

'So whose fault was it, Mrs Fraser?'

'*His*, of course. That Esmond boy.' And all at once the pieces shift into place.

I can feel the sweat trickling down my back. I've got far too many layers on for this place. The heating is on full blast. On the TV, tempers are fraying. '*I'm not the father of that kid – take any test you like – it ain't mine.*'

Muriel sits back again, her lips pursed together. 'Of course, he *claims* he didn't know anything about it. Well, he would say that, wouldn't he. The nasty little shit.'

Quinn smiles, despite himself.

I take one of her agitating hands and force her to look at me. 'That's what Michael said, was it, when he came to see you? That he hadn't known about the pregnancy?'

'But I know for a fact she wrote and told him.'

Quinn is taking furious notes. 'So she kept the baby – she's going to bring it up herself?'

'Not *it*. *Him*.' She smiles, immersed in memory. 'Such a beautiful child. He has her eyes. I told her – he'll be a charmer when he grows up, just you wait and see.'

'How are you all doing?' says the care assistant, bustling up with cups of tea. 'Do you think you'll be much longer, Inspector? Only I think Muriel's getting a bit tired now. We don't want to overdo it, do we?'

* * *

2 January 2018, 11.16 a.m.
Two days before the fire
Ladies' lavatories, Birmingham New Street station

'But I want to see the pirates! You *promised*! For my *birthday*!'

'Please be quiet, Matty. I'm trying to clean this poor lady up.' Sam pulls out another wet wipe and has another go at the sick stain on the tartan coat, but all she seems to be achieving is spreading it even further. The woman is fussing, 'It's really all right, you mustn't go to all this trouble – you need to continue your journey.'

'We do, Mummy,' says Matty quickly. 'If we don't get on the train we're going to miss the pirates!'

Sam glances at Zachary. He's sitting on the side of the sink, leaning against the tiles. He's silent now but he looks miserable. He's been sick twice since they got off the train.

She turns to Matty and bends to his level. 'I'm afraid we can't go to the pirates, Matty. Zachary is too unwell. We need to take him home.'

Matty's face crumples into a wail. 'But *you promised*!' he says.

'He can't help being ill, Matty –' she begins but he's stamping his foot.

'You said it was *my* treat – for *me*. For my *birthday*. Not for Zachary – for *me*!'

'I think I'll be on my way now,' says the woman, edging towards the door. 'You have your hands full without worrying about me.'

'I'm so sorry again,' begins Sam, taking a step towards her. 'He really didn't mean it.'

'That's what you *always* say,' says Matty as the door bangs closed behind her. 'You *always* say Zachary doesn't mean bad things to happen, but they *always do*. Like he didn't mean to kill Mollie but he still *did*.'

'Ssh,' she says quickly, wondering who might be overhearing. Overhearing and misconstruing. 'We can play pirates when we get home. Just you and me. You'd like that, wouldn't you?'

'You said you'd take me to the *real* pirates. I'm never going to see them now. Never. It's not *fair*!'

Her heart breaks, he looks so forlorn. And he's right. It's not fair. It's his birthday treat and she'd wanted it to be special and now it's all spoiled. She knows how badly injustice burns. Because there's nothing you can do to mend it.

She reaches out again and tries to hug him but he pushes her violently away. '*Leave me alone!* I hate you! I hate Zachary and I hate *you*. I don't care that he's ill – I wish he was *dead*!'

* * *

Out in the car, I realize I have a text from Baxter.

> Still can't find a Harry or Harold Brown. Doesn't help Brown is such a common name. But I'll keep looking.

> Mother's name is Jennifer, if that helps.

I send the text and turn to Quinn. He's on the phone. To the Griffin School.

'Make it three years either side just in case,' he says. 'You can send it now? Fabulous. Thanks.' He finishes the call. 'They're emailing me their school roll for when Esmond was in the sixth form.' He shifts in his seat so he can look at me more easily. 'So Michael got his girlfriend pregnant.'

I nod. 'And Harry was the result. It fits. He's the right age, similar colouring.'

'So what's the theory? He turns up on the doorstep last summer, announces he's the long-lost son and Michael gives him a job doing the garden?'

He's right to be sceptical. I don't think that adds up either.

'No,' I say slowly, 'I don't think Michael even knew he had another child. From what Muriel said, he must have known Jenny was pregnant, but he may well have thought she'd had an abortion. She may even have told him that.'

'And you don't think this Harry told him who he was either? Seriously?'

'What would you do if someone appeared out of the blue and claimed to be your child?'

With the sexual history Quinn has, this could be a lot more than hypothetical one day, which may account for the speed of his reply.

'Get a DNA test,' he says at once.

'Right. Only there's nothing remotely like that on Esmond's credit card or email records.'

He considers. 'Those sites always claim to be 100 per cent discreet.'

'Yes, but you can't pay them with cash, can you? There'd be *something* on the credit card, even if it was under some sort of anonymous corporate name.'

He nods. 'And if there was, Baxter would have found it. So – what? Harry was just checking him out? Sussing out the lie of the land before he did his big reveal?'

'Possibly. Only something must have happened – something that made Michael suspect who he really was. That's why he came down here. He knew that if Jenny really had gone through with the pregnancy, her grandmother would know.'

Quinn turns to look back at the building. 'Wonder why he went for the doolally granny, though? Must be someone else in the family he could have asked.'

Quinn has a genius for getting up my nose. But he does have a point.

There's a ping on his tablet and he opens the email. 'It's the list from the Griffin.'

He scrolls down, then back again. 'No Jennifer. No Jenny. Bollocks.' He sits back in his seat. 'We should go back in there and ask the old dear for the surname. She didn't look that bloody tired to me.'

I hold out my hand. 'Can I see?'

He passes me the tablet, clearly irritated that I don't trust him to have checked properly. But there was something in what he just said – something Muriel mentioned – I may be wrong –

But I'm not. That'll teach me to listen to what people actually *say*. Not just what I'm expecting to hear. I point at the screen. 'This girl – here – I think it's her. Ginevra Marrone. It wasn't *Jenny* Michael was seeing, it was *Ginny*.'

Quinn takes the tablet. 'Right,' he says after a moment. 'And she's in the list for 1995, but disappears after that.'

Because she got pregnant. Because she had Michael Esmond's baby.

'So she's, what, Spanish?'

'Italian would be my guess. It's an Italian name.'

He nods. 'So that explains why Michael came down here. Because the rest of the family –'

'– went back to Italy. Right. Presumably that's why Ginevra never returned to the school. And remember what Muriel said about a priest. I can well imagine how a traditional Italian family would have reacted to their unmarried teenage daughter getting pregnant. And this was twenty years ago, remember.'

'Not just teenage, boss,' says Quinn, looking at the list again. 'Ginevra Marrone was in Year 11 in 1995. We won't know for sure until we track down Harry's birth certificate but I reckon she could have been as young as fifteen.'

So not just unmarried but underage.

Quinn sits back. 'Jesus. First the harassment allegation and now this. No wonder Esmond was bricking it.' He turns to me. 'Do you think that was what the two grand was for? This Harry bloke was blackmailing him?

Threatening to go public if he didn't pay up? It would explain why he took out the money in cash.'

I'm not so sure. 'The sequence is wrong, isn't it? He'd have spoken to Muriel before he handed over any money. *And* done a DNA test.'

But Quinn is right too: the money still doesn't fit.

'Though there's one thing all this does explain,' I say, getting out my phone again, 'and that's why Baxter can't find anyone called Harold Brown. I don't think that's Harry's real name at all.' Because I've remembered now how Gislingham tracked down Jurjen Kuiper online. And didn't Alex once joke with me that Giuseppe Verdi would have sounded a lot less glamorous if he'd been plain English Joe Green?

It takes point nothing of a nanosecond on Google to prove I'm right. All those trips to Italy – I must have picked up something after all. I switch to the phone screen and dial the number. 'Baxter? It's Fawley. The man you're searching for isn't called Brown. His mother's name is *Marrone* – it's the Italian word for Brown. He's using the English version of his Italian name, and I bet he's doing exactly the same thing with his first name too. If I'm right, the person you need to be looking for is called *Araldo Marrone*.'

* * *

Even though it's barely five minutes from her front door, Everett has never actually been inside the Volterra bar. She doesn't own any clothes she could possibly wear in there, for a start, and as far as she's concerned gin is just gin and gives her a headache, as does the idea of trying to choose between fifty-seven different artisan varieties.

At this time of day there's hardly anyone inside. According to the blackboard on the pavement, they serve coffee all day, but the indigo walls and ornate chandeliers have an after-dark feel to them compared to the wholesome coffee shops and brightly lit patisseries round the corner. She makes her way to the bar and glances through the back to where a young man with a large sandy beard and a black shirt and trousers is stacking glasses.

'Can I help you?' he calls.

'DC Everett, Thames Valley Police.'

The young man reaches for a tea towel and comes through to the front. 'What's all this about then?'

She shows him her phone. 'I think you've been employing this man?'

He squints at the picture then nods. 'That's Harry. He's been working here about nine months.'

'When did you last see him?'

The young man frowns. 'Why – what's going on?'

'Just answer the question, please.'

He considers. 'New Year's, I think. Yup, that would've been it.'

'Was he due to be working since then?'

'Not sure. I don't do the rotas. But you could ask Josh. He's the manager.'

Everett takes down the mobile number. 'What's he like, this Harry?' she asks, closing her notebook.

The young man shrugs. 'He's a good barman. Knows his drinks, knows his punters.'

Ev's eyes narrow. 'What do you mean by that?'

'Oh, you know. He can read people. The ones who

307

want to be left alone. The ones who want a shoulder to cry on. The ones who want to flirt.'

'He does a lot of that, does he? Flirting?'

A dry grin. 'Fuck yes. Women are all over him. Lucky git. I mean, looking like that, he has his pick.'

Ev frowns. 'I thought he was gay?'

The young man gives a bark of laughter. '*Gay?* Harry's not gay. Where'd you get that from?'

'Sorry, must have got my wires crossed.'

He's still smiling. 'Take it from me, he is *not* gay. I caught him once, in the back room, with a girl. One of the punters. And believe me, they weren't discussing the bloody weather.'

'Right,' says Everett, more than a little nonplussed but endeavouring not to show it. 'And is there anyone special, do you know – an actual girlfriend?'

'Not that he talked about – at least, he never mentioned a name. Though I got the impression there could have been someone, the last month or so. But he was pretty cagey about it.'

'And this Josh, the manager. He'll have an address for him, will he?'

The young man shrugs. '*An* address, yes, but Harry's been moving round a bit so it may not be up to date. I know he was dossing with a mate for a while, and after that he was at that youth hostel on the Botley Road.'

Bugger, thinks Ev. Why didn't we think of that? We were parked virtually on top of the place.

The door opens and a couple of girls come in, laughing and looking at something on their phones. The young man glances across at them and then at Everett.

'Like I said,' he says quickly, 'I'm pretty sure he's not there any more. Last time I saw him he said he was going to be moving.'

'You don't know where?'

'Nope,' he says, picking up some drinks menus from the counter, 'but I think it was somewhere round here – somewhere decent too. I reckoned someone must have died.'

Ev stares at him. 'Say that again.'

He flushes a little. 'You know – he was getting some sort of legacy. He definitely said something about "getting what I'm due". I suppose that's why I wasn't surprised I haven't seen him. He probably doesn't need to bother with crappy bar work any more, the lucky bastard.'

* * *

2 January 2018, 3.09 p.m.
Two days before the fire
23 Southey Road, Oxford

Samantha shunts the front door closed behind her and drops the bags where she's standing. She's suddenly and overwhelmingly exhausted. She can hear Zachary careering about upstairs, shouting at the top of his voice. You wouldn't think there'd ever been anything wrong with him. He spent the last half hour of the journey back jumping up and down on her lap saying he wanted to play pirates. She knows he didn't mean to be tactless, but it was just about the last thing Matty needed to hear. He, by contrast, sat silent and pale the whole way, staring out of the window. Every time she tried to speak to him he just blanked her. She's seen him sulk before but this is different. He's never been this sullen, this locked in. And it's the first time he's ever spoken about what happened to the dog.

She goes into the kitchen to find him taking a juice from the fridge. He bangs the door shut and swerves past her, head down, not meeting her eye.

'Harry should be coming tomorrow,' she says quickly as he reaches the door, painfully conscious how desperate she sounds. 'I asked him to pop in while we were away. He was going to fix that tap in the bathroom but, if you like, he can help you with your volcano project instead.'

Matty still has his back to her.

'You'd like that, wouldn't you?'

She stands there, willing him to turn round, willing him to say something.

Then Zachary comes racing in. He has a plastic sword in one hand and a black patch lopsided over one eye. *'Nyah, nyah, nyah!'* he screams, banging the sword against Sam's legs. 'I'm the evil pirate, I'm the evil pirate!'

When she looks up, Matty is gone.

* * *

Sent: Fri 19/01/2018, 17.12   **Importance: High**
From: DCEricaSomer@ThamesValley.police.uk
To: DIAdamFawley@ThamesValley.police.uk,
           CID@ThamesValley.police.uk

Subject: Case no 556432/12 Felix House, 23 Southey Road

Baxter says to tell you there's still no activity on Harry's mobile, and the address Ev got from the bar came up empty as well – they haven't seen him for a couple of weeks. We're seeing if we can find any other way of tracking him down.

And I've spoken to Rotherham Fleming again and they're still refusing to divulge anything about the Esmonds without a court order. However, they did confirm that there's nothing in the wording to preclude illegitimate children from inheriting under the will. If Harry can prove he is definitely Michael's son he will be entitled to his share of the proceeds of the sale of the property and any insurance money. But that's only because clause five has been fulfilled. If the house had remained standing, as the child of the younger son he wouldn't have been entitled to anything.

* * *

'Fuck,' says Quinn, when I read out the email to him. We've just joined the M25 and the traffic is nose to tail. Friday evening; we should have known.

'That gives him a shit-load of motive, doesn't it? I mean, not just to burn the house down but to get rid of Michael *and* his kids at the same time. With them out of the way there's a hell of a lot more cash for him.'

The traffic edges forward and comes to a halt again.

'So he arranges to meet Esmond at the house that night, knocks him out cold, then sets the house on fire. I mean, let's face it, if anyone knew where that bloody petrol was it was him. He'd been mowing the sodding lawn all summer.'

Someone behind us is sounding their horn.

'*And* he probably knew Esmond was under pressure. Wouldn't have been hard to pick up on that if he was there all the time. He'd have known it was odds on everyone would assume Esmond set the fire himself – that everything had just got too much. I mean, even *we* did, didn't we?'

He glances across at me, wondering why I'm saying nothing. But I'm trying to think. Because yes, what Quinn is saying works in theory, but my copper's instinct isn't there – not yet anyway. You'd have to be one hell of a callous bastard to even consider doing something like that, far less carry it out, but then again we don't know he's not. We don't know the first thing about him.

I take a deep breath. 'It was Esmond who called Harry that night, not the other way round.'

Quinn shrugs. So what?

'And your theory only works if Harry knew about the will. He needed to have known he'd only be in line for the cash if the house had to be demolished. Otherwise the arson makes no sense.'

'Yeah,' says Quinn, signalling and moving out into the fast lane. Which is moving barely faster than we are, but patience never has been one of his key personal competencies. 'Well, if you ask me, he *did* know. Like I said, he's been in and out of that house for months; he might even have had a key. He could easily have got into that office and found that will, just like I did.'

I get out my phone.

'Who are you calling?'

'Philip Esmond. If Michael knew who Harry really was, his brother is the one person he might have told.'

'And Philip didn't think to tell *us*?'

'Well, you know what it's like,' I say grimly. 'Families. Families and secrets.'

* * *

Telephone interview with Philip Esmond, 19 January 2018, 5.45 p.m.
On the call, DI A. Fawley

AF: Mr Esmond? Sorry to bother you again. Do you have a minute?

PE: Sure. What is it?

AF: I'm afraid there's no easy way to raise this, but did you know your brother got a girl pregnant when he was still at the Griffin School?

PE: No I didn't. *Of course I didn't* – I'd have told you.

AF: Isn't it possible you were in Australia at the time?

PE: I'd still have known. My parents would have hit the bloody roof for a start – there's no way they could have kept that quiet.

AF: You said you remembered a girlfriend of his called Jenny.

PE: Yes, I told you that.

AF: It seems it was Ginny, not Jenny. Her father was Italian.

PE: If you say so. I don't remember her having any sort of accent. But like you said, I was in Australia most of that year. So it was her, was it – she was the one he got pregnant?

AF: We believe she went through with the
pregnancy, though your brother may have
thought she'd had a termination. He had
another child. One he knew nothing about.

PE: Fuck.

AF: We believe this child came to Oxford last
summer and met your brother. What we *don't*
know is whether they told Michael who they
really were. We thought he might have talked
to you about it. If that had happened.

PE: Absolutely not. Like I said – this is all news
to me. Mike didn't say a word. I mean, he was
a bit stressed but shit, I had no idea –

AF: Do you think he would have done? If he was
faced with a situation like that – if someone
had turned up claiming to be his child –
would he have talked to you about it?

PE: [*sighs*]
I honestly don't know. I'd like to think so,
but like I've said before, we weren't that
close. Not since we were kids.

AF: Thank you, Mr Esmond. I think that's all for
now. I expect you'll be wanting to speak to
your solicitor.

PE: My *solicitor*?

AF: This long-lost child. They will have a claim
on the estate, under the terms of the will.
Assuming they can prove who they are.

PE: [*pause*]
Fuck. Of course. I didn't think.

AF: As I said, I won't take up any more of your time –

314

PE: Hang on a minute. This child – doesn't that
     mean he – she – has a motive? You know – for
     burning down the house? Christ, even –

AF: For murder? Yes, we will certainly be looking
     into that.

PE: [*quickly*]
     But that means Mike may not have killed them
     after all, right? Sam and the kids? It may have
     been this – this *person* – instead. *He* might
     have killed them – he might have killed *Mike* –

AF: As I said, we need to examine this new
     information and decide whether we can
     eliminate this person from our enquiries. We
     haven't been able to speak to them as yet, so
     it's all guesswork at the moment. But please
     don't get your hopes up. I know why you'd want
     to exonerate your brother but we have a long
     way to go yet.

PE: Yes, yes, I know. But it is *possible*, isn't it?
     That *is* what you're saying?

AF: [*pause*]
     Yes. It is possible.

* * *

When the phone rings Gislingham and Baxter are the
only ones still left in the incident room, and Gis is on his
feet with one arm in his coat.

'CID,' he says, wedging the receiver under his ear.

'Is DC Somer there?'

Gis knows the voice, but he can't immediately place it.

'It's Giles Saumarez. Hants Police.'

Gis makes a face at the phone. What's this tosser up to now? 'Sorry, she's gone home already.' He hesitates, then thinks, bugger it. 'I think she had a hot date. Friday night and all that.'

But even Gis has to concede that Saumarez doesn't miss a beat.

'No worries. Can you leave her a message? That tramp she had a close encounter with – Tristram? We got him dried out and charged him with the damage to the hut, but he's swearing black is white it wasn't him. Says it was already like that when he got there.' A pause. 'Just thought you guys would want to know.'

'Great,' says Gislingham, 'I'm sure "us guys" are very grateful.'

Even though Saumarez is still talking he cuts short the call and heads for the door. 'Don't work too hard,' he calls over his shoulder.

'Yeah, right,' mutters Baxter as the door swings to behind him.

* * *

'I agree. It could well have happened that way.'

I'm in Gow's office. He's moving around, collecting papers, putting them into his laptop bag, pulling files off the shelf.

'Sorry about this,' he says distractedly. 'I'm off to Cardiff in the morning for a conference. Another bloody Marriott hotel. It would only be natural for this young man – Harry, Harold or whatever his name is – to have a deep antipathy to the man who abandoned his mother. Whatever version of the past he's been told over the years, Michael Esmond isn't likely to have come off very well. And you know as well as I do that childhood resentments go very deep, regardless of whether they have a basis in objective fact.'

That one goes painfully close to home. But Gow's not to know. It's not the sort of thing I talk about.

Gow puts another file in his bag. 'And when he grows up and comes over here to track his father down he finds him sitting on what appears to be a mountain of money, none of which is being shared with him.'

'And if his own upbringing had been less than affluent –'

'Right. You can easily see him deciding that it was high time the truth came out. High time he got his fair share.'

'But even granting all of that, to go from there to burning down a house where two children were sleeping – two children he *knew* – who were his own half-*brothers*?'

Gow shrugs. 'One of the great advantages of arson is that you don't have to look your victims in the face,' he says drily.

He takes one last look around his office. 'I think that's it. Give me a call if you need anything else. And let me know when you do finally track down Signor Marrone. I'd rather like to observe.'

* * *

3 January 2018, 5.59 p.m.
Six hours before the fire
23 Southey Road, Oxford

'It's so boring. *He's* so boring. He spoils *everything*.'

Matty is sitting on the edge of his bed. Harry is next to him. Matty is close to tears.

Harry reaches out and puts a hand lightly on the boy's shoulder. 'Hey, give him a chance,' he says softly. 'I know he can be a bit irritating, but he doesn't mean it. He's only little. He doesn't realize.'

'Everyone *always* says that. It's *boring*.'

'I know. But it's true. That's how it is. For all big brothers.'

'I *hate* him. I wish he was dead and it would be like it was before. Mum loved me then.'

Harry moves a little closer. 'She still does,' he says kindly. 'She really does.'

'She never talks to me any more. Not like before.'

'She's a bit sad, that's all. But she's trying really hard to get better.'

Matty looks up at him, blinking away the tears. 'I wish I had a big brother. One like you.'

Harry ruffles his hair. 'I'd like that too. But families are funny things. You never know who you might find one day.'

'What do you mean? I don't understand.'

Harry shakes his head gently. 'Nothing. Forget I said it.'

Downstairs in the hall, the grandfather clock begins to strike the hour.

'So where's this volcano thing then? The one your mum told me about? Only I saw something on the internet where they made lava out of baking soda and vinegar. It looked really cool.'

Matty is staring at his feet, kicking them against the base of the bed.

'Matt?'

'It's downstairs,' he says in a small voice, 'on the dining table. If Zachary hasn't ruined it.'

Harry gets to his feet. 'Shall we go down then? See if your mum has any baking soda?'

Matty shrugs. There are tears now, spilling over and sliding down his cheeks.

Harry bends quickly and gathers the boy in his arms, hugging him tightly. 'It's OK,' he whispers into his hair. 'I'm not going anywhere. It's going to be OK. You'll see.'

*　*　*

'Can I have a quick word, sir?'

'Of course, Adam. Take a seat.'

Harrison is looking unusually chipper. No doubt relieved to have got the University suits off his back.

'It's the Southey Road case, sir. There's been a new development.'

It doesn't take long, and when I've finished he's looking a good deal less perky.

'So you want to issue a statement saying we've concluded that it was a murder-suicide, even though we haven't concluded anything of the kind?'

'We're struggling to find him –'

'This – what was it – Araldo?'

'Araldo Marrone. That's definitely his surname, and Araldo is the Italian version of Harold so that's a reasonable working assumption. The problem is that we think the family went back to Italy so he was in all likelihood born there and we're struggling to get any birth records out of the Italian authorities.'

Harrison glances at his watch. 'Gone seven on a Friday night? I should say you were.'

'I don't want to run the risk of leaving it till Monday. And frankly, even if we do, Baxter isn't convinced the records we need will necessarily be computerized. Not from twenty years ago, anyway.'

'No,' says Harrison heavily, 'I wouldn't put any money on that either.'

I remember a holiday in Italy when people pushed my credit card away like I was trying to con them. And that was the nineties, for God's sake. *'No plastica'* became the running joke of the week.

Harrison, meanwhile, has sat back in his chair. 'So you think if we announce the case is closed this man Marrone will come forward?'

'If he *did* set that fire it was all about the money – about getting his share of the Esmond cash. He can only do that if he makes himself known. But he won't take that risk until he thinks the coast is clear – and that means convincing him we believe Michael Esmond was the culprit.'

'And if he didn't set the fire at all – if Michael Esmond really did do it? I assume you still think that's a possibility?'

'Yes, sir. Unless and until we can rule Marrone out. And we can't do that until we can question him.'

He picks up his pen and starts toying with it. 'I'm not keen on lying to the taxpayer, Adam. Public trust in policing and all that.' He sighs. 'But I suppose there are cases where the end justifies the means.'

'Yes, sir. I think most reasonable people would want us to do everything possible to establish the truth. Especially if that means catching a particularly brutal killer.'

I watch him thinking for a moment, then, 'All right, Adam. Go ahead and issue a statement. Let's just hope it works.'

* * *

BBC Midlands Today

Saturday 20 January 2018 | Last updated at 09:12

Police close case in Oxford house fire

Thames Valley Police confirmed last night that they are no longer seeking anyone else in connection with the fatal house fire in Southey Road on the morning of 4 January. Four members of the Esmond family died as a result of the fire, which is now believed to have been started by Michael Esmond himself, in a form of murder-suicide known to psychologists as 'family annihilation'. Esmond, 40, was an academic at the University's anthropology department. The University has not commented on rumours that Esmond was facing a serious disciplinary procedure, relating to an incident of alleged sexual harassment.

Speaking last night, Detective Inspector Adam Fawley again offered condolences to the victims' family and friends, saying that he hoped they would at least now have a degree of closure. He declined to speculate on reports that the man found at the Southey Road house was still alive when

---

the fire started. He also refused to comment on what might happen with the Southey Road property. Developers are already thought to be interested in the site, which extends to nearly an acre and is located in one of the city's most prestigious residential streets.

* * *

Sunday night. It's been a beautiful day. Clear blue skies, a ghost of warmth in the sun. The first daffodils. On days like this we would walk through Port Meadow and stop at the Perch, or go into town and have lunch in the roof-top restaurant at the Ashmolean. I could have done all of these things today, but I did none of them. It terrifies me – that Alex's absence could ever become that normal. That I could create an existence for myself that doesn't include her. Be someone other than the man she loves. Loved.

My life is on hold. In limbo.

I try to read but I can't seem to get beyond the first page. There's been no response to the statement we issued on Friday. Nothing useful, at least. Property developers and ambulance chasers don't count. I turn on the TV but the news is wall-to-wall Royal Wedding.

When it starts to get dark I go upstairs to draw the curtains. Spare room. Jake's room. Ours. The wardrobe that still contains almost all Alex's clothes (which I'm trying to see as positive), and the Indian wooden box that still holds every piece of jewellery I ever gave her (which I'm determined not to see as less so). The diamond earrings I bought for her fortieth, the grey pearl necklace for our tenth anniversary, the platinum ring I gave her when Jake was born. I had that made by a jeweller on North Parade. A broad plain band engraved with A and A and J entwined together. The three of us. Inseparable. As I thought. As I hoped.

I pick it up and feel the chill of it against my skin and wonder how long it is since she wore it. Whether she took it off when he died, because she couldn't bear the reminder. As if the memories weren't reminder enough. The photographs. The roomful of toys and clothes and games. I turn the ring in my hand, the letters catching the light, superimposed, so it's impossible to tell which comes first –

It's impossible to tell which comes first.

Five minutes later I'm in the car.

* * *

'DI Fawley? Sir?'

I wake with a start, disorientated. And cold. And with a banging headache. I look up into Somer's concerned face. The clock on the wall behind her says 7.09. In the *morning*. How the hell did that happen?

I sit up slowly, feeling the complaints in every joint.

'Are you OK, sir?'

'Yes, I'm fine.'

There appears to be a pizza box and the remains of a six-pack of Becks on the desk in front of me. And a saucer full of cigarette ash. That's not good. I gesture at it all vaguely. 'Er, do you think . . . ?'

'Oh, of course.' She rushes to consign the evidence to the bin and comes back towards me. 'I got the text. About the early meeting.'

I'm standing up now, rubbing the back of my neck. 'I meant to go home first.'

'You have something new, sir?' She's looking around, at the documents and photograph albums from Southey Road strewn haphazard on my desk, at the Post-its, the scrawled notes.

'Yes, I think so. That's why I wanted everyone here.'

She's standing right next to me now, our shoulders almost brushing. And then there's the sound of the door opening and when I turn round – Gislingham.

He stops, registers the state I'm in, the shirt that looks like I slept in it, the sudden flush on Somer's face.

'Fuck,' he stammers, bright red. 'I didn't realize –'

It occurs to me suddenly, with one of those jolts that wake you in the middle of the night, that he might actually think there's something going on between Somer and me. That he might even have been thinking that for quite some time. That he might not be the only one –

Shit.

'I've been here all night,' I say quickly, reddening myself now. 'And as you can see, DC Somer has only just arrived.'

His mouth is open, but nothing's coming out.

'Right,' I say, with as much professionalism as I can muster in my current state. 'I'm going for a shower. Round everyone up, would you, Sergeant?'

*

By the time I get back, the incident room is charged with expectation. At least, that's what I'm hoping it is.

'Right,' I say, walking up to the front and tapping the photo Davy Jones gave us. The picture of Harry, standing in front of the Radcliffe Camera glowing in golden light, hands on his hips, sunglasses slung around his neck. Harry, which we thought was short for Harold. Or I did. Only I think I got that wrong. That's what hit me last night: it isn't just the Royal family where 'Harry' is short for something else entirely.

'This man, who's been going by the name of Harry Brown, is the son of Michael Esmond and Ginevra Marrone, the girl he got pregnant when he was seventeen, and she was only fifteen. We were assuming his Italian first name was Araldo, but I think we were wrong. I think that in his case "Harry" isn't short for Harold, it's short for *Henry*: I think his real name is actually *Enrico* Marrone. And thanks to Esmond's grandfather's will he has an extremely powerful motive to set the fire at the Southey Road house. In fact, given his father was only the younger of the two brothers, burning the house down was the one and only way he *was* going to get his hands on anything.'

I glance around the room. That piece of information had already done the rounds; it wasn't news. But what I'm about to say next will be.

'There's something else. Something I didn't realize until late last night, though it's blindingly obvious as soon as you see it. If Harry's real name is *Enrico* Marrone, his initials are EM.'

Silence.

'The same as Michael's,' says Gislingham. 'Only backwards. Shit.'

'Right,' I say, pointing at a second photograph. The signet ring. 'EM. The same initials that are engraved on this ring, which we found on the corpse at Southey Road. Those letters could stand for ME, but they could just as easily stand for *EM.*'

I go back to the first picture. 'And as you can just about see in this photo, Harry is wearing a silver-coloured signet ring on his left hand.'

People are starting to look at each other now.

'I came back here last night and went through every single photo album we found at Southey Road and I can't find a single picture showing Michael Esmond wearing any sort of ring. Not even a wedding ring.'

Ev is gaping. 'But Philip identified that ring as his brother's.'

'I know he did, but all we have is his word for it.'

'But why would he lie?' she continues, before stopping in her tracks. 'Oh shit, that body isn't Michael, is it. It's Harry. Michael is *still alive.*'

The noise level is rising now. I hold up my hand.

'Which is precisely why I dragged you all in here at this godawful hour of the morning.'

'But wouldn't the post-mortem have picked that up?' says Asante. 'I mean, if the body was someone as young as that surely the pathologist would have seen it? Can't they prove it from the bones?'

But I'm shaking my head. 'I've come across this before. If a body is very old or very young you can age it from the skeleton, but between about twenty-one and forty-five the bones don't change much. And that's exactly the age range we're looking at here. It was a good question though, Asante, well done.'

I look around at the rest of the team. 'So, we need to think this through very carefully. If Philip Esmond deliberately misled us about that ring we have to assume it was because he wanted us to think Michael is dead. Because he wanted us to stop looking for him. And if Michael really is still alive – and right now that's a very big *if* – then it's *Philip* who must be helping him to hide. After all, he has his own boat – what better place for someone to lie low for a few days.'

'Or leave the bloody country,' says Quinn darkly.

'I don't think they've done that – not yet. Philip can't afford to leave before he's buried the body. Not if he wants us to believe it's Michael's. They won't want to arouse unnecessary suspicion.'

'We can contact Poole harbour,' says Gis. 'Make sure the boat is still there.'

'Good, and while you're at it, tell them to expect us. And to stop that bloody boat leaving.'

'What do you want the rest of us to do, boss?' Baxter now.

'That ring is pretty distinctive. Let's get Davy Jones in ASAP to see if he can identify it.' I look round. 'DC Asante – think you can handle that?'

He smiles. 'Absolutely, sir.'

'Right – Baxter, can you contact car-rental firms in the Poole area. Philip was driving a hired red Nissan Juke when I last saw him – that shouldn't be too hard to find. And when you do, have a look at ANPR – see if we can track his movements since he got back to the UK.'

'On it, boss.'

'And Somer, can you speak to the Tech unit again about that phone call on the afternoon of January 4th, when Philip rang in and spoke to you.'

She's frowning. 'But we already proved he was in the middle of the Atlantic then –'

'I'm aware of that. What I want to know *now* is where he was the day *before* that call was made.'

* * *

3 January 2018, 9.04 p.m.
Three hours before the fire
Southern Rail train service, near Haywards Heath

The passengers in the carriage have reached the grin-and-bear-it (and in some cases the gin-and-bear-it) phase of the delay. Anger is pointless, they just have to stick it out. Conversations have started up, and one little girl is going round offering people her Liquorice Allsorts. Several people look up as the man in the tweed jacket walks through the carriage for the second time. His clothes are respectable enough but everything else looks like it's coming apart. His shirt is untucked and there are sweat stains visible under the arms. As he passes the elderly black woman at the far end, adjacent to the guard's area and bike racks, she hears him muttering to himself, 'Is there nowhere on this entire fucking train you can make a private phone call?'

She shakes her head, tutting, and makes a comment to her husband in an undertone. She doesn't like swearing. And men like him, they should know better.

Five minutes later, she hears his voice again. She twists round and realizes he must be on the phone. He's keeping his voice low but the intensity – the vehemence – is unmistakable.

'I know who you are,' he's saying. 'Do you hear me? I *know who you are*.' He shakes his head. 'Not now – not on the phone. Meet me at the house. I should be back by midnight. We can talk about it then.'

* * *

'You were right, sir. To question where Philip Esmond was when he called me.'

It's Somer, on the speaker-phone. We're in Gislingham's car. Quinn is in the back, making a superhuman effort not to criticize his driving.

'He wasn't sailing south like we assumed,' Somer continues. 'He'd already turned round. He was heading back to the UK.'

'When did the boat change course?'

'As far as we can work out, it must have been in the early hours of the 4th of January.'

'So he knew,' I say quietly. 'He knew about that fire long before you told him.'

Long before it hit the news. And the only person who could possibly have told him is his brother. Michael Esmond. He didn't die in that fire. He's still alive.

'Philip got a call from a mobile phone at just after two that morning,' she says, 'which must have been right around the time he turned back. The caller was in the Southampton area. No prizes for guessing where.'

'Calshot Spit.'

329

'Right. Those witnesses who ID'd Michael were right after all. He *was* at the hut. We just didn't get there in time.'

I sense Gislingham shift in his seat next to me and when I glance up, he's frowning.

'Though the mobile number he used to call Philip was different,' continues Somer. 'It wasn't the same one as when he rang Harry from the train. He must have thrown it away because he thought we might be able to trace where he was.' Or – which if you ask me is much more likely – it was Philip who realized, and Philip who told him to dump it.

'So whose phone was it?'

'That's where it gets interesting. It belongs to a man called Ian Blake. He reported it stolen that very morning – January 4th. He lives in one of the blocks of flats on the Banbury Road, about half a mile from Southey Road.'

I must be missing something here. 'So how the hell did Esmond get his hands on it?'

I can almost hear the smile in her voice. 'Because it was on the front seat of his car at the time. You probably don't remember – uniform were handling it – but this chap Blake had his car stolen from outside his flat in the early hours that morning. He does shift work at the John Rad and he left the engine running to de-ice the car. Only when he came back out again it was gone. There was quite a bit of cash too – the wallet was in the car as well.'

So that's how Esmond got to Calshot. He stole a car. The one thing we hadn't thought of. The one thing a man like him would never dream of doing. Not if he was in his right mind.

'Has Esmond made any more calls on that number since?'

'No, but he did get a text later that same day. From Philip's satellite phone. I checked the timing – Philip sent that text *five minutes after he spoke to me*. Five minutes after I'd asked him whether he knew anything about a hut and he denied all knowledge. *That's* why Michael wasn't at Calshot when we got there, sir – his brother had already warned him we were coming.'

And just to be on the safe side, he left it the best part of three days before calling us to claim he'd 'remembered'.

'Good work, Somer. Anything else?'

'Oh yes, DC Asante said to tell you Davy Jones has ID'd the ring. Says he definitely saw Harry wearing it.'

'Tell him good work.'

'I will, sir. And Everett wants a word. Hold on.'

There are muffled noises on the line and then Ev's voice.

'I spoke to the Poole harbourmaster, boss. Turns out Esmond isn't in the main marina but one on the other side of the harbour. Took us half an hour to track down which one but we got there in the end. It's a place called Cobb's Quay. The manager there says Philip Esmond docked sometime in the afternoon on January *7th*. He'd phoned ahead to say there'd been a change of plans and he needed a berth.'

I'm trying to remember the timeline but Ev does it for me.

'When DC Somer spoke to him on the 7th he told her he hoped to be back in a couple of days. But he was lying. He was *already here*.'

I pound the dashboard in frustration. There was no reason to suspect him at that point, but all the same we should have checked. We should have been more thorough. *I* should have been more thorough.

'The boat's definitely still there?'

'Yes, sir. The manager at Cobb's Quay says he's spotted at least one man on board in the last couple of days. Quite tall, dark hair, he says. Though he's only seen him at a distance.'

And Philip and Michael look very alike. At least superficially. It's not conclusive.

'Tell him to let us know at once if he shows any sign of leaving. But with luck we'll be there ourselves in an hour.'

'Less,' says Gislingham as I finish the call. 'We're past Eastleigh now.'

He's still frowning, though.

'Everything OK?'

'Fine,' he says, checking his rear mirror before indicating to overtake. 'I think I forgot to mention that Hants Police called.'

'Oh yes?'

'It was late Friday. I was half out the door. It was that DI you spoke to. Saumarez. He said the tramp we found in that hut claimed someone else had already broken into it before he got there.'

'Well, that tallies. Michael Esmond wouldn't have had a key.'

'No, boss.'

But there's still something, and for the life of me I can't work out what it is.

And then my phone rings.

4 January 2018, 12.05 a.m.
23 Southey Road, Oxford

When Harry gets to the house, Michael is waiting for him. He opens the door in silence, and then walks away at once to the sitting room.

'What's this about?' says Harry lightly. 'Bit cloak and dagger isn't it – all this "meet me at midnight" stuff?'

'The train was delayed.'

Michael closes the door behind them. He hasn't switched on the lights. There's only the dull glow of the street lamp, casting a long thin stripe through the curtains and across the floor. In the shadows he looks different. Strange. You can almost hear the crackle of nervous energy. He has a half-empty bottle of whisky by the neck. For the first time, Harry starts to feel uneasy. Perhaps this wasn't such a good idea.

'What do you want?' he says, all lightness gone. 'Because there's somewhere else I need to be.'

'I know who you are,' says Michael.

'Look –'

'Don't try to deny it. I know who you are. And whatever it is you want, I'm telling you now you're not going to get it.'

Harry raises his eyebrows. 'Really? You sure about that? Because I spoke to a lawyer –'

'I don't care who you've spoken to. I'm not going to let you ruin my life. You have no right –'

'Oh, I think you'll find I have every right.'

Michael starts moving closer. Harry can smell the alcohol on his breath. There's something unfocused about his eyes. Harry begins to back away. 'Look, we can talk about this – but not now. Not when –'

'Not when what, exactly?'

Harry feels the wall crunch against his spine. Michael is so close his spit is on Harry's skin. He lifts his hands and pushes Michael away. 'You're pissed.'

'Too right I'm fucking pissed. In every sense of the fucking word.'

He never swears.

He never swears.

'I'm going,' says Harry, pulling his coat back up round his shoulders. 'I should never have come in the first place.'

'No you fucking shouldn't,' says Michael, drilling a finger into his chest. 'So why don't you just pack up your crap and go back to that shithole you came from.'

Harry moves a little closer. His voice is still low, but there's a menace in it now. 'Yeah, well, if I come from a shithole, whose fault is that? Because it can't be the genes, can it. There can't be anything wrong with those. I mean, look at you – your wife's in pieces, your son is struggling, and you don't even appear to have bloody noticed.'

'Don't you dare talk about my family like that –'

'Don't you *get* it? They're *not just your family*. Not any more. They're *mine*. And I've done more for them in the last six months than you have in six bloody *years*. Look at poor bloody Matt – how many times have you promised to do things with him and let him down at the last minute? There's always something more important, isn't there? Always something about *you* – about *you* and your career and your big important job that as far as I can see you've made such a fucking mess of they're going to fire your sorry arse –'

'I'm warning you –'

Michael is swaying now, slurring. Too drunk to take anyone on. Or so Harry thinks.

It's not the only error he's about to make.

* * *

Poole is bright but cold. The slap of ropes against fibre-glass. Seagulls. High clouds fleeting across a washed blue sky. I breathe a lungful of salt air and think – not for the first time – that I really should get out of Oxford more often.

'Couldn't have chosen a better place for a hideout if he'd bloody well tried,' says Quinn tetchily, slamming the door and making great show of stretching his legs.

But he's right. In the summer this place must be heaving – the social club, the chandlery, the shiny new yachts lined up for sale – but at this time of year it's almost deserted. And even if it wasn't, the pontoons stretch out two or three hundred yards into the water. If your boat was moored at the far end you could be on it for days and no one would even know you were there. It's almost too perfect.

We walk towards the water and the manager must have been watching for us, because the door to the office is already opening. And a few yards away, in the car park, I can see a red Nissan Juke.

'Detective Inspector Fawley?' says the man, looking at the three of us and plumping for me. I guess I should be flattered.

'Duncan Wright. I've been keeping an eye out since you phoned but I haven't seen any movement on *Freedom 2*.'

'And where's the boat?'

'Berth C31,' he says, pointing. 'Over there.'

Cobb's Quay must be top end because every boat we pass is either new or in pristine condition. Polished wood, colour-coordinated sails, gleaming chrome catching the winter sun. And right at the far end, tilting gently on the water, *Freedom 2*. It looks like something out of a Sunday supplement. I'd wondered about that name the first time I heard it, thinking it was just a rather adolescent lifestyle statement – Philip's way of thumbing his nose at the choices his brother made. 'Freedom to' do what the hell he liked, freedom to get out from under the weight of family expectations. But knowing what I do now about the life those two boys led, the home they had, I'm not so sure. Like everything else in this case, what's on the surface may not be as superficial as it seems.

There may have been no sign of life on the boat all morning, but there is now. By the time we get to the boat he's on the prow, waiting for us. Navy hoodie, padded gilet, Ray-Bans.

Philip Esmond.

'Inspector,' he says, taking off his glasses. 'I had no idea you were coming –'

'Neither did we, Mr Esmond.'

He glances at Gislingham and Quinn and then back at me. 'What's happened? Has there been a development?'

'You could say that,' says Quinn sardonically.

'Could you move away from the boat, Mr Esmond.'

'But –'

'Please.'

'All right,' he says heavily, holding up his hands. 'If you insist.'

He steps down on to the pontoon, and Gis moves past me and on to the boat, ducking down into the cabin.

'When you first came to St Aldate's you told my officer that you'd only just got back to the UK. That you had come straight to Oxford as soon as you arrived.'

He frowns. 'So? What's that got to do –'

'In fact, you'd docked here three full days before that. On January 7th.'

His face hardens a little. 'I don't see what difference it makes. I had stuff to do, that's all.'

'Really?' I say. 'The sort of "stuff" that includes driving to Calshot Spit to collect your brother and bringing him back here?'

'That's ridiculous – like I said, I'd forgotten all about that poxy place.'

'I doubt it, Mr Esmond. Judging from the photo albums we found at Southey Road, you went there at least a dozen times when you were a child. You wouldn't be likely to forget that. Not, of course, unless you had a very good reason.'

'You can't prove any of this – it's just speculation.'

'On the contrary, Hants Police have already found the car your brother stole, abandoned less than a mile from the beach hut. As for you, I have officers trawling ANPR data as we speak. It's only a matter of time before we find out exactly where you've been. So what was the plan? Lie

337

low till the funeral was over then head off back to Croatia where you'd claim the money from the will and set your brother up in a new life?'

Gis appears at the hatch and shakes his head. 'He's not here, sir.'

I take a step closer to Esmond. 'Don't make this harder than it needs to be. I can arrest you here and now, if I need to. We know Michael is alive and we know you've been trying to protect him. I have a brother – I get it. But it's over now. And it will be better for everyone if you just tell us the truth. There have already been far too many lies. Far too many and for far too long.'

Esmond turns away, takes a deep breath and then lets it out in a heavy, jagged sigh.

* * *

4 January 2018, 12.09 a.m.
23 Southey Road, Oxford

'And what about Sam?' says Harry. 'Stuck in this bloody great mausoleum day in, day out. No job, no friends, just wiping Zachary's arse and waiting on you hand and foot. No wonder she's fucking depressed – no wonder she turns to someone else for a little bloody affection –'

He knows even as he says it that he's gone too far. 'Sorry,' he stumbles, 'I shouldn't have said that –'

But it's too late. He can't take it back – can't unsay it –

Michael's eyes narrow 'It's *yours* – is that what you're telling me?'

'What – what are you talking about?'

338

'The fucking *baby* – that's what I'm talking about.'

Harry swallows. 'Shit – I didn't know –'

'She's your stepmother, you disgusting little pervert.'

Harry's eyes widen. 'No – you've got it all wrong – shit – is that what you think?'

The bottle of whisky may be half empty but it's heavy, easy to wield.

Harry stumbles as the first blow lands and he staggers backwards, a rush of blood breaking down his neck.

'You bastard,' he hisses, sprawled against the wall. 'You total fucking bastard –'

*   *   *

'It wasn't Michael we found at the house, was it, Mr Esmond? It was Harry. Or should I say Enrico?'

Philip still has his back to me. 'So you know about that.'

'We know your brother had a relationship with Ginevra Marrone and that she had a baby. We also know Harry came here last year looking for his father. And it was his body we found in the ruins of Southey Road.'

Philip turns slowly to look at me. Quinn has his phone in his hand and the voice recorder on.

'What I *don't* know, Mr Esmond,' I continue, forcing him to meet my eye, 'is how much *you* know about DNA.'

He looks baffled. 'I don't know what you mean.'

'Our lab concluded that the body at the house was Michael because it shared enough of your DNA to be your brother. And you knew that, didn't you? That's why you were so keen to give us that bloody sample – you'd looked it all up and you knew the conclusion we were bound to come to. But that's not the only possibility, is it? There's at least one other relationship that could produce exactly the same result.'

He's not saying anything now. Just staring at me.

'How long have you known Harry was your son?'

* * *

15 July 2017, 2.09 p.m.
173 days before the fire
23 Southey Road, Oxford

'You want me to prove it? You want to do a test?'

They're standing at the far end of the garden. By the summer-house and the compost heap, where a cloud of midges flitter in the July heat. Further up the lawn, Sam is dozing in a deckchair, and the two boys are kicking a ball about.

Harry is staring at him, waiting for an answer. 'I asked you – do you want to do a test, because that's fine by me. *I* don't have anything to hide.'

'It's not that I don't believe you –'

Harry's face hardens. 'You're just not sure who's the daddy, right? Whether it's you or your little bro.'

'You don't understand –'

'I understand all right. I *understand* that he dumped my mother and you moved in on her. That's what I *understand*.'

Philip sighs. 'It wasn't like that.'

Harry raises an eyebrow. 'So what was it "like", exactly? A quick fumble in the back of your car? Got her on the rebound, did you?'

340

'She knew what she was doing – she was hardly a –'

He stops, embarrassed.

'Hardly a virgin, is that what you meant? No, your brother saw to that, didn't he?'

'I didn't mean that – I meant she was mature for her age – she made her own decisions –'

'She was fifteen, for fuck's sake. *Fifteen.*'

Philip flushes now. 'I know. Look, you have to believe me – if I'd known she was pregnant –'

'What? You'd have married her? Fat chance. *Daddy* would have put paid to that.'

'I meant money. I could have given her money.'

The blue eyes are icy cold now. 'You'd have paid her to abort me.'

'Don't be ridiculous. You know that's not what I meant. If I'd known I'd have done the right thing.'

'Oh, don't worry,' says Harry with a bitter laugh. 'You're going to. I'm your son. The eldest son of the eldest son. And that means all of this is mine.'

He gestures up at the house. Philip watches as Michael comes out of the office and goes over to his wife. She looks up at him, shading her eyes against the sun. They exchange a few words then he unfolds another deckchair and sits down next to her.

'I got a lawyer to look at that will I found,' says Harry. 'I bet the trustees don't know your brother is living here, do they? In fact, I bet you didn't even bother asking them.'

Philip flushes. 'It's an informal arrangement.'

'I'll take that as a no, then. My lawyer says he's got no right to live here. That if you don't want to that's your decision, but after that it comes to me, not him. And as far as I'm concerned I've been waiting long enough. It's my turn. That's why I came here. Looking for you.'

341

'You can't expect me to turn them out – that's completely unreasonable.'

Harry moves closer. 'What's *unreasonable* is leaving a fifteen-year-old girl to bring up a baby alone. What's *unreasonable* is growing up on the breadline because your mother's family have disowned her. What's *unreasonable* is finding out your father's rolling in it and not a single fucking penny of it has ever come your way –'

'We're not rolling in it. We never were and we certainly aren't now.'

'Fine. Like I said. I just want what's due to me. My fair share.'

Philip takes a deep breath. 'You're going to have to give me some time. Something like this – out of the blue – it's going to be one hell of a shock. And you know as well as I do that he has a lot on his plate right now.'

'OK, I get that. I'm not about to make things worse for Sam and the kids if I can help it. You, frankly, I can take or leave, but them – they're my family.'

'I'll speak to him – find the right moment. I promise.'

'Six months,' says Harry, starting up the mower again. 'I'll give you six months. If you haven't told him by then, I'll do it myself.'

* * *

'So when did you tell him?'

Philip looks away again. 'I didn't.'

'You never told Michael that Harry was your son? You never told him he and his family were going to have to move out of that house?'

'There never seemed to be a good time. Mike was in

over his head already. What with Sam, and Mum, and all that crap with his job. I didn't think he could take any more.'

I take a deep breath. 'So instead of dealing with any of that – instead of facing up to the consequences of your own actions – you decided to swan off to Croatia and leave the shit to blow up behind you?'

'It wasn't like that,' he says quickly.

'So what was it like? Because I'm afraid from where I'm standing –'

'I spoke to the trustees,' he says. 'In July. Before I left the UK. I asked whether what Harry said was right.'

'And?'

He makes a face. 'It was pretty much exactly what he told me. They said that if Harry wanted to live in the house, they couldn't see how they could refuse, as long as he could prove who he was. The best they could come up with was him and Michael sharing the place, but there wasn't a snowball's chance in hell of that working. Even if they'd both agreed.'

'Did you do the DNA test?'

He nods. 'Yes. But it was just a formality. I knew he was telling the truth. He looks – looked – exactly like Ginny.'

He glances away again, past me, over my shoulder. Towards the quay.

'But Michael did find out, didn't he? How did that happen – did Harry tell him?'

He shakes his head. 'No. I managed to persuade him to give me a bit more time. But Michael worked it out for himself. He told me, that night when he called from the hut, that he'd overheard Harry telling Sam about some pudding or other his mother used to make at Christmas.

It's a speciality from Puglia – that's where the family come from. Mike remembered having some at Ginny's house. It was too much to be a coincidence. Especially with the bloody tattoo.'

He can see from my face that I have no idea what he's talking about.

'Harry had a tattoo on his chest. Juniper berries. He told Michael it was for his mother. That's what her name means. Juniper.'

'I see. So even if he didn't say anything explicitly, he wasn't exactly keeping it secret, was he?'

Philip makes a grim face. 'He's a risk-taker. Like his father. I think he enjoyed sailing close to the wind.'

We stand there a moment, staring at each other. I can feel the sun on my back, the pontoon moving gently beneath my feet.

'How did Harry die?' I say eventually.

He sighs heavily. 'When Mike called me that night he was barely coherent – I could hardly make out what he was saying – I couldn't believe it – that Harry was dead – that Mike had actually *killed* him –' He runs a hand through his hair. 'He said they'd argued, that Harry claimed he'd been having an affair with Sam and Michael thought the baby must be his and I think that was the last straw, coming on top of everything else. I think for one fucking ghastly moment it just sent him over the edge.'

'Was that true – the affair?'

Philip shrugs. 'I don't know. She was very unhappy, and she was lonely. I suppose I can see how it might have happened.'

'And Michael tried to cover up what he'd done by

setting fire to the house. With his innocent family asleep upstairs –'

'He *didn't know that*,' he says quickly. 'They were supposed to be in Liverpool. Some show or other. For Matt's birthday. You have to believe me.'

'I do,' I say gently. 'She left him a message on his mobile, to say Zachary was sick and they were at home.'

But I didn't realize till now exactly what that meant.

'He lost his phone – he never got that message –'

'I know. The phone's been handed in. We knew he'd lost it.'

And the rest, we can check. And in all this appalling mess, there is suddenly a tiny splinter of relief. He never meant to kill them. He was a family destroyer all right, but he never set out to be.

'Look,' he says, 'Mike's half out of his mind about Sam and the kids – he didn't give a shit about that house – he always pretended to love it but it was just a colossal millstone round his neck – round *both* our necks –'

And I remember, now, that office in the garden. Everything about it the polar opposite of the rest of the house: colour, furniture, atmosphere, light. That house wasn't a treasured legacy. It wasn't even a home; it was a prison. A curse.

'Where is he now, Mr Esmond?'

He opens his mouth and closes it again. 'I don't know,' he says eventually. 'When I heard you on the pontoon I thought it must be him. He should have been back by now –'

He looks up towards the quay again, visibly concerned now.

'He went that way?' I say, following his gaze.

'About an hour ago.'

There's something else. Something he's not telling me.

'What is it, Mr Esmond?'

He swallows. 'When Michael found out about Harry – when he worked out Ginny was his mother – he assumed, you know –'

And there it is – the last missing piece.

'He assumed Harry was *his* son. Not yours.'

He reddens. 'He never knew, you see – that she and I had had a thing. I mean, it was only once or twice. I didn't think it mattered.'

But once or twice can matter. Once or twice can be everything.

Philip sighs. 'And when he went to Brighton to see Muriel she just kept referring to "that Esmond boy". He had no idea she actually meant me.'

She said exactly the same when we saw her. And I jumped to exactly the same conclusions.

'Does he still think that?'

He glances at me and then away. His face is bleak with shame. 'He's barely spoken to me since he got here. I just didn't think he could take any more right now.'

'So what happened this morning?'

'I went to get some food and when I got back he was on my iPad. I've been hiding it in my stuff but he must have found it. There was that story in the news – on the BBC.'

'– saying that the man who died at Southey Road was still alive when the fire started.'

He nods. 'Mike was in a terrible state – he said that just made it worse – that if he'd known Harry wasn't dead he'd never have set the fire at all – that they'd *all* still be alive. He got hysterical – started saying he'd *seen* him – he'd seen Matty. I tell you, I was seriously worried by then – I thought he might actually be losing his mind. But then he seemed to calm down and said he had to get out – that he was going mad cooped up in the boat twenty-four hours a day and he needed to clear his head.'

'And you let him go?'

He shrugs miserably. 'What else could I do? He said he wanted to be on his own.'

Gis must have spotted something on the quayside because he gestures to me and I turn to see a man running towards us. But it's not Michael Esmond. It's the marina manager.

* * *

4 January 2018, 12.12 a.m.
23 Southey Road, Oxford

'Look,' gasps Harry, 'I didn't sleep with Sam – I swear – and she's not – you're not – seriously – you've got it all wrong –'

He tries to get up but slips heavily back. There's panic now, as he starts crawling towards the door. Michael watches him for a moment, then walks slowly round to stand in front of him, blocking his exit, gazing down.

'So what is it that I've got wrong, exactly?'

Harry's elbows buckle and he rolls over on to his back, his chest heaving hard. There's blood in his hair, down his face, in his mouth.

'I'm – not – your son – whatever you think – it wasn't you I came for – it was Philip –'

But if he thought that would make this all go away he couldn't be more wrong.

Michael stares down at him, and the fear he's lived with for all these weeks darkens quickly into something far, far worse. This man hasn't just broken into his family, stolen their love, taken his place, he's going to take his home – ruin his life – destroy everything he's worked so hard to get.

And suddenly there's something about the heft of the bottle in his hand that makes him feel, for one appalling moment, that he is free. Free from himself, free from that man everyone has always expected him to be and no matter what he does it's never been enough. Free to be angry and vindictive and out-of-control and who-gives-a-shit just like –

Something in his face must have changed because Harry tries again to get up but his body fails him and the words he needs to say spew in a bubble of blood. And then there's a foot against his neck and he's being forced back down, and the weight is pushing, pushing, pushing until his face hits the floor and there's bile in his mouth and no air in his lungs and darkness in his eyes.

* * *

'Inspector!' calls the marina manager as he comes within earshot, breathing heavily with the exertion. 'One of the other owners has just reported their inflatable stolen – I thought you ought to know.'

'When was this?'

'Can't have been more than an hour. Perhaps less.'

Philip Esmond has gone white.

'Does your brother know how to use one of those things?'

He shakes his head. 'I doubt it. He never comes sailing – he hates the water.'

I turn back to the manager. 'If he's heading out to sea, what's the best way to stop him?'

His eyes widen. 'Shit, I don't give an amateur much chance out there in a bloody dinghy –'

'I *said*, how do we *stop* him?'

'To get out to sea from here he'd need to go through the Little Channel – that's right by the lifeboat station. If he's still this side of the bridge those guys can probably intercept him – but if he's past that already, it'll be a lot harder.'

'How far is it?'

'Ten minutes by road – less.'

Gis and Quinn are already running back to the car.

'I'll come with you,' says Esmond.

'Call them,' I shout to the manager, starting back towards the quay. 'Tell them we'll meet them there and to be on the lookout for that dinghy.'

'Hang on,' he calls. 'What does this bloke look like?'

'Him,' I say, pointing at Esmond. 'He looks like him.'

* * *

4 January 2018, 12.22 a.m.
23 Southey Road, Oxford

Zachary sits up. He can hear voices downstairs. He slips off the bed and creeps to the door. He can definitely hear the voices now. It's Harry. And Daddy! Mummy said Daddy wasn't coming back yet but Zachary's sure he can hear him. Perhaps it's a surprise. Perhaps he isn't supposed to know. Zachary likes surprises. He likes presents and surprises and pirates and chocolate.

He pushes the door open and tiptoes over to the banisters in the dark. There aren't any voices now. He slides down on to the floor and looks over. And there he is. Daddy. Wearing his coat. But he looks funny. Just standing there. Sort of angry and sort of sad. Zachary is about to call out but Daddy suddenly turns and goes to the kitchen. Zachary hears the back door open and a few minutes later Daddy's back. He's carrying something. He goes back into the sitting room and Zachary can hear the sound of water sloshing about. Like when they played in the paddling pool when Uncle Philip was here. Perhaps that's what the surprise is. He edges closer and peers through the banisters. Then there's a funny 'pop' sound and suddenly there's a pretty yellow light in the sitting room. Like the bonfire they had with Harry when he did all those tricks. Zachary liked that. It was fun.

Daddy comes out again. He doesn't look so sad now. He looks like he did when the dentist told him he had to have his tooth out and then he didn't have to after all. Zachary watches his father take a long look around the hall, then let himself out. The front door closes and there's the sound of footsteps on the gravel.

Zachary stands up and starts slowly down the stairs, one step at a time, one hand clutching the banisters, his pale blue security blanket trailing behind him.

*   *   *

We pull up outside the lifeboat station in a screech of brakes. The boat is already in the water. One of the crew comes towards me at a run. The wind is getting up now.

It may be a dead calm in this channel but it'll be choppy out on the open sea.

'DI Fawley? Hugh Ransome. We think your man must have gone through already. One of the lads thought he saw a dinghy like that a quarter of an hour ago.'

He looks across at the four of us. 'We only have room for two.'

'I'll come,' I say quickly. 'With Mr Esmond. My officers will check in with Dorset police. Make sure they know what's going on.'

Ransome nods and turns towards the boat. 'There are helmets and life jackets on board,' he calls over his shoulder. 'They're non-negotiable.'

As we clatter down the gangway a small crowd is already gathering. There are two people in the boat already – a man and a woman in the same white hats and high-vis jackets. The engine is running and we move off in a surge as soon as we have our gear on. Safe to say Philip Esmond is quicker at it than I am.

'Will your man know what to do if he gets in trouble?' shouts the team leader over the spray and the boom of the engine.

Esmond shakes his head. 'Even if there are flares on board I doubt he'd know what they were.'

'He can swim?'

Esmond nods. 'But not well.'

It's a narrow channel and ferries and motor cruisers are pulling past us in both directions, sending huge bow waves in their wake that smack hard against the boat, but we're a lot more stable than a small dinghy would be. I can see from Philip's face that he's thinking the same thing.

And then we're heading into wider water, the dry docks and industrial units thinning out on the near bank and low woods on the far shore. The water glistens in the winter sun, and here and there a sailing boat is pulling against the wind, but that's all I can see. Ransome has binoculars, scanning the bay.

'Anything?' I ask.

He lowers the glasses and points. 'Over there.'

* * *

4 January 2018, 12.43 a.m.
23 Southey Road, Oxford

When Matty opens his eyes he knows at once something is wrong. He can smell burning. He sits up. And now he hears it again – the terrifying sound that broke into his dream.

Zachary.

Matty leaps out of bed and on to the landing. From the top of the stairs he can see Zachary below him in the hall. He's staggering, screaming – screaming in a horrific animal howl Matty has never heard before.

His pyjamas are on fire. His skin is on fire –

'I'm coming – I'm coming!' Matty yells, racing down the stairs, his legs giving way under him, nearly falling. Zachary lurches towards him, still screaming, but Matty can hear words now – *Daddy, Daddy* –

He seizes the blue blanket lying on the bottom step and rolls his brother up in it, like he's seen them do on TV. Tighter, tighter, until all the flames are out. The smoke is thicker now. The rug in the sitting room is on fire and it's spreading through the floorboards, running like little rivers of flame, like the lava they saw on the volcano film at school. He can't get to the front door – he can't get to the kitchen – the fire is everywhere and he doesn't have any shoes. And he has Zachary to think of. He looks around. It's as if they're on an island in a sea of flames. They can't stay here –

He scoops his brother up in his arms, staggering under the weight. Zachary isn't screaming any more. 999, thinks Matty, I need to call 999, like they told us in citizenship class – get an ambulance and the fire engine and the police – 'Don't worry, Zachary,' he says, his breath already raw in his throat, 'we'll go back upstairs and then I'll wake Mummy and find a phone –'

That's what he keeps repeating to himself, all the way back up the stairs, his burden heavier at every step.

Wake Mummy – find a phone – wake Mummy – find a phone –

When they get to the nursery Matty puts Zachary down on the bed. He keeps telling him that everything's going to be OK but he isn't moving and Matty is starting to panic. He goes back to the nursery door and opens it a couple of inches. He can see the red glow of the flames against the wall of the stairwell and he can feel the heat on his face. The fire is really big now. He can't go back down there.

He goes over to the window but he knows it's locked. Daddy's locked all the windows to keep them safe. There's no way out that way – he can't even call for help. He feels the hot wet pee running down his leg. Then suddenly, everything's OK again, because he can see Daddy – Daddy is on the other side of the road, staring at the house. Matty starts banging on the window, screaming *Daddy, Daddy, Daddy.*

His father looks up and his face stiffens in horror – for a moment he stands there, not moving, as if frozen to the spot, then he moves towards the house. First slowly, then at a run, but as he gets to the door there's an explosion from the sitting room and glass and burning debris rain down over the garden. Matty sees his father stagger back, his hands shielding his face, and then the flames climb higher and Matty can't see him any more.

'I'm coming, Daddy!' he shouts. 'I'm coming!'

* * *

The inflatable is empty, dipping and lifting in the quiet current. We come alongside and the crew pull it in and secure it to our bow. We must be a thousand yards from shore. Way too far for any normal person to swim. Even if there'd been time.

Ransome is still scanning the horizon, but we all know it's hopeless.

There's no one in the water.

Michael Esmond has gone.

One of the crew leans over and takes something out of the bottom of the dinghy. She looks at it briefly then hands it to Esmond. It's a pocket watch; a gold pocket watch on a red velvet pouch. Not left by mistake. Left to be found. And I remember now. That other Esmond family heirloom, handed down through the generations, just like that house. The pocket watch that has a motto engraved on it in Polish.

Blood is thicker than water.

Philip Esmond closes his eyes for a moment, then clenches his fist around the watch and, before I can stop him, flings it out and up through the soft and glittering air.

* * *

When I push open the door to the incident room at eleven the following morning I walk straight into a chorus of 'For He's A Jolly Good Fellow'. It's not that they're being insensitive; this has been a brutal case and no one knows that better than they do. But it's also been Gislingham's first big investigation and he's got a result. A neat tick in the 'solved' box, and Philip Esmond charged with perverting the course of justice. Harrison will be positively delirious. Even if our murder suspect is almost certainly dead. Even if we don't have a body. There was an email from Ransome on my phone first thing: 'We're still looking but don't hold your breath,' he said. 'The way the currents work round here it may be months. And if he meant to do it, he'd have weighed himself down. Cases like that – you don't find them again.'

And now I'm clearing my throat to say something but Quinn gets there first.

'I'd just like to say,' he begins, raising his voice over the din, 'that the Sarge has done a cracking job this last couple of weeks. Well done, mate, played a blinder.'

He smiles as he says it, and he means it too. And the rest of them can see that, and they know as well as I do that even if it's true, saying it can't have been easy. There are some shouts of 'hear, hear', which we all know are as much for Quinn as they are for Gis.

Gis grins at him. 'Thanks, mate. Appreciate it.' He looks around the room, then checks his watch. 'OK, guys, maybe a wee bit early for lunch but the drinks are on me.'

'Thought you'd never bloody ask,' says Quinn, to more laughter.

'Actually,' I say, 'I think this is probably my shout.'

More cheers, and as the noise dies down and people start to collect their coats and make their way to the door I see Somer pat Quinn lightly on the back as she passes by.

* * *

When the call comes through at the end of the day, Somer is in two minds about answering it. She's been lumbered with clearing up the incident room and the rest of the team left over an hour ago. Everett has stayed behind to help out, but with the files boxed up and the whiteboard cleared, even she's getting a bit impatient now.

Somer stares at the phone. If it rings more than five times I'll pick it up, she tells herself. Just in case it's important.

'Come on, Erica,' says Everett. 'A girl could die of thirst in here.'

Three rings, four, five.

Somer seizes the phone, trying not to notice Everett sighing and rolling her eyes.

'CID, DC Somer speaking.'

'I was hoping it would be you.'

She recognizes the voice, but can't place it. Not straight away. But in the half-second it takes her to give it a name her gut tells her it's a good voice – a voice she associates with good things. She will remember that, later, and hug the thought.

'It's Giles, Giles Saumarez.'

She blushes and turns quickly away, hoping Everett hasn't noticed (though, of course, she has). It's not business, this call, not if he's calling himself Giles.

'I'm going up to Banbury to see my stepfather next weekend and I wondered if you'd like to meet up. Lunch? A drink?'

Everett has come round to face her now, grinning and mouthing '*Who is it?*'

'Yes,' says Somer, holding the phone a little tighter, 'I'd love to. Actually, I need to ask your advice.'

'Oh yes?'

'I wonder if you have a view on mittens?'

His voice is still full of laughter five minutes later, when she puts down the phone.

* * *

I look around the sitting room one last time. The cleaners have been in and scrubbed the place to within an inch of its life, but I still want it to be perfect. I want her to see how much it matters to me that it *is* perfect. I glance at my watch, which shows precisely two minutes later than when I last looked. The nervous energy is getting the better of me and when I find myself squaring the corners of the magazine pile I know I'm in trouble.

The bell rings. I'm three-quarters to answering it before I realize it can't be her. She has a key. But after all this time, perhaps she doesn't feel able to use it. Perhaps she doesn't even think of this as her home. I feel slightly sick at that, and perhaps that's why I'm not smiling as much as I meant to when I open the door.

She's standing there. On the step, looking down the drive at the front garden. Where I spent three hours last week putting in new plants. She's wearing jeans, boots and a soft leather jacket I bought her in Rome because it was exactly the same colour as her hair. I haven't seen her wear it in ages. But she's wearing it now. She *chose* to wear it now. My heart contracts with the terror of hope.

She turns then and sees me. 'Wow,' she says, gesturing to the garden. 'Did you get someone in?'

I open my mouth to say something but she's already moved past me into the house. And I watch her, noticing the effort I've put in. Not just the cleaners. The flowers. The bottle of wine on the table.

She looks awkward now, and starts fussing with something in her handbag. I've done too much. I shouldn't have made it look so forced –

'Sit down, Adam, please.'

She chooses the sofa and I hesitate a moment, wondering if I should take the chair. Wondering how we ever let it get so damn stupid that I'm worrying where to bloody *sit* –

'I've been doing a lot of thinking, since I've been away. A lot of thinking.'

Two months, but it feels like years. Like decades.

'Being at my sister's gave me space to do that. Among other things.'

Other things – what other things?

'I'm seeing a lot more clearly now.'

I want to look at her. I want to look at everything I love about her that I haven't seen all these weeks, but I'm scared at what she'll see in my eyes.

She obviously wants me to say something and I try to make my voice work. 'OK.'

Her face clouds a little, but I can't tell whether it's because of what she's about to say or because she can sense my unease.

'We broke each other's hearts about the adoption, Adam. I wanted it so much, and you couldn't bear to do it, even though you'd do anything for me.' Her voice is softer. 'That's when I knew it would be wrong. You'd do anything for me, but not that one thing. You *couldn't* do it. That means I shouldn't ask you. I understand that now. And I won't. Never again.'

I swallow, stare at my hands. 'And you're OK with that? With us not adopting?'

It's a point of no return. Because one of the answers to that question is *Yes, because there is no 'us'. It's over.*

She's silent for so long I dare to look up at her. She's smiling. 'Yes, I'm OK with that. Because I love you. Because I want to be with *you*.'

When I take her in my arms, touching her is electricity. Two months' absence – and now her smell, her hair, her body – known and not known. Intimate and gloriously strange. She's the one, in the end, who pulls back. Takes my face in her hands, traces the tear on my cheek with her finger.

'You really thought I wasn't coming back?'

'I knew how much it meant to you. I knew how unhappy you were.'

She smiles again. 'Not any more.'

I stare at her a moment then reach forward for the bottle. 'We should celebrate. It's a Meursault.'

Her favourite. Her absolute favourite.

She shakes her head. 'No, thank you. Not for me.'

'OK, it's a bit early but it's the same one we had at the Boathouse last summer. The one you went mad about. Took me bloody ages to find it.'

She smiles. 'It looks wonderful and I wish I could, but I can't.' Her smile widens. 'I really can't. I did tell you, didn't I, that I wanted to be sure. And now I am.'

And now she's staring at my dazzled and incredulous face and nodding and my eyes are full of tears and I'm laughing and she's taking me in her arms and holding out a photo and my heart is in freefall as I look, for the first time, at the blizzard of grey and white dots and realize what it means. What all of it means – the weeks of pain and waiting and doubt.

A child.

Our child.

'I still can't believe you didn't guess,' she whispers, her eyes sparkling. 'Call yourself a detective . . .'

Acknowledgements

The first people I would like to thank are my readers. It's been an amazing year – only a year! – and I want to thank everyone who has bought, borrowed, read, reviewed and recommended the two Adam Fawley books that have gone before this one.

Thanks are due again to my outstanding 'pro team': Detective Inspector Andy Thompson for his help with police procedures; Joey Giddings for expert advice on forensics; Ann Robinson for her help with the medical side; my good friend Philip Mann for his knowledge of all things nautical; Nicholas Syfret QC for the legal aspects; and Jeremy Dalton for ensuring I didn't make a fool of myself when it came to online gaming. I'd also particularly like to thank Graham Turner and Steve Johns of Oxfordshire Fire and Rescue Service for their absolutely invaluable help and advice – I couldn't have done it without them. As before, I have exercised a degree of artistic licence in some areas, as all writers do, but any errors are solely down to me.

Thank you also to my agent Anna Power, who continues to amaze me, and the whole wonderful team at Penguin – my editor Katy Loftus, my superb PR Jane Gentle, Rose Poole for such great work on the campaigns, the whole team at DeadGood for their fabulous support, and James Keyte, who brought the previous two books to life on audio and will I hope be working on this one.

Thank you also to my excellent copy-editor Karen Whitlock, and a special mention to Emma Brown and the Penguin production team: every book has introduced a new design challenge (the fire report this time) and as always they have risen to it beautifully.

As with *Close to Home* and *In The Dark*, I have had wonderful support from my team of 'first readers': my husband, Simon (who also drafted the infamous Esmond will), and my dear friends Stephen, Sarah, Peter, Elizabeth and Andy.

A few final words on the book itself. As before, while there are some real Oxford places and roads in the novel, others are my own invention. There is, for example, no 'Southey Road' or 'Bishop Christopher's'. The news items are also entirely fictional; none of the people represented is based on a real person and any similarity between online usernames in the book and those of real people is entirely coincidental.

The BBC radio podcast I refer to is a fine and moving piece of broadcasting by Jon Manel, which you can still listen to by searching for *The Adoption* on the BBC iPlayer.

CARA HUNTER

All the Rage

DI Fawley Thriller 4

The first girl came back. The next won't be so lucky.

A teenage girl is found wandering the outskirts of Oxford, dazed and distressed. The story she tells is bizarre. Grabbed from off the street, a plastic bag pulled over her face, then driven to an isolated location where she was subjected to what sounds like an assault. And yet she refuses to press charges and claims the whole thing was just an April Fool gone wrong.

DI Fawley investigates, but there's little he can do without the girl's co-operation. Is she hiding something, and if so, what? And why does Fawley keep getting the feeling it's related to a case from his past, a case he's spent years trying to forget?

And then another girl disappears, and Adam Fawley no longer has a choice: he has to face his demons, whatever the cost, professional or personal.

Because unless he does, this victim may not be coming back . . .

Coming soon

Available to pre-order now

www.penguin.co.uk

The hit crime series
everyone is talking about

'Breathtaking' *Sunday Times*

How many have you read?

CARA HUNTER

Close to Home

DI Fawley Thriller 1

**Someone took Daisy Mason.
Someone you know.**

Last night, eight-year-old Daisy Mason disappeared from a family party. No one in the quiet suburban street saw anything – or at least that's what they're saying.

DI Adam Fawley is trying to keep an open mind. But he knows that, nine times out of ten, it's someone the victim knew.

That means someone is lying . . .

And that Daisy's time is running out.

CARA HUNTER

In the Dark

DI Fawley Thriller 2

**Do you know what they're hiding
in the house next door?**

A woman and child are found locked in a basement room, barely
alive.

No one knows who they are – the woman can't speak, and there are
no missing persons reports that match their profile. The elderly man
who owns the house claims he has never seen them before.

The inhabitants of the quiet Oxford street are in shock. How could
this happen right under their noses? But DI Adam Fawley knows that
nothing is impossible.

And that no one is as innocent as they seem . . .

www.penguin.co.uk

Sign up to

CARA HUNTER's

Newsletter

Get **exclusive offers**, Cara's
recommendations for the
best crime books around and
insider information on her **new novels**
before anyone else.

**Use the following link to receive
regular emails from Cara:**

https://www.penguin.co.uk/newsletters/carahunter/

He just wanted a decent book to read ...

Not too much to ask, is it? It was in 1935 when Allen Lane, Managing Director of Bodley Head Publishers, stood on a platform at Exeter railway station looking for something good to read on his journey back to London. His choice was limited to popular magazines and poor-quality paperbacks – the same choice faced every day by the vast majority of readers, few of whom could afford hardbacks. Lane's disappointment and subsequent anger at the range of books generally available led him to found a company – and change the world.

'We believed in the existence in this country of a vast reading public for intelligent books at a low price, and staked everything on it'
Sir Allen Lane, 1902–1970, founder of Penguin Books

The quality paperback had arrived – and not just in bookshops. Lane was adamant that his Penguins should appear in chain stores and tobacconists, and should cost no more than a packet of cigarettes.

Reading habits (and cigarette prices) have changed since 1935, but Penguin still believes in publishing the best books for everybody to enjoy. We still believe that good design costs no more than bad design, and we still believe that quality books published passionately and responsibly make the world a better place.

So wherever you see the little bird – whether it's on a piece of prize-winning literary fiction or a celebrity autobiography, political tour de force or historical masterpiece, a serial-killer thriller, reference book, world classic or a piece of pure escapism – you can bet that it represents the very best that the genre has to offer.

Whatever you like to read – trust Penguin.